"The start to Blackburn's [new?] series is an exciting story [that?] offers a more intense focus on the characters' histories with emotional trauma, interracial and blended families, and the damage of two-faced faith."

Booklist

"My first trip to Gossamer Falls, through the pages of *Never Fall Again* by Lynn H. Blackburn, is one that will have me coming back to visit again and again."

Reading Is My Superpower

"Romance, danger, and deadly crime-fighting scenes make this a perfect read. With Lynn H. Blackburn, I know I will always be getting what I want—plus some."

The AR Critique

"A fabulous story with characters who will live in your head—and heart—long after the last word. I'm eagerly awaiting the second book so I can return to Gossamer Falls and catch up with all my new besties!"

Lynette Eason, award-winning, bestselling author of the Lake City Heroes series

"Lynn Blackburn is a rising voice in romantic suspense! This book had it all—a delicious romance, obsession, found family, redemption and reconciliation, edge-of-your-seat suspense, and the kind of ending we all root for!"

Susan May Warren, *USA Today* bestselling and RITA Award–winning author

"With an exceptional gift for writing relatable characters who touch deep places of the heart, Lynn Blackburn's voice is unrivaled! I quickly fell in love with Landry, Cal, Eliza, and, in fact, the entire compelling cast of characters in this brand-new romantic suspense series."

Elizabeth Goddard, bestselling author of *Cold Light of Day*

BREAK
MY
FALL

Also by Lynn H. Blackburn

GOSSAMER FALLS · 2

BREAK MY FALL

LYNN H. BLACKBURN

Revell

a division of Baker Publishing Group
Grand Rapids, Michigan

© 2025 by Lynn H. Blackburn

Published by Revell
a division of Baker Publishing Group
Grand Rapids, Michigan
RevellBooks.com

Printed in the United States of America

Library of Congress Cataloging-in-Publication Data
Names: Blackburn, Lynn Huggins, author.
Title: Break my fall / Lynn H. Blackburn.
Description: Grand Rapids, Michigan : Revell, a division of Baker Publishing Group, 2025. | Series: Gossamer Falls
Identifiers: LCCN 2024035102 | ISBN 9780800745370 (paperback) | ISBN 9780800746681 (casebound) | ISBN 9781493448586 (ebook)
Subjects: LCGFT: Christian fiction. | Romance fiction. | Novels.
Classification: LCC PS3602.L325285 B74 2025 | DDC 813/.6—dc23/eng/20240802
LC record available at https://lccn.loc.gov/2024035102

Cover design by Laura Klynstra

Baker Publishing Group publications use paper produced from sustainable forestry practices and postconsumer waste whenever possible.

25 26 27 28 29 30 31   7 6 5 4 3 2 1

To the entire Huggins family.
I hope you know you're
the inspiration for the Quinn family.
I love you all.

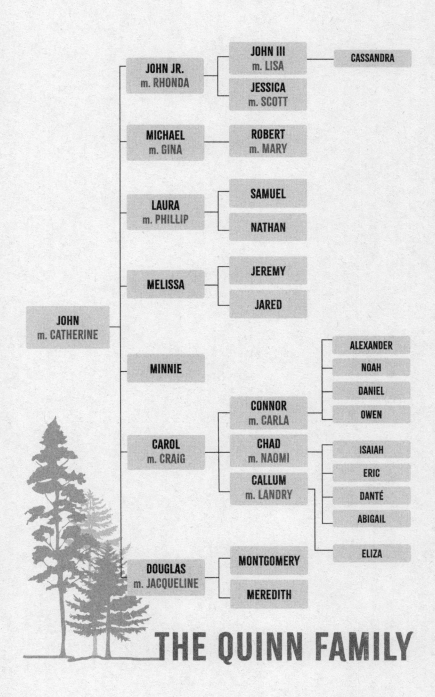

THE QUINN FAMILY

ONE

"No more peppermints, Mrs. Frost, or next time it's a root canal."

Mrs. Frost chortled with laughter, her veined and sun-spotted hand holding her cheek where it was still numb from the filling. "Don't you get sassy with me, Dr. Quinn." She put heavily sarcastic emphasis on the "doctor" part of that sentence. "I knew you when you were nothing but a shocked look on your mama's face."

Meredith Quinn removed her gloves and tossed them in the trash before helping Mrs. Frost climb from the dental chair. "I think surprise babies make the best babies. At least that was certainly true in my mother's case."

Mrs. Frost patted her hand, and her hooded eyes were kind and gentle when she asked, "How *is* your mama, child?"

Meredith made sure the elderly woman was steady on her feet before she responded. "She's good. So far no sign of a recurrence. The doctors said her cancer was growing rapidly, but they treated it aggressively and we're happy for all the days we have with her."

"I know you are. You're a good daughter." Mrs. Frost fumbled in her purse for her wallet. "How much do I owe you?"

"Nothing, Mrs. Frost. It was my pleasure." The woman had family who helped take care of her as much as they could, but she was on a fixed income and didn't have anything extra.

"Nonsense. I have to pay you something."

"I'd take some hot chocolate before I leave."

Mrs. Frost gave her a shrewd look. "You've sure turned into a Quinn woman. I see that as clear as day. Sweet as sugar. Stubborn as a mule."

"I'll be sure to tell Granny you gave me such a lovely compliment."

"You'll do no such thing. You can't talk about your patients. I know. There's laws about it now."

Meredith laughed at her superior tone. "I can't talk about your dental condition. But there aren't any rules preventing me from passing along well-wishes to my granny from an old friend."

"Pshaw." Mrs. Frost waved a hand at her. "Who're you calling old? I should tell your mama to wash your mouth out with soap." She opened the door that led from Meredith's mobile dental van and stepped out. "Come inside when you're done. I'll have the cocoa ready."

"Yes, ma'am." Meredith watched until Mrs. Frost was safely through her front door before she closed herself back into the small space.

Her mobile dental clinic had been a gift from her parents and grandparents when she'd moved back to Gossamer Falls a couple of years earlier. She loved it with every fiber of her being. It was small. There was only one chair. And most of the time she had to be hygienist and dentist. But with it housed in the back of a diesel-powered Sprinter van, she could navigate the winding roads of the Western North Carolina mountains and bring basic dental services to the underserved populations who would otherwise do without.

At least one Saturday a month, sometimes more, she would drive to a nearby county and set up her van. Usually it was in the parking lot of a small church. She'd clean the teeth of anyone who came by. Most of her patients were kids, and she typically gave them a good cleaning, a thorough checkup, and instructions for them and their parents on proper dental health.

But today had been the first time she'd made a midweek house call. Mrs. Frost lived forty-five minutes away from Gossamer Falls in what she generously referred to as a cabin.

Meredith's brother, Mo, called it a shack. Mo was correct.

Still, as she'd pointed out, Mrs. Frost had known Meredith since before she was born, just ten months after her brother, Mo. Meredith's arrival had shocked the extended Quinn family and the town of Gossamer Falls. A story she'd heard many, many times in her youth.

She didn't hear it quite so much anymore. Only the real old-timers ever brought it up. To most people, she was Dr. Meredith Quinn, town dentist. Sister to Mo. Cousin to . . . well, about half the town. Daughter to Douglas and Jacqueline. Granddaughter to John and Catherine.

Gossamer Falls had been her home for all but ten of her thirty-two years. She'd finished her bachelor's degree in three years. Went straight to dental school for four years. Then worked for three years in an urban setting where her days were a mixture of typical dental practice and charity dental clinics.

She'd been talking about being a dentist since she was a tiny girl. But no one knew what she'd hoped for most. Not her parents, Mo, or her cousin Cal who was more brother than cousin, not even Bronwyn Pierce, her childhood best friend. Meredith had prayed that someday she would move back to Gossamer Falls with a husband who would want to make his life there.

She'd dated in college and a little bit while in dental school, but husband material was thin on the ground.

But when the opportunity to open a dental practice in Gossamer Falls had presented itself, she took it. Even though it meant giving up on the dream of finding a spouse. Because she already knew everyone in Gossamer Falls, and a husband-to-be surely wasn't there.

And when her mother was diagnosed with aggressive breast cancer within a year of her return, Meredith knew she'd made the right choice. Even if the cost was high.

She shook her head at the way her thoughts had wandered as she went through the motions of securing all her equipment for the drive home. Once everything met her stringent requirements, she stepped outside, locked the van, and joined Mrs. Frost for hot cocoa.

And hopefully cookies.

An hour later, full of hot cocoa and more no-bake cookies than she wanted to admit to eating, Meredith climbed into the van and headed home. She typically took Wednesdays off, and her plans for this morning had been to sleep in, clean her tiny home— which with its seven hundred square feet took her all of an hour at most—and then spend the rest of the day working on her taxes.

The sleeping in and cleaning wouldn't be happening. Sadly, the taxes would. It wasn't even lunchtime yet. She should be able to return to Gossamer Falls and park her van in its normal spot in the garage off her dental office without anyone getting their shorts in a twist about her absence.

She *had* promised not to go out alone anymore, but that promise had been for her charity clinics where the clientele, admittedly, could be a bit on the shady side. Today's trip had been a response to an SOS from Mrs. Frost. Meredith had been in absolutely no danger. There'd been no reason to take an escort. Certainly not a police escort.

Not that Police Chief Grayson Ward would agree with her assessment. If he found out, he would blow a gasket.

No. Nope. Not thinking about Gray. Not today. She was happy. She was smiling. The world was beautiful. Mrs. Frost wasn't hurting anymore. Meredith kept her speed steady as she maneuvered through the mountain roads without a care. They didn't intimidate her. She'd learned how to drive on this very stretch of road.

Uncle Craig, her cousin Cal's dad, had put her behind the wheel of his pickup when she was almost fifteen and said, "Take it away, sweetheart."

In a family as large as the Quinns, it was hard not to have favorites. Meredith didn't even try. Uncle Craig was her favorite uncle. He didn't fuss when she hit the brakes too hard. Didn't grab the door when she took a turn too quickly. They rode around for two hours before they made their way back home.

She'd never forgotten how her father greeted them. "Well?" He looked at Uncle Craig like he had some explaining to do.

"She's a natural." Uncle Craig gave her a hug and a wink and walked inside with her dad.

Mo and Cal swarmed her. "How was it?" Cal asked. Mo studied her.

"It was awesome!"

Mo gave her a hug then and they went into Cal's home where her parents, Uncle Craig, and Aunt Carol were standing in the kitchen drinking coffee.

It wasn't until ten years later that she learned that her dad had told Uncle Craig that he just didn't think he could do it. His baby girl, out on the road? The idea of teaching her to drive terrified him.

So Uncle Craig had volunteered and took full credit for the fact that Meredith was, hands down, the best driver in the family.

As if in response to her prideful thought, the van stuttered as she accelerated through a curve. She patted the steering wheel. "What's the matter, baby?" She glanced along the panel, and the light of the low-fuel indicator caught her attention.

"That can't be right." She'd filled up this morning. She should have at least three-quarters of a tank. No way she could be on empty.

The shudder that ran through her vehicle put the inaccuracy of her assessment into sharp relief. None of this made sense. Her low-fuel indicator usually flicked on when she still had a quarter of a tank. And even when she was all the way on empty, she had enough diesel to get to a gas station.

But her fuel gauge didn't care about her logic. The van jerked. Jolted. Jumped forward a few times. Died. Her downhill momentum kept the van going long enough for her to ease off the road and park on a small shoulder between the road and the mountains towering above her. She was still ten miles from home.

She was eight miles from anything.

The ground on the other side of the road went straight down.

She glanced at her phone. This was going to hurt. She dialed Mo's number.

Or tried to. No signal.

Not unusual in the mountains. No cell phone provider had figured out how to make phones work in all the nooks and crannies of the forested area she called home.

Meredith dug around in the passenger seat for her coat. She hated driving while wearing one. And it wasn't safe to do that anyway. But she kept one in her van at all times. She'd put it on and go find a spot that gave her a view of the road coming into and out of the curve. She'd be able to flag down anyone who happened to come by.

The good news was that she was back in Gossamer County. Barely. But she was in Gray's jurisdiction.

It shouldn't matter, but Chief Kirby was crooked, and she didn't trust the officers from Neeson the way she trusted the Gossamer Falls officers. Gray, for his many faults, was a cut above when it came to police chiefs. He was irreproachable.

Donovan Bledsoe, one of Gray's officers, had recently stolen the heart of her baby cousin Cassie. They were so in love it was disgusting. Sweet. But disgusting.

If Meredith ever fell in love, she was going to keep the PDA to a minimum. No need for smooching *every single time* you see each other. No lingering looks that left little to the imagination.

Nope. Meredith planned to keep her personal relationships personal.

If she ever managed to have a relationship to keep personal.

But her relationship status, or lack thereof, wasn't a pressing issue. She was stuck on the side of the road in a dead Sprinter van with no cell service. It was January, and it was cold as whiz. Not that she had any idea what that meant. But that's what she'd always heard. "Cold as whiz" meant that things were freezing.

Like her nose. And fingertips.

Both of which she needed. And her gloves weren't in her coat pocket. Where were they?

She rested her head on the steering wheel. This was not how the day was supposed to go. Not at all.

The crunch of gravel on the road behind her pulled her to an upright position. A quick glance revealed flashing lights. A frisson of fear trickled through her until a closer look settled her. This was a Gossamer Falls patrol car.

She was safe.

Then Grayson Ward climbed from the vehicle and stalked toward her.

Maybe not.

Grayson Ward took his time approaching Meredith's van. He had questions.

So many questions.

But the first one, the one that mattered the most, was answered when she opened her door and hopped out.

Something inside him settled at the sight of her. Uninjured, but with blue eyes flashing. He braced himself for what she would say.

Meredith Quinn wasn't a petite woman. She was five-seven and there was nothing that would compel him to try to guess her weight. She owned a shirt that said, "You can tell I work out but also love pizza," and that seemed like a perfect description. She had plenty of muscle, and she loved to go hiking, but there was also a softness about her—particularly in her face—that many people found compelling.

Not that any of that softness was directed toward him at the moment. "Are you following me? Did you put a tracker on my van?" She'd walked closer as she talked and now stood just a foot away. "How did you find me?"

He leaned back and crossed his arms. "Why are you on the side of the road?" He had no idea how or why, but his question took the fight right out of her.

"I don't know!" she all but wailed. "Everything was fine. I was cruising toward home, thinking about how my uncle Craig taught me to drive on this road, and then"—she reached back and patted her van—"Flossy started acting funny."

Flossy? She'd named her van Flossy? "Define funny."

"She jerked a few times. At first I thought something was in the fuel line." She wrinkled her nose. "But now I'm wondering if something is wrong *with* the fuel line. Do you smell that?"

"Oh yeah." He'd noticed it as soon as he got out of his car. "Smells like diesel."

"Yes! And that makes no sense. I had a full tank before I left town this morning. I always fill up right before I come because"—she flung a hand toward her van—"getting stuck on the side of the road in the mountains is never a good idea." She patted the van again. "At least it's broad daylight."

"Not a fan of the dark?" Gray attempted to keep his tone neutral.

"Not a fan of being outside alone in the dark. There are critters. Big ones. Small ones. I prefer to keep my distance from all of them."

"Understood." Gray looked at the van, then back to Meredith. "You keep an eye on the road. I'm going to see if I can figure out why you're losing fuel."

Gray removed his duty belt and laid it in his cruiser.

"Why aren't you in your Explorer?" He never drove a regular Gossamer Falls cruiser.

"Because"—he grabbed a flashlight from the car and returned to her van—"my Explorer needed new tires." Then he lay on his back and shimmied his body between the ground and the underside of the van. This was going to be the end of the shirt he was wearing. He managed to wait until he was well and truly under the van to ask, "Who needed their teeth cleaned so urgently this morning that you couldn't wait for me to come with you?"

The silence that greeted him told him he'd done a lousy job in his attempt to be calm.

Shoes—completely impractical shoes—appeared in his line of sight. "For your information, it *was* urgent. And it didn't require your professional presence. I wasn't hosting a clinic. It's my day off, but Mrs. Frost called me at home at six thirty this morning. She had a toothache that had kept her up all night. She's eighty-seven and everyone knows she shouldn't be driving anywhere under any circumstances. Speaking of which, can't you take her license? Isn't that in your job description?"

Gray slid the flashlight between his teeth and found the fuel tank. "Not my jurisdiction."

The words were garbled, but she must have understood because she responded, "Gotcha. And that means Kirby should do it, but he's not going to do anything he doesn't have to do. Mrs. Frost would probably swat him on the nose with a rolled-up newspaper if he tried. She doesn't suffer fools."

Meredith was correct on all counts. Even the part about her not needing his assistance. They had an agreement that she wouldn't do any clinics alone. She'd promised to take someone with law enforcement experience with her, and she'd stuck to that for the past six months without complaint. He'd gone several times during the fall. Donovan, one of his most trusted officers, had gone in December. Her brother, Mo, and cousin Cal, both of whom had military experience and were, technically, consultants for the Gossamer Falls Police Department, had gone with her in early January when she'd made a rare weekday trek to try to catch as many children as she could before they returned to school after the Christmas break.

"You still haven't answered my question, Chief Ward."

Uh-oh. When she started "Chief Ward-ing" him, it meant he'd lost control of the conversation. At this point, all he could do was institute emergency measures.

"I was on patrol." True. "This"—he shifted—"entire"—he scooted again, and a piece of gravel dug into his back. A grunt escaped.

Meredith's face appeared between the ground and the bottom of the van. "What happened? Are you okay?"

"I'm fine."

"Are you sure?"

"It was a rock, Meredith. I'm lying in the gravel on the edge of the road looking at the bottom of a van. It's not going to be comfortable."

"Right. Sorry about that. Maybe I—"

"Don't even think about it." He had no idea what she might be thinking. But the last time she'd had a bright idea, she'd redecorated the break room at the police station. If she'd stopped there, it might have been okay. But she hadn't. She'd redecorated his office and the locker room too.

It was still masculine. But now, each stall had little odor sprays and each shower had an array of soaps and lotions, which at times meant his officers walked around the station smelling like they were headed out on a date instead of on the way to keep the peace.

The towels, well, no, he couldn't complain about the towels. The towels she'd brought were plush and large, and he had shamelessly checked the invoice and bought some to use at home.

But still. Meredith had no off button. Once she decided something needed to be done, there was no stopping her.

A low *humph* was her only response to him shutting her down, but even without looking in her direction, he could picture her. Blue eyes flashing in outrage. Full lips pouting. There were curls in her brown hair today, and they were probably flying around her face in the wind.

"Don't think I missed the fact that you have yet to explain what you're doing here, Chief Ward."

When Gray next glanced in her direction, all he could see was her feet as she paced beside the van. He smiled around the flashlight. Meredith was bighearted and bullheaded and the reason he walked around with a bruised heart. The blasted thing insisted on beating hard every time she was in the vicinity, and nothing his brain said could convince it to chill and accept the truth.

Meredith Quinn was his to protect, but she could never be his.

TWO

Meredith had a moment of startling clarity. Regardless of why he'd happened to be driving by—and she put mental quotes around "happened" because she had no doubt he'd either followed her, tracked her, or come looking for her—he was currently under her van, lying on a rough road, and doing it without any complaint.

And she had him all to herself for a few minutes.

Why was it that when that happened, and it happened rarely enough, she always seemed to find a reason to snap at him. She took a deep breath and made a heroic effort to rein in her sass. "Mrs. Frost is a sweet lady. I went to help her. I didn't even think about her being in another county. And even if I had, I would have gone anyway. Because, again, Mrs. Frost is precious, but she's also a menace on the road who shouldn't be allowed to drive anywhere ever again. So I told her not to come to the office. I would bring the office to her."

Her magnanimous explanation earned her a grunt. And then a low whistle. Well, that was a weird response.

"Meredith."

She bent over so she could look under the van again. Not that she could see Gray's face well, but it felt rude to continue talking into the air when he was just a few feet away. "Yes?"

"Could you hand me your phone? I need to take a few pictures."

She pulled her phone from her pocket. "Pictures of?"

"The hole in your fuel line."

She got down so she could reach under the van and handed the phone to Gray. A few clicks later, he held it out to her. "Can you take this? I'm coming out."

She considered offering to pull him out by his legs but bit her tongue. That would probably hurt his back. And it would be awkward. And she wasn't even sure if she could move him. The man was a wall of muscle.

But she did do what was clearly the only polite thing. She watched him like a hawk as he shimmied himself out from under the vehicle and then leaned over to rub his hands in the grass. Which might be the reason she was a little bit breathless when he finally got to his feet and asked to see the phone.

"Huh?"

"The phone? The pictures?"

"Oh. Right." She handed it over and gave herself a mental slap. He turned the screen toward her. "See this?"

She studied the photo. "That's where my diesel leaked?"

"Yeah. It's hard to see, but when I wiped the line dry, I could see the cut. I don't suppose you, I don't know, ran over a large branch, or took the van through a ditch, did a little off-roading?"

His questions, albeit increasingly facetious, held a tinge of hope. He would have been thrilled if she could give him an explanation other than the one she could already see forming in his mind.

She wanted to say that she made it a habit to take her freakishly expensive dental office on wheels through random fields, but she refrained and answered truthfully. "Mrs. Frost has a gravel driveway, but her sons smoothed it out last week. I didn't so much as hit a pothole today."

Gray's mouth twisted into an unpleasant grimace. "Stay here."

It wasn't a request, and she considered ignoring it. But given that there were now two vehicles and two people on the side of the road, she chose to remain where she could flag down any oncoming motorists before Gray, who was now walking up the middle of the road, was flattened into a police chief pancake.

He walked around the curve and out of sight. Rude. He could have said something like, "I'm hot on the trail." But no.

She opened her van door and reached inside for her coffee. It was still hot, and she was on her eleventh sip—and yes, she was counting—when Gray reappeared. He didn't say anything as he returned to her side. When he reached her, he looked at the insulated tumbler she held. It was a lurid pink. "I didn't think you liked pink."

"I don't particularly."

"Then why?" He waved a hand toward the cup.

"Because Cal and Mo used to have a bad habit of raiding my kitchen when they can't find their own mugs. I bought four of these in lovely neutral shades before I gave up and started buying the most obnoxious colors they make."

"Clever girl."

Meredith nearly dropped her coffee. Was Gray flirting with her? This was flirting. Right? "Would you like a sip?"

"What's in it?"

"Coffee."

"I gathered that. What else is in it?"

"Oh, um, oat milk creamer?"

He rolled his eyes but took the tumbler and raised it to his lips. He took a cautious sip. Then another. "That's not bad." He blew out a breath. "We have to consider the possibility that someone punctured your fuel line while you were at Mrs. Frost's house today."

Meredith leaned against her van. "Why?"

"I have a few theories."

"Care to share?"

"Not here. Not now."

"Does that mean later?"

Gray shifted his feet. "I'm not sure."

"I deserve to know."

"You do. But I don't want to scare you."

"Please." Meredith pointed a finger at his chest. "You've been trying to scare me off for months. This is the moment you've been waiting for. Why aren't you jumping at it?"

"Because this is different."

"How?"

Gray walked toward his car. "Not now." He reached inside and used the radio. "Tell Donovan I need him here with a gas can. But it needs to be diesel. Yeah. At least ten gallons." He rattled off a few more things that he wanted and signed off.

She had walked to his door. "Thank you. My phone doesn't have a signal."

"Want me to get a message to Mo?"

"No." She dropped her head in defeat. "But yes. They'll freak out if they can't reach me. Although by now someone in my family has probably already started a phone tree."

"How would they even know?"

"Police scanner. Someone will have heard it and called my parents, or Papa, or Mo directly. Poor Donovan. He'll probably be leading a caravan of Quinns here."

"Let them come." Gray didn't seem to think this was as serious a situation as he should have.

"I don't need to be rescued."

Gray quirked an eyebrow.

"Yes. I *did* need to be rescued. But you've already rescued me admirably, so now I'm fine. Perfectly safe. I don't need a parade."

Gray studied her for a moment, then returned to the radio, where he made it clear to Donovan that he should risk the wrath of his soon-to-be in-laws and make sure most of them stayed home. "Mo can come if he wants. Or Douglas. But we don't need the whole family."

Donovan said he understood and he'd do his best.

"Happy now?" Gray asked Meredith.

"Yes. Thank you."

Gray went to the back of his car. "I'm going to see if I can wrap that up enough to at least slow the leak until we can get you to a service station."

For the next ten minutes, Meredith sat on the ground beside Gray's legs and handed him the various items he requested. When he shimmied back out, she went to the front of her van and retrieved her stash of baby wipes. She returned after he'd gotten to his feet.

He wiped his hands clean and glared at her van. "Meredith?"

"Gray?"

"I know I don't have any authority, any right, any . . . well, anything to ask this. But I'm going to ask it anyway. Please don't leave the county by yourself. Not just for clinics. For any reason. I—" He ran a hand over his close-cropped head. "There's something going on and you're involved. I don't know how. I don't know why. I don't know what the end game is. I don't want to scare you or make you jump at shadows. But I need you to be careful."

He took her hands in his and squeezed. "Please. I'm . . . I'm begging you. Please."

She stared at their hands and tried to keep her face from showing her shock. He'd never touched her before. Never. His hands were so big, so warm, so firm and sure. But there was so much pain in his gaze. So much fear. For her. She wanted to explore the emotion. Wanted to understand where his intensity came from.

Wanted to have permission to slide her hand into his anytime she wanted.

But now wasn't the time or place. So she nodded and said the only thing she could that would alleviate some of Gray's distress. "I promise."

Donovan arrived with Mo's Jeep close behind him. Mo hopped out and ran to Meredith. "What on earth have you gotten yourself into now, baby sister?"

Anyone hearing just the words would have thought Mo rough and angry. But Gray could see the emotion, feel the tension, and more importantly, watch the way this often-taciturn man grabbed his sister in his arms and squeezed her close.

The sight rubbed at the place in his heart that would never heal. He envied them this moment in a way neither of them knew. He left them to their conversation and walked over to Donovan.

"She was at Mrs. Frost's house for approximately two hours." While Mrs. Frost didn't live in their jurisdiction, she did drive into Gossamer Falls. And Meredith was right. The woman was a menace behind the wheel. All of Gray's officers knew Mrs. Frost. "She had a toothache, so Meredith came up here and took care of it rather than turn Mrs. Frost loose on the unsuspecting citizens."

Donovan chuckled. "Wise woman."

"Indeed. Meredith said she was in the van for about an hour. Then went inside to visit. Mrs. Frost made her hot chocolate and cookies."

"Are you thinking the damage was done while they were in the house?"

"Probably. When I asked Meredith if she heard or saw anything strange, she said no, but that Mrs. Frost had the TV on and the

27

volume was so loud she wouldn't have noticed if a train had come through."

"Opportunity or planned?" Donovan asked.

"Maybe a little of both? A plan that was implemented as soon as the opportunity presented itself?" Gray looked to where Mo was talking to Meredith, one arm casually thrown over her shoulder, her head against his chest.

"I don't get it." Donovan waved a hand in her direction. "She goes there to help. That's it. She's not causing any trouble. She's cleaning teeth and filling cavities. It's not like she's busting up meth labs."

"No. But the kids love her. And kids talk. They talk a lot of trash, but some of it's legitimate. Back when Landry was taken, Meredith made a comment that if Kirby didn't cooperate, she'd share some incriminating information. I didn't have to threaten Kirby with that. But I do wonder if her comment got back to him somehow."

"What does she know?"

"She's never said. From what I've been able to put together, there've been little comments here and there. A lot of small stuff that, taken on its own, means nothing. But when combined? Could mean we have a dirty cop. Maybe more than one. And that the meth and cocaine coming through the mountains has found a safe harbor right on the other side of the county line."

"Those Atlanta dealers don't play." Donovan's face clouded. "I don't like having that stuff right across the county line." Donovan had almost lost his fiancée, Cassie, to some locals mixed up in the drug trade just a few months ago. The wound was raw. "It would help if she didn't go traipsing off alone. But she's a Quinn. And the Quinns—"

"Believe me. I know. But we've talked. She promised not to leave the county alone."

"How did you manage that?" There was more innuendo in those five words than Gray thought possible.

"Drop it."

Donovan gave him a small salute. "Yes, sir." There was no attitude in his remark. Maybe a little disappointment, but nothing else. "Ready for me to try to get the van moving again?"

"Yeah. Fill her up. Then we'll caravan into town."

"Sounds like a plan."

Donovan went to his truck to get the diesel while Gray walked over to the huddle where Meredith and Mo stood in tense conversation. "Excuse me."

Meredith and Mo turned to him and their familial similarity hit him hard. The way they stood and the set of their mouths were identical. And even though he was sure they'd been arguing, there was still a closeness, a comfort level, between them.

If things had been different, would he and Jasmine have had this kind of relationship? Would people have been jealous of how close they were? Would she have looked at him the way Meredith looked at Mo now, with a mix of exasperation and fondness?

Meredith tilted her head in Mo's direction. "My big brother thinks I've made poor life choices today."

"You left town. Alone!" Mo pointed at Gray. "Tell her."

"From what she told me, there wasn't any reason for her not to pay a visit to Mrs. Frost."

At Meredith's triumphant "Told you," he focused on her.

"Although, it would have been wise to let someone know you were headed out."

"Exactly," Mo growled.

"But it isn't something we need to worry about." He turned to Mo. "Meredith's promised not to leave the county alone anymore, so that's settled."

Mo's eyes widened, and he turned on Meredith. "You didn't tell me that."

"You didn't give me a chance. You went all overprotective big brother on me. Gray and I had an adult conversation with no yelling and no threats. I recognize there's a problem far greater than what any of us realized, and I'll take all necessary precautions."

Mo stuck a hand toward Gray. "Man, I don't know how you did it. But thank you."

Gray shook Mo's hand, and when their eyes met, Gray saw something that he didn't want to know.

Mo approved.

He didn't need Mo's approval. Especially not when it came to Meredith.

Meredith shoved Mo's arm. "I'm right here, you moron."

"Yes. I see that. In the middle of nowhere out of diesel."

"I had a full tank!"

"It doesn't matter if it leaks out all over the road!"

Meredith turned to Gray. "We need to call Mrs. Frost. She has animals. If it leaked out at her house—"

"I'll go see her." Mo's voice was reassuring.

She gave him a hug. "You're the best big brother. I don't care what I said earlier."

"Yeah, yeah." Mo made eye contact with Gray, and Gray gave him a quick nod of appreciation.

Gray would have loved to go to Mrs. Frost's home and investigate the scene, but he couldn't. It was out of his jurisdiction. Mo had no such limitations. He could do a favor for his baby sister, and Mrs. Frost would flirt and ply him with cookies and hot cocoa. She might even tell him things she hadn't thought to mention to Meredith.

Mo Quinn was an interesting guy. Quiet in a crowd. Funny and sarcastic with the people he was close to. A favorite of all the little Quinns, and goodness knew there were a lot of them, and the first one to volunteer to hang out with his aunt Minnie when his granny needed someone to look after her.

He also had a mind that understood patterns and loved spreadsheets. He'd been something secret with Army intelligence, and no one knew for sure why he'd left when he did. He claimed it was because his mama had cancer and he decided it was time to move home.

Gray figured that was about 30 percent of the story. The remaining 70 percent had yet to be told.

Regardless, Mo wasn't a man to be trifled with. He could handle himself and whatever came at him.

"Meredith, who do you want to work on your van? Do you want to take it to a mechanic?"

Her eyes widened in horror. "Are you kidding? Daddy would strangle me. I'm driving Flossy straight to my parents' house."

"I refuse to call your van Flossy."

Meredith patted her van. "Why not? It's the perfect name. The kids love it. Flossy, the mobile dentist van."

Donovan stood nearby with the gas can at the ready. "I still say you should get a vanity plate."

"I tried." Meredith's expression was so disgruntled that Gray had a sudden and intense urge to call the DMV and insist they provide her with whatever she wanted. What was wrong with him?

It was time for him to get away from Meredith. He did fine as long as he kept his distance, and today had topped him off for at least a week. Gray clapped his hands together. "Okay. Let's get out of here. Donovan, fill her up. Mo, if you'll pay Mrs. Frost a quick visit?"

Donovan and Mo nodded.

"Meredith, Donovan will take the lead. I'll follow. We'll stay with you all the way to your parents' house. And if you need a ride back to your office, one of us will take you."

Meredith flashed him her trademark smile and dropped into a sugary-sweet Southern drawl. "Why, officers, I just don't know how to thank you for coming to my aid." She fluttered her eyelashes to dramatic effect.

Donovan bowed dramatically. "It was our pleasure, ma'am."

"You're just sucking up so I'll make that obnoxious flower arrangement you asked for."

Donovan shrugged. "I'll do whatever I have to do."

"I'm *not* making it. It's a crime against nature."

Donovan poured diesel into the tank. "Meredith, you make flower arrangements out of wood. I'm not saying they're a crime, but they aren't exactly following the nature of things."

"They're gorgeous, and they never die." Meredith defended her creations. And she wasn't wrong. Gray had never paid any attention to flower arrangements until Meredith had brought a bouquet to the station that even he had to acknowledge was stunning.

When he realized that the flowers were made from paper-thin sheets of wood that had been shaped and dyed, he couldn't believe it. And then she casually mentioned that she'd been the one to design and dye each flower and that she'd created the arrangement.

He'd made sure the flowers were in a prominent spot, and he smiled to himself every time he saw them.

Not that he told her that.

"What does Donovan want you to do?"

Meredith groaned. "He wants me to make an arrangement so gaudy it could possibly cause permanent retinal damage to anyone who views it for more than a few seconds. And he wants me to present it to Cassie as the real thing. I've tried to explain to him that no one pranks their bride on their wedding day."

Gray adjusted his belt. "Can you make the arrangement? I mean, is it possible to make it?"

"Yes, but—"

"Why don't you make it and let him have his fun *before* the wedding. She could carry it during the rehearsal, and then it can be the bouquet she tosses during the reception."

Meredith gaped at him for a few seconds, then threw her arms around him. She squeezed him close and then leaned back and looked into his face. "Gray! You're a genius!"

Eyes alight, she looked at Donovan. "What do you think?"

Donovan rubbed the back of his neck. "I think it's great, but if it's all the same to you, I'm not going to squeeze the stuffing out of Gray to express my approval."

Meredith, body still pressed to Gray's, hands still on his arms, scrunched up her face at Donovan, then turned a radiant smile on Gray. "I'm so happy! Thank you!" She rose on her tiptoes, and before he saw it coming, planted a kiss on his cheek. Then she hugged him again before releasing him to run over to Mo.

Gray stood frozen in place. He heard her explaining his solution to "this bouquet issue that's been giving me literal nightmares" to her brother, but he couldn't quite get his brain and body in sync. He should move. He should get in his car.

He should drive far, far away from Meredith Quinn.

But five minutes later, he was in his car, following Meredith to her parents' home.

THREE

Meredith checked her rearview mirror.

Still there.

Gray was following her home, as promised.

She'd kissed him. What had she been thinking? It wasn't that big of a deal. She liked Donovan. A lot. And she loved Cassie. She was so happy for them and so excited about their pending nuptials. Cassie had a very specific idea in mind for her flowers, and Meredith had used up far too many brain cells trying to figure out how to redirect Donovan from making a truly horrible mistake.

Gray's solution was fabulous, but it wasn't that big of a deal. She'd overreacted. She'd been goofy and ridiculous, and in her glee, she'd kissed Gray's face.

Ten minutes outside of town, her phone rang. She answered it through the Bluetooth. "Beep! What's up?"

"That's what we want to know," Bronwyn said. "I have you on speaker. I'm with Landry. Cal's on the phone with Mo. But Cal is just doing a lot of grunting, and we can't figure out what's going on. Are you okay?"

"I'm fine." Meredith broke down the events of the morning. "I'm almost back in town. Donovan's going to peel off and return to the police station. Gray's following me to Mom and Dad's. Then he'll give me a ride back to my office to get my car."

"Someone punctured your fuel line." Landry, Cal's wife, chimed in. "Why? What were they hoping to accomplish?" Given that Landry had been targeted by a stalker a year ago, her questions held an edge of worry that didn't surprise Meredith.

"I don't know. I'm sure Gray will do everything he can to find out. But I was in Neeson County."

"You're going to have to stay out of there." Bronwyn used her CEO tone.

Their friendship had resolidified enough over the past couple of years that Meredith wasn't afraid to push back. "I'm not your employee."

"I never said you were. But I'm sick and tired of my friends and employees being in danger. First Landry. Then Cassie. Now you? It needs to stop."

"We're all good. Better than good." Landry's voice filtered through the speaker. "And, Bronwyn, I get that you're afraid for Meredith, but taking that fear out on your oldest friend isn't going to solve anything."

"Go, Landry!" Meredith crowed. "I do love having you for a sister." Technically, Landry was her cousin-in-law, but Quinns didn't get too fussed about actual familial titles.

"I love having sisters." Meredith could hear the smile in Landry's voice. "And as your new sister, I have to tell you that while I don't agree with Bronwyn's approach, I can't disagree with her overall message. There's something going on over there, and I'm afraid for you. Cal and Mo need you. So do Bronwyn and I."

Somehow, Landry's gentle reproof shattered the wall Meredith had erected to keep herself calm, and she had to work to keep from crying. "I know. You're right. I don't understand it. But I'll be careful. I've already promised Gray I won't leave the county alone. And if I go anywhere out of my normal routine, I'll make sure someone knows what's happening."

"Good. I'm sorry I was so bossy. I'm just . . ." Bronwyn went silent.

"What she isn't saying," Landry said, "is that when she gets scared, she tries to control everything and everyone around her. She's working on that."

Landry's comment made Meredith laugh. And she could hear Bronwyn's laughter as well. "Can we talk more tonight? Firepit?"

"Sure," Landry agreed immediately.

Bronwyn hesitated. "I don't know. My presence adds a layer of tension to the proceedings. I don't want that."

Meredith turned into her parents' driveway. Bronwyn wasn't wrong. The rift between Bronwyn and Mo was so deep that Meredith had almost given up hope that it would ever be healed. "Mo doesn't talk to me about you. He never has. I'm not sure if he ever will. But he did tell Cal that he was glad you're back in my life. And in Cal's life. I don't think he wants to keep us from spending time together. Please come."

"I'll think about it."

"I'll work on her," Landry said.

"Thanks. Listen, I'm at Mom and Dad's, so I need to run."

"Give them my love," Bronwyn said. "And let us know if you need us to do anything."

"Will do."

In her rearview mirror, she saw that Gray had parked in the driveway. Meredith continued on behind the house and straight to her father's shop. Every Quinn male had a shop of some kind. Meredith suspected it was because they all carried a packrat gene and they knew better than to try to bring all their junk inside their homes.

Papa Quinn's shop mostly had tools and gardening equipment.

36

Her dad's shop held similar items but also an assortment of specific tools for car repair. He'd had a passion for cars since he was a kid. A passion Papa Quinn didn't share but had encouraged all the same.

She parked the van, climbed out, and came face-to-face with two men who, on the surface, couldn't be more different. Her dad was lean but still straight and strong. His once-brown hair was shot through with gray, most of which had come over the last few years. He wore glasses and gave off a bit of an academic vibe. And he was the best dad a girl could have. He'd held her heart safe for every single moment of her thirty-two years.

Beside him, Gray stood a couple of inches taller and about a foot wider in the shoulders. Gray had a muscular frame that made people ask him if he'd played football in high school (no) or been in the military (yes, a Marine). His dark hair was cut short. His ethnicity was a mix of African American, Hispanic, and White, and his skin stayed brown year-round, although it did darken a little in the summer. At thirty-five, he didn't look old, but there was already a gravitas and maturity to him that screamed "I've got this." Even when he was relaxed, he gave off a protective vibe.

When he wasn't relaxed, like now, the vibe morphed into a fierce energy that radiated from him and gave the impression that he was a microsecond away from throwing his body in front of a bullet. He was the best police chief Gossamer Falls had ever had. And he'd held Meredith's heart in a stranglehold since the moment she'd laid eyes on him two and a half years ago.

Gray must have already assured her dad that she was unharmed, because he wasn't nearly as freaked out as she'd expected him to be. In this situation, the best defense was offense.

"Hey, Dad! Some idiot cut my fuel line. Do you think you can fix it?" She was going for more outrage than fear.

"Nice try, munchkin." Her dad sounded stern, but his eyes crinkled and he held out an arm. She snuggled against him. "Gray told me someone had cut it. He hasn't gotten around to telling me why."

"He doesn't know, Dad. It just happened."

"And why am I just now hearing about it?"

"Because I didn't want you or Mom to freak out. I'm fine. Perfectly safe. And . . ."

She trailed off as his arm tightened.

"No more solo trips." There was no budge in his voice.

"Dad—"

"No more, young lady. I know you're grown. I couldn't be prouder of you. But my heart can't take it. Please."

She caught Gray's eye, and he dropped his gaze and studied the ground. But not before she caught the flicker of satisfaction on his face.

"I promise."

"Thank you." He kissed her temple and released her. As he walked around her van he called over his shoulder, "When do you need Flossy back?"

Gray tensed and quirked one eyebrow at her. She'd stood in front of a mirror once and tried her best to mimic the look but had failed miserably. The best she could do was get one eyebrow a fraction higher than the other.

"Not for two weeks. I don't have anything planned next weekend." She pitched her voice loud enough to carry to him on the other side of her van. "I'm still working on Cassie's flowers, and I got a new wedding order this week that I wanted to create a few samples for. I'm planning to be in the shop this weekend and next."

Gray's shoulders dropped a few inches, and her dad's grunt of approval filtered to her. "Do you need a ride back to your office?

Or do you want to go in and see your mom?" Gray's question sent a prickle of . . . something . . . along Meredith's spine.

This man. He kept himself so closed off that sometimes she wondered if he even liked her. Not in a romantic way. She'd given up on that. Or, tried to give up on it. But she did suspect that he knew how she felt and her presence annoyed him. She was sensitive to things like that, and she was aware that he made it a point to avoid her. Not always. But enough that she'd noticed and had tried to stay out of his orbit as much as possible too.

And then he went and did something like this. Something so thoughtful and gracious. He had other things to do, but he was willing to wait for her to say hello to her mom because, somehow, he knew she'd feel bad if she didn't.

Following her train of thought to what seemed like a logical conclusion, she decided that Gray did like her. He did pay attention to her. He did know things about her that she didn't make a point of sharing. It made her want to hug him.

But she'd already kissed him today. It wouldn't be wise to force herself into his personal space again. "Can I have five minutes?"

"You can have as long as you want." His voice was low and gravelly. "I'll be out here. Come find me when you're ready."

"Thank you. I'll be fast."

Gray watched as Meredith jogged to the house. He would never tell her she couldn't speak to her mother. One of the things he appreciated most about her was her connection to her family. The way they loved each other so openly and so well.

But he had a couple of ulterior motives today. One, he wanted to talk to Doug Quinn without Meredith overhearing. And two, he needed some space before he drove her to the office.

Doug leaned against the van. "What do we need to do to protect her?" he asked Gray. "Keeping her in the county isn't a permanent solution."

Gray took a position beside Doug. "It's a start."

"I'll talk to the boys."

"The boys" would ultimately include every male member of the Quinn family, but it would begin with Mo, Cal, Cal's brothers Chad and Connor, and Cal's dad, Craig Shaw.

"And I'll be having a chat with the mayor."

Gray frowned. What would the mayor have to do with it?

"We're long overdue for some changes around here. How would you feel about being sheriff?"

The police/sheriff situation in this part of the state was muddled at best and full-on chaotic at worst. North Carolina's constitution called for each county to have a sheriff, but through some quirk of distance and muleheadedness, Gossamer County, Neeson County, and a few other neighboring counties had never gotten the memo.

Even though it was a murky legal area, Gray handled the law enforcement for the entire county. Chief Kirby did the same in Neeson County and for the town of Neeson.

They'd had few major crimes, and no one had questioned Gray's authority to enforce the law in Gossamer County.

But Doug wasn't wrong. No one wanted a criminal to get by with their crimes due to technicalities over jurisdiction limits.

Gray wasn't sure how he felt about the position, but before he could answer, Doug continued. "Think about it. If it turns out that you'd have to run for sheriff, are you willing to do it? I can assure you, you'll win. You'll probably run uncontested."

"I don't love the idea of running for office."

"I know. But times are changing. We need to get ourselves sorted." He looked toward the house where Meredith had opened the door. "Right now, though, we just need to keep our girl safe. I don't want this sheriff stuff to distract you."

"Then why'd you bring it up?"

"Because I don't want you hearing about it from the wrong person or being blindsided by it. You've done a great job as chief of police. This town and this county are too small to need a sheriff and a police chief. If we have to change the titles we will, but when it comes to how things get done? No one wants anything to change."

Meredith came to a stop beside them. "That could be Gossamer Falls' motto. 'We don't want anything to change.'" She bumped her dad's shoulder. "But what specifically don't we want to change?"

Doug looked at Gray, then at Meredith. "Just talking to Gray here about the whole sheriff/police situation."

Gray had expected Meredith to shrug off the words, but her face grew serious. "We really do need to fix it. We need to be sure everything is buttoned up tight so there's no wiggle room for criminals here. It's bad enough that it's on our doorstep. Kirby's dirty, and I don't trust his mess not to bleed over."

Doug put an arm around his daughter. "You ever gonna tell us what dirt you have on him, baby girl?"

She shook her head. "I have more suspicion than specifics. My specifics are legit, but I hear things. Kids talk. Patients talk. There's stuff going on in Neeson County that we wouldn't let fly here. And Kirby looks the other way. I suspect they have something on him."

"Who are *they*?" Gray asked.

"*They* are whoever's really running the show. I have an idea of who that is. But no proof. But there's hinky stuff going on. The last time I was up there, I had three patients who had injuries that indicated abuse. I saw a teenage girl who I suspect is being trafficked by her stepbrother. And two moms who sported bruises that looked an awful lot like someone had used them as a punching bag."

Meredith pulled away from her dad and paced. "One of those moms is the wife of a sheriff's deputy. The fox is in the henhouse, and those poor people can't do anything about it. They can't afford to move. They can't risk speaking up. So they deal with it."

She focused on Gray. "You wouldn't know this because you didn't grow up here, but I've been told my entire life to 'stay out of Neeson.'" She glanced at her dad, and Doug confirmed it with a nod. "When I was young, I thought it was overprotective parents being paranoid. Then, when I hit my late teens and early twenties and knew everything"—she winked at her dad— "I was sure it was some kind of better-than-thou attitude. Like Gossamer Falls folks were too good to associate with the likes of people in Neeson. And I thought that was because everyone here had a serious case of entitlement."

She shrugged. "Then I moved home and spent some time in Neeson. If I had kids? I'd tell them to stay out of Neeson too. There's something going on up there, and it isn't right. There are good people there, but they're overshadowed by bad people who've decided Neeson is theirs."

Nothing Meredith said was news to Gray. But he hadn't realized how much she'd seen and absorbed. To his knowledge, the only time she was ever in Neeson was when she did a clinic. Which meant her patients *were* talking. And Meredith might know more than she realized she did.

Whether she did or didn't know anything specific, someone in Neeson thought she did.

Had the goal today been to scare her? To abduct her? To kill her?

His chest tightened at the thought. "We'll get to the bottom of it." The words were a vow he had no problem making. Failure wasn't an option because to fail would mean leaving Meredith at risk.

As far as Gray was concerned, Meredith was dangerous, but she should never be *in* danger. And whether she liked it or not, he intended to make sure she was protected.

The world needed people like Meredith Quinn. Shoot. He needed people like Meredith Quinn.

Or maybe he just needed Meredith Quinn.

But he couldn't have her. He'd closed that door a long time ago. His role in her life wasn't to be the one she came home to. It was to be the one who made sure she was safe and able to go home . . . to whoever awaited her.

Right now, that meant driving her back to her office and then finding out what was going on in Neeson.

FOUR

Gray's car smelled like leather and Gray. She didn't think he wore cologne. But it might have been some kind of aftershave or lotion or soap or something. Whatever it was, it was a scent she associated only with him. And she liked it too much for her own good.

She dropped her head back as he climbed into the driver's seat and buckled his seat belt.

"Tired?" The concern in his voice settled over her like a fleece blanket.

"Not really. I'm frustrated. Annoyed. Confused."

"But not afraid?" There was genuine curiosity in the question, so she answered it in the spirit it had been asked.

"I was afraid this morning until I realized I was back in Gossamer County. And I'll probably be afraid later when I'm by myself and have time to process everything. The idea of someone sneaking around Mrs. Frost's place? And slicing my fuel line? That's creepy." An involuntary shudder rippled through her.

"Creepy's one word for it." Gray's low rumble had her turning in her seat to look at him more fully.

"What word would you use?"

His hands flexed on the steering wheel. "Criminal."

"Ah. Yes. It's criminally creepy."

He smirked a little, but that's all her lame joke got her. She wanted to keep him talking. "Not to poke the bear or anything, but you never did explain how you happened to drive by right when I needed you."

If she hadn't been watching him, she wouldn't have noticed the guilty expression on his face. "Gray? Were you following me?"

"No." The word came out quick and sharp.

"But?"

He tapped the wheel a few times. "I was on patrol this morning. And I saw your 4Runner at the office and that the van was gone."

"So you decided to drive toward the county line?"

"I continued patrolling."

"At the county line?"

"I drive that road at least once a week."

"You're impossible."

"I'm just doing my job, ma'am."

She stared out the window and hoped he didn't see the smile she was fighting. He'd come looking for her. Why? She wanted to ask, but she didn't. "Under the circumstances, I'm glad you found me. I was contemplating how long it would take me to walk to town, and I'm not dressed for a long trek." She held out a booted foot. "These boots were most definitely not made for walking."

He did laugh then. Not a long laugh, but it was real and more relaxed than she'd heard from him today. She gave herself a mental gold star.

"I've never understood why women wear shoes that hurt their feet and make it impossible for them to move quickly."

"Sometimes it's vanity. We like the way we look while wearing them or the way they make our legs look. But mostly I think some women just like cute shoes. Abby and Eliza both love shoes, and

45

they're only six." Abby and Eliza were her cousins' daughters, which made them her cousins once removed, but they called her Aunt Meredith, and she thought that was perfect. She loved both of their fathers like brothers.

Her mind flew to a different topic, and she blurted it out before she thought about it. "Did you hear that Cal's adoption of Eliza is final and her name change is official? She's now Eliza Shaw, and she's ecstatic about it."

Gray's smile was a flash of white in her peripheral vision. "I heard. Cal told me she's been going around introducing herself as Eliza Shaw and writing her name on everything."

"Did he tell you about the gift?" Cal had given Eliza a monogrammed necklace with her new initials on it.

"I was with him when he picked it out." There was a bit of smugness in Gray's voice.

"Y'all did a good job. Landry told me Eliza wears it every day."

"Cal was so excited to buy it. He couldn't love that child more if she was his flesh and blood, but making everything legal and official has settled something in him."

"I agree. He said Aunt Carol already asked when they're going to give her a new grandbaby."

"Oh, he told me." Gray laughed, and the conversation settled into an easy flow until he pulled into the parking lot of her office. "Where are you headed from here?"

The question was asked innocently enough, but Meredith caught the protective edge in it. Normally, she would have bristled, but today, she appreciated knowing someone was looking out for her.

"I'm headed to my desk. It's tax time."

"Have fun with that."

"Oh, I won't, but I promised myself tacos tonight as a reward for my good behavior and hard work."

"Tacos are a reward?"

She opened the door, climbed out, but then leaned back across the seat. "Tacos can be anything you want them to be. They can be a reward. They can be a treat. They can be therapy. They can be breakfast, lunch, or dinner. But most importantly, tacos can't be limited to Tuesdays." She grinned at him and closed the door.

And had the intense satisfaction of seeing him laugh as he drove toward the police station.

Followed by the ever-present dissatisfaction that plagued her when she was away from Gray.

"He's not interested." She reminded herself of that painful truth, walked inside, made a sandwich from the supplies she kept in the office kitchen, and then lost herself in the tedium of tax preparation.

It took Gray forty-five minutes to get to his desk. When he finally sat down, he dropped his head back onto his chair and closed his eyes.

He was so tired.

He'd only taken four breaths when his intercom buzzed and Glenda, his secretary/daytime dispatcher, spoke. "Chief Ward, Cal Shaw is here to see you."

Gray leaned forward and pressed the button that allowed him to speak to her. "Send him back."

A minute later, Cal entered his office. Maisy, Cal's faithful golden retriever, was right on his heels. She came around the desk and pressed her muzzle into Gray's stomach. "Hey, girl. Hello, beautiful." He crooned a bunch of nonsense that for some reason made perfect sense when spoken to a dog.

Maisy wasn't officially a trained therapy dog, but she had an uncanny ability to sense tension. She would always comfort Cal first, but she was wildly generous with her affection and had a knack for arrowing in on the most stressed-out person in the room.

"Well"—Cal sat in the chair across from Gray's desk and nodded toward Maisy—"I guess that answers my first question. You're having a crummy day."

"You talked to Mo?"

"Mo and Uncle Doug."

"Meredith?"

"Came here first. Going to see her next."

Gray ran his hands over Maisy's head. She rested it on his knee and didn't seem inclined to move. Not that he minded. "I don't know any more than I did an hour ago. Someone intentionally punctured her fuel line. I can't prove it, but I'm not trying to prove it in court. Given the way it was leaking, there's no way it happened before she left town. That means someone did it while she was at Mrs. Frost's home."

Cal leaned forward and snagged a mini Reese's cup from the bowl on Gray's desk. "Mrs. Frost is a terrorist on the road, but she's harmless otherwise."

"Agreed. And Meredith said the tooth pain was real. Mrs. Frost wasn't faking it. And Mo sent me a text. He drove up to Mrs. Frost's place. He wound up spending an hour doing stuff around her house but looked around while he did it, talked to her as he did. She didn't know anything, and he didn't find any smoking guns."

They sat in silence for a few moments. "None of this makes sense, Gray. Why target Meredith?"

"No clue."

More silence.

"I heard she promised not to leave the county alone."

Gray grunted acknowledgment. Cal was fishing, but Gray wasn't in the mood to bite.

"You asked. She promised." Cal reached for another Reese's. "Funny."

"She's an intelligent woman, and what happened scared her. She doesn't know what's going on either. I gave her an excuse to protect herself. That's it."

"Right." Cal slapped his hands on his legs. "Good talk." He stood, leaned over the desk, and dropped his voice to a low whisper. "I don't care how much you've deluded yourself about your relationship with Meredith. But I appreciate that you're doing everything you can to keep her safe. Thank you."

In a normal voice, he called Maisy to him. She gave Gray one last snuggle and then followed Cal to the door, where he paused. "We'll be out by the firepit tonight."

"It's freezing."

"True. But it's a good place to have a conversation that no one can overhear. We'll build the fire up big. It will be toasty."

"It would be toastier inside." Gray didn't mind sitting by a firepit in the fall or spring. Or even in the summer after dark when the mountain air could still be a bit chilly. But in the dead of winter? North Carolina winters weren't nearly as cold as Chicago winters, but it still got nippy at night.

"Wear gloves."

"I'll think about it."

"You do that."

Cal and Maisy left. But Cal's question lingered. Why Meredith? Why today? And who was behind it?

The town was still reeling from the events of the fall when a prominent member of the community, Steven Pierce, had been arrested for drug dealing and attempted murder.

The Pierce family owned and operated The Haven, an exclusive resort for the uber-wealthy, connected, famous, and reclusive. Bronwyn Pierce had grown up with Cal, Meredith, and Mo and was now the CEO of The Haven. Steven was her cousin, and he'd tried to have Cassie Quinn, the new chef at The Haven's fine dining restaurant, killed.

Ironically enough, the drama between the Pierces and Quinns had cooled noticeably in the aftermath. The majority of the Pierce family had been horrified by Steven's actions. The Pierce/Quinn conflict was long-standing, but it had never been violent.

That had been the only good thing to come from the arrest. It had brought unwanted press to the usually quiet and safe town of Gossamer Falls. The media, always quick to scent blood in the water, had used the events to highlight the ongoing drug issues in the mountains of Western North Carolina specifically and the Appalachian region in general.

While Gray had no problem acknowledging the real problems in their area, the thing that made him see red was that his hands had been tied. While the attacks on Cassie had been in Gossamer Falls, the root of the problem was across the county line in Neeson. And outside his jurisdiction.

But he'd found a possible way around that.

Criminals could be savvy and slick, but they could also be incredibly stupid. And some of the drug traffickers in Neeson had crept across the county line. Gray doubted they knew they'd slipped into his jurisdiction.

He wasn't about to enlighten them. Not until he had proof and the kind of evidence that would bring in the state investigators who would turn Neeson upside down and inside out.

He hadn't lied to Meredith this morning. He had gone toward the Neeson County line because he suspected that she'd gone in that direction. What he hadn't told her was that while he was near the county line, he sometimes parked, got out of his Explorer, and did a little hiking.

If Meredith knew what he'd been up to, she'd lose it.

The first time it had been an in-the-moment idea, but since then, he'd made more jaunts into the forest. Always alone. And he was willing to admit that it hadn't been a smart decision. He wasn't a skilled outdoorsman. After the events of today, he was done going solo. But it was what he'd seen on his hikes that had convinced him that some of the drug traffickers had spread a bit too far south. The jurisdictional lines were blurry in the area, but he'd confirmed that at least one house he suspected of being a meth lab was solidly in the town limits of Gossamer Falls.

Gray had friends in Raleigh and in the State Bureau of Investigations. There were people, the kind of people who could do something about it, who didn't like what was happening in Neeson. The mess with Steven Pierce had given them the ammunition they'd needed to stop gathering information and move toward making arrests. But they weren't there yet.

The investigation that had been launched was so secret that none of his officers knew anything about it. That was about to change.

He picked up the phone and called his contact at SBI. It was time to spread the net wider.

FIVE

"I hate to say this, but it might be too cold for a firepit night."
Meredith had started the evening in her warmest coat, gloves,
toboggan, and lined boots. But even though the fire Mo had built
was reaching bonfire proportions, she was twirling around like a
rotisserie chicken to stay warm. "I'm going inside to get a quilt."

"Me too." Cassie jumped up from where she'd been sitting on
her fiancé's lap and ran to her own house.

"Hurry up!" Donovan called out. "You were keeping me warm."

Meredith paused at the door to her tiny house and looked back at
the firepit where Donovan sat talking to Cal and Mo while Landry,
Cal's wife, roasted a marshmallow for their daughter, Eliza.

Things changed. And this change was good.

Meredith, Mo, and Cal had built their tiny house compound
a few years earlier. They all owned adjoining land, gifted to them
on their twenty-fifth birthday—a rite of passage for the Quinn
grandchildren and now great-grandchildren.

Given that they were all single at the time, it made more sense
to build small homes. The hope, though no one had voiced it, was
that eventually they would all find spouses and build their forever
homes. The tiny houses had been meant to be temporary.

So far, Cal was the only one who'd found the love of his life.

He and Landry moved into their home on Cal's land last July. The house was less than a quarter of a mile from the tiny houses. During the winter, when the trees were bare, you could see their porch from the firepit.

Since Cassie had needed a temporary place to live, Cal had offered his tiny house to her until she and Donovan married. They would eventually build on Cassie's land, but they weren't in a hurry.

Cassie's addition to their little compound had been a good fit for all of them. And this past summer, Mo and Cal had demolished the original firepit and expanded it. Where once there had been three permanent chairs, now there were eight.

The sound of an engine caught her attention, and the sight of Gray's Explorer sent Meredith running inside her house. She'd had a long day and it wouldn't hurt to touch up her makeup and run a brush through her hair before she went back out.

Ten minutes later, wrapped in an old quilt and carrying two others, she rejoined the group, which now included Gray and Bronwyn Pierce.

"You came!" She hugged Bronwyn and handed her a quilt, then turned to Gray. "Would you like one? I told Mo it was too cold. His answer was to throw more wood on the fire."

Gray took the quilt and pointed at Cal. "I told you it was too cold."

"It's never too cold." Mo and Cal spoke in unison, and the whole group burst into laughter.

They chatted for another ten minutes before Landry stood and pulled Eliza up with her. "We're going to head home." She gave Cal a kiss that probably was intended to be a short peck but turned into something more. When she pulled back, she whispered something to him and he grinned.

"Disgusting." Bronwyn blew on her hot chocolate. "And yes, I'm a bitter old harpy."

Landry laughed at Bronwyn's insincere griping. "See you tomorrow." She hugged Meredith, then Bronwyn. "Don't stay out too late. You have a busy day."

"Yeah, yeah." Bronwyn truly sounded disgruntled now, and Landry gave her another hug. "You've got this. I'll be praying."

"Thanks."

They weren't trying to keep their voices low, so Meredith had no guilt about asking, "What's tomorrow?"

Meredith caught the way Mo watched Bronwyn with a look that gave her the courage to keep hoping for a reconciliation between her brother and her best friend.

Bronwyn groaned. "A board meeting."

Everyone around the fire groaned with her. Even Eliza.

"Aunt Bronwyn hates board meetings," Eliza informed them. "She says they're the worst way to waste a day."

Bronwyn wasn't Eliza's aunt by blood or by marriage, but once Eliza realized that she now had a huge family that included lots of aunts and uncles, she immediately put Bronwyn into the same category.

Bronwyn grinned at the little girl with all the affection and adoration a doting aunt could have. "You got that right, sweetheart. Now come give me a hug and let your mama take you home and get you warmed up."

No one brought up the board meeting again until Landry and Eliza waved their flashlight from the large wraparound porch of their home.

Landry would settle Eliza into bed and then come back out with a monitor. Assuming they hadn't all frozen to death by the time the bedtime routine was over.

"Board meeting?" Cal directed the question to Bronwyn, who'd taken her usual seat. "They giving you trouble?"

The "they" in question was a faction of the Pierce family who didn't approve of Bronwyn's leadership. They were the same faction who insisted that Steven Pierce was innocent of all charges, even though Cassie had heard his voice and they had other witnesses and tons of evidence regarding his role in her abduction.

"When are they not giving me trouble?" There was a weariness in Bronwyn's voice that was new. "It will be fine. My side of the family supports me, and we have the majority stake. But I can't shake the feeling that they are up to something."

"A hostile takeover?" Gray's question gave Meredith the excuse she needed to look at him again. He looked tired too. And worried. There was a line between his eyes that she had an urge to smooth out with her fingertip.

"Maybe? After what Steven did? I wouldn't put anything past them. I have to go into every meeting armed to the teeth."

"Literally?" Gray's eyebrow did that thing it did, and Meredith couldn't quite tell if he was concerned or merely curious.

"Literally." Bronwyn wasn't joking. "Don't worry, Chief. I have my concealed carry permit."

"I know you do." Gray wasn't joking either. The tension around the firepit had spiked higher than the flames. "Want some backup? I'm sure Donovan wouldn't mind hanging out in Hideaway with Cassie if you want someone close."

Hideaway, the fine dining restaurant at The Haven, was Cassie's domain. And Meredith was sure Gray was right about Donovan's willingness to spend time with her.

"I'll be there too." Mo's deep rumble came from the other side of the firepit. "You won't mind my company, will you, Cassie?"

Bronwyn looked at her mug, and Meredith blinked back tears. Mo and Bronwyn's relationship was so complicated it made quantum physics look straightforward. To Meredith's knowledge, the two had still somehow managed not to speak directly to each other in . . . over a decade? It had been a very, very long time.

Cassie, bless her, piped up, "Mo! You know you're one of my favorite cousins." She winked at Meredith as she said this. "Of course you can come."

"One of?" Mo's voice was almost a purr. "It's okay, Cass. I know you don't want to hurt their feelings by telling the truth, but we all know I am *the* favorite."

During the not-really-heated exchange that followed as Cal made his case for favorite cousin status, Meredith saw the moment when Gray made eye contact with Donovan. There was a chin lift and a nod, and she knew Donovan would be in Hideaway tomorrow during the board meeting. And if Mo said he would be there, he would.

She leaned over and patted Bronwyn's hand. "We've got your back."

"So it would seem." Bronwyn gave her a small smile and leaned back into her chair. It was like she was trying to hide in plain sight, and Meredith's heart hurt for her friend. So she did what she could.

She clapped her gloved hands together, and while they made almost no sound at all, the motion directed everyone's attention to her. "I hate to be the one to cut this frivolity short, but I'm freezing to death. Cal? I'm assuming there's a reason you wanted us all out here tonight?"

Cal propped his feet on the stone wall around the fire. "Yeah. I think it's high time you told us what you know or think you know about Chief Kirby and the mess going on in Neeson."

Gray sat straighter as Meredith stared at Cal. Her mouth was open in a little "O" of surprise, but she didn't say anything.

"I know you don't want to gossip or slander. And that's admirable. I love that about you. You're gentle and kind, even with people who don't deserve your favor. But, Mer, someone cut your fuel line today. It's time to share with the class what you know, think you know, might know, or might maybe possibly kinda sorta suspect." Cal pointed to Gray. "He's doing everything he can to keep you safe." He pointed to Mo. "So is he. So am I." He waved his hand around the circle. "Everyone here will protect you to the best of our ability, but you have to give us something to go on."

Meredith dropped her head, and Bronwyn leaned toward her. "He's right, you know."

Meredith looked up and her gaze snagged Gray's. "Did you know this was what he wanted tonight?" There was pain in the question and a hint of betrayal in her expression.

"No clue. He told me we needed to talk and that I should come over tonight. It was all very cryptic."

Her entire body relaxed at his words, and Gray wondered if she had any idea how expressive she was. She should never, ever play poker. Or go undercover.

It was a miracle she'd gone this long without sharing what she knew about Kirby. At the risk of bringing her ire down on him, he kept going. "For what it's worth, I agree with Cal."

Before she could respond, Mo chimed in, "So do I."

Donovan, not to be left out, said, "Same."

Cassie and Bronwyn shared a look, and Bronwyn said, "I'm all for the sisterhood and everything, but I'm with the guys on this one."

Landry rejoined them and flopped into her seat beside Cal. "Are we making Meredith spill?"

Cassie said, "I believe so."

"Oh, thank goodness." Landry grinned at Meredith. "You know I love you, but you're stressing us out."

Meredith's shoulders dropped and she said, "Fine," with the same attitude a teenager might use on their parents. But when she spoke again, her voice was clear and held a confidence and concern that told Gray she'd spent a lot of time thinking and processing what she was sharing. "I first noticed something was weird in Neeson on my third trip. My schedule has me in the county three times a year. The first time I'd been there had been in April. But it was December this time, and it was bitterly cold."

She scooted closer to the fire and took a sip of her drink. "You know how kids are. Teenage boys will wear shorts and a hoodie no matter how cold it is. And I'm not like Mrs. Flanders."

Bronwyn, Cal, Mo, and Cassie all laughed. Gray looked at Donovan and Landry, and the three of them shared the same look. The one that said, "I have no idea what's so funny."

Meredith caught his eye and reined in her laughter enough to explain. "Mrs. Flanders is about eighty now. But when we"— she waved her hands to include her cousins and brother—"were younger, she was the town librarian."

Mo threw back his head and laughed louder than Gray had ever seen him. "Do you remember?" That was all he got out before he doubled over laughing again. Cal joined him and then, to Gray's shock, Bronwyn laughed so hard she snorted.

Bronwyn and Mo shared a look while they were laughing, and while Gray didn't claim to have a romantic bone in his body, even he could feel the sparks and tension coming off those two.

Meredith again pulled it together first. "Mrs. Flanders had been widowed about three months after she got married. She wasn't really that old, but when we were little, we thought she was ancient. She would be so mad when we came in without a coat. She'd say, 'You're gonna catch your death' and 'I know your mother can afford to take better care of you' and, my personal favorite, 'I'm going to have a chat with Catherine about this.'"

Mo wiped his eyes. "She had so many chats with Granny. I never understood why Granny didn't tell her to shove off."

Meredith put her hand on her chest and widened her eyes in obviously mock outrage. "Granny would never."

Landry scooted to the end of her chair. "What did y'all do to this poor woman?"

Bronwyn raised her hand. "To be fair, it wasn't Meredith or Cal."

Mo looked to the stars, and his entire body shook with the laughter he still hadn't gotten under control. "It was my idea. Bronwyn was a little bitty thing. And we were sure she'd fit."

Fit?

"The book drop slot was a lot bigger than it is now. We'd seen it on a tour our class took of the library. It was more of a chute. Like a slide." Bronwyn held out her hands. "I mean, it was just begging for someone to try it."

"You went down the book return?" Donovan's question held all the same surprise that Gray was feeling. It was hard to imagine the normally cool and professional Bronwyn Pierce as a little hooligan terrorizing the librarian.

"I tried to."

Mo still didn't have complete control of his laughter. "I got down on the floor on my hands and knees. She climbed onto my back and put her arms and head in. Then I tried to push her the rest of the way through by her feet."

Meredith and Cal both howled at his words.

"There were so many books in the bottom that I couldn't squeeze my entire body into the bin." Bronwyn wiped at her eyes. "And the chute was too narrow for me to pull my legs up."

Meredith managed to speak in between bouts of giggles. "We came around the corner, and all we saw was Mo standing beside the book return and Bronwyn's feet kicking."

Cal picked up the tale. "And that's when Mrs. Flanders caught us."

"What happened?" Landry and Donovan asked at the same time.

The four miscreants were all laughing so hard they couldn't answer. Cassie spoke up. "You have to understand that this story is a family legend. I've heard it my entire life. Mrs. Flanders panicked and started screaming. Aunt Carol was in the nonfiction section and came running because she thought someone was hurt. She gets the story from Mo, calls into the chute, and hears Bronwyn insisting that she's fine, just stuck. She turns to Mrs. Flanders and says, 'For crying out loud, Janet. Pull yourself together and go get the child out of the book return.' But Mrs. Flanders is frozen. So Aunt Carol goes into the office area where the book bin is and extracts Bronwyn from the chute. By this time, Mrs. Flanders has stopped screaming, but she's furious and she tells them to leave and never come back." Cassie took a breath. "The story goes that Aunt Carol took all four of them out for ice cream after."

"Mom told me later that she thought the whole thing was hilarious. Especially because it was Beep that went down the chute. She would have expected it of me or you"—Cal pointed to himself and then Meredith—"but never Mo and Bronwyn."

It took a couple of minutes for the laughter to turn to chuckles and then to random huffs of amusement.

"Anyway," Meredith said once she was fully in control, "Mrs. Flanders never had children, but she had a lot of opinions about children. No one could make her understand that kids don't like to wear coats. That if they're cold, they will put one on. And that they won't get sick from walking from the car to the library without a jacket."

She pointed to herself. "As the favorite aunt of many delightful children, I'm not like Mrs. Flanders. I don't judge the moms when the kids walk into my office wearing nothing more than a sweater. To be honest, I'm more likely to judge if they come in covered up in a scarf, toboggan, and puffy jacket when it's not that cold outside. It's not safe for kids to be in car seats when they're all bundled up like that. And it's inefficient to expect them to put on that many layers to walk fifty feet."

Gray had to remind himself that a toboggan in North Carolina wasn't the same thing as a toboggan in Chicago. He didn't know why they didn't just call it a hat. Or a knit cap. Both of which were shorter than saying toboggan. And less confusing. But now wasn't the time to bring it up, because all the humor drained from Meredith's face as she continued to speak.

"It's different in Neeson. When I do the clinic up there, I park in a church lot. They let me hook up to their power and water. They typically open the building, but they don't turn the heat or A/C on."

"Why not?"

Gray knew the answer to Cassie's innocent question, but he wondered how Meredith would answer it. "Part of it is ignorance. They think they're doing a good deed by giving me access to the water and power, and they are. But they mainly open the building so I have access to the bathroom. The people who come to the clinic don't go to their church. The pastor knows Papa and Uncle John, and they asked the pastor there if I could have access to the building. I think in the minds of the people in the church, they're already going above and beyond."

"That's dumb."

Gray gave Cassie an air fist bump. She wasn't wrong.

"They don't really see the people who are coming to my clinic. I mean, they think what I'm doing is great. They're in favor of it. But that doesn't mean they trust the riff-raff in their building. So they won't make it convenient or comfortable for them. Even when it's blazing hot or freezing cold."

Meredith gave Cassie a sad smile. "It's entitled and completely not what Christianity is about, but I'm playing a long game. That church parking lot is the best spot in Neeson for me to set up. There's plenty of room. Easy access to the water and power. They have bathrooms. And even the criminal element in town would hesitate before coming after me on church property. It's the safest spot in town. And every time I go, I pray for their hearts to soften."

Meredith propped her feet up on the firepit edge. "The problem is that their concerns are valid. I didn't realize it at first. I thought it was just snobbery and elitism and a holier-than-thou attitude. And it is some of that. But it's also prudence. I do see adults, but I'd say seventy-five percent of my patients are children and teenagers, and I've discovered that their parents aren't always upstanding citizens."

It required an intense effort for Gray to keep from making a comment on Meredith's understatement.

Donovan either didn't succeed or didn't try. "I think when you said they aren't upstanding citizens, what you meant is they're drug-running hardened criminals."

Cal and Mo had gone from relaxed and laughing to serious and alert.

"I wish you were wrong." Meredith looked into the fire. "The parents . . . I know they're up to no good. But the kids? They're adorable. Chubby cheeks. Funny stories."

When she didn't seem inclined to continue, Mo asked, "What kind of stories?"

"Oh, you know." Meredith wiped at her eyes, and when she spoke, her voice was high and childish. "My dog got into the shed last night. I think he heard something, but Daddy said it was just an animal. But he ran out of the shed with a sock! A purple sock! I think he might be magic because I don't have any purple socks."

Gray expected her to stop, but she didn't.

Meredith's voice shifted to that of a young boy. "My daddy has two jobs. He works at the jail. But he also has a special kitchen in our barn. I'm not allowed to go in there, but he goes in there a lot. He said he's perfecting a recipe. And sometimes people come buy his special treats late at night."

It was like someone had opened the floodgates because, this time, her voice had changed, and she was a frightened girl. "I don't know how that happened, Dr. Quinn. I'm just clumsy. I bruise super easy so I don't know . . ."

Meredith—his sweet, funny, innocent Meredith—looked around the circle of people who now stared at her, their faces a mix of horror and worry. And when she spoke, her voice was harder than he'd ever heard it. Angry in a way that he hadn't known she was capable of. "Those stories? Those came from children who have fathers in law enforcement. There's at least one officer who's physically abusing his family. One is cooking meth. And I don't even want to think about the purple sock. Best-case scenario? He's having an affair. Worst case? Trafficking—drugs and people."

SIX

Meredith slid back into her seat. She'd told them. It was out. But not the worst of it. "I went to Kirby."

Gray nearly came out of his chair. "You did what?"

"I'm a mandated reporter, Gray. And I was in his jurisdiction. I'm required by law to report cases of suspected abuse. I went to Chief Kirby and told him what I'd heard."

Gray stared at her, mouth open and apparently unable to form words.

"What did he say?" The question came from Mo, who was nearly vibrating with fury.

"He took my report. Told me he'd look into it. Told me he appreciated me doing my job. He was kindness personified."

"So, basically, he patted you on the head, told you that you were a good girl, and sent you on your way assuming you wouldn't worry about it anymore?" Bronwyn's words dripped with derision.

"Essentially."

"When did he realize you weren't going to drop it?"

Meredith could have hugged Landry for her words. "The next time I filed a similar report."

"What did he say?" Gray's voice was a low rumble, and it sent a shiver down her spine. The shiver wasn't entirely one of fear.

"He wasn't quite as friendly. He told me he appreciated the position I was in as a mandated reporter but suggested I shouldn't take everything that came from the mouths of toddlers as gospel."

"Idiot." Cassie smirked. "How'd that work for him?"

"I sent my next reports to social services, but nothing happened. I've concluded that there's no one in Neeson County who is safe. The children aren't safe. The adults aren't safe. I'm not saying there aren't any good people there. There are. But there's so much fear there. Someone, and I'm not convinced the someone in question is Kirby, has them all under his thumb. The social worker told me she'd received my report and she would look into it. I keep sending reports. She sends me the same canned response each time, so I asked Mo to find out about her."

Mo was not pleased. "You didn't tell me why you wanted the info."

"I didn't want to bias you."

He gave her a curt nod, then took up the narrative. "I didn't know the backstory. What I found out is that the social worker assigned to Neeson is Marvin Johnstone's daughter-in-law. Marvin is in his sixties, and he's doing awfully well for a man who hasn't held down a job in thirty years. Large home. Multiple cars. The family lives on the property."

Donovan snorted at that. "The way you do?"

"No." Mo wasn't angry, but he was firm. "Not even close. We own our land. We own our homes. Even these homes." He waved at their tiny homes. "It's different for them. Johnstone owns the property and houses. His kids live in them. They pay rent. I didn't dig more at the time."

His expression told Meredith that he would be digging now. Probably tonight.

"Johnstone's the one we suspect is behind most of the drug trafficking in Neeson." Gray closed his eyes and leaned back into his seat. "Meredith? How do you do this?"

"Do what?"

"Get mixed up with the absolute worst possible people?"

"Hey!" Cal objected.

"I'm not talking about your family." Gray rubbed his hands over his face. "I'm talking about Johnstone and the dirty cops."

"It's not like I went looking for them." Why was this so hard for everyone to understand? "I offered free dental care. That's it. I didn't think anything of the officers bringing their kids. It's not like police work is a high-paying job. I was happy to take care of anyone who needed some help. No problem. And I didn't know Johnstone had a lot of money. I have a lot of little Johnstones in my files, and their parents don't look like they're living large. The kids are in cheap clothes. The moms look . . ." Meredith considered her words.

"I'm not a mom, but I know it's exhausting and hard work," she said. "So please understand that what I'm about to say is not a criticism of these women. It isn't. But these moms look defeated. Worn. Desperate. They're trying. But they don't think they have any choices. I don't think they believe they can leave. They're stuck. And their kids are stuck."

It was the stuckness that broke Meredith's heart. "I don't know how to help them. I don't know what else I can do. I try to be kind. Try not to make assumptions. Try to pray for them. And I've told more than one of them that if they ever decide to make a change, they can call me."

Gray sucked in a breath. Cal shared a look with Mo that Meredith didn't like at all. And then Donovan let out a huge groan. "You've ticked off the entire criminal population of Neeson. Which means anyone—from Johnstone to Kirby—could be coming after you."

"Yes."

"You have to stay out of Neeson." This came from Mo. "You see that, don't you?"

Meredith didn't respond.

"Meredith?" This time it was Cal. "You don't have to do clinics in Neeson. You really don't. You've done quite a few. Let things settle down."

"I can't."

"You can't or you won't?" Gray's tone told her he already knew the answer.

"I've given my word."

"Is that worth dying over?"

"They aren't going to kill me!"

"What do you think the plan was for today, Meredith?" Gray's voice had lost all of its usual control. "They intended to leave you stranded. They probably hoped you'd be stranded in Neeson County. If you'd run out of diesel a mile earlier, I wouldn't have seen you. Do you not see how easy it would be? We find the van on the side of the road. You're missing. A week from now, we find your body. No one is to blame. It's a tragedy. You decided to hike and got turned around."

Meredith's throat constricted at his words. No one else spoke as they watched the conversation bounce between them.

"There is nothing in Neeson worth taking that kind of risk."

"There's a wedding."

"A wedding?" Gray snorted. "Why do you have to go to a wedding?"

"I'm doing the flowers."

"When?"

"In late February."

"Can they not come to Gossamer Falls to pick up the flowers?"

"I have a contract to decorate the church and the reception hall.

The girl getting married is precious. Her little sisters are adorable. The mom is so tired and worn. I need to help them."

"At the expense of getting yourself killed?"

"It's a wedding!"

Gray glared at her. She glared back. "You cannot go into Neeson alone. At all. Ever. For any reason."

"I don't have a problem with that. You don't have to worry about me sneaking off to Neeson. I'm not stupid, Gray. And I don't have a death wish. But I can't live with myself if I can't keep my word." She wanted to ask him why he cared so much. Why it mattered so much. But with her family looking on, she kept her questions to herself.

"Are you invited to the wedding?"

"What?"

"The wedding that you're doing the flowers for. Are you invited to the ceremony?"

"Yes."

"Then I'm your plus-one."

"You—you're—what?"

"I like it." A slow smile crept across Cal's face. "They wouldn't dare do anything with Gray there."

Gray ignored them. His eyes were focused on her. "Well?"

This was a bad idea. Going to a wedding together? "I'm going to need to make a couple of trips to Neeson over the next month or so."

"I'll go with you."

"Gray." She didn't mean to whine. She cleared her throat. "I promise not to go alone. But you don't have to go. I'm sure my brother would be willing to be my plus-one."

She looked at Mo. The traitor shook his head. "Not a chance, baby sister."

"Why not?"

"I don't do weddings."

"You were Cal's best man!"

"It's a recent decision."

"Mo isn't a good choice for this. It has to be me." Gray's tone said it was decided.

"Why?" She was panicking. She could feel it. She'd been spending way too much time with Gray lately. If she had to go to a wedding with him? Dressed up? Gray in a uniform nearly undid her. Gray in a suit?

She wasn't a sadist. Spending time with him was a form of torture. She wanted to be with him, and she dreaded being with him. What fresh disaster would happen while she was in his presence? How much more would it hurt to want him and see for herself just how much he didn't want her?

She'd done her best to avoid him. And now?

"I have reasons." Gray held up a finger. "The first one is that if I go, they'll know I'm carrying. They'll know I'm prepared for anything, and they'll be less likely to try something. It might not hold them off forever, but it should make the wedding safe for you."

She wasn't convinced.

"Meredith, if I go, there's little chance of danger. If Mo goes? Not only will you be at risk, but you'll be putting him at risk as well. I know you don't want that."

"Of course not. But I don't want to put *anyone* at risk." She couldn't very well tell Gray that putting *him* at risk made her feel queasy.

"Then don't go to the wedding."

He had her and he knew it. Jerk. "Fine. You can be my plus-one for the wedding."

He nodded. It wasn't a date. He hadn't invited himself because he was falling for her. He'd invited himself because he was worried about her.

"And you won't go to Neeson alone?" This came from Mo. For a man who might not survive the night, he was being awfully pushy.

"I won't go to Neeson alone for any reason." It wasn't hard to make that promise. Going to Neeson terrified her.

Not that going to the wedding with Gray wasn't also terrifying. But her choices were limited. She either risked her life or her heart.

She was pretty sure she was going to lose one or the other.

Gray wanted to lock Meredith in a padded room for her own protection, but locking innocent people up was frowned upon. "I do have another reason for going to the wedding." His announcement pulled everyone's attention to him.

"I've already talked to Donovan, and what I'm about to tell you can't leave this group."

Everyone nodded.

"I can't go into details, so don't ask for them. But I want all of you to be on guard. We aren't the only ones who know things in Neeson are disintegrating. We aren't the only ones who want to do something about it. We've been picking on Meredith tonight."

"For good reason." Mo's stage-whispered comment made Meredith hold her hand up to him.

Her "You're dead to me" look was met with a grin from Mo.

Gray decided to ignore the exchange. "I can't make any of you do anything, but I'd prefer it if none of you go to Neeson for the next few months. And Bronwyn?"

Her eyes met his, and they were full of questions. Mo went on alert, and Gray suspected he didn't realize his demeanor had changed.

"I know you're above reproach, but you need to be careful at

70

work and around your family. I'm not convinced that Steven was the only Pierce involved in some of the enterprises in Neeson."

Bronwyn didn't argue. "I know. My parents are worried. Dad talked to Uncle Ronald and wasn't pleased with the response. Steven's parents have circled the wagons around him, and that entire branch of Pierces is furious with our side of the Pierces because we haven't supported Steven in"—her voice pitched up—"his time of need."

Her disgust with that statement was evident. "Dad isn't having it," she continued. "He's furious about all of it. He even called Cassie's dad."

There was a collective gasp.

"You didn't tell me that!" Meredith looked torn between excitement and outrage.

"I didn't know until today. Dad came by the office." She nodded at Cassie. "He ate at Hideaway and agreed with me that Cassie is the best thing that ever happened to the restaurant.

"Apparently he decided he should call John Quinn and tell him that."

"Wow." Cal rubbed his chin.

"I didn't see that coming." Cassie's comment summed it up well.

Bronwyn turned her attention back to Gray. "I appreciate the heads-up. And I am taking it seriously. So is my family. Dad is doing a lot of talking behind the scenes, trying to figure out which factions will be difficult and which will be reasonable. If you know of anything specific, I'd be happy to hear it."

"I wish I did, but if and when I learn more, I'll pass it along." Gray decided to press his luck. "Would you consider a police presence inside the gates of The Haven?"

Bronwyn's eyebrows nearly flew off her head. "What kind?"

"Random patrols."

"We have security."

Gray didn't react, but they all knew The Haven's security wasn't up to snuff. "Think about it. And don't be surprised when you see more overt law enforcement presence in the general area."

The long, quiet moment that followed was pierced by Mo's deep voice. "What are you worried about specifically at The Haven? A threat toward Bronwyn? Or the issue with drugs being sold and used?"

Gray looked at Mo. What he said next would send a ripple through their small group. "Both."

Bronwyn slumped in her seat while Landry, Cassie, and Meredith all scooted toward the end of their chairs. Cal, Mo, and Donovan gave him nearly identical looks he didn't need help interpreting. They were ready to protect Bronwyn, no matter the cost.

"I'm not trying to scare you."

"Sure you are." Meredith's eyes flashed in outrage. "And that's okay. But I'm confused about why they would be coming after either of us."

"I don't know what's going on at The Haven," Gray said. "I just know there are rumblings about the Pierces being unhappy. And given that Steven was prepared to go farther than anyone expected, I think Bronwyn needs to be on guard."

Bronwyn met his statement with a nod.

He turned to Meredith. "As for you? You know specifics. Maybe you know more specifics than you realize. Maybe they've decided they want you to stay out of Neeson. Maybe today was just about scaring you off. Maybe it was something more. I don't know. And I don't know how they're connected beyond a hunch that some of the criminal element that Steven Pierce was mixed up in is some of the same element who have been sending their kids to your clinic."

Gray laced his fingers together. "It's a tangled knot of family ties and outside criminals coming in. It's like trying to solve a puzzle when we don't have a picture to go on as a guide. We have lots of pieces. Some of them are definitely border pieces and we're making progress on that aspect. But the middle? It's a jumble."

He turned to Meredith. "I know this is a big ask, but would you be willing to come to my office tomorrow and help me connect some dots?"

"I'm happy to help, but I have a full schedule tomorrow."

He'd expected that, but he wasn't ready to give up. "I'm not sure if you've noticed, but I don't keep normal hours."

"Okay. I can come by after my last patient."

He'd been prepared for her to offer to talk on Saturday. Tomorrow night was far better. "That works for me. Thank you."

Meredith slid back in her seat. "Now that we're all depressed and scared, can we talk about something else?"

Her words hit him hard. He knew she hadn't meant to hurt him. Meredith didn't go around intentionally being mean. But still. He wanted her to be safe and happy. He didn't want her to live in fear. Jasmine had lived in fear for most of her eleven years. He would spare Meredith that if he could.

"I tried to teach Cal how to make a vase this week."

Gray sent Landry an appreciative smile and did his best to keep the conversation going. "How'd he do?"

"It had to be better than the last time." Mo turned his head and scratched his neck. He mouthed the word "disaster" to everyone.

"It wasn't a disaster." Landry's rebuttal lacked conviction. "It wound up being an . . . interesting shape."

"Why do you keep trying?" Meredith asked. "He's hopeless!"

Landry leaned into Cal and kissed him. There was no heat in the kiss. Nothing inappropriate. But there was so much tenderness in the moment that Gray looked away.

And when he did, he looked straight at Meredith. And found her looking at him.

Then in a completely junior high move, he bounced his gaze to the fire. And when the opportunity to leave presented itself a few minutes later, he took it.

He was five minutes down the road before the heat left his face and his heart rate settled. He had no idea how he'd survive the next few months of close proximity to Meredith.

But he would. There were lines he couldn't cross. And she was on the other side.

 **SEVEN**

Meredith brushed her teeth and ran a brush through her hair. It had been a long day, and she was exhausted. But yesterday she'd promised to talk to Gray, so that's where she was headed.

She pulled her phone off her desk and looked to see if he'd canceled.

Hey. I know it's late. I was thinking about ordering a pizza. We can eat while we talk?

He'd sent the text thirty minutes earlier. Ten minutes ago he'd added.

Pepperoni? Mushroom? I know you don't do olives.

So, they were having pizza. Fine. And how did he know she didn't like olives?

I like pepperoni. Or Hawaiian. Or meat lovers. Or white pizza. Or margherita.

The dots popped up.

Sounds good. You headed this way?

In five minutes.

She closed everything up and locked her office. When she stepped outside, she saw Gray walking toward her, phone to his ear. "Yeah. Can you deliver it to the station?" A pause. "Perfect. Thanks."

He slid the phone into his pocket. "Pizza will be ready in about thirty minutes."

"Do we need to talk outside?" She hoped not. It was freezing.

"No."

"Did you think I would get lost?" She pointed to the police station that she could see from her office.

"No."

"Then is there a reason you came out here to meet me?"

Gray was surprised by her question in a way that made her think he wasn't entirely sure of the answer. "Would 'I'm a gentleman' suffice?"

Surprisingly enough, it did. "Yes."

"Good." He held out a hand in the direction of the office. "It goes against my nature to have a woman walking around outside in the dark alone. Even here."

"By here, you mean Gossamer Falls?"

"Yes. I grew up in a city. It wasn't safe after dark." His words were clipped, and she got the distinct sense that whatever had made him think that was a painful thought. A bad memory.

"So this isn't because you think someone's going to snatch me off the street in between my office and yours?"

Gray didn't answer.

"You do think someone's going to snatch me?"

"No."

"You didn't quite stick the landing on that one, Chief Ward. If you're going to say no and expect me to believe it, it would help if you believed it yourself."

"I don't think you're in danger in the middle of town."

76

"But you haven't ruled it out as a possibility?"

"I never rule out anything."

He held the door to the station open and ushered her inside.

He nodded to the officer behind the desk but didn't speak. Meredith didn't feel like letting it slide. She turned around and walked backward as she greeted the man. "Why good evening, Officer Dawkins. How are you?"

He stood and winked at her. "I'm just fine, Dr. Quinn. And yourself?"

"Lovely. Thank you."

"I heard tell you kept Mrs. Frost from threatening public safety yesterday. Sure do appreciate that."

Meredith gave him a faux salute. "You aren't the only one who can serve and protect."

She turned and flashed a smile at Gray. The expression on his face made no sense to her. Was he angry? Frustrated? Annoyed? "What? You didn't expect me to walk past him without speaking, did you? He was two grades ahead of me in school. I've known him my entire life."

He leaned closer. "I'm not opposed to you speaking to people, but I didn't expect you to stroll in here and flirt with my officers."

Oh no he did not go there. "Are you serious right now?"

"Do I look like I'm joking?"

She waited until they were in his office to respond. He helped her with her jacket, and she allowed it, but that didn't mean she was going to take a seat until this was resolved. "First, I was not flirting. I was being friendly, unlike—oh, I don't know—you, who walked in and barely acknowledged him. It would have been rude for me not to say hello. *I* am not rude."

She tried to flip her hair, but somehow it got caught in her earring. Annoying, but not enough to make her stop talking. "Second, it was one officer, not multiple officers." She tried to find the strand of hair that was stuck. "Third, he's married. He and his wife teach the first- and second-grade Sunday school class at my church. He's a friend. I speak to my friends when I see them." She'd managed to get most of the hair loose, but not the final little piece that must have wrapped itself around the hoop twenty times while she was trying to untangle it.

"And fourth, if he wasn't a married man and I wanted to flirt with him, it wouldn't be any of your business."

A vein throbbed in Gray's temple. "It would be when he's on duty."

"Nope. Still not then."

"How do you figure that?"

"I figure that because, unlike poor Jeremiah out there, I'm not one of your employees." She was verging into "you're not the boss of me" territory, and she didn't want to go there. "I'm allowed to flirt, or not flirt, with anyone I want. You're too good of a boss to penalize an officer for something that's out of their control."

She managed to get the earring out of her ear, but it was still tangled in her hair. She looked around the office. "Did I not put a mirror in here? I need to fix that." She tried to see her hair and the earring in it but couldn't twist around enough to find it.

"Let me." Gray was there. Right in front of her. His hands were in her hair before she had a chance to argue. And then she had no oxygen to manage it. "There's a small mirror by the coat tree." His voice was low and soft.

She managed to suck in some air, but it was embarrassingly loud. "I can—"

"No. You can't. You've really managed to make a mess of this, and there's no way I can let you cut your hair. You love your hair."

She did, although she had no idea how Gray knew that. She'd had shorter hair when she was younger. And then she'd cut it after a breakup, which had been stupid because one of the big rules of breakups was not to make any major hair decisions without talking to your best friends first. But she'd been short on friends at the time. And she'd thought a pixie cut would make her happy.

She'd cried for an extra week, and everyone thought it was because of the guy when it was really because of her hair.

His fingers brushed against her jawline. "We can't be defeated by an earring."

"No." Her voice was a whisper.

"As for your earlier comments, you're right. I was rude to Dawkins. It wasn't intentional. I was just trying to get you inside and safe."

He pulled the earring free and handed it to her. "And you have always demonstrated that you are a much better person than I am. Which is why I shouldn't have been surprised when you made the choice to be kind even when I wasn't. It's good for me to be reminded that kindness from you isn't the same thing as flirting. Please accept my apology for jumping to conclusions."

Meredith couldn't figure out what was happening. He wasn't mad anymore. But even though he was being calm and gentle, she couldn't shake the sensation that he was further away from her than he'd ever been before.

Gray took a seat behind his desk. He needed the desk between them. No. He needed miles between them. Maybe a few states. A country?

If he moved to the Caribbean, he could find a job as a dive instructor and forget that he'd ever known a girl with gorgeous hair, a smile that could stop the world—or maybe just his world—and who he could never, ever have.

Right now what he needed was for Meredith to go home. But

he'd invited her here. He'd ordered pizza. Better to get this over with.

He pulled a legal pad from his desk and then put his laptop in front of him. "Okay. Let's see how much we can cover before the pizza arrives."

Meredith blinked a few times, then put the hoop earring back in her ear. "Okay. What do you want to know? And full disclosure, I'm bound by HIPAA regulations. I can't talk about my patients."

"I understand that. I don't want you to discuss anything dental or medical. Although I would like to know more about the reports you gave to Kirby and the social worker."

Meredith reached into her bag. "I thought you might say that. I made copies." She handed him a stack of forms. "My guess is that these documents don't exist in Neeson County. They've probably been destroyed. Or lost. Kirby made it a point to mention to me, twice, that they 'aren't as fancy' as we are down here in Gossamer Falls."

"He's using their paper system as a way to hide things?"

"I can't prove it. I can't prove anything. I'm a dentist, not an investigator. But if it walks like a duck and quacks like a duck . . ."

Gray scanned through the documents and then set them on his desk. "Are these your only copies?"

"No." She rushed to add, "Not that I don't trust you. I do. But if this building burned down, I wouldn't be shocked. Especially now that Steven Pierce has been moved."

Steven Pierce had been moved for his own safety. Ideally, few people would have known about his presence in their jail. But with the way his mother was squawking to the press at every opportunity, there'd been no way to keep it under wraps.

"True. Although if he'd stayed here, that might have made us an even bigger target. I suspect his criminal overlords are none too happy with dear Stevie right now."

"I can tell you for a fact that Steven never went by anything other than Steven. That whole 'dear Stevie' thing of his mother's is an act." Meredith hopped out of her chair and went to the mini fridge in the corner of his office. She opened it, extracted a bottle of water, and looked at him. "Do you mind?"

"Help yourself." He tried not to think about how much he liked how comfortable she was in his space.

"Do you want one?"

"No. I'm good." He pointed to the thermos on his desk.

"Coffee? For supper? How do you sleep?"

"It's water. I don't drink coffee after two p.m. Well, not usually anyway. And I sleep just fine, thank you very much." It was true. Sleep had never been his issue. His nightmares usually found him while he was wide awake.

She opened the bottle of water, took a sip, and flounced into the chair. "Good to know." She took another sip, then put the lid back on the bottle. "Look, I'm not sure if I have the answers you want. But I've been thinking about it today, and I might know how to find them."

Gray didn't like where this was going, but he knew Meredith. He had no chance of stopping her unless he heard her out. "I'm listening."

Meredith handed him another piece of paper from her bag. "After we talked last night, I decided it would make our time more efficient if I organized my thoughts. So I wrote this up at lunch today. I wouldn't recommend letting anyone see it."

Gray scanned the page. He was only two lines in before he stopped and looked at Meredith. "You heard this?"

"I did. And now that you know, you can understand why I won't discuss it with my family. I won't put them at risk any more than they already are by association with me. If it got out that they knew?"

Gray pinched the bridge of his nose. "Yes. And I agree. Let's start at the beginning."

Meredith glanced behind her at the closed door. "Can anyone hear us?"

"No."

"Okay. Fine. For context, as I mentioned before, the Neeson church opens their doors for me, mainly so I can use the facilities. I was inside one day, and before I came out, I heard voices in the hallway. Deep voices. I didn't recognize them. I assumed they were a couple of dads, although I typically see the moms. Not a lot of dads bring their kids to the dentist."

Gray fought to keep an impassive expression on his face. But the thought of her alone in an empty building, even if that building was a church, sent a shiver of terror across his skin.

"I heard the first guy say, 'Kirby's ours. You don't have to worry about that.' Then the other guy said, 'What about Nichols? He's a straight arrow.' And the first guy said, 'We have a plan for him.' And then the other guy said, 'Really? Because I don't think we can turn him.'"

Meredith swallowed hard, and her expression was grief-stricken when she continued. "The first guy used a few curse words and then he said, 'The only kind of man who can't be turned is a man who has nothing to lose. A man like Nichols has a lot to lose.'"

"There's a Nichols on Neeson's police force. Do you think that's who they were talking about?"

"Yes."

"Do you know what they have on him?"

She shook her head. "No, but I might be able to get it."

He wasn't touching that. Not yet. "Do you know who the other two men were?"

She nodded.

"How do you know?"

"They were still talking when I came outside. I didn't think they saw me, but it's possible they did. And given what happened with my van, I'm leaning more toward the idea that they think I overheard them."

"Who are they, Meredith?"

She looked at the paper she'd handed him. A paper that didn't have any names on it. "Does it change anything if I tell you?"

"It might." When she continued to hesitate, he asked, "Why don't you want to tell me?"

"What if I'm wrong?" She threw out her hands. "I don't think I am, but what I'm accusing them of is serious. I could ruin their lives. I won't swear under oath about this. Hearsay is inadmissible. And this is all hearsay."

"I'm not going to try to get a warrant based on what you tell me. And I promise to keep an open mind."

She leaned toward him. "Trace Ledbetter and Winston Hardaway."

Gray sat back. Winston Hardaway was Chief Kirby's son-in-law. "How do you know them?"

Meredith ran a hand through her hair. "Winston is the same age as Cal's older brother, Chad. Gossamer Falls High played Neeson High in most sports. We don't play them as often now because they're a smaller school. Winston was a phenomenal basketball player. He and Chad weren't friends, but they were friendly. They wound up at a lot of the same camps and got along reasonably well. He has a scar on his temple. The story was he got it mountain biking."

"You don't believe it?"

"I never thought to question it until I started hanging out in Neeson. Lots of folks with random scars in Neeson. Makes you wonder."

Gray made a note on the legal pad to mention the scars to the undercover agent. It might be nothing. Might be important.

"What about Trace?"

"Never met him or heard of him until this past year. His wife brings his kids in."

"And?"

"He comes with them."

"And that's weird?"

"It doesn't have to be. It isn't always. But with him? Yeah. It's weird. My clinic is tiny. I let an adult come in with the kids, but just one. He doesn't like that. Wanted to know why he couldn't come in too. I told him he was welcome to if he could fit. Or he could come in instead of his wife. He didn't want to do that."

"So he gave you a bad vibe?"

She gave him an apologetic look. "I told you I don't really know anything. It's a lot of thoughts, maybes, inklings, vibes. Not facts."

"You don't have to have facts to be right."

"Fine. Then yes. He gives off a bad vibe. His kids aren't afraid of him, but they're still very young. His wife is flat-out terrified and so are other people. When they show up, there's tension in the people waiting. Last time, there were at least five people in front of them, but somehow they wound up next in line. When I asked about it, Mrs. Ledbetter said her husband had somewhere to be and had asked the others if they would mind if they jumped the line."

Despite the seriousness of the conversation, Gray had to bite back a smile. Meredith was such a mother hen. It had offended her, on the others' behalf, that they'd been taken advantage of.

"There wasn't anything I could do." Meredith hopped up and started pacing the small area in front of his desk. "I wouldn't have caught the subtext the first time. Maybe not the second. But by the third, I knew the people and the routine. Mrs. Ledbetter would never jump the line, but Trace didn't hesitate. He has something on those people."

"Did anyone say anything about it?"

"Obliquely. When the Ledbetters left, my next patient was someone close to my age. She's friendly. We talk about music and hiking. So I said something like, 'Mrs. Ledbetter sure did appreciate you letting them take your spot in line.'"

Meredith tapped the back of the chair with her fist. "She looked at me and said, 'Dr. Quinn, he don't wait in line in Neeson. Not at the post office, not at the diner, and sure enough not at the dentist.' Then she looked like she wanted to cram every word she'd said back in her mouth so I just said, 'Good to know.' And I changed the subject."

"You didn't leave it there, though, did you?"

Meredith looked like a kid caught with her hand in the cookie jar. "No. I used a database of Mo's to look up Trace Ledbetter."

"And?"

"And I think he might be the scariest man I've ever met."

EIGHT

Meredith walked to the bookshelf in Gray's office. She couldn't deny the way her confession had lifted a burden from her. A weight she hadn't noticed until it was gone.

It was nice, having someone else understand. But why did it have to be Gray who shared the load?

"You're good at that." She touched a small rock that sat on the shelf, shiny and smooth like it had come from a river. Or maybe it had been handled so often it had worn down.

"I'm going to need you to be more specific."

The teasing tone had her turning to face him. "Are you messing with me?"

He widened his eyes at her, and there was a grin tugging at his lips. "I would never."

"Fine. Since you're good at so many things, I'll clarify. You're good at getting people to talk to you. To open up. To spill their darkest secrets."

"Have you spilled your darkest secret?"

Oh. He was good. She had a secret. It wasn't dark, but it was private. And somehow she suspected that he knew. "I think I've gone as far as I'm willing to go." For tonight, anyway.

"Fair enough." He went from teasing, or was it flirting? Maybe?

No. It must have been teasing. Regardless, he went from whatever it was to business in a nanosecond. "You're right. Trace Ledbetter is a scary man. He's second in command to Marvin Johnstone and definitely the one in line to take over the criminal enterprise when Johnstone steps down. I don't suppose you can avoid them?"

She dropped her head. "No."

"Why do I get the feeling there's more to this story?"

"No. I mean, yes. I mean. Not exactly."

He picked up the pen and held it over the notepad. "I'm ready. Hit me."

It was going to hit the fan, but better now than six weeks from now. "It's about the wedding."

"The wedding you're doing the flowers for? The wedding where I'm going as your plus-one?"

"What other wedding would it be?"

"Meredith, right now, if you told me you'd left out the part where you'd seen a mountain troll in a cave and you were sure he was terrorizing the town, I wouldn't be surprised."

"What's that supposed to mean?" She didn't have to fake her outrage.

"It means you dribble out information in no particular order. I'm waiting for you to tell me you've committed to giving Marvin Johnstone a root canal or something."

It annoyed her that he wasn't wrong. Or that she had more to say. "He could use a dentist. His teeth." She shuddered. "It's the meth. I see a lot of it."

"I don't doubt it." Gray waited.

"Fine. The thing about the wedding is that the girl getting married—"

Gray closed his eyes like he was facing a firing squad. No. That wasn't right. If he faced a firing squad, she guessed he would do it with his eyes wide open.

"Why are you closing your eyes?"

"I'm praying for God to give me strength to handle whatever you're about to say."

"Fine. The bride is the niece of Johnstone. I didn't know it when I agreed. Her last name is Finley. And the groom is Officer Nichols."

Gray dropped his head to his desk and lightly tapped it on the surface. Repeatedly. She let him vent his frustration.

"Is this the same Nichols you overheard Ledbetter and Hardaway talking about?"

"I assume so. He's young. Moved to Neeson about eighteen months ago. Met Lydia Finley the first week he was here. Lydia's in her early twenties. Precious. She has four younger sisters, all of whom will be bridesmaids. I didn't know they had any connection to Johnstone until a few weeks ago when they gave me a list of people who needed bouquets and boutonnieres. Lydia's mother, Mrs. Finley, is Marvin Johnstone's youngest sister."

Meredith gave up on her roaming around his office and took a seat again. "The bride is lovely, and unless I'm very much mistaken, the wedding is a love match. I don't get any sense that she's being coerced. They're adorable together. They're poor and probably always will be, but he came to me and asked if there was any way I could do the flowers for the wedding because Lydia's a big fan of my work. It was a surprise for her. I couldn't say no."

"Because they're young and in love?" Did Gray sound bitter? Or sad?

"What better reason? She's found her person. She loves him, and he loves her back. They're young, but they'll grow up together. She wants to travel, and he wants to take her places. She hasn't lived a fairy-tale life. But in this one area, I can help make her dreams come true. At least, I think I can."

"Besides the obvious possibility that Marvin Johnstone is going to show up at the wedding, what has you worried?"

"What if the bad guys are planning on using this? The wedding. Their love. Her. What if she's the way they're going to turn Nichols to the dark side? Am I aiding and abetting?"

"You're doing the flowers. You aren't complicit in any criminal act."

"You know what I mean."

Gray looked at her. "As much as you might want to, you can't fix everyone. Some situations can't be resolved. Some people can't be made whole. It isn't your responsibility to make it happen."

A buzz coming from the phone on Gray's desk interrupted whatever else he might have said. Gray pushed a button and spoke. "Ward."

"Chief." A voice she didn't recognize came through the speaker. "Your pizza's here."

"Thanks. I'll come get it." He turned to her. "Just a minute."

When he left the room, she dropped her face into her hands and took several slow breaths. She'd told him everything he needed to know. She should leave. Maybe take a few slices for the road. She didn't need to stay.

But he'd ordered pizza for her. And it would be rude to leave. Wouldn't it?

She had no idea what was happening tonight. Were they flirting? Was he telling her to stay away? Or was she making this more than it was and it was all about the work and she should just focus on doing what she could?

"You okay?" Gray startled her from her mental rambling.

"Yeah. Why?"

He set the pizza on the small table in the corner of the room and beckoned her to join him. "Because you were moaning?"

Crud. "Sorry."

"Care to share?"

"Nope." Decidedly not. No sharing. No way. No how.

He opened the pizza box, and the scent of garlic and tomatoes filled the room. She inhaled deeply. "I love pizza."

"I know." His smile was small but real. "I ordered the margherita. Hope that's okay."

"Perfect."

For the next few minutes, they ate and talked about random stuff. Despite her tension, it was easy to talk to Gray. He was interesting and had this way of focusing on her that made her feel like her words were important.

She'd been hungrier than she'd realized, and the pizza was exactly what she needed to settle down. She finished off her second slice and took a sip of water. "So, Gray, I feel like you know everything there is to know about me. But I don't really know a lot about you before you showed up in Gossamer Falls. Fill me in?"

Why had she said that? She was sliding into date territory with questions like that. But once she voiced it, she couldn't bring herself to regret it. She wanted to know. Needed to know. Maybe the secret to Grayson Ward was locked in his past.

Gray took a bite of pizza to give him a few moments to order his thoughts. She wanted to know about him, about his past and his family. How could he have this conversation with her?

"I was born in Chicago."

Meredith took a bite and nodded.

"Never knew my dad. Not even sure if my mom knew my dad."

"That's tough." Meredith said the words as fact, with sympathy but not pity. He had no idea how she managed it, but he appreciated it.

"My mom was . . . well . . . she tried. She tried hard. She loved me. Loved my sister."

"You have a sister?" Meredith's eyes glowed with interest.

"No. I had a sister." His words extinguished the delight on Meredith's face.

"I'm so sorry."

He was too. The radio on his desk squawked an alert.

Meredith sat up straighter. "Do you need to get that?"

"Not yet. I don't respond to every call. My men are good at what they do, for the most part."

"But?" Meredith prompted him with a smile.

"But there are only so many of them. I wait for them to decide if they can handle it, and they know I'm here tonight. If they need another set of hands, they'll message me."

Meredith wiped her hands on a napkin. "You're a good boss."

"I don't know about that. I try to be the kind of boss I would want to have. Give them the support they need but not get all up in their business. It's a fine line. I'm not always successful."

"That's not how I hear it."

The blare of voices coming through the radio pulled him away from the question he wanted to ask in response. As he listened to his officers explain the situation, he couldn't stop the mix of relief and regret that flooded through him as he realized he was going to have to cut his evening with Meredith short and wouldn't need to continue the conversation about his past.

Being with her was agonizing, and yet, he craved it. He didn't want to think about what a psychologist would do with that.

"You have to go." Meredith stood and put the lid down on the pizza box. Then she gathered the plates and napkins.

"I do. But don't clean up. It will be here when I get back."

"Oh no it won't. Your office would smell like stale pizza. Stale pizza smell is revolting. You don't need revolting when you return from a call. Go. I've got this. I'll clean up and head home. We'll talk more later."

She looked at him then, her hands full of trash, and caught him staring. "Go! Fix the problem. I'll be praying for the family." She gestured toward his radio. "I got the gist of that. Car in the ditch. Crying kids. Kids love you. They'll settle down when you get there and charm them."

He blinked a few times. There'd been nothing but honesty and maybe even a little bit of respect in her words. She wasn't teasing. She believed what she said.

Her confidence warmed him more than the heavy jacket he pulled on, and he held onto that as he walked into the night.

An hour later, he was sitting in Meredith's office with a sobbing eight-year-old. The little girl had latched onto him and refused to let go, so now he was sitting in a dental chair as Meredith prepped her instruments.

She'd had time to go home and change, but she hadn't been in bed when he called and asked her if she could come back to see what could be done about sweet Lisa's teeth.

"Okay, Lisa." Meredith said he could charm kids, but he had nothing on her ability. "Dr. Shaw told me that except for these broken teeth, you're good to go. Once we get you fixed up, you'll be able to head home with your family."

Lisa's mother was on her way to the hospital in Asheville with what Dr. Shaw suspected were shattered tibias. Lisa's father was still at Dr. Shaw's office with her younger brother, Caleb.

The car came around a curve, an animal ran out across the road. The dad swerved. Lost control. Slammed into the side of the mountain, which was bad, but not as bad as if he'd gone off the other side of the road and slid *down* the mountain.

Airbags deployed all over the car. Lisa's mom had her feet

propped up on the dash at the time of the wreck, and the resulting tibial fractures were why Gray never allowed anyone to put their feet up in any vehicle he was driving.

Lisa had been buckled in, but she'd been taking a drink from a cup. At some point during the swerving, hitting the side of the mountain, and the side airbags deploying, the cup met her mouth and broke two teeth off.

There'd been a lot of blood and Lisa had been full-on hysterical. Understandably so. But when Dr. Shaw got to her, she looked her over, told one of Gray's men to call Meredith, and assured everyone that Lisa would be fine.

Meredith, for her part, had never failed to respond to an emergency request in Gossamer Falls since she'd moved back to the area and set up her practice. Her aunt, Carol Shaw, was the only doctor in town. Meredith was the only dentist. If Carol said Meredith was needed, Meredith came.

That was the kind of person she was.

Gray brushed Lisa's hair from her face. "I know your mouth and face hurt, sweetheart, but I need you to sit in this chair and lean your head back so Dr. Quinn can take a look."

Lisa grabbed him with more strength than an eight-year-old should possess. Gray looked to Meredith for guidance.

"Lisa, I get it, baby. I do. You've landed the biggest catch in the county, and you don't want to let go. I don't blame you. But he's too big to sit in the chair with you."

Gray had been focused on Lisa but found himself unable to look away from Meredith as she continued to coax Lisa to relinquish her hold on him. Did Meredith really think that? That he was the biggest catch in the county?

He couldn't allow himself to be caught. Yet the idea of being Meredith's had his heart doing its best to overrule his brain.

But his brain was in work mode and insisted on staying present, and he caught Meredith's next words to Lisa. "How about if you sit in the chair, and he comes around to the other side and holds your hand? Would that work?"

Lisa didn't seem to like it, but she didn't fight him as he eased her into the dental chair.

"Excellent." Meredith pointed to the seat where the hygienist usually sat, and he took it. "Gray, go ahead and hold Lisa's hand. In fact, why don't you hold both of them."

Gray leaned forward and grabbed both of Lisa's hands. He rested all four of their hands on her tiny stomach. Meredith gave him a nod and he understood that one part of his job was to comfort Lisa. The other part was to make sure Lisa didn't move.

Smart Meredith.

Meredith cajoled and sang and teased until she was able to see the problem teeth. Then she assured, confided, and joked until the teeth in question were no longer jagged and Lisa's mouth was no longer bleeding.

About halfway through, Lisa's dad and brother had walked in. The poor man looked like someone had taken a baseball bat to his nose. By tomorrow, he would look like he'd gone a few rounds in the octagon with a mean MMA fighter.

But he gave Gray an appreciative smile, cooed to the son in his arms, and stroked a finger down the cheek of his daughter. There was so much love in this man. He was a big guy. Beard. Kind of rough looking but clearly a marshmallow on the inside. At least where his family was concerned.

Gray had seen it before. This man could hold his own in a fight, but his wife and kids were his whole world.

"Landon Jefferson." Gray had blanked on his name until he'd introduced himself to Meredith. "Can't thank you enough, ma'am." His voice quavered a bit at the end.

"Lisa's going to need more dental work," Meredith said. "I'm sure you have a dentist at home. You need an appointment with him or her as soon as you can." She handed Landon her card. "Feel free to have them call me. I'll send over my notes."

The car was a total loss, but Doug Quinn had volunteered to drive the family to the hospital in Asheville. They had family meeting them there who could take care of the kids and get them what they needed.

When they drove off, Meredith let out a satisfied sigh. "I love my job."

NINE

Meredith bumped Gray's arm. "Are you done for the night? Or do you have to go back to the office and fill out paperwork?"

He couldn't help but grin at her. She was clearly amped up from her work tonight, and he didn't mind admitting that it was one of his favorite things about her.

Meredith didn't help people because she had to or because she should. She helped people because she wanted to. It filled her up and left her overflowing.

"I have to shut down my office. We left in a hurry. But then I'm done. One of the perks of being the chief. The officers have to deal with the paperwork."

"Don't they turn that paperwork in to you?"

"Yes. But I don't have to read it tonight. I can go home, go to bed, and go to sleep."

"Brilliant." She beamed at him. "You go home and sleep, Chief. I'm going to go home and . . . not sleep."

He should've said good night right then and there. Which is why it made no sense to him that he said, "If you aren't going to sleep, what are you going to do?"

"No idea." And he could tell that she didn't care. "I might

read a book. Or go to the shop and work on some arrangements. Or sit by the firepit until Mo comes out to talk to me. He hates to see me out there alone." She leaned in closer. "Don't tell him, but it's my secret weapon. When he's been inside too long, or he's getting all moody and grumpy, I go sit out there by myself. It doesn't take long. He can't stand it. So even if he doesn't want to come out, he will."

She said that last bit with a little bit of a laugh. "Cal says I shouldn't manipulate him. I say it's not manipulation when the person knows they're being manipulated. Mo knows I'm doing it on purpose, but he can't stand it, so he caves. Every time. And then I make him talk to me until he's less of a grouch and more of a teddy bear."

"Mo? A teddy bear?"

"I'll have you know that Mo Quinn is a world-class hugger."

Gray held up his hands. "Don't take this the wrong way, but it will be okay with me if I never learn that from personal experience."

"Please." Meredith waved him off. "Guys need hugs too."

"They generally prefer those hugs to come from women."

"Point taken. But I've seen him hug Dad. And Cal. And Papa Quinn. But he's the best with the kids. Our baby cousins adore him. He's a family favorite."

Gray had seen it for himself but still found it hard to believe. "I don't see that side of Mo often."

Meredith's happiness bubble didn't pop, but it did deflate a bit. "He hasn't been the same in a long time. But he's still in there. I keep hoping he'll let the real Mo out to play more often. He did last night around the firepit. The way he laughed?"

Gray had never seen Mo laugh that way. "I didn't fully appreciate how far back the four of you go. I knew you, Mo, and Cal have known each other your whole lives, but I didn't realize Bronwyn was part of your terror cell."

Meredith swatted his arm. "Hey! I'll have you know we were the most adorable tiny terrorists who ever ran amuck in Gossamer Falls."

"I have no doubt."

"But yeah. Beep has been part of our merry band since kindergarten."

Beep. The only people who called Bronwyn that were the three cousins. Bronwyn Elena Elizabeth Pierce did not seem to mind it when those three used the childhood nickname, but he couldn't imagine anyone else calling her that.

Gray wanted to ask her more. He wanted her to tell him stories about her childhood and dental school, and he wanted to know why she'd wanted to be a dentist in the first place. He wanted to slip her hand in his and walk through Gossamer Falls beside her.

What he did was take two steps away from her. "Sorry to be abrupt, but I need to go make sure everything's squared away and call it a night."

Meredith lifted her chin, put her face to the sky, stretched out her arms, and spun around in a circle. "I need something to do. I'm too keyed up. I think I'll go make some flowers before I torture Mo."

She dropped her arms and gave him a look he couldn't interpret. "Good night, Gray. You made a difference tonight. Don't forget that."

Why did he feel like she wasn't saying good night, but goodbye? She didn't look back, wave, or acknowledge him again as she walked back into her office, leaving him standing on the street. He pulled himself together and returned to his own office.

It took him twenty minutes to wrap up, and when he picked up the jacket from the chair where he'd tossed it earlier, he saw Meredith's bag.

It must not be a purse. She'd had her keys, her phone, and everything she needed to get into her office. There was no telling what was in the bag, but since she'd brought it in, she'd eventually start looking for it. He picked up the phone and dialed her number.

"Hello?"

"Meredith. It's Gray."

"Oh! Hi!" Did she sound . . . guilty? Or upset? Something was wrong with her voice.

"I'm sorry I didn't notice it earlier, but you left a bag in my office."

"Thanks. I'm still in my office. I'll be right there."

Why was she still in her office? "No need. I'm walking out. I'll run it over."

"It's no problem."

"Meredith. I'm walking out the door."

"Okay. Thanks."

When he saw her standing by her office door a minute later, he couldn't figure out what was wrong. But something was.

She tried to hide whatever it was with a cheery smile. "Thanks. I didn't realize I'd left it." She reached for the bag, but he held onto it.

"What's the matter?"

She looked straight at him and dropped the facade of happiness. With that barrier gone, her pain was so evident it hurt him to look at her.

"It's nothing you can fix, Gray. But it isn't life-threatening or dangerous. Don't worry about it."

"Meredi—"

"Gray, I don't want company." There was no give in her voice. "Thank you for bringing the bag."

"You're welcome." He stepped back. "Good night."

"Good night." She closed the door in his face, and he had no choice but to leave her alone in her office.

Crying.

Meredith closed the door completely before she allowed the tears to flow free. She dropped the bag on the floor and lay down on the sofa. It took fifteen minutes for the tears to dry up and take the shards of her broken heart with them.

She'd had such a great night. Gray was easy to talk to. And he made her want to tell him everything she'd thought or noticed in every trip she'd made to Neeson. He somehow made it seem like he really wanted to know her, and that she was worth knowing.

Worth knowing. Yes.

Worth loving? No.

She walked into her private bathroom and splashed water on her face. The woman in the mirror looked so sad, and Meredith knew why.

She'd never believed that people could fall in love at first sight. Still didn't. But she did believe they could fall in love fast.

She had.

She'd nearly swallowed her tongue the first time she saw Grayson Ward standing in the police station. He was talking to Cal, and it was clear that they were good friends. She hadn't hesitated to interrupt them, introduce herself, and wish him well on the interviews.

Cal told her that Gray had saved his life. She wasn't sure if that was literal or figurative. Cal had gone through some hard stuff, and Gray had known him before and after the worst of it.

That fact alone would have made him interesting to Meredith. But then he got the job and moved to Gossamer Falls, and her interest morphed into something that bordered on an unhealthy obsession. She would bump into him—accidentally, of course—at the coffee shop. She'd suddenly feel compelled to work on her arrangements when he was visiting with Cal while Cal worked on his side of their shared shop.

She'd invited him to join them around the firepit and to every family gathering at Papa and Granny Quinn's. She made sure Cal knew she was fine with Gray joining them when it was supposed to just be her, Cal, and Mo for dinner.

She'd thrown herself in Gray's path, and all she'd gotten for her efforts was a bruised ego and a shattered heart. When her mom was sick, she'd put all her focus into taking care of her, and until tonight, Meredith had believed that by getting some distance and spending less time around Gray, the hold he had on her had broken.

Nope.

Not even a little bit.

Tonight, she'd accepted his offer to join him for pizza. And then she'd told him she was available this evening. When she realized what she was doing and how tense Gray was, probably because he had this woman throwing herself at him, she'd shut herself down, told him good night, and all but ran to the safety of her office.

How many ways did a man have to make it clear that he wasn't interested before she would accept it and move on with her life?

Cal had indicated that Gray had some trauma in his past and that in all the years he'd known him, he'd never had a serious girlfriend. That right there should have been enough to send her running. Of course, Mo hadn't had a girlfriend in years, either, but that was different.

Wasn't it?

Or was that it? Was there a girl out there somewhere who'd already taken up residence in Gray's heart? Was his heart claimed by someone she'd never know?

Did it matter?

Yes. It did.

Did it change anything?

No. It did not.

Her phone rang. Again. She'd ignored it three times. This time she looked and was unsurprised to see that it was Mo calling. "When I don't answer, that means I don't want to talk."

"Gray called Cal. Told him you were in your office crying and wouldn't talk to him. What did he do to you?"

"Nothing."

"Then why are you upset?"

"Given that you've known me my entire life, I'm not sure why me having a crying jag is big news. I'm allowed to cry when I'm upset."

"You are, but that doesn't mean I have to like it."

Mo never liked it when she cried. Bless him. "I'm sorry you got stuck with a big-emotion sister."

"I'm not. I love you exactly the way you are. I just don't like it when you're upset. And to be clear, I'm not sorry that you got stuck with an overprotective big brother. Two of them if you count Cal, which I know you do. Big-emotion baby sisters who wear their hearts on their sleeves need big brothers to go to bat for them."

"I love you too."

"I know. Now, what did Gray do?"

"I already told you. Nothing."

"And that's the problem?" When she didn't answer, he muttered, "Oh boy. Okay. Come home. I'll start a fire."

"Okay."

"Be careful."

"I will."

She slipped out of her office and went straight to her car. She only cried a little on her way home. And when Mo met her by the fire with arms open wide, she stepped into his embrace and let him hold her until the tears again stopped.

"Why am I not good enough?" She whispered the question into his chest.

"Did he say that to you?"

"No."

Mo waited. He was annoyingly good at waiting.

"I've all but painted a sign that says, 'I have feelings for you,' but he's not interested. Why? I'm not ugly. I'm smart. I have a job. I'm not a criminal. I mean, on paper, I'm a catch. But in real life? Not so much. No one has ever wanted to catch me, at least not anyone I want to be caught by."

Mo rested his chin on her head. "I don't have an answer other than that it isn't that you aren't good enough. I know for sure that is not it." He squeezed her closer. "Maybe it's us. Some kind of family curse that skipped a few generations and landed on us and now we're destined to love people who don't love us back."

They stood by the fire until her left arm got too hot. She spun them around so her right side was to the fire, but didn't break the embrace.

When Meredith spoke next, she chose her words very carefully. "I don't know how to do this. Be his friend but nothing more. I need some space."

"I'll tell Cal. We'll get you some distance."

"I don't want Gray to know. It's embarrassing enough as it is."

"I'm not convinced he knows to begin with. But if he does, he should be honored that you'd notice him, much less want to know him . . . better."

"Trying not to think about how I'd like to know him?" she teased, and he pulled back from her.

He made a face that looked like he'd sipped pickle juice straight from a jar. "I never think about that. You're my baby sister. The thought of you . . . no. I don't think about it." He tapped her nose. "At the same time, I want that for you. A man to love you the way you deserve to be loved. And a man who can be the safest place you've ever known."

Meredith had nothing to say to that.

"Gray could have been that man. But if he can't move past the things holding him back from you, then there's someone else."

"There might not be." Meredith voiced the thing she'd been thinking of lately. "Maybe I'm going to be the coolest aunt, best cousin, and sweetest friend, but not a wife and not a mother. I feel like if that's what God wants for me, I should be okay with that."

Mo chuckled. "Maybe God wants us to be like Matthew and Marilla." He winked at her, and she remembered her long-ago promise to never, ever tell anyone how much her big brother adored *Anne of Green Gables*.

"You think God wants us to grow old and grumpy and then adopt a redhead who will turn our world upside down?"

"It could happen."

"That wouldn't be so bad."

"Nope."

"Love you, Mo."

"Love you."

She walked to her door, and right as she opened it, she heard him say, "I could give his computers a virus . . ."

"No!"

"Offer stands."

She went inside, and while she wasn't happy, at least she'd stopped crying. She was loved. Dearly and deeply. But Mo and Cal, her parents, her family, all of them loved her, but they didn't have a choice. Not really. And because they didn't have a choice, it didn't count.

She wanted someone to choose to love her.

But that someone wasn't going to be Grayson Ward.

TEN

Meredith woke up the next morning with a headache, puffy eyes, and a renewed determination to live the life she'd been given without trying to force it to take a different shape.

She made it until ten a.m. when Lucy, her office manager extraordinaire, leaned into the room where she was finishing up a filling. "Dr. Quinn, when you're done here, you're needed in your office."

Meredith looked up, and Lucy mouthed "police chief."

Meredith nearly dropped her instruments. "Ten minutes." She was proud of the way her voice didn't waver.

She wasn't proud of the way she took her time and ten minutes turned into fifteen before she walked into her office and faced Gray. "How can I help you this morning?" She hoped her cheery voice and bright smile would distract him from any thoughts he might have about last night.

Unfortunately, he didn't respond immediately. He studied her face. She'd read about the idea of "studying a face" in books and never appreciated how disconcerting it was to be on the receiving end of such focused attention.

"How are you?"

"Good. And you?"

He frowned, and it was like a little thought bubble popped up over his head. She could tell he wasn't happy with the way she was deflecting. Too bad.

"I've been better. Are you planning to be here all day?"

"Yes." Where was he going with this?

"Good. Could I borrow your car?"

"If I'd had time to imagine every possible thing you could have said to me, borrowing my car wouldn't have made the list." She tried for amused surprise, but based on his expression, she didn't quite manage it.

"I need to take your car to your dad's shop."

"Why?"

"Because he found a tracking device on the van."

Meredith started to say something. Stopped. Tried again. Gave up and took a seat behind her desk. Gray didn't seem bothered by her response, and he waited patiently for her to focus. When she did, she asked the first thing that popped into her head. "Why would anyone want to track me?"

"Probably so they could find an opportunity to puncture your fuel line."

That made sense. Except it didn't. "That would explain how they knew where I was. But that still doesn't explain the why of it."

"No. It doesn't. We don't know why, and until we do, it makes keeping you safe significantly more difficult. We don't know where the threat is, so we have to guard against anything and everything."

"And you think they might have put a tracker on my car."

"I would. The dental clinic van gives them the best chance of catching you out of Gossamer Falls and alone. But your dad mentioned that you make regular trips out to see the Colliers and the Newmans."

"They're old and lonely. I pick up groceries and stop in for a chat. And they're in Gossamer County. Going to see them wouldn't put me at risk."

The Newmans lived up a steep drive that was frequently impassable in the winter, sometimes for days at a time. Once, when she was in her early teens, it had been two weeks before anyone could get a vehicle up there. They'd been okay because seven days into the freeze, she, Bronwyn, Mo, and Cal had hiked up the drive with backpacks filled with groceries. When they got there, they'd spent two hours splitting firewood and being entertained by Mr. Newman's tales. Then they'd mostly slid down the driveway on their backsides.

"True, but the drive out there is windy. No one else lives that way. If someone stopped you . . ." Gray balled his hands into fists and then released them. "I'm not saying you can't continue to roam the county the way you usually do. But if you're being tracked, we need to know. And if someone has put a tracker on your car, then I'm going to have to make some big decisions about how to handle it."

Meredith wanted to push for more information, but it was Friday and she had a full patient load today. She rarely worked more than two Fridays each month, and they were always packed. She opened the bottom drawer of her desk and took her keys from her purse, then tossed them to Gray, who caught them one-handed.

"I have a full schedule. Please let me know what you find." She stood and Gray followed her lead.

"Thank you. I'll return these to you later today."

"No problem. You can leave them with Lucy."

Was that a flash of hurt in his eyes? Maybe. But did it matter? No. She needed distance if her heart was going to heal, so she had to avoid him as much as possible.

"Sure thing. I'll text you if I need anything further."

"Sounds good." She sailed out of her office with a little wave and didn't look at her phone until lunchtime.

There were five texts.
From Gray:

Found it.

From Dad:

Baby girl, we need to talk.

From Mo:

You're grounded.

From Cal:

Please don't leave the office until someone can
follow you home.

From Mom:

Sweetheart, I made banana bread today. I'm
going to send some home with Gray. Make sure
you get it from him and don't leave it in your
car.

She nearly cried from relief at the normalcy of her mom's
text. She replied in reverse order to the way she'd received the
messages.
To Mom:

Yum. Thank you. You're the bestest mom ever.

To Cal:

I can't leave the office because I don't have a
car. And I don't need an escort home.

To Mo:

Whatever.

To Dad:

> Should I plan to come over tonight?

To Gray:

> Oh joy.

It wasn't professional or impersonal, but what was she supposed to say?

Her dad responded first.

> Your mother's making chicken and dumplings.

She replied as fast as her fingers could type.

> I'll be there.

Mo responded while she was typing.

> Not kidding. Mom's making chicken and dumplings. Dinner with them?

She replied.

> Yes to dinner. Still not grounded. You're not the boss of me.

Cal responded next.

> Your car is headed back to you now. Chad's driving my truck home so I'll need a ride. Can you pick me up at 5?

She replied.

> Sneaky. Underhanded.

Cal responded.

> You say sneaky, I say effective. See you at 5.

Gray responded.

Left your keys with Lucy. Car's in your spot.
Tracker still in place. We need to talk.

Meredith considered the merits of destroying her phone. If she threw it hard enough at the wall, it might break. Maybe. Water would be better. But no. It would be a nuisance to have to replace it.

She replied to Gray.

Tomorrow? I have dinner plans tonight.

Gray responded.

See you at dinner. We'll talk tonight.

She did throw her phone after she saw that. She couldn't help it. The blasted thing bounced off the wall and lay on the floor. She imagined it was judging her for her temper.

She left it where it was and went back to her patients. That worked until Lucy, all smiles and sunshine, handed it to her. "You dropped this, Dr. Quinn."

She turned it off, and despite pulling it from her pocket multiple times, she made it until her last patient left at 4:45 before she powered it back up.

This time the only text she responded to was from Cal.

I'm ready whenever you are.

On my way in ten.

The thumbs-up told her he'd seen it. She closed everything up for the weekend and went out to her car. Where was the tracker? Did it track her location only? Or did it listen in?

Her cheeks flamed as she slid into the seat. How embarrassing would that be? She'd had Mexican a few days ago and the

110

ride home had been . . . well . . . it hadn't been quiet. She had manners, but she should be free to let go in the privacy of her own car.

And then there'd been the ranting she'd done on the way home last night. She bit back a groan. If anyone was listening, she didn't want to give them anything else to mock her with. She turned up the local Christian music station. If they were going to listen, they were going to listen to worship music from now on. Maybe they'd be convicted of their wicked ways.

When she parked in Cal's office lot, she hopped out and met him at the door. "Do you know about my car?"

"Yes."

"Does it listen in or just track location?"

"I'm not sure. We should assume they're listening." He pulled her arm through his. "I'm sorry. We'll figure this out." He tugged her toward her car. "Want me to drive?"

She was grouchy now, and her response was a petulant, "No."

Cal, to his credit, laughed, climbed in, and kept a steady stream of mindless chatter until she dropped him off at his and Landry's new home. "I'll talk to you later. Thanks for the ride."

She gave him a small salute and made the short trip to her parents'. Mo's Jeep was already there. As was Gray's Explorer. She pulled herself together, as much as she could, and walked inside.

Gray didn't know what had happened after Meredith went home last night. He'd sat where he could see her office door. It had been over thirty minutes before she'd walked to her car. He was sure she'd been crying, and if the way her eyes looked this morning was any indication, she'd cried a lot last night.

Based on the cool reception he received from Mo when he'd walked into the Quinns' home, he had a bad feeling that the tears had something to do with him.

He replayed their conversation. He thought the evening had been fine. Better than fine. It had been hard not to think of it as a date. Hard not to let his mind wander to what it would be like if she was his and if he could always have her to come home to after a call. And harder still not to ask her to come back to his place when she was so amped up.

He almost suggested it, but then she'd shut down and said she needed to go home. His relief had been heavily tinged with regret. But relief had won out. Meredith Quinn was an extraordinary woman, and if he was the kind of man who was looking for a partner, she would be it.

But he wasn't that kind of man. The women he loved died. All of them. And he'd known since he was in his teens that he would be single for life.

He'd take care of the people in this town and be the best police chief he could be. But he wouldn't be a husband. Wouldn't be a father. He'd decided a long time ago that he didn't want that. Even if the sight of Meredith walking straight into her father's arms did send a pang of regret through him.

"Supper's ready. Let's not let it get cold." Doug Quinn gestured them to the kitchen table. "Then we'll talk."

Mo and Gray sat on one side of the table, Meredith on the other, with Doug and Jacqueline on either end. Doug asked the blessing, plates were filled, and they dug in.

"Mrs. Quinn, this is phenomenal." It wasn't hyperbole. Gray hadn't grown up eating chicken and dumplings, but he was pretty sure they were now his favorite food. "This is what I would request for my last meal."

Mo and Meredith laughed. Doug gave his wife a look that was a combination of pride and adoration, and Gray suspected a whole lot of gratitude that she was here.

Jacqueline had survived an intense battle with cancer last year. There was still a hint of frailty to her physically, but the eyes that pinned him now held a mama bear's strength. "Thank you, Gray. But, sweetheart, if you ever call me Mrs. Quinn again, I will wash your mouth out with soap."

Gray choked down the bite he was working on. "Ma'am?" He hadn't grown up saying ma'am, either, but after moving to Gossamer Falls, he'd learned fast.

She pointed her fork at him. "You heard me. Jacqueline or Jacque will do fine."

He would go to great lengths to avoid addressing her directly in the future, because he wasn't sure he could manage to call her by her first name. But what he said was, "Yes, ma'am."

"Now that we've settled that, I'm glad you're enjoying the dumplings because you'll be taking some home. I made enough for a crowd."

"You always make enough for a crowd, Mama." Meredith shared a look with Mo. "Not that we're complaining."

"Of course you aren't. I have to make enough for a crowd because on the rare occasions I don't make enough to send home, you two get all pitiful and dramatic about it." She turned to Gray. "They're shameless."

"It's not our fault you're the best cook in the family." Mo took another serving and piled it on his already empty plate. "We're spoiled."

"Oh, you're spoiled all right." Jacqueline winked at Mo, and to Gray's astonishment, Mo blew her a kiss. It was clearly a long-standing tradition between them, because she caught the kiss and then brought her fist to her lips. And then, without missing a beat, she looked at Meredith and said, "Merry-girl, what did you ever decide to do about Cassie's bouquet?"

Merry-girl? Gray had been around the Quinns a lot, and he'd never heard that nickname. He hadn't been around Jacqueline Quinn much, and never in as intimate a setting as a family meal. But he understood now why the whole family adored her and why she was Cal's favorite aunt even though he would never admit it.

She made everything comfortable and somehow managed to make him feel like he was one of them rather than what he was—an outsider intruding on their time together.

The meal was so enjoyable that Gray almost forgot about the weird tension he'd sensed from Meredith and the cool way Mo had welcomed him.

Almost.

Under their mother's influence, both of them warmed up and the conversation flowed easily. Meredith talked about the crazy bouquet she was making for Cassie's rehearsal, and Mo entertained them with his latest adventures with Abby and Eliza.

But when Jacqueline—he would never get used to that—brought a chocolate pie to the table, there was a shift in the atmosphere he couldn't quite figure out.

After everyone had their pie and those who wanted coffee were sipping decaf, Doug said, "Gray, we have a rule in this house. No heavy stuff during dinner."

"That's because everyone knows that a spoonful of sugar helps the medicine go down." Jacqueline tapped her pie. "Dinner is for conversation. Dessert is for communication."

"That's Mom's way of saying we play nice during dinner and get serious during dessert." Mo picked up his coffee mug. "Depending on what's going on, sometimes that saying is switched up."

"'Dessert is for confrontation.'" Meredith made big eyes at everyone. "That's always fun."

Mo raised his mug to Meredith in an air toast. "Let's not forget 'Dessert is for confession.' That one's a real winner."

Doug wiped his face with his napkin. "My personal favorite was 'Dessert is for conflagration.' That one was very popular when they were teenagers and if you looked at them funny, they lost their tempers."

"I'm shocked that you only remember the negative options." Jacqueline feigned outrage. "There were positive ones too. 'Dessert is for celebration' comes to mind."

"Nice try, Mom." Mo squeezed his mom's hand. "I'm afraid that's not what we're dealing with tonight."

"No. Tonight is definitely not a celebration." Jacqueline blew out a deep breath and turned to her husband. "Okay, honey. Take it away."

Doug nodded gravely. "I have to give credit to Gray for insisting we look over Meredith's 4Runner. There were location trackers on both your 4Runner and Flossy." Doug patted Meredith's hand. "Baby girl, I don't know what you've gotten yourself into, but we have to figure it out before someone gets hurt."

"I know, Daddy." Meredith gave him a gentle smile.

Mo rested his elbows on the table. "Gray and I talked this afternoon. I did a little bit of digging around, and I think I have what you need."

"What who needs?" Meredith asked.

Gray jumped into the fray. "I asked Mo if he had a way to check for bugs. He's already checked this house, and it's clean. But we need to check your house tonight. And your shop. And your office."

Meredith's face paled. "You think someone bugged my house?"

"I think it's more likely that they've bugged your office. Mo's security around your home is tight, and it would be very difficult for anyone to find a way onto the property, much less get inside, without triggering an alarm. They, whoever they are, might have a better shot at getting into your shop, but I think the likelihood is small. Still, I wouldn't be doing my job if I didn't check."

"I think you need to come back to our place tonight, Gray. We'll scan everything." Mo held out a hand toward Meredith when she huffed. "Not optional. I agree with Gray. It's unlikely, but I won't rest until we know for sure. And tomorrow we'll check your office." He frowned. "Or, maybe Monday. I don't want to make it obvious that we're looking."

Gray considered that. "Let's wait until we see if there's anything in your home. Then we'll decide."

"Wait." Meredith held up a hand. "Why are we checking for bugs? That's not the same as the tracking device. I thought it was a location tracker. That would just tell people where I was."

"That's true." Mo nodded at Gray.

Great. It fell to him. It *was* his job, but Gray hated to be the one to have to do it. "Meredith, after I brought your car back to you this afternoon, I talked to Mo. He came over here to look at your van, and he found a listening device inside the exam area."

ELEVEN

Meredith heard the words, but they didn't make sense. Why would someone bug her van? Tracking her wasn't enough? Why did they want to hear what she had to say?

Or did they want to hear what she said to her patients when no one was supposed to be listening? "That could be a problem."

"What do you mean?" Her dad set his fork down with a clink.

She cleared her throat. "Sometimes, I tell people who look like they might need some help that they can call me. I give them my phone number." She tried to find the words that wouldn't make everyone at the table freak out, but she wasn't sure those words existed. "I might tell them there are safe places in Gossamer Falls if they decide they need to escape."

Everyone at the table closed their eyes as they absorbed her words.

"Merry-girl"—her mom sounded tired—"you know how much I love your big heart, but you can't save the whole world."

"I'm not trying to save the whole world. I'm trying to save a few people who live less than twenty miles from me and who I believe are being abused. I can't walk away without giving them some hope. What kind of person would I be if I did that?" Meredith scraped up the final crumbs of her pie to keep herself from saying anything else.

Her dad reached for her free hand and gave it a squeeze. "We know. And we're proud of you. We don't want you to change, but we do want you to be careful."

"I think that ship has sailed." Mo took another slice of pie and placed it on Gray's now empty dessert plate, then put another slice on his own. "Anyone else want more?"

Meredith almost said no, but then she changed her mind. "Me. Chocolate can't fix everything, but it sure can't hurt."

"Well said." Mo slid the pie onto her plate.

"What's this?" She pointed from her pie to his. "You gave me a skinny piece."

"That's because you're going to eat half of it and decide you don't want more."

She took a huge bite out of spite, put her hand in front of her face to keep anyone from seeing her chew, and spoke around the food. "You just want leftovers."

Mo blinked at her like a baby owl. "I'm sure I don't know what you mean."

She took another bite and, to her annoyance, realized that her agitation was leading to an unhappy tummy, which led to the decision that she was done. For now. "I guess we should head over to my place and get this done."

She spared a glance at Gray. He hadn't messed around. His second slice of pie was almost gone.

"We can help clean up first. If the house is bugged, an extra thirty minutes won't change anything." Gray took a sip of his coffee. "Before we go over there, I need to hear more about these people who are being abused."

Meredith's heart, the traitor, swooned at his words. He didn't doubt her words or her conclusions. How was she supposed to get over him when he kept being sweet and considerate? When he insisted on respecting her opinion and seeing things the way she saw them?

She was doomed.

She forced her wayward thoughts back to the question. "There was a teenager, the first time I went to Neeson. The bruises and the way he flinched from contact . . . it gave me shivers to think about what his life must be like. I gave him my card and made up a story about how he shouldn't hesitate to call if he had any trouble with his teeth."

Meredith would never forget that boy. He'd been so tough and so scared at the same time. "I almost didn't go back after that—I wasn't sure I could take it—but the next time I didn't see anything particularly problematic. Nothing that I knew in my gut was an abusive situation. Not in Neeson at that time," she clarified. "I'm convinced there are two girls being trafficked in another county, and there's a family that I saw a few months ago who had some dental injuries that didn't match with their explanations. I'm afraid the dad, and maybe the mom, are alcoholic meth users."

Everyone at the table grimaced.

"But the last time I was in Neeson, I spoke to two women. One was single, and I think she's a meth addict. I assured her we could help. Gave her my card."

"And the other?" Gray asked.

"The other was a mother. She was wearing long sleeves, but when she picked up her son, the sleeves rode up and I could see bruises on both arms that looked an awful lot like someone had grabbed her and shaken her. She also had a black eye. It was skillfully covered with makeup. But we were sitting close together in my tiny office, so it was easy to see. And she was moving gingerly."

The memory made her heart ache. "I've seen battered women before, and I'd bet a new dental clinic that she'd been beaten. Probably had bruised ribs. Maybe broken."

Meredith forced herself to take a breath and a drink. Recounting the visit was making her blood boil. "She's young. Probably not even twenty-five. She reminded me of Cassie. Blond hair. Blue eyes. But where Cassie, despite the hard things she's been through, is full of life and laughter, this woman . . ."

She shuddered at the memory. "Her eyes were . . . blank. They lit up when she talked to her son. She's obviously trying to be the best mom she can be to him. My guess is that her abuser hasn't been violent with her son. That might be the tipping point. But she's broken inside.

"I gave her my card, and I put my cell number on the back. Told her I had friends who could hide people who didn't want to be found and who would be willing to help."

Gray studied her. "How do you know you have friends who know how to hide people?"

Meredith hesitated, but Mo jumped in before she had a chance to explain. "Because this isn't Meredith's first foray into saving people, is it, baby sister? I notice how you left out the other girl you talked to a few visits ago."

"I was going to mention her next."

"Sure you were."

"Have you checked on her recently?"

Meredith hadn't asked before because she was afraid of the answer.

"I have." Mo gave her a reassuring smile. "She's good."

"Wait a minute." Gray pointed at Mo, then at Meredith, then back to Mo. "You knew about this? You're in on it? Helping her?"

"Of course I'm helping her. I wasn't going to leave her by herself to drive through the state with a nineteen-year-old on the run."

Both her mom and dad wore similar expressions of shock, but there was something else. Pride maybe?

Meredith jumped in. "She was being forced into a marriage with a man twenty years older than her. I'm not saying all age gaps are bad, but that's a big one. And, again, she was being forced." Meredith enunciated the last few words for emphasis. "She came to see me because her groom wanted her to have whiter teeth. He wanted veneers and a bunch of cosmetic stuff, and I don't do that in my clinic. I told her she'd have to come to my office, and she'd have to pay for it. She did. But that kind of work doesn't happen in one visit. I talked to her each time. It took a few visits to get her to open up, and when she did, the whole story poured out."

Mo took up the story from there. "Meredith came to me. So I did some investigating and determined it was all true."

Meredith didn't want to implicate anyone who had helped, but it was important that Gray and her parents understood that she hadn't been reckless. "I have friends in the middle of the state from when I lived and worked in Raleigh. They have experience with helping human trafficking victims. We got her to them, and they took it from there."

Gray pinched the bridge of his nose. He did that a lot. Usually when he wasn't happy. "Just so there's no confusion about anything. In the last six months, you've helped a young woman escape Neeson and you've given a young mother your cell number and a promise of sanctuary in Gossamer Falls, all while providing dental care from your van?"

"That's a succinct summation. Yes."

"And you didn't think to mention this when I asked you if anyone might have it out for you?"

Meredith took another drink to avoid having to speak. The tactic worked because Gray turned his ire on Mo. "And you? You let her do this?"

"I'm sorry." Meredith had no trouble speaking now. "Did you ask him if he *let* me? I am my own person. No one *lets* me do anything."

Gray's eyes sparked with something Meredith had never seen

from him before. It might have been anger, but that wasn't quite right. "I would *never* let my baby sister take that kind of risk."

"Then I guess it's lucky for all of us that I'm not your sister."

———

Gray stood from the table. "Jacqueline." He swallowed hard and forced out, "Doug, would you excuse me for a moment?" He glared at Meredith and Mo. "I need some air."

He made a beeline for the door and was unsurprised when no one came after him. He heard a low thrum of voices from the dining room, but he couldn't make out what they were saying. Not that it mattered.

What was Mo thinking? Meredith was a treasure. She should be protected at all costs, even if that protection meant she was angry. Angry beat dead. He pulled his phone from his pocket and dialed a number that he had memorized.

"Hello." The woman on the other end never used her name, but no one else answered this call.

"A new wrinkle."

"Let's hear it."

"Turns out the individual under threat has been aiding abuse victims. She and her brother got at least one out of town. You might know the people who helped her with that."

"Oh, really?"

"You know anyone in the middle of the state who would be inclined to help someone being trafficked get out?"

He took her prolonged silence as a yes. And he let the silence linger.

She broke it. "Do you have names? Timelines?"

"Not yet. But I think it was only one so far. Shouldn't be too hard to find out. It was within the last six months."

"I'll see what I can find out on my end." There was a pause, and when the woman next spoke, the concern in her voice was so real, Gray could feel her tension in his bones. "You need to rein her in."

Gray snorted.

"She's not equipped for this."

"I agree with you one thousand percent, but you don't know her. She's tenacious. And she . . ."

"She can't say no."

"Exactly!" He'd expected this FBI agent to be a bit more hard-nosed about this. Her reputation preceded her, and everything he'd heard was that she was not someone you messed around with. But from the way she talked, he thought she understood. "I'm not sure if she could live with herself if she did. It's like she needs to help as much as she needs air."

"She probably does. And that means you're in big trouble. You're going to have to find a way to protect her but also not clip her wings. She'll never forgive you for it."

"I'm learning that. I think I made her entire family mad because I made it clear that I think they've dropped the ball on her protection."

There was a hiss of sound. Had she opened a soft drink? "I understand where you're coming from. I have a sister who I fully intend to blame any and all gray hair on. She has absolutely no sense of self-preservation. But take some friendly advice. You can't protect everyone. You can try, but if you take it too far, you'll smother them or stop them from doing what they believe they're called to do. And they will not thank you for it. They may even turn on you."

Gray didn't like the advice, but he couldn't argue that her words rang true. "I think I may be teetering on the edge of doing that."

She laughed. "I'd bet you ran right past the edge and don't even realize it yet. But it's probably not too late."

"I don't know." Gray looked back at the house where he could see the family moving around, clearing the table, and taking dishes to the kitchen. "As far as I can see, the only real solution is to solve the problem on this end. As long as that exists, she won't stop."

"I don't know your friend, but you're probably right. The good news is we're closer than ever to solving that particular problem."

"It might not be soon enough."

There was a long pause, and he thought she might be about to end the call. But instead, she said, "We want to keep everyone safe. And that sounds noble. It feels right to us."

"Yes. It does."

"But that's not our job."

"I'm pretty sure it *is* our job."

"We're to protect and serve and do everything we can to bring criminals to justice. By doing that, we help provide safety for our citizens. But it *isn't* our job to keep everyone safe."

"I don't mind taking the risks, but I don't want *her* to take them."

"Not your call, my friend."

"You can be very annoying."

"I've heard that. My husband, sister, and my friends would agree. I choose to see it as them being annoyed because I'm so often right. It's a burden I'm willing to bear." Her laughter ruined her attempt at being a snob. "Sorry. I couldn't resist. When this is over and we've fixed the mess up there, we'll have to come pay you a visit. I'd like to meet this girl who has you all tied up in knots."

"You're welcome to visit anytime. As for meeting her . . ." Gray let the sentence hang for a moment. "That will depend on whether we're still speaking."

"You'll find a way. Good luck. Call me if you need me."

"Will do."

He slid the phone into his pocket. Mo came outside and walked toward him. The best offense was a good defense, so Gray started talking before Mo reached him. "I was out of line. I apologize."

Mo frowned at him. "I'm not so sure that you were. Mom's ready to make you a chocolate pie every day, and Dad's ecstatic that someone beside him is on the hot seat with Meredith. You said what he's been trying to say for a while." Mo pointed toward the house. "You haven't been around enough to realize this, but Meredith gets her stubborn nature from Mom."

Gray tried, he really tried, to keep his expression neutral.

Mo's unamused snort told him he'd failed. "I know. I'm the most stubborn of the bunch. But that doesn't change the fact that Meredith is like Mom. Big brains and marshmallow hearts, both of them. Dad and I figure that means they can get themselves into even bigger messes than they could if they weren't quite so smart or if they cared a lot less. We love them for who they are, but they make life challenging."

The door opened and Meredith stepped onto the back porch. "You've been out here long enough that you missed the cleanup. If you're done, I think it's time we went back to the house and checked for bugs."

"We who are about to die salute you," Mo muttered under his breath.

"You aren't gladiators," Meredith said. "You won't die. But you might want to." She disappeared into the house.

"How did she hear that? Does she have super hearing?" Gray followed Mo toward the deck.

"I say it a lot. She probably caught just enough to know what it was. But yes, her hearing is freakishly good. Don't ever say anything anywhere near her that you don't want her to hear. I think some of it comes from being a dentist. She spends her whole day translating what people are saying, and somehow, she's turned that into something she considers a useful life skill. I find it frustrating."

"Why do they do that?" Gray asked as they walked into the house.

"Why does who do what?" Meredith was gathering up a bag of leftovers.

"Why do you talk to patients when you're working on their teeth? They can't answer you."

"It's rude to ignore them or leave them out of the conversation." Meredith said this as if it was the most logical answer and she was stunned that Gray had needed to ask such a question. "I'm good at figuring out what people are saying. Comes with practice."

Gray nodded, said his goodbyes to Doug and Jacqueline with far less awkwardness than he'd expected, and walked to his car with half a chocolate pie and enough chicken and dumplings to keep him fed for at least three days. Proof that the Quinn legacy lived on in this branch of the family. "Feed your friends and feed your enemies, and don't worry if they aren't sure which they are." He'd heard Granny Quinn say that a few months ago, and he couldn't decide if it was comforting or terrifying.

He was pretty sure he was still in the friend column with everyone except Meredith. She'd put him in the enemy column, and he should try to stay there. But he couldn't protect her if she wouldn't speak to him. For now, he had to stay in her good graces until they took down whoever was behind the bugs, the punctured fuel line, and the rest of the mess in Neeson.

After that? Well, after that, she'd be safe. And he could let her go.

TWELVE

Meredith stood by while Mo checked her 4Runner for bugs. It came up clean. "This makes no sense. Why put a location tracker but no listening device?"

Mo moved on to check Gray's Explorer and his own Jeep, but Gray stayed by her. "I don't know." He sounded . . . sad? Defeated? Angry? A toxic mix of all three? "We're shooting in the dark. We have no way to know when the devices were planted. It could be that they planted both on the van while you were at Mrs. Frost's house. They might have planted the one on your car while it was in the parking lot at your office at any time. Maybe they only had one listening device they could keep up with. I don't know."

Meredith tried to stay angry with Gray. She had every right to be. He'd snapped at her like she was a toddler with no sense, and he kept treating her like she was a brainless twit.

No. That wasn't entirely accurate. He believed her when she told him what she'd seen, heard, and suspected. And there was no mistaking that his outburst had been motivated by concern for her safety.

It was hard to stay mad about that. But she was going to try.

Mo gave both vehicles the all clear. They loaded up and drove the few miles to their houses.

Cassie wasn't home, and she wouldn't be there for hours yet. The Friday dinner shift at The Haven was always a busy time for her. The thought of cooking over and over again had never appealed to Meredith, but Cassie had been happiest in the kitchen since she was no bigger than Eliza and Abby.

And it wasn't like she could comment. She was a dentist. Definitely not a profession for everyone. Most people couldn't fathom what had driven her to pursue dentistry or why she loved it so much.

Meredith parked her 4Runner in its usual spot in their carport, climbed out, and waited by the firepit for Gray and Mo. Mo pointed to the houses. "Let's check here first. I called Cassie earlier and asked her if she'd mind if we walked through her place. She said that was fine."

"Let's start with Meredith's." Gray didn't wait for them to agree or disagree but walked straight to Meredith's porch.

"Sir, yes, sir." Meredith didn't try to hide her sarcasm, but it fell on deaf ears. Gray was a man on a mission and didn't react.

Ten minutes later, he'd morphed into an angry man ready to tear the world apart. The tiny listening device on the scarf she'd left draped over the back of a chair mocked all of them. Mo motioned for everyone to talk normally, and Meredith did her best.

"Did I tell y'all what Mrs. Frost told me?"

"There's no telling." Mo sounded a little grouchy, but he usually did, so maybe whoever was listening wouldn't notice. Especially since they couldn't see how his mouth had pinched to the point that little white lines formed along his lips.

"She claims that fifty years ago, one of Mrs. Staton's cousins, or maybe it was a sister? She was a little vague on the relation. Anyway . . ." Meredith followed Mo and Gray as they finished the scan of her living room and moved toward her kitchen. "She claims that one of them ran off and joined an actual circus."

"Fifty years ago? That was the 1970s. Did they have circuses you could run away to in the '70s?"

"No idea. This was Mrs. Frost's story. I wasn't expecting accuracy."

"Fair point." Mo motioned for them to be still while he checked her bathroom.

Meredith had a moment of panic. If they'd bugged her bathroom, she . . . well . . . she had no idea what she would do. It was so violating. Her home was her safe place. Her sanctuary.

Mo came out of the bathroom, gave them the all-clear signal, and then motioned for Meredith to keep going with her story.

She found her voice again and continued. "Anyway, she said that this girl disappeared, no one heard from her for a few months, and then she sent a postcard from New York that told them she was having a blast."

"Did they look for her?" Gray gave her a dark look. "I'm not going to love this story if it's going to add a cold case to my files."

"Oh, that's the best part. She sent regular postcards for the next two years and then sent them a wedding announcement. Not an invitation, mind you. Mrs. Frost was quite clear that this was the big news in this story. She didn't invite them to her wedding, just let them know it had already happened."

"Scandalous." Mo had finished downstairs and climbed the steps to the small loft area first.

Meredith and Gray waited for Mo to scan the area. When he came back down, she continued. "Mrs. Frost claims that this cousin-slash-sister is still held up in their family as the archetypal black sheep."

"I'm sure." Mo took the opposite stairs to her bedroom. "Why did she feel compelled to tell you this?"

Meredith held her breath while Mo walked around her room. She couldn't see him, but she could picture him waving his device over her bed, nightstand, bookshelves, and television.

The space was small compared to a lot of bedrooms, but it was perfect for her. She loved it, and when Mo gave her a thumbs-up, she could have cried in relief. Instead, she finished her tale. "According to Mrs. Frost, this girl didn't run off alone."

"No?"

"Nope. Mrs. Frost claims she ran off with Aunt Melissa."

Mo gaped at her.

Gray's expression shifted from angry to confused. "Who is Aunt Melissa?"

"She's Dad's sister. She came between Aunt Laura and Aunt Minnie."

"There's another one? I've never met her." Gray frowned. "I've never even heard of her."

"Yeah, well, we don't talk about her much. It makes Granny cry. And Minnie remembers her and gets very upset when she doesn't show up for family events."

"Does she ever show up?" he asked.

"No. We've never met her." Meredith included Mo in her statement. "As far as I know, once she left town she never came back."

Gray turned to Mo. "Do you know where she is?"

Meredith understood the question. Mo could find people, and there was no way he wouldn't have tried to find her. And, of course, he had.

Mo's response was a short nod. "She's got two kids. Boys. No husband. Don't know if the boys have the same dad or not. They're younger than we are, but not by much. I reached out to her. Gave her contact info. Told her the family would love to see her."

"Not interested?"

"Apparently not. And the thing is, it's not like she doesn't know where we live. Papa and Granny Quinn haven't moved. The town's still here. She could come home if she wanted to." Mo cut his eyes at Meredith. "But the circus angle didn't come up in my research."

"It may be completely bogus." Meredith followed both men back to the firepit. "You know Mrs. Frost. She's getting confused. It might have been true. It might have been a rumor. It might be that she combined a couple of different stories into one."

Meredith dropped her cheery storytelling persona as soon as they reached the firepit. "What do we do about it?"

Mo looked at Gray.

Gray heaved a frustrated sigh. "When did you last wear that scarf?"

Meredith didn't have to think about it. "Monday. Aunt Minnie always comes to work in the front office on Mondays. We walked to the restaurant for lunch. I always walk with her. The only time we drive is if it's raining. She needs her exercise, and a quarter-mile walk in the cold won't hurt her. Or me."

Meredith dropped her head and then threw it back to stare at the sky. "I took off my jacket and scarf and put them on the back of the chair when we went to order. I had Aunt Minnie with me, so you can imagine the scene. We talked to a bunch of people while we were in line."

"It would take the merest brush to deposit a bug like that on your scarf." Mo saw the same problem she did.

"Exactly. It could be anyone. And if it's that easy? They could have done it while I was walking down the street."

"Maybe, but I like the restaurant for this." Gray considered his words but seemed comfortable with the assertion. "And you go there for lunch most Mondays. I don't think it's a stretch to assume that anyone who's been paying attention to your routine would know they'd have a chance to get close to you."

Meredith leaned forward, resting her hands on her knees, and took deep breaths like she'd just finished running a race.

"What is it?" Gray knelt beside her. "Meredith?"

"I took the phone call from Mrs. Frost in my living room. They would have heard me tell her I was coming."

Gray couldn't stop himself from taking Meredith's hands in his. "Breathe." She did as he said, and he squeezed her hands. "That's it." When she paused, he urged her again. "Breathe." When she took several breaths without prompting, he stood up and used the motion to pull her back into a standing position. He didn't release her until Mo stepped up to her and pulled her into his arms.

"They really are coming after me." She spoke into Mo's shoulder, but Gray heard the broken words.

"They can't have you. You're a Quinn, and Quinns don't negotiate with terrorists. We don't sit by when our neighbors are being abused and violated, and we don't back down when things get tough." Mo spoke to Meredith, but his eyes were on Gray.

Gray got the message. The Quinns would rally around Meredith. They would do whatever they had to do to protect her. And while her personal actions might have precipitated the attention of the criminal element in Neeson, the entire family would move heaven and earth to get to the bottom of it.

"I didn't mean for this to happen." Meredith shuddered, and Mo squeezed her tighter.

Even though it would have been the polite thing to do, Gray didn't give them privacy. He didn't look away. He didn't try not to overhear. He didn't think he could have made himself move even if he wanted to.

"I know." Mo patted her back. "You didn't do anything wrong."

Meredith snorted.

"It might not have been wise, baby sister, but it wasn't wrong. You acted in love. You took a chance because you couldn't pretend the problem wasn't real. You're a force for good, and good will prevail."

"It doesn't always." Her argument held an edge of defeat that Gray couldn't bear to listen to.

"That doesn't mean we don't keep fighting." Gray placed a hand on her back. "If more people refused to look away when they saw wrongdoing, the world would be a much better place."

Meredith twisted in Mo's arms and narrowed her eyes at Gray. "An hour ago, you were furious with me."

"I'm still furious with you. But that doesn't mean I don't admire you, and it doesn't mean that I'm not in awe of your courage." He leaned closer. "And I agree with Mo. Good will prevail. There are other forces at work to change things in Neeson. You aren't alone. And while it's good that your family has your back, you have a lot of other people behind you too."

"What are you talking about?" Mo asked.

"I've been worried about Neeson since I got here. And I have friends on task forces that deal with things like this. When I found Meredith's fuel line cut on Wednesday, I made a few phone calls and got some balls rolling. Then when I heard about the other activities in Neeson tonight, I went outside and made a phone call to the person in charge of the overall investigation. She's the best federal agent I've ever interacted with. She has a solve record that makes her a rising star at the FBI. She could be at their headquarters by now, but she doesn't want to leave Raleigh."

"Do I know her?" Mo asked.

"You might." Gray considered his words and then added, "You definitely have mutual friends."

Mo nodded in understanding and didn't press for more information.

Gray patted Meredith's back and stepped away from them. "Let's go check your shop. I really don't think we'll find anything there, but let's clear it from our possibilities. Then we can decide what to do about your scarf."

"Okay." Mo kept his arm around Meredith's shoulders but turned her so they could walk down the small path that led to the shop she shared with Cal. Gray walked beside them. "I still think we should check my house and Cassie's."

Neither Mo nor Meredith seemed to need a flashlight, but Gray didn't feel as confident about taking a walk through the woods in the dark. He turned on his phone flashlight and kept it trained on their path. "I don't expect them to have planted anything in your homes, but they could have gotten something on some of Cassie's clothes."

"A scarf . . ." Mo trailed off.

"Yeah. It's diabolically brilliant. She's not likely to throw it in the wash, she could have it in her car, in her office, her home, or wrapped around her neck while we all sit around the firepit and talk."

Meredith let out a tiny moan. "What if I'd worn it Wednesday?"

"But you didn't. We can't get caught up in the what-ifs and should-haves. We have to stay focused on what we know and what we can control."

Meredith leaned into Mo, and no one spoke while he opened up Cal's side of the shop, turned on the lights, and then stepped back.

Gray didn't need an invitation. He stepped in, weapon drawn, and cleared the space. When he nodded at them, they went to Meredith's side and repeated the process.

Then while Gray and Meredith watched, Mo scanned her shop. It came up clean. "I'm going to scan Cal's side. Be right back."

He slipped out the door, and Gray was left alone with Meredith.

She walked over to a flower arrangement that even his untrained eye could see was a crime against floral design.

"This"—she pointed to a random piece of what might have been a weed—"is all thanks to you."

"I'm not sure that's a flattering statement."

"Oh, but it is. I'm having a blast designing it. When I'm convinced it can't be any worse, I think of something to add that will make it even more awful." She touched a petal, then twisted it around so he could see the full effect. "I was thinking I'd work on it tonight. Maybe finish it. But I don't think I can. I need to make something beautiful."

She walked to the far wall where shelves were filled with tubs of paper-thin wooden flowers. "I used to make every single flower by hand, but that became too time-consuming and completely ruined all my profit margins. I found places I could buy the types of flowers I use most often in bulk. Now I only make the truly unique blossoms."

Gray walked over to stand near her. She opened the lids of several tubs and removed multiple stems. "They're all cream."

"I dye everything." She pointed to the long table covered in dyes and pigments, and a sink that looked more like a kaleidoscope than the stainless steel that peeked out randomly from under all the colors. "Which means I can make flower arrangements to match any decor, any outfit, any style. I can make any shade of green or pink or orange, and I love playing around with different tones. Sometimes I'm in the mood for a riot of color. Sometimes I want the soothing peace of twenty cohesive blues."

She opened a book and flipped through it. It was a photo album of her designs. She paused on one and tapped her finger on it. "What do you think of this one?"

"It's my favorite. I walk by it every day."

She stepped away from the book. "I didn't think you noticed it."

"I notice everything."

She huffed out a small breath. "Yeah. I guess you do."

"You make it sound like that's a bad thing."

"Not bad. But frustrating."

He threw his hands up. "Why is that frustrating?"

She mimicked his hand gesture. "Because you notice everything. If you're choosing not to act on something, it isn't because you're clueless. It's because you don't want to."

Mo chose that precise moment to come back. He glanced between them and said, "Everything's clear. I'm going to walk back and check my place and Cassie's. Just to be safe." And he was gone.

Meredith turned her back to him, but not before Gray caught the way she wiped her finger under her eyes.

"Meredith."

"What?" There was a tiny quaver in her voice. She sniffed, cleared her throat, and faced him with a cheery smile.

If she'd been angry, he might have been able to keep his distance. But she was so brave. So strong. She'd been put through so much hard stuff tonight, and she was trying to smile. He couldn't leave her confused or hurting over something when it was in his power to . . . what?

He couldn't fix it. Would clarifying help? Maybe not. But would it make things worse? Before he'd made up his mind, his mouth took the decision out of his hands. "Just because I don't do something doesn't mean that I don't want to. Sometimes I do want to. Very much. But I can't."

"Can't?" Meredith moved toward him until they were only a foot apart. "Or won't?"

He shook his head. "Both."

"Why?"

"I have my reasons."

"Care to share?"

Had she moved closer?

"No."

"Maybe you should." She gave him a small smile. "I could tell you if your reasons are valid."

She was definitely closer.

He took a step away, and the hurt that flashed across her face short-circuited his brain. He didn't remember deciding to reach for her. He had no idea when his feet moved. Or when he rested his hand under her chin. But he did know that once she was in his arms, there was no amount of logic or reason that could stop him from leaning his face toward hers.

Had she closed the final inches or had he? His lips moved across hers, and he confirmed things he had long suspected. Her lips *were* soft. Her kiss *did* scramble his brain. And her body *was* a perfect fit against his.

He also discovered things he hadn't known, like the way Meredith tasted of chocolate and whipped cream and the way her skin warmed under his touch. And when she let out a soft sigh against his lips, he learned that it was possible for a woman to make him forget his own name.

Eventually, he remembered who he was, where he was, and who he was with, and he also remembered why he shouldn't be doing what he was doing. He broke the kiss and took a step back.

Meredith's eyes were closed, and when they opened, the way she looked at him would haunt him for the rest of his life. There was so much . . . no. He wouldn't even let himself think that word. But the joy and excitement, the smile on her lips, the flush on her cheeks, all of it faded when he increased the distance between them.

"Gray?" The confusion and hurt cut through the last haze of desire and idiocy.

"I'm sorry, Meredith."

"Was it that bad? I'll admit I'm out of practice, but I thought—"

"No. It—"

"Cassie's place is clear." Mo's voice crashed through the moment. "My house is too. We need to decide what to do with the scarf."

Meredith turned her back to them. "You decide. Burn it. Bury it. Throw it in the wash and drown it. I don't care. I'm going to stay here and work for a while."

THIRTEEN

Meredith kept her back to Gray and Mo as they discussed the best way to handle the bug. She was so focused on not paying them any attention that she didn't realize they'd come to a decision until she heard Mo say, "Let's take care of it."

She turned enough to make eye contact with her brother. "Have fun with that." Her voice sounded mostly normal. Or maybe it didn't. She didn't care. It didn't matter.

She wanted them to leave her alone.

And when they finally did, she waited a full minute before she slid down the wall until her rear hit the floor. She pressed her head to her knees and waited for the tears.

But they didn't come.

They should be streaming down her face. She wasn't a weeping willow, but she wasn't a cactus either. She cried when tears were called for.

And tonight called for tears. She needed the tears.

But they wouldn't come.

She sat on the floor, eyes dry, mind blank, heart bleeding, until a strong arm wrapped around her. Some part of her consciousness must have known it was Mo. There'd been no fear, no spike of alarm, no sense of danger. But that might have been because she was numb to her core.

Gray had broken her.

"Are we going to sit here on this cold floor all night?" Mo asked. "I don't care. Just want to prepare myself."

She shrugged.

"Well, if you don't care, then I'm going to vote no." He stood and pulled her to her feet. He ushered her to the door, turned out the lights, tucked her against him, and walked her home.

When they reached her door, he opened it, then turned her so she faced him. "I'm here whenever you want to talk about it."

She nodded.

"Promise me you won't make *any* decisions about *anything* until we talk."

She nodded again, walked inside, and closed the door. She'd taken three steps when the import of his words registered. He was worried she might hurt herself. Or worse.

She went back to the door and opened it. She didn't call his name, but Mo must have heard her because he stopped walking to his house and turned back.

"I would never do that." She heard the conviction in her voice.

"I'm glad you think so. But never's a long time to hurt."

She considered his words as she went through the motions of getting ready for bed. She washed her face. Moisturized. And the more she thought about it, the more she realized that Mo was right.

She was never going to have Gray in her life.

And never would be a long time to hurt.

What had happened? What had gone wrong? He'd wanted to kiss her. He'd participated fully. He'd been warm and inviting and oh so strong and gentle.

And then he'd turned to ice. There'd been no give in his body or his voice. No room for argument. No place for debate.

But if he thought she'd let it go, he was wrong.

So very wrong.

Meredith gave up on sleep at 5:30 a.m. She drank coffee that tasted like sludge. Ate breakfast that might as well have been sawdust. Made her bed. Dusted. Cleaned her bathroom. At 7:30, she gave up on sitting around. She had taxes to do.

She sent Mo a text so he wouldn't wake up and freak out when she wasn't home, then drove into town. It took her a few minutes to get into her office, set the heat to a temperature higher than the normal weekend setting, and find the right files for her accountant.

She tried to lose herself in the monotony of expenses and bills, and at some point, she lost track of time.

Until a deep voice pulled her from her concentrated focus.

"Meredith?"

She didn't scream, although it was a near thing. "How did you get in here?"

Gray pointed over his shoulder. "The door was unlocked."

"Well, that was stupid of me. You can see yourself out, and I'll lock up behind you."

"We need to talk."

She opened a random file and pretended to read it. "About what?"

"You know what."

"Oh, you want to talk about how you kissed me senseless and then informed me that it had been a mistake and then disappeared." She'd thought about that sometime around 2:00 a.m.

He could have come back to talk to her, but he'd left. Was he that big of a coward? Or that big of a jerk?

"Yes." He pointed to the chair across from her desk. "Could I sit down?"

It would be petty to tell him no, but she made him wait a full ten seconds before she said, "I guess so."

He sat and placed his ball cap on the chair beside him. He was in his "off-duty" outfit, which for him typically meant khaki or black combat-type pants and some kind of boots. In the winter he wore a thermal long-sleeved shirt, and a T-shirt in summer.

He leaned toward her and shook his head a few times. "I don't know where to start."

She had a few suggestions, but she wasn't going to make them.

"I owe you an apology."

He was right about that.

"And an explanation."

Also a good idea.

"I should never have let things go as far as they did."

Screech. The needle scraped along the record in her mind. "What?" She hadn't meant to say that out loud.

"I knew you were attracted to me. That you were interested in being more than friends. And instead of keeping my distance, I encouraged you."

"What?" She had to stop saying that.

"I should have told you a long time ago."

Was he married? Because really, that was the only thing she could think of that would justify this.

"I can't have romantic relationships. I can't get married and have kids. That life won't ever work for me."

Meredith waited for him to continue, but he didn't say more. "Would you care to elaborate?" She could feel her anger and embarrassment rising. "Because, and please understand that this is

142

just a random suggestion, but if you can't have romantic relationships, you probably shouldn't go around kissing women."

Now that she'd started, there was no stopping her. "What's so wrong with romantic relationships? With marriage and kids? And while we're at it, I realize that I've made a total fool out of myself by wearing my heart on my sleeve, but do you think so little of me that you don't think I know the difference between a kiss and a marriage proposal?"

"I—"

"And I'm hardly an expert, but there were two people kissing. It's not like I jumped you and there was nothing you could do. You outweigh me by at least fifty pounds. I think you could have found a way to disentangle yourself if you'd wanted to."

"I—"

"So you can understand my confusion when you say you should have ended this, whatever this is, a long time ago. But you were right there in the thick of it. I'll admit that I'm not entirely clear on who started it. But I am crystal clear on who ended it. And then you left."

"Mo—"

"You could have come back to discuss it."

He inhaled slowly. "Mo was supposed to tell you. I got a call while he was scanning his house. I had to go to the scene of another car wreck. There was a fatality."

Guilt shot through her. "He didn't mention it. Was it . . ."

"No one you would know. Kentucky license and plates." He blew out a breath. "We've had more vehicular fatalities than I think is reasonable. I don't have any evidence, but I'm wondering if some of our neighboring counties and their criminal activities are drawing people to the area who then drive through Gossamer County while buzzed, stoned, high, drunk, or all of the above. There's no toxicology yet, obviously, but I can't figure out how this guy wrecked. It was like he just drove off the road. We're probably lucky that it was a single-car accident and that he didn't hit someone else. Two big wrecks this week, and I don't have a way to stop them. It's not like I can straighten the roads."

Meredith could almost see the weight of responsibility resting on Gray's shoulders. She could almost feel sorry for him.

Almost.

She kept her mouth closed and waited for Gray to remember why he came by. Because she seriously doubted it was to tell her that a motorist had died.

"I didn't get back to the office until five thirty this morning. At that point, I went home, showered, and crashed. When I woke up, I started to head to your place, but I saw your 4Runner so I stopped here."

"Okay." It was a lame response, but what did he expect her to say?

Gray leaned back in his chair. "There's no way for you to know this, but every time I see you and Mo together, I have to fight off a twinge of jealousy. If my sister had lived, I think we would have had something similar to what you and Mo have."

Gray laced his hands together and stared at them as he continued. "Her name was Jasmine. She was three years younger than me. We lived in a not-so-great part of Chicago. It wasn't the worst place in the city, but it wasn't safe. Our mom . . . she couldn't afford anything else. She tried. She worked two, sometimes three jobs. Kept us fed. We didn't have the coolest clothes or the latest styles, but we never went hungry."

He didn't realize he'd stopped talking until Meredith shifted in her chair. He made eye contact, then looked out the window.

"She was eleven. Gang violence broke out in our neighborhood. Drive-bys and random shootings. One night, they shot up our house. She ran into my room. Took a bullet to the chest."

Meredith gasped.

"She died in my arms. Mom was at work. I held her until Mom got home."

Meredith was crying now.

"We never slept another night in that place. Mom moved us in with a guy from one of her jobs. Samson offered, and she said yes. I figured out pretty quickly that he was romantically interested in Mom, but she'd never given him the time of day. I had never known her to date anyone. Jasmine and I were her priority."

Meredith grabbed a tissue and blew her nose.

"I still don't know if she felt forced or coerced, or if she developed feelings for him, but she married Samson nine months later. He was okay, except for when he went on a bender. It didn't happen often, but he was a mean drunk. He liked my mom, and I didn't think he'd do anything to her. But I could tell he was just waiting for me to be gone. So I went to school and worked and stayed out of the house as much as I could."

He rubbed his hands over his face. "Maybe it was worse than I realized. I was a teenage boy. My brain wasn't fully formed. My heart was broken. I missed Jasmine and the friends I had where we used to live. I don't know, but I know I wasn't paying attention."

He closed his eyes as the scene unfolded before him. Coming home late from an evening shift to a police barricade. The neighbors outside. The look on the officer's face when he came out to tell him that his mother was dead.

"Samson shot a cop when they tried to intervene. The cop survived. But the other cops returned fire and Samson died. When they got inside, it was too late for my mom. He'd beaten her to death."

He couldn't look at Meredith. He could see her in his peripheral vision. Her hands were over her mouth and tears streamed down her cheeks, but if he looked at her, he would fall apart. And he couldn't do that.

"They put me in foster care, which sounds bad but wasn't. The family they put me with was amazing. John and Leslie were Christians. Their own kids were grown and none of them lived close by, so they decided they would foster older teenagers. I was their first placement. They helped me get my grades up, helped me decide about college and the military. Led me to Christ. I owe them so much."

He leaned forward, elbows on his knees, and tried to slow his heart rate. The wounds that he'd thought had scarred over? Turned out they could still bleed if he picked at them enough. He'd expected telling Meredith to be uncomfortable. He hadn't been prepared for it to hurt so much.

"I was a senior in college and had already signed my life away to the Marine Corps when John showed up at my apartment. I could tell he'd been crying. They'd fostered two more boys after me. One was a sophomore in college. The other was a junior in high school. Leslie had been taking him to an SAT preparedness class and got caught in a high-speed chase. The driver hit her head-on. She died instantly."

Meredith was crying so hard her entire body shook.

"I've been to too many funerals, Meredith. The women I love? They die. And not of old age or natural causes. They die horrifically. And that's why I can't fall in love. Ever."

Meredith didn't speak for several minutes. Gray had no idea what else there was to say. He'd dropped a lot of heavy information on her, so he sat there as she processed what he'd said.

146

Then she looked up at him, her eyes red and puffy, mascara tracks on her cheeks, and whispered, "Three women you loved died, Gray. That's unbelievably awful. And if you told me that was why you're afraid of love, or had kept yourself from forming close relationships in the years since, I would understand that."

"That's exactly what I'm saying."

"No, it isn't. You're acting like you're cursed or something."

"Maybe I am."

"That's a load of horse manure. You're no more cursed than anyone else is. You *decided* that you didn't want to fall in love. Fine. That's your prerogative. But if you thought coming in here and telling me your tale of woe would make everything okay between us, then you'll be leaving here sorely disappointed."

She wiped her face with a tissue. "Your experiences are heartbreaking, but you're a grown man. And you *knew*. You knew how I felt, and instead of coming to me and telling me right up front, or at the very least, explaining it to Cal and having him tell me, you let us carry on for a couple of years. Years, Gray! Wasted years, apparently, when I thought you just needed some time. That was cruel. And the worst part is, it's all a lie."

Gray's pain had morphed into anger. How could she be so insensitive? "Not one word of that was a lie."

"Oh, I have no doubt that you believe this curse is real and that you're doing all you can to avoid any more deaths. There's just one problem."

"Just one?" Sounded to him like there were about a thousand.

"For the past few months, you've been playing some kind of weird hot-and-cold game with me. Some days, I thought there was hope. Some days, I was sure you were clueless. But one thing that can't be disputed is that you've been taking extra care of me. You've provided extra security and done the kind of things that, oh, I don't know, a man might do when he has feelings for a woman but he hasn't acknowledged them."

"Or maybe"—Gray leaned over her desk—"they were the kind of things a man might do if he'd already lost a sister, a mother, and a foster mother, and didn't want his friends to experience the same pain."

Meredith sat back in her desk chair like she'd been punched. "Can you honestly tell me that's why?"

"I can honestly tell you that's why I thought I was doing it." Although he now realized that there was clearly more going on.

"Here's what I know." Meredith stood and walked around her desk. "I will always be sorry for what you've experienced. While I never met them, neither your sister, your mother, nor your foster mother would have ever wanted you to live a loveless life. But you've lied to yourself about what you want and why. You've lied to yourself about me." She pressed her hand to her heart. "You kissed me, Gray! And you had an opportunity to break free of the deception you've been operating under, but you chose to dive back into it instead of taking a leap of faith and exploring something that could have been beautiful."

She walked to her door and paused on the outside, arm extended in a clear sign that he was dismissed. "But you no longer need to expend any energy worrying about me. Should I require any further assistance from Gossamer Falls law enforcement, I will direct my inquiries to your officers. Goodbye, Chief Ward."

Gray didn't know how he'd expected this to go down, but he hadn't seen it ending this way. He paused as he walked past her. "I realize it's cliché, but—"

She held up a hand. "I realize you don't plan to have children, so maybe you don't care, but if you place any value on the tenderest parts of your body, I strongly suggest you do not say anything about friendship to me."

Gray stepped away from her. He didn't want to give her any opportunity to follow through on her threat. She didn't follow him, and he paused at the door and looked at her. "I *am* sorry, Meredith."

There was no give in her face. No compassion in her eyes. And when he'd gone outside, the only goodbye she gave him was the click of the door as she locked it behind him.

FOURTEEN

One week later, Gray sat at his kitchen table and reread the email that had landed in his inbox on Thursday.

> Our man on the inside says there's a wedding coming up in a few weeks. Any chance you can crash it?

He'd lost count of how many times he'd read that message. And it was the same every time.

He pulled the legal pad he'd been taking notes on toward him and studied the circles and lists and arrows. There was a connection here. There had to be. Something that would make it all clear.

But he couldn't find it.

He flipped the pages over and started with a blank sheet. At the top of the page, he wrote *The Problem in Neeson* in block letters.

Underneath it he wrote three headings: *Drugs, Trafficking, LEO Involvement.*

When he'd come to Gossamer Falls, one of the first things the hiring board did was cover the issues in the nearby counties. There were unique conflicts with each of their neighbors, but Neeson was the problem child. Everyone knew it, and as Meredith's comments at dinner had indicated, they'd known for decades. They might not have had a handle on the specifics, but the people of Gossamer Falls knew enough to keep their kids out of Neeson.

His brain hiccupped as the image of Meredith sitting at her parents' table wormed its way into his thoughts.

He'd seen her twice since the debacle last Saturday. He still had no idea how he'd gone from sharing his greatest heartache and her sobbing like her heart was shattered to her calling him a liar and telling him she never wanted to speak to him again.

He'd been a jerk. He would own that. But he wasn't a liar. He'd told her the truth. And after the way she'd reacted? He hadn't known she had that level of mean in her. So it was probably for the best.

He tapped the pen on the table.

But . . . had he lied with his behavior? He could see her perspective on that. She had no way to know how hard he'd worked to keep his distance. Or how much he'd wrestled with his feelings toward her.

And then there was the kiss. He didn't believe in accidental kisses. It was extraordinarily difficult to fall into someone else's lips with your own. And then to stay stuck there? Spend a few blissful moments exploring? No. Kisses might not be planned, but they weren't accidents.

The knock on his door dragged him back to the present. "It's open."

"Shouldn't the police chief set a good example for his citizens by keeping his door locked?" Cal Shaw came in and walked straight to Gray's kitchen.

"I *am* setting a good example. I'm saying, 'We're safe here.' I'm also saying, 'I can take care of myself.' And both of those are things the citizens should want from their police chief."

Cal took a mug from the cabinet and poured himself a cup of coffee. "Someone's feeling a bit touchy this morning."

Gray ignored the remark and turned back to the legal pad. Behind him, he heard the fridge open, the splash of cream, the clink of a spoon, the sip. Another thirty seconds passed as Cal rinsed his spoon, put everything away, and joined Gray at the table.

The only sounds around the table were the scratch of Gray's pen and Cal's slurping.

"You're doing that on purpose." Gray cut his eyes at Cal.

Cal's response was another, even louder, gulp.

"I'm going to kick you out if you don't stop that mess."

"I'm going to keep doing it until you tell me what's got you growling at everybody you see."

Gray set the pen down. "Then I hope you enjoy hanging out in an empty house. I'll go work at my office."

He held Cal's stare, and to his surprise, Cal gave in. He took another sip, this time at a normal volume, and set the coffee on the table. "She hasn't shared. You won't share. I think Mo knows more than he's telling. Landry says I have to stay out of it until you want to talk about it. I'm trying to take her advice. I know there's something up. I'm guessing it's bad. I don't know who's to blame—"

"Me." Gray wouldn't give him details, but he also wouldn't let Cal think any of this was Meredith's fault.

Cal gave him a long look. "Okay. Thank you for that. I think."

"You're welcome. Just know . . . that's all I'm going to say."

Cal frowned. "Then know that this is all I'm going to say. You're my best friend. You saved my life—"

"You saved mine."

"Yeah. But you don't seem to think that your life matters or that you deserve anything beautiful in it. I don't know what happened, and I'm not saying Meredith is the answer. But God might have big plans for you that you can't even imagine, and you refuse to consider them because you've decided your own path. Trust me on this. I wouldn't have chosen the path I took to be where I am today, and there's still heartache on the edges of my life that I've realized will always be there. But I've learned a lot since Landry blew all my ideas out of the water. And the main thing is not to expect God to go along with your plans. He has his own plans. And they're better." Cal adjusted his ball cap and grinned. "And that's all I have to say about that. So, why am I here? You called this meeting."

For his entire adult life, Gray had done his best to keep his relationships to a minimum. But Cal Shaw had shown up in his life and refused to stay out of it. He knew Cal would keep his word, and unless Gray brought it up, he wouldn't press for more information.

He also knew that he'd be thinking about Cal's words for a long time. He'd thought his plans were in line with God's will for his life. But were they? Or had he made plans and then assumed God was on board? And if the plans were his and not God's . . .

He set that aside for later. Right now, he needed Cal's brain. "What I'm about to tell you can't leave this room."

Cal straightened and fired off a crisp salute. Which was ridiculous—they'd been the same rank. But he got the meaning.

"A month after I took this job, I was approached by an FBI agent in Raleigh. Special Agent Faith Powell. She's part of a task force that is made up of FBI, Secret Service, SBI, ATF, DEA, and pretty much a member of every state and federal alphabet-soup agencies you can imagine, including a few you've never heard of."

Cal whistled. "Big time. What did she want?"

"The task force was created to address police corruption across the state. They have multiple cases they're working. But the reason she called me is that it's her job to fix Neeson."

"What's her plan?"

"It's a long game. They don't want the small fish. They want the whale. DEA has a man undercover in Neeson. He's been there a while, and I have a feeling they want to get this wrapped up."

"Did our former police chief know about this?" Cal gave him a knowing glance.

"No. The task force deemed him to be too big of a question mark to take him into their confidence. They ran the whole thing without his input, but they brought me on as soon as they could. They've kept me in the loop, but most of what I've done is provide information when needed and a bolt hole in case their undercover agent needs to run."

"What changed?"

"Steven Pierce."

Cal's knuckles went white. "If you tell me they want to cut a deal—"

"No. Nothing like that." The entire Quinn clan would lose their collective minds if the man responsible for Cassie's kidnapping wasn't punished for his actions. "It's because of the press. The attention on Gossamer Falls and Neeson didn't sit well with our drug-running neighbors. They've enjoyed years of virtual autonomy. And now there's a new police chief next door in Gossamer Falls and one of their wealthy and influential clients is arrested for kidnapping and attempted murder. I'm not saying Meredith shouldn't have helped those women, but the timing stinks. If Steven's actions kicked the hornet's nest, Meredith's may have poured gasoline on it."

Cal looked at his already empty mug. "I'm going to need more coffee."

"Not sleeping?" Gray asked as Cal went to the kitchen.

"Landry wasn't feeling good. She was up several times last night."

"You should have told me, you moron. We could have talked at your place."

Cal returned to the table. "Landry's in her studio. Eliza's with Mom."

"No Abby?" Abby and Eliza were best friends. Now they shared a Nana. They were growing up the same way Cal had grown up with Meredith and Mo, and everyone involved was thrilled.

"Mom's trying to spend time with them individually. She doesn't want Abby to resent Eliza, and she wants to get to know Eliza away from Abby. She's set up a plan where the girls go hang out with her one-on-one, and then later the other one joins in the fun. I think they're planning to pick Abby up for lunch. Who knows what will happen after that."

Cal looked out the window. "It's hard to believe all this is going on right next door. I want it to be as safe for the kids as it was for me, Mo, Meredith, and Bronwyn."

"I'm doing the best I can, brother."

Cal toasted him with his mug. "I know. What do you need from me?"

"I had a message about the wedding."

"By the wedding, do you mean the one Meredith's doing the flowers for?"

"That's the one."

"Do you want me to figure out how to convince her not to go?"

"No. I want you to figure out how to be sure she takes me as her plus-one."

Two hours later, Meredith stopped on the trail they were hiking, picked up a pine cone, and threw it at Cal's head. "Have you lost your mind? You ask me to come for a little hike, and then you drop this 'you still have to take Gray to the wedding' on me?"

Cal didn't look ashamed of himself. He'd tricked her. Convinced her that what she needed was some fresh air and a hard hike to clear her head.

And she'd been scatterbrained enough to believe him. She'd enjoyed the hike. She always enjoyed the hike. When they were kids, they would go on hikes and pretend that Mo and Cal were Lewis and Clark while she was Sacajawea. It worked great for her because, in her version of the story, she bossed everyone around and told them where to go. The consensus was that she had a better sense of direction than the rest of them, and she'd led them out of a few close calls.

She couldn't believe Cal had done this. "I'm telling Granny on you."

"No you won't."

"Oh yeah?"

"Yeah."

"What makes you think that?"

"Because if you tell Granny, she's going to make you tell her what happened with Gray."

Meredith picked up another pine cone and threw it.

Cal batted it away. "Quit that. You're mad because I'm right."

"What I want to know is how you drew the short straw."

"What do you mean?"

"Why is it you and not Mo having this super-fun conversation with me?"

"Oh, that's easy. Mo doesn't know anything about it yet."

Meredith trudged up the trail and didn't speak to Cal for a full five minutes. She paused after crossing a small creek and waited for him to join her. "Tell me why."

Cal did.

And when he finished, she picked up a smooth rock and tossed it into the creek. "Y'all are going to give me whiplash. 'Don't go to Neeson. It's dangerous in Neeson. Stay away. You shouldn't go to the wedding at all.' And then you find out someone wants to be sure Gray is at the wedding and it's all, 'You have to go to the wedding, and you have to take Gray.' What happened? Not worried about my safety anymore?"

Cal leaned against an ancient pine and let her vent.

"Why can't you or Mo go with me?"

Cal pinched his lips together. Was he fighting a smile? "Which one of us do you want to go?"

She opened her mouth to say anyone would be better than Gray, but defeat warred with desperation as the complexity of the situation became crystal clear. "I don't want either of you to go." She pointed a finger at Cal. "And you can wipe that smirk off your face."

"Would you prefer the smirk or for me to point out that I knew this is what you would do?"

"Neither. I want you and Mo to come up with a better plan."

"Oh, that won't be hard. Don't go to the wedding."

"I have to!"

"You don't."

"If I don't go, how will Gray get in?"

"Gray is the chief of police. He has access to all sorts of people who can figure it out. You, my dear, are a dentist and a civilian. There's no reason for you to put yourself in danger to make it easier for him to put himself in danger."

"I'm going."

"You've made that abundantly clear. And as your cousin-brother I've already concluded that there's no way to talk you out of it, and as such, I want you to take Gray. I can protect you. So can Mo. But we have no legal authority to act if things go haywire."

"Gray doesn't have jurisdiction in Neeson."

"He will if he's acting as part of the task force."

Meredith gaped at him. "He lied to me. He told me he didn't have any authority outside Gossamer County."

Cal frowned at her. "I'm not taking his side, but it isn't like you to accuse someone of something like that. I don't know what's going on with you two. All he would tell me was that it was his fault and to stay out of it."

He'd told Cal it was his fault?

"He didn't lie." Cal enunciated each word. "The way he explained it to me is that day in, day out, he has zero authority outside Gossamer Falls. But if things go south in Neeson, he has the authority to act but only on matters that are specific to the issues that fall under the task force's purview. He can't waltz in there and start arresting people willy-nilly."

Meredith considered his words. "Fine. I'll concede the point."

"Big of you, since I'm right and you overreacted."

"Don't push me, Cal."

"What happened?" Cal's brow wrinkled in confusion. "Where did my sweet, gentle, compassionate Meredith go?"

Despite the tender way the rebuke was delivered, the words stung. "She's still here."

"Really?"

"Yes. But not for him. He doesn't deserve gentle, compassionate Meredith."

"Why not?" Cal's frustrated question split something open in her.

"Because I thought I was falling in love with him. Because he's the only man I've had any interest in since the first moment I saw him. Because he's decided that he's cursed and can't have any kind of romantic relationship. And because he didn't share that fact with me until after he kissed me." Meredith gasped in a breath. "Or maybe I kissed him and he kissed me back." She waved a hand. "It's a blur. The point is, we kissed, and I was so stupid that I actually thought it meant something."

She wiped a rogue tear from her cheek. "It meant something to me. And I think it meant something to him, but not enough. I'm not enough to pull him out of his self-imposed emotional black hole. And now"—she wiped another tear, or seven—"now I have to go to a wedding with him. A wedding, Cal!"

He winced.

"A wedding with a man I might still be a little bit in love with, and with whom I am definitely a lot in hate with."

"You don't hate him."

"Well, no." Quinns were taught young not to throw that word around lightly. "I don't hate him. But I despise him. And I despise myself. I can't stand to see him, to be around him. It hurts every time. And it's embarrassing. I've been all but throwing myself at him for a couple of years and the whole time, he wasn't interested."

Cal looked at the ground. "I'm not convinced he's not interested."

She thumped her chest. "I was there for the conversation. Oh, he's attracted to me. He'll acknowledge that. But he isn't interested in a relationship. And I'm interested in nothing less."

The tears had gotten completely out of hand, and her nose was running. Cal reached into the small backpack he always carried and extracted a handful of napkins. He approached her the way he might approach a rabid raccoon. She probably looked like one.

She took the napkins and tried to dry her face. Cal returned to his spot against the tree and didn't speak.

When she'd pulled herself partly together, she spoke into the silence. "Now, you tell me that you want me to take him to a wedding where he could be hurt. My choices are to take my brother, my cousin, or the man who stole my heart but doesn't want it. I don't want to take any of you! I'm so angry with him that I can barely say his name without feeling the need to go to his house and . . . I don't know . . . take all his shoelaces and

159

belts, or replace his coffee with decaf, or put hair remover in his shampoo. That doesn't mean I want him in harm's way. How am I supposed to live with myself if I take him to the wedding and he gets killed?"

Panic welled inside her at the idea.

Cal stepped forward and pulled her into his arms. "Mer, I hear you, but if you can't handle the idea of taking him to the wedding, there's no way a relationship between the two of you ever would have worked. He's the police chief. He puts on a bulletproof vest every single day. He carries a weapon to work, and even when he isn't at work, he's always armed. He's always a target."

She shuddered at his words. "It's not like he's in Chicago anymore. He's in Gossamer Falls. It's safe here."

"It usually is."

Meredith knew Cal was thinking about Landry's stalker, about Cassie's kidnapping, and about her punctured fuel line.

Gossamer Falls hadn't been safe lately.

She pressed her forehead into Cal's chest. She didn't want to spend a second with Grayson Ward. Not even one.

But did she have a choice? She'd already stuck her nose in the mess in Neeson. And they knew it. This wasn't about her, her feelings, or how awkward it would be to spend an evening with a man she was desperately trying to get over. This was about the moms, the kids, the scared faces, the bruised arms, the broken teeth. This was how she could fight back. "He can be my plus-one, Cal. But not my date. You tell him that. He shouldn't care. It's not like he wants anything more from me than a ticket to the reception. I'll do my civic duty. Nothing more."

Cal squeezed her close. "I'm sorry he hurt you."

"Me too."

"Want me to hurt him back?"

"No. He's your best friend."

"Want me to break up with him?" There was a tiny bit of humor in Cal's words, but a strong vein of sincerity as well.

"Don't you dare."

"Want to come back to the house and eat ice cream and watch old movies?"

"You hate old movies."

"But I love ice cream. And I love you. I can endure the movie."

Meredith stepped away from him and pulled the last dry napkin from her pocket. "This is why you rock at being a girl dad. You're good with tears and drama."

Cal looked like he did when he was a kid and got caught doing something wrong. "I'm not really. If you say no to the ice cream, I'm pretty much out of ideas. Also, full disclosure, Landry suggested it."

Meredith laughed until she cried a little more, but this time the tears were gentle and cleansing. She slid her arm through Cal's. "I'll take the ice cream. And then I'll go work in my shop. I have wedding flowers to finish."

FIFTEEN

At 8:30 on Monday morning, Gray's phone rang. He took a look at the incoming caller and almost dropped the phone. Why was Meredith's grandfather calling him?

He'd seen Papa Quinn on Sunday at church, but they hadn't spoken. Not that he typically spoke to him at church. Gray preferred to sit in the balcony so he could slip out if he got a call, and the Quinns sat on the main level. Which meant he'd had a lovely view of Meredith sitting in between Mo and Cal. And he didn't miss the way Mo draped his arm around his sister in what, to Gray's mind, looked like an attempt to comfort her. And maybe protect her.

Gray hadn't paid as much attention to the sermon as he should have because he'd spent part of it wondering if something had happened that he didn't know about. He trusted Donovan to tell him anything that related to the situation in Neeson. But what else was bothering her?

Was it possible she was still upset about him? About the kiss?

Would she hold a grudge forever? He deserved it, but he didn't think she had it in her.

He dragged his mind back to the phone call. He'd never know

what the man wanted if he didn't answer the call. He cleared his throat and answered the way he always did. "Chief Ward here."

"Chief, this is John Quinn." A pause. "Senior."

"Yes, sir. How are you today?"

"Fine. Fine. I know you're a busy man, but I was hoping you could come over to the house around lunchtime."

Gray glanced at his calendar even though he already knew there was nothing on it. "I could do that."

"Excellent. Let's say eleven thirty."

"Sounds good."

"See you then."

The phone disconnected, and before he did anything else, Gray put the lunch appointment on the calendar. He had no idea how long it would take, so he blocked out three hours to be safe. He tackled the reports left in his inbox overnight and, at 9:30, made a phone call.

The woman he was calling answered on the third ring. "Hello."

"I have an invite to the wedding."

"How'd you manage that?"

"Meredith is doing all the flowers for the wedding. I'm her plus-one."

A long silence. "You sure that's a good idea?"

"She's going no matter what. I might as well be there to help keep her out of trouble."

Another pause. "I don't like it."

"Honestly, I don't either. But it's the best I can do."

"Does she know you have other motives than keeping her safe?"

"It's complicated, but yes. We had a huge fight last week and I wasn't sure she would be okay with me going. I haven't even spoken to her since the fight. But she told her cousin to be sure I understood that I could be her plus-one but not her date. She made that very clear."

"You had a fight?" Was that amusement in her question? Or concern? Gray didn't know her well enough to tell. "How did you convince her to let you go anyway?"

"She's doing it for the people of Neeson. She wants to see the situation resolved, and she's treating it as her civic duty." Cal had rolled his eyes when he told Gray that, but it was on-brand for Meredith. The woman had no self-protective instincts at all.

Or he hadn't thought she had. She'd developed some fast when it came to him.

"Okay. We have about four weeks until the wedding." Faith groaned. "I don't like this. I want our guy out of there and I want Neeson back on the straight and narrow. And I do not like knowing a civilian is going to be in the middle of it."

"I don't disagree, but she's already in the middle of it. And while she didn't do it on purpose, she did put herself there. No one else is responsible. Short of sending her off to Europe for a few months, I don't see how we have any options but to work with the situation we have."

"You're right. Let's pray we can resolve everything peacefully."

They chatted for a few more minutes, then disconnected. Gray worked until 11:15 and then made the drive out to John and Catherine Quinn's.

He parked beside a familiar car. What was Mrs. Frost doing here?

Doug Quinn walked out of the house and paused on the front porch. When Gray met his eyes, the look he received wasn't hostile, but it wasn't friendly either. Doug strode down the steps, a set of keys in his hand, and met Gray at the bottom. "Chief."

Great. They were back to Chief instead of Gray.

"Mr. Quinn."

Doug shook his head and extended a hand to shake Gray's. "Good to see you. I hate to run. Mom tried to convince me to stay for lunch, but I promised Mrs. Frost I'd have her car checked out while she's here." He cut his eyes to the house, then whispered, "She wants to sell it. Asked me to give it a look and tell her how much it's worth."

Gray kept his voice low. "Please tell me she doesn't plan to buy another car with the proceeds?"

Doug grinned. "She told Mom that she's thinking about a truck."

Gray dropped his head in defeat.

"Mom told her she needed to stop driving because she was going to hurt somebody."

"Did it work?"

"Not yet. But Mom's pretty persuasive."

"Everyone in a ten-county radius will be safer when she stops driving, so let's pray Granny Quinn can work a miracle."

"I'm on it." Doug climbed into Mrs. Frost's car and had to adjust the seat significantly before he cranked the engine and drove away.

Gray watched him go, then climbed the steps to the front door. He'd survived Meredith's dad. Now to see if he could survive her grandparents. And Mrs. Frost.

"Come on in, son." Papa Quinn held the door open before Gray reached it. "My Catherine has been cooking up a storm this morning."

Gray entered the Quinn home, and despite his concern about how Papa and Granny Quinn might feel toward him, his entire body relaxed. He had no idea how Granny Quinn did it. The house was large and old, but it never felt cold or remote. Walking into their home was like walking into a hug.

And today, it smelled like heaven. Something with onion and garlic, maybe tomato? Whatever Granny Quinn was cooking, it was going to be delicious.

Papa Quinn led him to the kitchen where Granny Quinn sat at a large round table. Mrs. Frost sat beside her. They looked up when Gray walked in, and while Mrs. Frost's smile was polite, Granny's was warm. "Well, well. I told John you'd come."

"Yes, ma'am."

"Catherine." There was a chiding note in Papa's voice.

"What? We're not gonna dance around it. He's at odds with our Meredith. But she won't give us any details, so I don't reckon he will either. Still, he came when asked. He's got a spine, and I like a man with a spine."

Mrs. Frost nodded in agreement. "Don't got no use for the ones with no spine myself."

"Come sit." Granny Quinn pointed to a chair. "And don't worry. I won't ask you for details. I have too many children and grandchildren to let myself get caught up in their relationships. I let the Lord sort it out. He knows what he's doing."

Gray wasn't quite sure if he should be comforted by the idea of Granny Quinn setting the Almighty on him or not. But at least she wasn't mad at him. He took the seat and said yes to the cup of coffee Papa Quinn offered.

"I've got a pot of soup on and cornbread in the oven. It'll be ready in a few minutes." Granny patted Mrs. Frost's hand. "Janet brought me some of her homemade muscadine jelly, so we decided to make us a batch of biscuits too."

Papa leaned toward Gray. "I'd appreciate it if you don't mention that to Carol. She wants us to eat less bread, but I don't see the point in it myself."

"Young people these days." Mrs. Frost raised her eyes to the heavens. "They mean well, but sometimes I just don't know."

Gray mimed zipping his lips. "I won't say a word. Especially since I fully intend to be complicit in your illegal activities. Wouldn't want to incriminate myself."

The conversation was easy after that, and Gray did his best to absorb everything he could. He'd learned early on that while the town elders might be deadly on the roads, and might have tongues that could be sharp, they were also a wealth of information. They had the wisdom of years and the experience to spot patterns that younger citizens simply couldn't grasp.

In the space of twenty minutes, Gray learned about two pregnancies, a scandalous love affair going on "right under everybody's noses" at the local bank, and how two teenagers he'd had his eye on were, according to Granny Quinn, selling pot at the high school.

Granny Quinn served vegetable beef soup that she'd canned in the fall with cornbread she'd cooked in a cast iron skillet and, of course, the contraband biscuits and jelly. All of this was washed down with sweet tea. And then she brought out a peach cobbler and vanilla ice cream.

At that point, Gray had to say something. "Do you eat this way every day?"

Papa Quinn shook his head. "Nah. My Catherine can't bear to have guests and not put on a spread of some kind. She'll feed me leftovers tonight."

Granny Quinn cut her eyes at her husband, but then took his hand and squeezed. "Poor dear. It's a hard life." And then they smiled at each other.

Gray wondered, not for the first time, what it would be like to have someone look at him the way Granny looked at Papa. It wasn't the way she'd probably looked at him when they were young and in the first days and years of love. It was intentional love. On-purpose love. It was the kind of love that came about after decades of choosing to love.

Granny Quinn took a bite of her cobbler and tapped the edge of her plate with her fork. "Janet, tell us what's going on in Neeson these days. We're hearing some things."

"Oh, Catherine. It's a sorry state of affairs. I never would have dreamed it. Marvin and Dennis were such nice young men. And now? I tell you. The things you hear! I mean, I've known for years that Marvin was into all kinds of shady things, but I thought he kept it a secret from Dennis. But now I hear that Dennis knows all about it and won't do anything."

"Surely not." Granny took a sip of her coffee, and her eyes met Gray's. "Seems like the police chief ought to arrest a man if he knows he's up to no good."

Mrs. Frost gave a prim nod. "I agree with you. But you know those two. They weren't ever the same after that McAbee boy got hurt."

Papa Quinn hummed in acknowledgment. "That was a long time ago."

"Oh yes." Mrs. Frost shook her head. "He died a couple of years ago. Lived all these years, but he wasn't ever the same."

Gray couldn't take it. "I'm sorry, but the McAbee boy? How did he get hurt?"

"No one knows." Mrs. Frost gave him a blank look.

Did she really not know? Or did she not remember? Gray shot a look at Papa Quinn, and thankfully he jumped in.

"I remember when it happened. Heartbreaking. Do I remember this right? That Kirby, Johnstone, and McAbee were close friends?"

Mrs. Frost nodded. "Never saw one without the other two. Until Lawrence, that was his name, went missing."

"They didn't find him for three days." Papa Quinn looked grim. "We helped look. A bunch of us from the church went up there. Walked through the mountains. I remember the boys were questioned about it at the time, but they claimed they had no idea where he was."

Gray found that an interesting choice of words. Papa Quinn obviously didn't believe their "claim."

"Found that poor boy in the woods, beaten near half to death." Mrs. Frost shuddered. "Took him to Asheville, then on to Duke. Did all they could for him, but . . ."

"He had severe brain damage from the assault," Papa Quinn explained. "Most of his physical abilities came back after he healed, although I believe he had a significant limp. But his cognition never returned to what it had been before. He didn't know his name or where he was. He could speak, but not much."

"The worst of it was, they never found out who did it." Mrs. Frost took another bite of cobbler. "The rumor was that he'd accidentally come upon some outlaw types. And he might have. Our mountains can be a good place to hide if you're of a mind to."

The conversation spun off in a different direction for a while with Granny and Mrs. Frost reminiscing about some criminal who'd hidden out for a few years before he was caught. But eventually Granny steered the conversation back to Neeson.

"I hear y'all are about to have a big wedding up there. Our Meredith is doing the flowers. Were you invited?" Granny asked Mrs. Frost.

"Oh yes. I believe they invited the whole town."

Neeson wasn't large, but the whole town? There wasn't a church big enough to hold everybody.

"But just to the reception," Mrs. Frost added. "They're having the church wedding for family and close friends, and they invited everybody to the reception out at the river. Which is all well and good, but what if it rains? Or snows? Who has an outdoor party in March?"

Gray had no idea where "out at the river" was, but it shouldn't be too hard to find out.

And he hated it for Mrs. Frost, but as far as he was concerned, rain or snow might be the best thing that could happen that day.

Gray didn't learn any more useful information from Mrs. Frost that afternoon, but when he returned to the office, he called Mo.

"Quinn," Mo answered.

"I could use your help on something."

A long pause. "And what would that be, Chief?"

Gray explained what he'd learned from his lunch with the Quinns and Mrs. Frost. "I know your grandfather wanted me to understand the connection between Kirby and Johnstone. But just because they were friends in high school, that doesn't explain why Kirby continues to look the other way. It might be a dead end, but I'd like to know more about Lawrence McAbee and the case surrounding him. Can you look into it?"

Mo was a consultant for the Gossamer Falls Police Department. He was paid a one-dollar-a-year retainer and then paid on a contract basis when he did actual computer forensic work, which was rare. But there was no one in the mountains of North Carolina who could do the job better than Mo. He made his living as a forensic accountant, but he'd been in Army intelligence before he got out shortly after his mom's cancer diagnosis. He had contacts everywhere—from law enforcement to the military to the dark web.

"This is an old case, Gray. I'll look into it, but it will take longer than normal. A lot of these records won't be online anywhere. I wouldn't be surprised to learn that they're on microfiche somewhere in a storage building in Neeson. If they exist at all."

"I know. But this is a stone we can't afford to leave unturned. Everybody knows Kirby's dirty, but no one knows why. This could be our why."

"Or it could be a story old people tell when they get together to gossip over soup and cornbread." Mo might have been annoyed

170

at the request, or that he'd been left out of the lunch invitation. It was hard to tell. And either way, he wasn't wrong.

"You know how this goes."

"Story of my life, man. Open every bar of chocolate until you find the golden ticket. If you're lucky, you'll be the one who finds it and not some entitled billionaire brat with an expensive lawyer."

"I'm not sure if you're talking about Willy Wonka or real life."

"Both. I'm on it. I'll be in touch."

"Thank you."

"Yep."

Gray was hanging up the phone when he heard "Gray" yelled through the line.

"Yes?"

"I may need to bring in someone to help with this. That going to be a problem? She's legit. Consults for law enforcement all over the country."

Gray considered it. "If it gets out that we're looking, it could cost a man his life."

"I'd trust her with mine."

That was a serious endorsement. "If you have to, then yes."

"Okay. Later."

This time, the call disconnected without interruption. Gray considered the implications of what he'd learned today.

If Dennis Kirby and Marvin Johnstone had been friends since they were kids, what did that say about their relationship today? If Mo or Meredith or Cal had gone off the deep end, how would the other two have handled it? Would they have been open in their disapproval, but at the same time would they have looked the other way?

He needed more information about Kirby and Johnstone's relationship, where they'd gone after high school, and what had led them back to Neeson. But he also knew his own strengths and weaknesses. If he could have gone into town and asked questions, that would have been ideal. But that option wasn't on the table. He'd have to wait for Mo to work his magic, and hope he got back to him sooner rather than later.

SIXTEEN

It had been sixteen days since she last had a conversation with Gray. Sixteen days of carrying on with her life as if it hadn't fallen apart. She'd always been an overachiever, but hitting the criminal radar and having her heart broken in the same week was taking it way too far.

She didn't want to be out on the town with Bronwyn. She should be at home, in her bed, eating ice cream straight from the carton and watching TV, but even that had lost its appeal.

It was just as well. It turned out that watching true crime documentaries hit differently after you learned your scarf had been bugged.

Last night, she'd watched a documentary on the making of the Blue Ridge Parkway. She loved her mountains. Loved hiking them. Loved exploring. She even loved camping in them. But last night, she'd watched TV and searched for cheap flights to anywhere that was far from home.

She tried to shake off the gloom. Tonight, she would be young, carefree, and fun, even if it killed her. But she wouldn't order anything caffeinated. She had enough trouble sleeping without hamstringing herself with late-night coffee.

"I'll take an iced decaf Americano with oat milk creamer." Meredith studied the small menu in front of her and added, "And a triple berry muffin." When the waitress turned to Bronwyn to take her order, Meredith took a few moments to refamiliarize herself with her surroundings. It had been a long time since she'd been out on a weeknight for, well, any reason. But when Judy, a longtime friend and the co-owner of Mountain Brew, Gossamer Falls' one and only coffee shop, said she wanted to have a music bingo night on the first Monday of the month, Meredith had promised to attend.

The idea was straightforward enough. Judy provided bingo cards and daubers, and at 7:00 on the dot, she would start playing music. Thirty seconds to "name that tune" and find it on your bingo card. Whoever won each round would receive a free drink to be used on another visit to the coffee shop. Judy planned to have at least three rounds if there was enough interest, with each round having a different theme.

Meredith looked at the sheet of paper in front of her. Four bingo cards on the page, each filled with song titles from the '80s. A solid place to start.

"We don't have to stay." Bronwyn tapped a perfectly manicured finger on the bingo card in front of her.

"Yes we do. Until the end. I promised."

Bronwyn pinched her lips together. "Yes, yes. You Quinns and your promises. Heaven forbid you break one."

Meredith focused on her oldest friend. "What is that supposed to mean?"

Bronwyn waved a hand. "Nothing. It's a good character trait, but you're clearly miserable, and promise or not, if you told Judy what's going on, she would understand."

"No."

Bronwyn flinched at the word, and Meredith realized she'd been

174

far harsher than she'd intended. "I'm sorry. I don't want to talk about it."

"And by *it*, you mean the part where your heart is broken?" Bronwyn placed a hand over her own heart. "Because it's not like I have any experience in that department or anything. I wouldn't know anything about what it's like to fall in love with someone who doesn't love you back."

"This is different."

"How so?"

"I'm thirty-two. You were sixteen, and he was a creep."

A flash of old pain crossed Bronwyn's face before she sighed. "Yeah. He was. I'm not trying to say my experience is the same as yours, but it's not like I've never had my heart broken. I'm here for you if you want to talk about it."

"I know. Thank you."

The silence that stretched between them wasn't uncomfortable. It was the kind of pause in a conversation that began decades earlier and had never really ended.

Judy brought the drinks and muffins and waggled her eyebrows in delight. "Bronwyn, thanks for being here. And for sharing the word with your staff. I've counted five Haven employees so far." She leaned in closer. "And Meredith, thank you for talking it up around town. We have a full house. Y'all are the best." She set the food on the table. "Good luck tonight!"

Meredith took a sip of her coffee and whispered to Bronwyn, "And now you know why I can't leave. Judy's poured a lot of energy into this. I want it to be a success. Especially since I'll be single forever. Might as well make an effort to be sure I have social options that don't require a date."

Bronwyn raised her own glass, filled with sparkling water and a lime slice, and toasted Meredith. "Good call."

The next hour and a half was more fun than Meredith had

expected it to be. She didn't win, but she enjoyed dancing in her chair to the different songs and cheering for the winners. On the final round, Judy called out that to get bingo, you had to fill your entire board. It took longer, but eventually an elementary school teacher who had been a few years behind Meredith in school won the grand prize of a ten-dollar gift card.

Simple pleasures. Fun atmosphere. Friendly people. No one acting a fool. Her life wasn't bad. Not even a little bit. She would focus on the beauty and try not to dwell on the way her chest ached almost all the time now. She knew the "heart" that loved others wasn't physically located in the heart that kept her blood pumping. But something pulsed with painful tremors anytime her mind replayed that kiss. Or, as she'd taken to mentally calling it, her "trip to the dark side."

She pulled on her heavy coat and wrapped a thick scarf around her neck. A scarf that she'd had Mo check for bugs before she left for the evening.

Bronwyn tucked her arm through Meredith's, and they walked out into the frigid February night. They'd stayed to talk to Judy, and the street was empty except for their two vehicles.

"Do you have a full schedule tomorrow?" Bronwyn asked as they paused by her BMW.

"Packed. If it keeps going this way, I may have to add another workday to my schedule."

"What? You mean you might have to work five days a week? The horror!" Bronwyn gave Meredith a cheeky grin. "It's a good problem to have."

"It is." Meredith had set a three-days-a-week schedule when she'd moved home, originally because there weren't enough pa-tients to justify being in the office more often. Then it was because she wanted to be available to take care of her mom while she went through chemo. But her Mondays, Tuesdays, and Thursdays had been so slammed that she'd added two Fridays a month as soon as her mom was back on her feet. "I'm thankful for the patients, but I don't want to be so busy that I can't run the clinic."

"Do you have any clinics planned for this weekend?"

"I would have, but my only choice for a protector is Gray. Cal and Landry are going somewhere for an early Valentine's Day weekend. So are Mom and Dad. Mo will be in Charlotte all day on Saturday for some kind of meeting with a client who lives in the Pacific Northwest and wants to meet with him in person. And Donovan is working."

Bronwyn grimaced. "What about Connor or Chad?"

Cal's older brothers, who were like Meredith's older brothers, would probably have stepped in. "I couldn't bring myself to ask them. I mean, what if something did happen? They have wives. Kids. I can't risk that."

Bronwyn threw her arms around Meredith and gave her a huge hug. "Your heart is ridiculous, and I'm so glad I know you."

They rocked back and forth, laughing, and as they broke apart, Meredith caught a glimpse of a dark figure hurtling toward them.

Before she could process what was happening, she was shoved into the middle of Main Street. She'd taken the hit in her stomach, and either the blow or the landing had knocked all the air from her. She lay in the middle of the road, desperately trying to pull in some oxygen and clear her head when she heard a sound that some part of her recognized as a vehicle.

She managed to sit up, but the dizziness drove her back down, elbows resting on the pavement.

Bronwyn lay a few feet away, eyes blinking rapidly. "What—?"

The headlights were probably what saved her life. Meredith saw them and had a flash of insight. The fast-moving vehicle was headed straight for them. She scrambled to her knees. "Run!"

Neither of them could get up, but they crawled into the empty space between her 4Runner and Bronwyn's BMW seconds before a large truck screamed past them.

Meredith had no memory of getting from the street to the door of the coffee shop. But she and Bronwyn reached it at the same time and pounded on the door until Judy rushed forward and unlocked it.

"What's going on?" she asked as they shoved past her.

"Lock the door. Quick." Meredith managed to gasp out the warning before she collapsed into a chair.

Judy locked the door and turned to where Meredith and Bronwyn were huddled together. "What's happening?"

"Call the police." Bronwyn bit the words out. "Please."

Judy nodded. "My phone's in the back. Hang on." She jogged away from them.

"Judy," Meredith called after her, "make sure the back is locked."

"I'm on it. I'll set the alarm too."

Meredith wasn't sure when the shaking started. But once it did, there was nothing she could do to stop the full-body tremor that racked her frame. Bronwyn, for her part, had managed to pale underneath her normally brown skin. Her eyes were wide, and her breathing was coming in short little gasps that didn't seem healthy.

Not that shaking from head to toe was healthy.

"I think we might be going into shock," Bronwyn forced out as Judy returned to the main room.

"I don't know what happened. That's what I'm trying to tell you," she said into the phone. "Meredith Quinn and Bronwyn Pierce just beat down my door. They look like someone roughed them up. And they told me to call the police."

A pause.

"They might be going into shock. There's some blood on Meredith's face." Another pause. "Yeah. Call her. Okay." She held the phone away from her ear. "Jeremiah Dawkins is on the desk. He can't leave the station, but he has someone on the way here. And he's calling Dr. Shaw."

Judy walked behind the cash register and came back with two towels. She handed one to Meredith and one to Bronwyn. "You, um, there's some blood." She pointed to Meredith's face and Bronwyn's hands.

"It doesn't hurt." Bronwyn looked at her hands like they belonged to someone else.

"Same." Meredith held the towel to her temple and brought it away. "That is actually a lot of blood." She should be worried about that. Shouldn't she?

Judy pressed the towel back to her head. "Hold it there. Keep pressure."

A second later, the front door rattled. Judy ran to it, peered outside, then opened it. Donovan came inside, took one look at Meredith and Bronwyn, and spoke into the walkie-talkie contraption on his shoulder. "Tell Dr. Shaw she might want to hurry. And call the chief."

"Don't call the chief." Meredith shook her head to disagree, and the pain that split through it had her dropping her head to the tabletop.

"Meredith!" Voices. Loud voices. Bronwyn. Donovan. Judy. And then everything was quiet.

Gray lived five minutes from the coffee shop. He made it there in three. He slammed his Explorer into park and ran to the knot of first responders standing by the door. They parted like the Red Sea as he approached, and one young volunteer firefighter held the door open for him.

Inside, Donovan leaned over Meredith.

A bloody, not moving Meredith, lying on the floor. A phone beside Donovan was on and the voice that came through was that of Cal's mom. "Okay, I'll be there in two minutes. Keep an eye on her."

"Yes, ma'am." Donovan had his hands on Meredith's wrist.

He didn't look up when Gray knelt on the other side of Meredith and took her chilled hand in his own. "What happened?"

Donovan shook his head. "Still don't know. I got here and she passed out."

Judy Galloway, the coffee shop owner, leaned over Bronwyn, who sat at a nearby table. "Dr. Shaw said for you to take a sip of this. Can you do that for me, sugar?"

Bronwyn reached out trembling hands and took the mug Judy handed her. She didn't drink. She looked at Gray. "Someone shoved us into the road."

Judy gasped. "What?"

"Then a truck. Big. Dark. Headlights. We managed to get out of the way. It would have hit us." She held his gaze. "Someone tried to kill us."

The door to the coffee shop opened on that pronouncement. Dr. Shaw entered, glanced at Bronwyn, then gently but firmly nudged Gray out of the way. "Move over, baby. Let me see what's wrong with our girl." Gray adored Carol Shaw. She was the closest thing he had to a mother now, and he was so thankful that Cal was willing to share her.

She did the things doctors do, pulling open Meredith's eyes, flashing a light in them, taking a pulse, and listening to her heart. While she did that, she spoke to Bronwyn. "Bronwyn, honey, where are you hurt, baby?"

"Hands. Knees. Maybe an ankle. I think Meredith may have hit her head on the pavement."

Gray had never felt so out of control, so helpless, since he joined the military. This chaos in his soul. This desperation as he watched Carol run her hands over Meredith's scalp. This was why he couldn't have relationships. This was why he couldn't fall in love.

"Tell me what happened, sweet girl." Carol's voice was calm. If she was rattled, there was no outer evidence. How could she be so solid? Gray knew that Meredith was her favorite niece. She loved her like the daughter she never had.

"Aunt Carol? Is she going to be okay?" Bronwyn's voice was shaky, and Carol reached over and placed one hand on her ankle.

"My girls are tough."

Bronwyn must have taken that as confirmation, because she took a deep breath and when she spoke, the words were quiet but clear. "We came to the music bingo night and then we stayed to chat with Judy. When we went outside, we were standing by my car, saying good night. Then someone came up and shoved us into the road."

Carol returned to her examination. At one point her hands paused and covered the same area on Meredith's head again. "There's a bump here. She definitely hit her head at some point."

The knot in his chest crawled up to his throat and threatened to choke him.

"Breathe, Gray. She's strong."

Bronwyn continued speaking, and her voice lost the certainty she'd had before. Now, her confusion and shock were evident. "It was like some kind of football tackle. And as soon as we were down, he ran off. No idea who it could have been or where he came from. I don't know if Meredith saw anything or not. I was pretty stunned. It took a few seconds—I don't know how long, really—to sit up. Then Meredith yelled for me to run. But I couldn't. I don't think she could either. We kind of crawled in between our cars. We barely made it out of the road when a huge truck screamed by."

She took a sip of whatever Judy had brought her. "We came here and Judy let us in and called for help. I don't know who they were targeting. It could have been either of us."

"Or both," Donovan muttered.

Gray didn't think Bronwyn heard him, but he gave Donovan a look that must have gotten his aggravation across because Donovan's next words were an even softer, "Sorry, Chief."

Meredith stirred beside him. The hand he held clenched around his. A soft moan fell from her lips.

"Meredith? Baby? I've got you, sweetheart." Carol Shaw was not one to hold back on the endearments under any circumstances, but when she was soothing an injured patient, a crying child, or a frightened parent, her bedside manner was something that couldn't be taught. Gray had seen her in action many times, but he'd never realized how much comfort she brought to the people watching.

"Aunt Carol?" Meredith's voice was a low rasp. "What—?" Meredith tried to sit up. "Bronwyn!"

Bronwyn was beside her friend in a heartbeat. She wrapped her hand around his and squeezed Meredith's hand through him. "I'm right here. I'm okay. Gray's here."

Meredith collapsed back onto the floor. "We'll be okay, then."

Gray didn't know what to do with that so he tucked it away in his mind for later. Bronwyn leaned against Gray's shoulder as they watched Carol run Meredith through a few tests before she allowed her to sit up.

"I have the mother of all headaches." Meredith squinted at her aunt.

"You may have a concussion. You have a goose egg on the back of your head, a nice scrape on your face that's going to be fun for you for the next few days, and your pants are ripped. Were they ripped before? Or is that new?"

Meredith grinned at her aunt, and when she did, Gray finally allowed himself to believe that she really would be okay. He couldn't keep sitting here. He was no one to her. Not even a friend. Not anymore. And he had a job to do. Even still, it took everything he had to stand up and walk away.

He stepped outside.

Donovan met him on the sidewalk. "Chief, I've got both of their purses. They were beside Bronwyn's car. I'm guessing they dropped them when they were tackled."

"They weren't tackled." Brick Nolan, one of Gray's deputies, shook his head. "You tackle someone standing still, everybody goes down pretty close to where they started. They landed in the middle of the daggum road. I found a bracelet a foot from the center line. I think it's Bronwyn's. Whoever hit them shoved them into the road. This wasn't no accident. It was attempted murder."

SEVENTEEN

After a trip to the ER to confirm that her head wasn't permanently damaged, Meredith spent Monday night into Tuesday morning in her childhood bed so her mom could check on her every few hours. She'd forgotten how uncomfortable it was to sleep in a twin-size bed and insisted on going home on Tuesday.

She slept better in her own bed but woke up on Wednesday morning with a raging headache, a body that hurt everywhere, and a deep sense of dread.

Sounds from the kitchen told her that Mo was in her house, making her breakfast. "Mo?"

"Yo," he called back.

"Go home."

"You want eggs? Or oatmeal?"

She rolled over and bit back a scream.

"Smoothies for everybody." Mo sounded way too cheery.

"Everybody?"

"Morning, Mer." Cal's voice floated up the stairs.

She eased from her bed and down the stairs. The two men in her kitchen watched her with unconcealed protectiveness. If Mo was a boiling cauldron of anger, Cal was a swarm of hornets. Both of them kept their emotions in check when they were with her, but she knew them too well. They were primed and ready for battle. The slightest hint of danger would set them off.

"How's the head?" Cal asked.

She ignored him and walked into her bathroom. She took care of business and then looked in the mirror while the whirring of the blender drowned out the sound of her dismayed whimper. The scrapes were a little better. The bruising was worse. She'd have to text Bronwyn later this morning and see how she was doing. At least Bronwyn had had the good sense to keep her head from the pavement. But her knees and elbows were probably several times their normal size by now.

She walked into her kitchen, went straight to her medicine cabinet, and grabbed some pain reliever. Mo shoved a smoothie in her direction, and she took it. "Thank you." She swallowed the pills and squeezed in between her brother and her cousin. "Good morning."

The arms that came around her were gentle.

She took a sip of her smoothie and bumped her head against Cal's shoulder, wincing at the jolt of pain. "I know why Mo is here. Why are you here?" When he didn't respond with a pithy comment, anxiety licked through her veins. "What is it?"

"Gray called this morning."

Meredith didn't want to think about Gray. The look on his face as she climbed into Mo's Jeep Monday night kept popping into her brain. He didn't have any right to look at her like that. He didn't want her. He didn't choose her. He didn't get to hold her hand. He didn't get to make her feel safe.

"He got a hit on the truck that tried to run you down. It was stolen from Tennessee three days ago."

"Are we surprised by that?" Meredith took another sip. Mo

really did make fabulous smoothies. "You have to be a special kind of moron to try to run someone down in your own vehicle."

Meredith walked around her small counter and settled into a seat at the kitchen table. Tiny house living was awesome for one person. Maybe two. But three, especially when two of the three were men in a bad mood? Things were a little cramped in that situation.

Cal joined her at the table. "Not sure if you've noticed, but most criminals are all Sheetrock and no studs."

Mo laughed. "I prefer to say their cornbread's not done in the middle."

"Papa says they're as smart as bait." Meredith grimaced.

"Yeah. Pretty sure that's what happened in this case." Cal reached for her hand and squeezed it. "The bait didn't survive."

Meredith looked from Cal to Mo.

Mo leaned against the counter. "Gray confirmed that the truck was stolen. No real surprise there. But he got a call late last night from a deputy with Buncombe County. They found the truck. Two dead bodies inside."

A shiver rocked through Meredith. "How did they die?"

"Hard to say," Mo answered. "The interior of the truck went up in flames. Isolated area. No identification on the bodies yet. But they got a partial match on the tag and general body style. Then, they found a VIN that hadn't been destroyed in the fire. The fire happened late Monday night or early the next morning. They investigated when someone noticed the smoke on their way to work Tuesday."

"Obviously, there's no proof yet. But it's a good bet that the two bodies were the assailants. They failed. They died for it." Cal's expression was grim.

"My guess is they were going to die anyway." Mo frowned down at the table. "Success or failure. It didn't matter. They had to go."

"Who are these people?" Meredith had no appetite but forced herself to keep drinking her breakfast.

"These are the people who are coming after you." Mo had no give in his voice.

"I hate to say this, but has it occurred to you that maybe I wasn't the target? Maybe they weren't coming after me at all? Bronwyn's family is . . . some of them are okay, but they aren't always rational."

"Oh, believe me. The thought has more than crossed my mind. The bottom line is that we don't know and we may never know. So you both have to be on guard until we resolve the situation in Neeson once and for all." Mo ran a hand over his scruff. "I can't see a scenario where you're in danger from anyone other than the Neeson crowd. The Pierces have no bone to pick with you. So when Neeson is dealt with, that gets you off the hot seat. I'm not so sure it will get Bronwyn in the clear."

Cal nodded in agreement. "Her family is messed up. And this whole mess with Steven being in jail. I don't understand it, but I know there's drama there."

"She's tough," Meredith reminded both men. "She survived her board meeting last month, and she'll survive whatever they throw at her now."

Mo didn't comment, but the white-knuckled grip on his cup spoke volumes.

Cal's phone rang, and he answered with a clipped, "Shaw."

Meredith didn't need to put him on speakerphone to hear Gray's voice. "Cal, I need to interview Meredith and Bronwyn today."

"So why are you calling me?"

Meredith pressed her leg against Cal's, and when he looked at her she mouthed, "Be nice."

She didn't want to be nice to Gray herself, but she didn't want to mess up Cal's friendship with Gray either.

"You know why I'm calling you." Gray sounded . . . tired? Frustrated? Lost? "Look, do you think she's up for it or not?"

"It just so happens, I'm sitting right beside Meredith. Hang on." Cal didn't mute the phone or cover the speaker or anything. "Meredith, Gray needs to interview you today. Are you up for it?"

She glared at him. "After lunch. Yes. I'll come to the station."

Cal put the phone back to his ear. "You heard that?"

"I hate you." Gray didn't sound lost anymore. He sounded furious.

"Too bad." Cal looked at Meredith again. "You want to call Beep?"

She nodded.

"She'll probably have Bronwyn with her."

"Thanks for nothing."

"Anytime."

The call disconnected.

"What was that about?" Meredith pressed a finger into Cal's arm. "Why did you do that?"

"He's too chicken to call you himself, so he called me and put me in the middle of the two of you when he knows full well that I'm trying very hard not to be in the middle. So he can deal with it."

Mo's low chuckle had an ominous edge to it. "Remind me never to make you mad, brother."

"Oh, you're next on my list, so buckle up." Cal stood and took his glass to the sink. "I've had it up to my eyeballs with men who don't have the sense to see the beauty that's right in front of them."

Meredith watched Mo and Cal face off.

"And yeah, Mo, I'm talking about you too."

"You think you're some kind of macho-man cupid or something?" Disbelief tinged Mo's question.

"No. I think I love you guys too much to let you keep being

stupid." He kissed Meredith on the head, grabbed his coat from the sofa, and paused at the door. "I do, you know. I love you both." He slammed the door behind him.

"Didn't see that coming." Meredith waved a hand to where, on the other side of the window, Cal strode to his truck.

"Me neither." Mo took his own cup and rinsed it in the kitchen sink. "I gotta get to work."

"Yeah. You do that. I'll call Bronwyn."

"Don't leave without letting me know." Mo followed Cal's path out the door but turned to his own house a few yards away.

Meredith was left alone at her tiny table with an empty glass and a heart that didn't know if she should be grateful to be so loved or angry that the people she loved most were all mad at each other in large part because of her.

She called Bronwyn, made plans to meet at Gray's after lunch, and got ready for the day.

Gray was not ready for the way his heart dropped when he looked up to see Meredith and Bronwyn standing in his office door at 1:00 on the dot. Bronwyn's taped wrist made him want to throw a stapler at the wall. Meredith's bruised face made him want to rampage through the streets of Neeson until he found the men responsible.

There were two dead men in a truck, and they might be the ones who committed the act, but they weren't the ones behind it.

He stood and waved them in. "Please come in. Have a seat. Would you like some water? Coffee?"

Both women said no.

He sat down behind his desk and tried to scrape together his last ounce of professionalism. "I don't want to make any assumptions.

I know we talked Monday night, but it would help me if you could go over what happened again."

They nodded, and Bronwyn spoke up first. "We've known Judy forever. Went to school with her. When I left town, she and Meredith did a lot of stuff together for a little while."

Meredith and Bronwyn shared a look, and Bronwyn continued. "Okay, it wasn't long. Judy started dating Jason in the middle of junior year and that was that. But we've all stayed friends. So when she said she wanted to have music bingo night, we told her we'd do all we could to support it."

Meredith nodded but didn't contribute. Bronwyn continued. "I told the staff at The Haven. Meredith had signs at the office. We mentioned it to everybody we saw. Invited them to come out. Told them we'd be there with bells on."

This wasn't something he'd known before. "So the fact that you were going to be at Mountain Brew on Monday night was common knowledge?"

"Anyone who was making any kind of effort to know our plans wouldn't have had any difficulty finding out where we'd be. We posted a selfie with Judy before things got rolling and reminded people of where we were."

Meredith cleared her throat. "I think we even said we'd be staying to the end and that it wasn't too late to come out and join us."

"Yeah, you're right." Bronwyn shrugged. "In hindsight, that seems like a dumb thing to do, but I don't think either of us could have predicted that someone would try to run us over."

Meredith nodded. "It doesn't make any sense. How could they have predicted it well enough to have someone shove us in the road and try to run over us? That seems too coincidental."

Gray wished he could agree with them. He tapped his pen on the planner on his desk. "I get what you're saying." He focused on looking at both women, even though every time he looked at

Meredith a nasty rage roiled through him and then was followed by an almost overwhelming compulsion to pull her onto his lap and hold her and tell her he would never let anyone hurt her ever again.

"I need to ask you something, and I need you to try to keep an open mind."

Both women gave him wary nods.

"How well do you know Judy?"

"We went to school with her." Bronwyn turned to Meredith and Meredith nodded. "We've known her forever."

"Would she have any reason to want to see you harmed? Or any reason to be willing to share your location with—"

"You think Judy set us up for this?" Meredith's disbelief rang through her question. "No way."

"I'm just aski—"

"What motivation would she have?" Bronwyn frowned. "There's no reason for her to come after us."

"Ladies, I'm not saying there is. I'm doing my job. Asking tough questions. I don't know Judy well, and the way you described her keeping you around until the very end . . ."

"It wasn't Judy." Meredith's voice was firm.

"I agree." Bronwyn gave him a stern look. "You'd have to have ironclad proof before I'd believe it."

"Look, I'm not saying it was, but you need to understand that these people who came after you didn't get a harebrained idea and run with it. Unfortunately, there've been a couple of incidents in Georgia, Tennessee, and South Carolina that could be related to what happened to you."

"What?" Meredith's gasp was so full of worry and shock that he had to force himself to continue.

"I have some contacts who've been very helpful. When I told them what happened on Monday, they put it through some kind

191

of computer program that looks for patterns. I don't know how it works exactly, but it generated a few leads. They forwarded the results to me, and one pattern stands out."

He stood and walked over to the board he had on the interior wall of his office. "There are five cases. In each one there were two assailants believed to be working together. In three of the five events, the individuals involved"—Gray made it a point not to use the word *victims*—"were shoved into traffic. There were three fatalities, two serious injuries, and one case where the man rolled to the other side of the road and suffered nothing more than a few scrapes."

"And seeing his life flash before his eyes," Meredith whispered to Bronwyn, who nodded her agreement.

"I'm sure that's true," Gray said. "In those cases, a large vehicle, which was later confirmed to be stolen, raced along in the aftermath. It didn't hit the people in the street but flew past and picked up the perpetrator. The vehicles were later found abandoned. In one case, the vehicle did hit the victims. That's the one where there were two fatalities. Clear case of hit-and-run, but it was a small town with few cameras. They didn't catch the event. Witnesses told them what happened and that they caught a glimpse of a large vehicle speeding away. Didn't see the plates. It's assumed that the driver picked up the man who did the shoving and took off."

"So these people have worked this out and done it before? Multiple times?" Meredith asked.

"Yes."

"What happened in the fifth incident?"

He didn't want to answer Meredith, but he had no choice. "In that incident, there were two individuals standing outside on the street. They climbed into their cars. Once one had pulled away, a large truck followed them and ran them off the road. The other person hadn't gotten out of the parking spot yet when an individual in a ski mask opened their car door, knocked them out with the gun, shoved them into the back seat, and drove off."

Bronwyn and Meredith both stared at him now, eyes wide.

"The woman was assaulted and left in her car. The police found her later that night about fifteen miles away."

Fear had a scent. A taste. And the air in his office was full of it. He didn't have to spell it out for them. They understood. He could see it in their eyes, and in the way they now clutched each other's hands.

"They have DNA from the victim. The Buncombe County officers know and will be running DNA on the two men in the truck to see if they match."

Meredith's eyes were wet. Bronwyn had tears streaming down her face. He rose and handed each of them a tissue before returning to his seat. "I'm sorry. I promise my goal in this is not to frighten you but to protect you."

Meredith spoke first. "You think whoever came after me, bugged me, and tracked me hired these men to . . . what? Kill me? Abduct me?"

Gray had no way to soften the blow. "Yes. We think the plan was hit-and-run. But if they couldn't make that work, they'd go for plan B. The task force has started running searches to see if they can find any other hits that match the profile."

"What do we do now?" Bronwyn blew her nose.

Meredith looked at her and said, "I'm so sorry, Beep. I didn't mean—"

"Hush. It could have been you or me. They have reason to get rid of both of us and you know it. It doesn't really matter who the main target was. We have to be careful." Bronwyn turned to Gray. "Right?"

"One hundred percent."

"I still don't think Judy was involved." Meredith shuddered. "No way."

"I never said she was." Gray hated what he was doing to Meredith and Bronwyn, but he didn't have a choice. "But you need to use caution with everyone. Even your friends."

Ten minutes later, Gray watched Meredith and Bronwyn leave, followed by the two officers who'd been assigned to shadow them. He should turn the case over to someone else. Donovan would do a good job. Brick would as well.

But no one would care as much as he did.

He'd been an idiot. And he might have to live with his stupidity for the rest of his life. But if anything happened to Meredith?

Lord, I'm gonna need some help here. It wasn't healthy to feel this level of panic about a woman. Although, if he gave himself a little bit of permission to be human, a certain level of terror was normal when someone you loved was in danger.

Because despite his best efforts, he'd fallen hard for Meredith Quinn. He couldn't ignore the facts. But that didn't mean he could pursue her. If anything, it meant he should try to stay away from her.

Although, that wasn't going to happen. He cared too much to do anything less than everything possible to keep her alive and healthy.

And when this mess was over, he'd step back—way back. She would find someone else.

The very idea of another man touching her made his chest burn. The idea that she would give her heart to someone else?

It would be torture to watch.

There weren't that many eligible men for her in Gossamer Falls, though. She was related to half the town.

Maybe he wouldn't have to watch her fall in love and get married after all. No. That didn't make him happy either. He wanted her to have everything she wanted and more.

But she wants you. Or, she did. Until you messed it up.

Seriously, Lord. Why did you bring her into my life? I was happy on my own.

No. He hadn't been. But he'd thought he was. Now he knew it'd been a lie.

He took some time to pray for direction and wisdom and peace and hope. And when he was done, he got to work.

EIGHTEEN

The following Sunday afternoon, Meredith walked along the river that ran between her property and Bronwyn's. There was a big football game on, and she didn't care about it at all. Mo had been out of town all weekend and would be driving home later tonight. Cal was with Landry at The Haven, watching the football game with a few actual pro football players whose season had ended in January. Bronwyn had decided to throw a big viewing party. Landry, The Haven's art teacher, had made some football-themed serving bowls that Meredith had to admit were awesome, and Bronwyn had asked Landry and Cal to help her host the event.

It hadn't been a hard sell. Cal had jumped at the opportunity and had already sent her a photo of him between two men who were apparently famous. Meredith didn't recognize them, but she was happy for Cal.

Bronwyn had asked Meredith to come too, but she declined. She hadn't been alone in days. Gray had made sure that there was an officer in shouting distance at all times. He'd even had one follow her home from work on Thursday and Friday.

She had gone to The Haven to help with the decorating and

had made a few quick arrangements for the party, but then she'd happily returned to the safety and solitude of her own home. A place where she didn't have to fake being happy.

A few months ago, her life had been quite lovely. She'd been reasonably content. Maybe even a bit on the self-satisfied side. Now? The man she thought she loved had rejected her. And her do-gooder ways had put her on a hit list.

Pride goeth before the fall.

She'd heard that her entire life. She hadn't expected the fall to be quite so . . . brutal. Or to last so long. She was so tired. Tired of hurting. Tired of being afraid. And tired of everyone feeling sorry for her.

She'd tried to hide her misery. But based on the way people treated her, she'd done a poor job of it. The Sunday after the kiss that shouldn't have happened, her mom called her out for being a grump. She had to come up with an explanation. One that didn't involve saying, "Gray kissed me and then apologized for it. And then he explained, and it was heartbreaking and stupid at the same time. I told him that, and now we aren't speaking to each other. And probably won't ever. At least not until I attend a wedding with him in a few weeks, but I can't think about that."

She'd blamed her gloom on the short days and long nights. Many people suffered from seasonal affective disorder. Why couldn't she?

Her parents hadn't pushed her, but she didn't think they'd fully bought it. Nonetheless, her mother continued to send her links to articles about combating the winter blues, which was why she'd been walking along the river every afternoon for the past couple of weeks. Trying to get some sunshine. Light exposure. Vitamin D. Whatever.

It hadn't worked.

She caught a whiff of something floral. And there on the bank

. . . the paperbushes had bloomed. The flowers were tiny and delicate and had always been a favorite of hers, both for their scent and their blossoms. She felt a kinship with the hardy bush that had the audacity to bloom in late winter.

She'd never decided if the paperbush was a late bloomer or an early one. Not that it mattered. Either way worked. But she imagined it as a warrior that not only survived the winter but refused to be contained by the cold. It was tough but beautiful, and it showed off delicate blossoms while everything else was still cowering in the soil, not daring to peek out for fear of an early frost.

She gave herself a mental slap. Getting philosophical over a shrub? She needed to get a grip.

If she could snap a decent picture, she might be able to recreate the paperbush blossoms. They'd look lovely in Cassie's real bouquet. Meredith knelt at the top of the bank, phone in hand. Ugh. The angle was all wrong. She leaned farther over the edge in an attempt to get a better shot.

The soil under her knee gave way, and her body tilted forward in an almost slow-motion crash. The phone fell from her hand, and she stretched her arm to catch it. Her hand and the phone did an aerial dance as she tried to grab it, but the phone slipped away and bounced down the bank with her body following behind.

Unlike the phone, she didn't bounce. She slid, face first, straight toward the river.

The phone left the bank and entered the river with an ominous kerplunk, and she skidded to a stop a foot from the freezing water.

She lay gasping for air before the image of her phone splashed across her closed eyes. She jumped to her knees and reached for the device. The water was ridiculously cold, and for a split second she wondered if the same thing was true for drowned phones as it was for drowned people. Maybe it wasn't truly dead until it was warm and dead.

She plucked the phone from its watery landing spot and groaned. Not even Mo would be able to fix it. The screen wasn't shattered. It was punctured.

She stared at the spiderwebbed screen for a moment. One of her nephews was fascinated with electronics and gadgets. He'd enjoy taking her phone apart. She tossed the phone to the top of the bank and then did a modified bear crawl up the side until she reached the top. When her torso was on level ground, she didn't bother standing up. She rolled over and lay down, leaving her legs to dangle over the slope.

She'd tried sunlight, fresh air, and movement, and what had it gotten her? A destroyed phone and an even worse mood than she'd started out in. She hadn't even managed to snag the photo she'd been trying to capture.

"Lord, I give up." That was the best she could do in the prayer department. She didn't feel like talking. She stared at the clouds and willed her body to relax. The sun would be setting soon, and the sky was a glorious riot of color. It was quiet here. Peaceful. Safe.

And wasn't it just about the most annoying thing ever that none of that made her happy? She wanted to be safe. But peaceful? Not so much. She liked excitement. She'd expected her life to have more spice.

Instead, she'd turned into a hobbit. She lived in a tiny house surrounded by family. There was a lot of delicious food, and she could eat second breakfast anytime she wanted. But at thirty-two, she was beginning to give up on the idea that anyone would come along and invite her on an adventure.

She had no idea how long she lay there. She wasn't praying or consciously thinking about anything. She wasn't trying to solve all of her problems or come to terms with the drama that had unfolded.

She took deep breaths and tried to be where she was.

"Meredith!"

She opened her eyes. Had she fallen asleep? She didn't think she had, but she must have if Gray was yelling at her in her dreams.

"Meredith!"

That had not been a dream. The sheer terror in the voice drove her to a seated position. "Gray?"

The man in question ran toward her. He didn't walk. He didn't stalk. He was in a full-on sprint. When he reached her, he dropped to his knees beside her. His hands touched her shoulders. Her arms. Her hair. "What happened? Are you okay?"

"What?" She'd been so relaxed. And now Gray was yelling and examining her the way she'd seen her papa check out a cow that he was worried about.

Gray spoke between gasps. "Got . . . a call . . . Mo said . . . you fell."

And just like that, it all became crystal clear. She would have to kill Mo. She'd miss him, it was true. But there was simply no other option.

Gray continued. "Your phone . . . signal . . . you didn't answer . . . he called . . . me." His breath slowed and he straightened.

She moved to get up, and he held a hand in her direction. "Wait. Did you hit your head?"

She ignored him, scooted her tush back so her feet were on level ground, and stood. "No, I didn't hit my head. I'm completely uninjured. And until you came caterwauling through my property, I was spending some time grounding." She thought that's what it was called.

"Grounding?" Gray pulled his phone from his pocket, but his tone made it clear that he wasn't buying her explanation. "I'm pretty sure most people who spend time 'grounding' don't look like they slid down a bank and into a freezing-cold river."

"I didn't go into the river."

He ignored her and spoke into his phone. "She's fine."

"Who is that?"

In answer, he handed her the phone.

She took it. "Hello?"

"Meredith? Your phone sent me an alert that you'd fallen. Then you wouldn't answer. I didn't know what to think." Mo's terror-tinged relief siphoned all her anger away. Well, most of it.

"You told me that fall detection app you installed probably wouldn't work, and now you've gone and gotten everyone all hot and bothered over nothing."

"I'd say it worked even better than expected. It sent out the alert."

"Yeah, and then it died before I could tell everyone what had happened." She spared a glance at Gray. "I think you nearly gave the police chief a heart attack."

"He'll live." Mo paused. "So the phone is toast but you're good?"

"The phone is ruined. And I'm fine."

"What happened?" His voice was settling into its normal range.

"The paperbushes are in bloom. And they're so beautiful. I thought I'd snap a few pictures and see if there's any way I can recreate them. But I leaned too far over the bank."

At her words, Gray pinched the bridge of his nose and shook his head.

Mo huffed. "You fell down the bank?"

"I dropped my phone. I tried to catch it and lost my balance."

"So, you fell down the bank."

"Technically, it was more of a slide. The phone, though. The phone definitely fell."

"And you didn't think to, oh, I don't know, go home?" His volume and pitch went up quite a bit on those last few words.

"I *am* home, you moron. I'm on my own property. I'm as safe as can be. If I want to lie here and contemplate the sunset, I don't need to ask you"—she cut her eyes toward Gray—"or anyone else for permission."

"I know that, Meredith. I also know there's every reason for us to be concerned about you. You're being targeted by people who do not have your best interests at heart. Or have you forgotten that someone tried to run over you?"

"I have not forgotten. I can't forget. I think about it all the time. But was it necessary to call the chief of police to come look for me?" She could hear the embarrassment and near-hysteria in her voice and tried to pull it back down to its normal register. "There are about a hundred Quinns in spitting distance. I don't think my dropped phone requires law enforcement—"

"He volunteered."

Now it was Meredith's turn to pinch the bridge of her nose. "Excuse me?"

"I tried Cal. I tried Dad. I tried Chad. I tried Connor. No one was nearby. In the midst of my calls, Gray had called Cal, who told him what was going on. Gray was nearby and he volunteered. I realize he isn't your favorite person right now, but I was fairly certain you wouldn't shoot him on sight. And if you had been in trouble, he has the skill set to help."

Gray watched as Meredith took three slow breaths. When she spoke, her voice had lost the edge of outrage it held earlier. "Okay. Given that I have no phone, it's up to you and Cal to let the family know that I'm not dead in the river. You created this situation. You fix it. I don't want to be deluged with concerned family members."

She looked to the sky. Gray got a definite, "Why me, Lord?" vibe from her as she shook her head, nodded, and finally said, "Fine."

No man alive had ever heard the word *fine* spoken in that tone and believed that everything was, in fact, fine. Gray had a moment to be thankful that her ire was directed toward Mo, but then she focused in his direction and said, "He's leaving." And she waved him away, then turned her back on him.

If she thought her dismissive gesture would work, she had a lot to learn. He waited as she continued to listen to Mo. What was he saying to her now? Mo wasn't known for being talkative. Maybe he was talkative, but only with a very select few? And, of course, Meredith would be one of the few. She adored her brother. Anyone could see it.

The old pain pierced through him. He'd been adored that way. Once. And he'd given up on having anyone care about him with that kind of loyalty and devotion ever again.

But . . . Meredith. Not that his feelings toward her had ever been brotherly in nature. His feelings were the kind that would get a man punched in the face by a big brother. He'd been fighting them since the day she waltzed into his office and told him she was giving the place a makeover.

And he'd succeeded in ignoring them, or at least not thinking about them too much, until that moment in her shop when she'd slid into his arms and he'd known he was hers.

And then he'd stupidly convinced himself that he could stay away from her and that eventually his feelings would go away.

He'd been so wrong.

She turned then and slid the phone into her back pocket. "You're still here." She was going for cool, calm, and disinterested. He could tell. But she was too frustrated, maybe even angry, to be successful.

"I am."

She tilted her head to the side and gave him the fakest smile he'd ever seen. And he'd seen some doozies. "Chief Ward." Her voice was sweeter than cotton candy.

"Yes, Dr. Quinn?"

She kept up the smile and the accent and the ditzy attitude. "I sure do appreciate you performing your civic duty and rushing out here to rescue me, but as you can see, I'm no damsel in distress." She stood straight and lost the vapid expression. Her next words were clipped and so hard they could have cut through granite. "You're on private property. *My* property. And I'd like you to leave."

She had a point. He glanced around to get his bearings, then walked ten yards away from her and sat on a fallen log.

She blinked. Ah, yes, there was the princess coming out. She'd expected him to do as she requested. Well, demanded.

And he had. Technically. *Your ball, Meredith.*

"Was I unclear?"

"Nope."

"Then why are you still here?"

"I'm not."

She blinked twice. "Excuse me?"

"I'm not on your property, Dr. Quinn."

She glanced around, and he saw the precise moment she understood. He gave her a few seconds to stew about it before he spoke. "I'm not here as the chief of police. I came as a private citizen at the request of a friend. And, as a private citizen, I have an open invitation to the property of Cal Shaw." He pointed to the tiny marker that Cal had shown him once. "And I'm on his property now."

If she'd fought back, he could have kept up the pretense, but she didn't. She threw up her hands. "Fine. Sit there. I don't care. I'm going home."

She turned and walked away, and there was so much hurt and defeat in her posture, Gray couldn't take it. He called out to her, "I'm sorry."

She whirled around. "Don't say that to me." Her voice vibrated with fury and pain. "Don't."

He wanted to go to her. To grab her and hold her and beg for forgiveness, but he didn't have that right. He could have had it, but he'd been an idiot. If he wanted those rights, he'd have to work hard, so hard, to earn them. He shouldn't try. He'd made his choices and he should live with them.

She turned to go, and he lost the battle. "Meredith?"

She didn't turn but she did stop. He expected exasperation, maybe anger. What he got was a sad, "What?"

He didn't know if this was the time, place, or right way to do this. But he couldn't let her walk away from him thinking he didn't care. "I'm a flawed, broken man. I know this. I've known it for a long time. And I used that knowledge to build walls around my heart that no one has ever breached. Until you. And when the walls fell, instead of saying thank you, I pushed you away and tried to rebuild them, higher and stronger and even more impenetrable than they were before."

She wasn't moving, so he kept talking.

"But the thing is, I can't seem to manage it. Every time I try, I remember how it felt to hold you, and they crumble around me. I hear your laughter and the stones I've gathered disintegrate to dust."

She didn't respond, but she didn't run away. That was good. Maybe.

"I *am* sorry that I hurt you. I'm sorry I pushed you away. I'm sorry I fought against my feelings and yours. I don't expect you to forgive me, but I do want you to have fair warning. I'm going to try to win you back."

She turned then. Her eyes were dry. Her expression pained but not gentle. "You can do whatever you want, Gray. I can't stop you. But fair warning. When I see you, my walls grow higher. When I hear your laughter, they harden. And when I remember what it felt like to have you hold me, then push me away? I build faster."

Her words ripped through him like shrapnel. He had no idea what she saw when she looked at him, but he made no effort to hide the pain. He didn't enjoy the agony searing through him, but he'd take it. Their relationship was like a broken limb that hadn't been set properly. It had to be rebroken so it could heal.

She turned and left without a backward glance.

He watched until she was out of sight, then returned to his vehicle. It wasn't until he was almost home that he realized Meredith still had his phone.

And hope, that audacious rascal, settled into his bruised heart.

NINETEEN

Meredith woke the next morning and, for the first time since she'd moved home to Gossamer Falls, considered calling in sick. She could have her office manager reschedule her patients. She could stay in her pajamas. She could read or watch TV. She could sleep. Sleep would be good.

She didn't hurt in her sleep.

In sleep, she didn't have to slow her heart rate and breathing rate when she remembered the way Gray said she'd torn down his walls and that her laughter had the power to destroy the stones he wanted to rebuild with.

In sleep, she didn't flush with remembered embarrassment every time she thought about what she'd said to Gray.

She'd been cruel. She'd taken the loving things he'd said to her and used them as weapons against him.

She'd hurt him, and then she'd walked away.

She piled on the self-recrimination until her snooze went off. Then she threw back the covers and went downstairs. The phone—his phone—sat on her counter. Taunting her. It was his private phone, not his work phone, so she hadn't stressed about returning it last night. But she would have to return it to him this morning.

The best plan would be to take it to the police station. She could leave it with the front desk and make sure they told him.

But taking it to the police station meant running the risk of seeing him. It wasn't a large building. He could hear her talking, or see her park, and come out. She couldn't handle seeing him today.

Or, maybe, ever.

But definitely not today.

She left for work, still undecided about what to do with the phone that now rested in her purse. Her new phone rang five minutes after she pulled onto the main road.

Mo had been in Asheville and had stopped by their cell provider and had everything transferred from her backups on the cloud and onto a new phone before she even went to sleep. She still had her old number and everything. It was good to have a tech geek in the family.

Mo had known she was upset last night, but he hadn't pressed her to spill her guts. Instead he'd handed her the phone, hugged her tight, and then when the dam broke on her emotions, he held her while she cried.

She was so tired of crying. But she was also tired of being afraid. Of looking at every friend with suspicion. Of asking Mo to scan her home, her car, and her clothing for bugs. Of being relieved when they weren't there, but also afraid that they might have missed something.

She missed singing in her car and talking to herself as she got ready for the day. But how could she do any of that when there was a chance someone was listening?

And mostly she was tired of being alone with all of it. She couldn't talk to Gray. And she didn't want to keep burdening Mo or Cal with her drama.

Poor Mo. He'd been the one to bear the brunt of her emotions lately, and last night was no exception.

When her tears had finally dried up, he rested his chin on her head and asked, "Are you sure you don't want me to kill him?"

"I'm sure."

"I have some new ideas—"

"No."

"Offer stands."

She knew he was joking. She also knew he was so angry with Gray that he could hardly see straight, which made the fact that he'd sent Gray after her even more telling. Mo had been truly afraid for her last night.

Gray had been afraid too.

Maybe all those sweet nothings had been a reaction to fear and today he'd be back to normal. He'd remember that he didn't want to have a relationship with her or anyone.

Or maybe he'd gone home after she'd viciously fired back at him and decided that he'd dodged a bullet when he'd broken her heart.

The phone rang again, and she tried to answer with her Bluetooth, then realized that it wasn't going to work until she connected the new phone to her 4Runner's sound system. She accepted the call on her watch. "Hello."

The voice on the other end was frantic. "Oh, Dr. Quinn. Are you on your way in?"

"Yes, Lucy. What's wrong?" Lucy had run her front office for the last two years. The young woman was a managerial whiz, but she could be a bit dramatic.

"It's Lottie Green." Lucy was nearly hyperventilating. "Her mom has her in the lobby. I think she has an abscess. Poor baby is crying. I think she's in so much pain that she's panicking."

The poor baby in question was eight, and while she probably was crying, Meredith suspected that Lucy was embellishing the details.

But on the bright side, she now had an excuse to delay the phone return.

She winced at her own thoughts. Grayson Ward had truly driven her over the edge.

"I'll be there in five minutes, Lucy. Tell Lottie to hang on."

"Oh, thank goodness. Should I call Sheila?" Sheila was Meredith's hygienist. An excellent one. But she had kids to take to school in the morning. "No. We'll manage."

"Okay. See you in a few."

An hour later, Lottie was no longer crying, and her mom was taking her to school. Meredith was two patients behind, and she'd only had one cup of coffee. She dashed into the kitchen to grab a second cup and caught a glimpse of someone—a male someone, a male someone in uniform—leaving through the front door.

"Meredith!" Her aunt Minnie came into the kitchen with a huge smile on her face.

"Oh, Dr. Quinn!" Lucy followed Aunt Minnie, holding a vase filled with gorgeous paperbush blossoms. "These are for you!"

"What?" Meredith looked from her aunt to Lucy.

"Your policeman brought them." Aunt Minnie grinned at her. "Mama says he's your man, and last night she prayed that you would see that."

"Please tell me she didn't." Meredith tried to hide her shock with laughter.

"Oh, she did." Minnie's earnestness couldn't be doubted.

Lucy doubled over with laughter but kept her hold on the flowers. "Dr. Quinn, if your granny is praying about you and Gray, you should probably go ahead and marry the man."

Meredith ignored her and stared at the flowers. Her mind refused to process what she was seeing.

"Don't you like them, Merry?" Aunt Minnie reached out and touched one blossom. "They're pretty."

Lucy looked from Aunt Minnie to Meredith to the flowers and then put on a huge smile. "Come on, Aunt Minnie." She pointed back to the reception area. "Let's go put these on the front desk where everyone can enjoy them today."

"Lucy, wait." Meredith practically chased her down and grabbed at the vase with trembling hands. "Thank you. I'll put them on my desk."

"Are you sure?"

"Yes."

Meredith tucked the vase in the crook of her left arm and pulled Aunt Minnie in for a hug with her right. "You're right, Minnie Moo. They are beautiful. You won't mind if I keep them on my desk, will you?"

Aunt Minnie's face lit, and she spoke with innocent sincerity. "You should keep them in your office. He brought them for you."

"Excellent. Thank you both."

Lucy chatted with Aunt Minnie as they returned to the front, and once they were back at the desk, Meredith forced herself to take measured steps as she returned to her office. Once inside, she closed the door, then set the vase on her desk and plucked the tiny white card from the blooms. The scrawl on the note was firm and bold, much like the man who had written it.

I kept a few of these for myself, and I put them in a vase in my office. They are yet another something that reminds me of you.

She stared at the words. The paperbushes grew on the side of the bank. They weren't convenient to reach. He would have had to climb down to pick them.

Meredith studied the arrangement, then picked up the vase. Sure enough, on the bottom there was a tiny anchor. Landry's mark.

He'd picked the flowers, then he'd gone to Cal and Landry's for a vase. Then he'd hand delivered the arrangement to her.

"Dr. Quinn?"

Lucy's voice came through the speaker on her office phone. "Yes, Lucy."

"You have patients ready in rooms 1 and 3."

"I'm coming."

Meredith took three long breaths. Each one drew the scent of the paperbushes toward her, but she set down the note on her desk and forced all thoughts of flowers and cryptic notes and men who made her want to scream from her mind.

She had patients to see.

And at lunch, she had a phone to return.

TWENTY

At 11:55 a.m., Gray answered his office phone. "Chief Ward."

"Can you meet a friend of mine tonight?" The female voice on the other end of the line was filled with urgency.

The words were a code. The undercover agent in Neeson had information he needed to send out, but he didn't feel safe using any of his electronic resources or any of the normal methods.

Since Gray had been aware of him, he'd only used this method once before. And knowing what Gray now knew, the timing lined up with the week when Meredith helped that young woman escape from Neeson. He suspected that things got so hot that the undercover agent hadn't dared take any risks.

Which begged the question, what was happening in Neeson now? He wanted to know, but he didn't ask. "I'll be there."

"Thank you." Faith sounded stressed in a way he hadn't heard before.

"Anything else I can do?"

"You can hide him if he needs out?"

"Yes."

"I don't want to lose him to these people. He's determined to stick it out, but—"

"I'll make sure he knows it's safe to come in from the cold."

"Okay."

"I'll call you tonight with an update."

A light blinked at him from his office phone. It was the one that told him Glenda wanted to talk to him. He disconnected the call and hit the intercom button. "Yes?"

"Dr. Quinn to see you."

Finally. He wasn't ashamed of the way his hands went damp in anticipation. "Send her in."

Twenty seconds later, Meredith stood at his door, phone in hand. "I planned to return this earlier. But I had an emergency—"

"Lucy told me."

Meredith's brow crinkled. "It's not like her to talk about patients—"

"Oh, she didn't. Not specifically. She said you had an emergency first thing and that it threw your whole morning off. And then Aunt Minnie told me you were behind by two patients." He held up two fingers the way Aunt Minnie had.

Meredith's shoulders dropped. "Yeah. It's been busy." She stepped in and put the phone on his desk, then took three steps back. "Anyway, here's your phone. And, um . . ." She pointed to the paperbush blossoms in the bud vase on his desk. "Thank you for the flowers. I'll return the vase to Landry."

Her words hurt, but he didn't think she'd meant for them to. "The vase is yours, Meredith. I got it for you."

"Oh."

Was she surprised? Pleased? He wanted to think she was, but he wasn't sure.

"Well, it's perfect for the blossoms. Thank you." She nodded, turned, and all but ran from his presence.

He stared after her. That could have gone better.

But it could have gone worse.

Meredith Quinn spoke to him. She didn't yell. She said thank you. He looked out his window in time to see Meredith, Aunt Minnie, and Lucy walking up the street.

Meredith usually let Aunt Minnie choose where she wanted to go for lunch, and she typically chose pizza or the coffee shop because they made a mean grilled cheese. He watched as the women paused to admire a puppy, then continued on until they went into Mountain Brew.

He'd been debating what his next step would be in his win-Meredith-over plans. But thinking about coffee and Meredith's love for all creamers and milks and toppings and syrups, he had a flash of inspiration. Unfortunately, it would have to wait until tomorrow.

Tonight, he had to go talk to an undercover agent.

Nine hours later, he stood hidden in the woods surrounding Gossamer Falls. The public parking area at the trailhead held seven cars. When Gray finished meeting with the agent he was here to see, he'd have to bust up the party.

He recognized two of the cars. Those kids' parents would not be pleased to know that their children were continuing the tradition of bringing their dates to the falls for some late-night canoodling.

He smiled at the memory of Granny Quinn using that word when she told him that each generation thought they were on to something new, but that John Quinn Sr. had taken her for a moonlight walk at the falls when he was courting her.

He'd been sure she was kidding. Papa Quinn had pastored a Gossamer Falls church for decades.

"You young people think you're the only ones who know anything about romance. You look at us old people and assume we're clueless." She'd tsked at him. "How do you think you got here in the first place? Hmm?"

Papa Quinn had walked by as she said that, and the look that passed between them wasn't what anyone would call sultry or steamy, but it was intimate and powerful. The kind of look a man shared with the woman he'd chosen not once, but over and over again, and the one he would continue to choose until death parted them.

"Catherine, don't embarrass the boy." Papa Quinn winked at her, then turned his attention to Gray. "What my bride failed to mention is that the moonlight walk was her idea." He waggled his eyebrows, and Gray couldn't decide if he was amused or horrified.

"Oh, you rascal." Granny blushed. She actually blushed! And when the laughter faded, the conversation shifted to other matters.

The memory of those two warmed Gray as he waited, his rear freezing into ice as he rested on a large boulder. What would it be like to share a lifetime of memories with a woman? To flirt and laugh and tease about the shenanigans you got up to in your youth and then transition seamlessly into gloating about the accomplishments of your grandchildren?

He wanted that.

A figure emerged to his left. Gray glanced in that direction only long enough to confirm that the man was alone and not under duress. After that, he kept his focus straight ahead. He knew little about the undercover agent. He wasn't even sure if the name they'd given him was his real name. On the off chance that it *was*, Gray made a point to never use it. He wouldn't do anything to risk the man's life.

They were far enough away from the waterfall that his hearing wasn't compromised, and his visitor made no effort to disguise his movements. Gray heard him take a spot on the rock behind him.

"Sorry I'm late." The gruff voice was low. "I made a few laps around. Based on what I saw, no one out here will disturb us."

Tonight, there was a group near the water. They'd brought speakers and were slow dancing by the river. Gray hadn't no-

216

ticed anyone doing anything inappropriate, but the night was still young. He'd chase them out before anything went too far. "Agreed."

To his left, he saw the man drop a stack of papers on the rock. Gray scooped them up, folded them, and tucked them in his jacket. "Do you need out?"

"No."

"She's worried about you."

"She worries about everyone. You tell her I'm fine and remind her that I know what I'm doing. I've been in here too long to be yanked out now. It will mess up everything."

"I'll tell her."

"I learned something this week that might blow the case wide open."

"I'm listening."

"There used to be a lot of meth in this area. Still is. But there aren't as many cooking it as there used to be. A few of the more enterprising have teamed up with groups out of Atlanta. They bring it up here and distribute it. They also, at times, provide a safe place for individuals who are too valuable to lose but are in danger of being scooped up by the police in larger cities."

"It's easy to hide here."

"It can be. Yes. But some of them, they chafe at the restrictions of small-town life."

"Voluntary house arrest beats prison any day." Gray shifted on the boulder.

"Sure. But these men . . ."

Gray wondered what this man had witnessed in Neeson that put that tone of absolute loathing in his voice.

"They're proud. Used to having people do what they want. But the local crime lords aren't interested in bowing and scraping. They figure it's an equitable arrangement."

"How many are in hiding right now?"

"Two. Brothers. These two take evil to a whole new level. I wouldn't trust them to watch a ferret, much less let them anywhere near my wife and kids."

"You have a wife and kids?" The question came out before Gray could stop it.

"Are you kidding? You think I'd be doing this if I had a wife and kids at home? No. But the men in Neeson do. They have wives, kids, grandkids. They dote on them. Some of them I genuinely believe adore them. Others not so much. But even the ones who aren't obviously protective of their families won't let them anywhere near our current guests."

There was a long pause before he continued. "It's messed up, man. Sometimes I can't figure out if these men are like this because they've done too many drugs over the years, or maybe they drank too much moonshine at an early age? Maybe they're just evil. I don't know. But at least one family is in debt to our guests in a way that means they've been providing for them. And I don't just mean food and water."

Gray wanted to throw something, punch something, or maybe shoot something. What he didn't want was to hear the details. He braced himself for what was coming.

"They've brought in at least three girls from out of state. One of them died the first night. The other two died last week. I didn't know anything about it until yesterday." Anger burned so bright from the agent behind him, Gray could imagine that he would show up as a bonfire on a heat scan. "I didn't know."

The last words were a whisper.

"I've been swimming in filth with the minnows, trying to hook the sharks, but you need to tell our mutual friend that I won't sit by and let this happen again. If I find out about it in time, I *will* do something. And it might get me killed."

Gray let the weight of the words settle on his shoulders. "Respect."

"I don't deserve it. I've been beating my head against walls for months. Trying to infiltrate without rousing suspicion. Then Steven Pierce went and blew everything up. It's good you moved him. They'll try to kill him before it goes to court. If his mama doesn't shut up, they might kill her too."

"Why?" Gray didn't understand what they would gain from taking out Pierce. "He tried to kill someone. There's so much evidence that it's the definition of an open-and-shut case. What's the point?"

"They're afraid of what he might know. And they're angry about the attention his mom's constant grandstanding is bringing to the drug issues in the area. They're convinced it will make state, federal, or other law enforcement take notice."

"It already has."

"Yeah, but they don't know that."

"What do you want me to do? How can I help?" Gray would do anything he could.

"Those papers I gave you have everything I know and everything I suspect. There's also a letter to my mama, in case I don't make it. I wrote one before I went under. But this one's updated."

"Let me get you out now. We have enough to—"

"No. We don't. They have lawyers of their own. They've covered their tracks. And they have the law-abiding citizens terrified. These folks know they're up to no good, but I don't imagine that they know how bad it is. Most of the time, the people in Neeson just live their lives. Going to work, going to school, going to church, mowing the grass, buying groceries. They know there's shady stuff happening at Johnstone's. I think most of them know Kirby is dirty. But they assume if they mind their manners, the dirt won't rub off on them."

"It always rubs off."

"Yep."

"What can you tell me about this wedding?"

"From what I know, the wedding itself is legit. The bride and groom are young and they're so in love. The problem isn't them. The problem is that Johnstone *won't* be there. He's taking his wife to the Caribbean for their anniversary. My money's on him using it as a business trip while she gets some plastic surgery, but that remains to be seen."

Gray almost turned around to look at the agent. "Don't take this the wrong way, but how is Johnstone not being there a problem? From where I sit, that seems like a good thing."

"Oh, it is for the bride and groom. But I have a bad feeling that I can't shake. And I've learned to trust my gut. When Johnstone leaves, he'll put Ledbetter in charge. Trust me on this, if Ledbetter ever takes over completely, Neeson won't be safe for anyone. For now, I'm more worried about some of the young bucks thinking this would be the ideal time to take out Ledbetter. Get rid of Trace, and there's room for a new number two in town."

"I appreciate the tips, but I still don't see why it's important for me to be at that wedding."

"Simple. Your dentist girl is going to be there. She can't be there alone. They haven't given up."

"Wait, you sent that warning because of her? Because you don't want her there alone?"

"I did."

Gray went cold. "What have you heard?"

"It hit the fan last week. That attempted hit-and-run? Not random. I assume you know that."

"Oh, I know."

"Wiser heads understand that to mess with a Quinn would bring fire and brimstone down on them. They won't touch her. They might harass her, but no harm would come to her."

"Well, somebody is gunning for her."

"Young bucks who want to prove themselves. And when I say young, I don't mean teens. I mean twenties and thirties. Old enough to know better but still dumb as rocks."

"I appreciate the warning. She's already promised to stay out of Neeson unless someone is with her. And I've got my officers keeping an eye on her. Her brother's tracking her phone. We know where she is at all times. But she's determined to do the flowers for that wedding. Couldn't talk her out of it, so I'm her plus-one."

"These idiots are opportunists. I don't see them coming after her with you around."

"Will you be at the wedding?"

"I'll be nearby if I can. The kids getting married are good kids. They don't deserve drama."

Gray didn't try to hide his amusement. "I don't know you, but I didn't expect you to be a romantic."

"Man, the only way I survive is to keep believing there's some good in the world."

"I hear you." Police work, even in small towns, could destroy a man's soul. Undercover work? That was brutal. "I'll do my best to be sure you can keep on believing."

"Appreciate it. I'm gone." Gray heard him take a few steps, then pause. "Hey, not my place to say, really, but don't be too hard on the kids tonight. They're young and stupid, but they aren't messing people up or doing drugs."

Gray kept his words in mind as he walked into sight, and in the dim light of the small lanterns they'd set up, he watched the teenagers pale under his gaze. "There's a sign at the trailhead that says this place is closed after dark," he called out. "I suggest you head on back home."

The place was empty of everyone but him within two minutes. But Gray couldn't shake the sense that someone was out there.

Watching. Maybe listening. He'd scanned his car and checked his clothes for listening and tracking devices before he left the office. He didn't want to put the undercover agent in any more danger than he was already in by accidentally giving him away.

Gray walked into the trees and waited another thirty minutes. None of the kids returned. And no one came after him.

Had someone been out there and slipped away? Would tonight's meeting end the life of the agent who was trying to take down the criminals in Neeson?

He drove back to his office and studied the documents the undercover cop had given him.

He'd pass them along to Faith tomorrow and hope that everything would come to a head soon. There'd been too much death. It needed to stop.

TWENTY-ONE

Tuesday morning, Meredith trudged through the icy air, then froze in mid-step when she saw Gray standing at the door to her office, a large thermal box held in his hands. She tried to squash the little flutter that skittered through her body at the sight of him.

No. She was not happy to see him. She was mad. She was not going to fall into his arms because he brought her flowers and . . . whatever was in that box.

She kept her mouth closed until she stepped beside him and entered her code to unlock the door. "Good morning, Chief Ward. How are you?"

"I'm fine, Dr. Quinn."

"That's good. I'm surprised to see you this early. I heard you were out busting up the lovebirds at the falls last night."

"How did you hear that?"

"Aunt Minnie left some markers at my place yesterday. I ran them by Papa and Granny's on my way here. Papa had been listening to the police scanner again."

Of course.

"And I believe there might have been a certain young Shaw present?" She was fishing, but she was almost positive one of Connor's

223

boys had been in the group that decided dancing by a waterfall in February was a good idea. Kids these days.

"I'm afraid I can't say. Confidentiality and all that."

She humphed. She didn't offer to let him in, but he followed her inside anyway and set the box on her desk.

"Enjoy." He turned to go.

"What is it?"

He slowed but didn't stop walking. "What's what?"

"What's in the box?"

"Coffee." He winked at her and walked out the door and up the street to the police station. Meredith opened the box and gingerly lifted out four small cups. They were numbered. The numbers corresponded to the notes on a card tucked in the middle of the box.

Four different flavors of lattes. Each one unique.

He'd brought her a coffee flight.

A text popped up on her phone. It was from Judy.

What do you think of your latte flight? The chief walked in this morning and asked if I could do something like that. I never have, but I may put it on the special menu. It was so fun mixing the flavors and creamers. And I had to throw in one iced just for you. Hope you enjoy. And don't even think I won't be spreading it all over town that Gray Ward is courting you. What?! He was so cute. He watched me make each drink and asked me a ton of questions. Adorable.

Lovely. Just what she didn't need. And this wasn't courting. This was . . . well . . . she had no idea what this was. She wasn't sure Gray knew what it was either. Was this some long drawn-out apology? Because if it was, it had to stop.

At least she knew they weren't poisoned. Gray had watched

Judy make each one. And poor Judy. She'd thought it was sweet. It wasn't sweet. He still suspected that she might have been aiding and abetting the people who attacked her and Bronwyn.

She sipped her hot lattes and iced latte and couldn't decide which was her favorite. Then she stared at her phone. She would have to say thank you.

Again.

Was this part of his plan? To keep her talking to him?

Because if it was, it was working.

The coffees are all delicious. Thank you.

You're welcome. I'm glad you enjoyed them.

And that was that.

She definitely did not check her phone throughout the day on Tuesday to see if he commented further, but Wednesday came with no answers, and no random deliveries of special treats arrived at her home. And she wasn't disappointed, because that would be silly.

But on Thursday morning, she was completely gobsmacked when a delivery arrived at 10:00 a.m. with a tray of Chick-fil-A biscuits and minis.

There was no Chick-fil-A in Gossamer Falls. The closest one was forty-five minutes away. And she missed her biscuits and minis. So much. She'd even tried to make her own. They were okay. But they weren't the same.

There was a note. She took it to her office, closed the door, and opened it.

I overheard you say once that the only thing you missed about Raleigh was the easy access to CFA, specifically for breakfast. I didn't know if you were a biscuit girl or a mini

girl, and really, can you go wrong either way? I think not.
Hopefully there will be enough here to satisfy your craving.

He didn't sign it, but did he need to? No. He did not. This really had to stop.

But she didn't know how to make that happen.

And deep, deep in her soul, she didn't want to. She wanted to see what he would do next.

The knock on her office door had her shoving the note into her jacket pocket.

"My, my, my." Bronwyn Pierce stood in the doorway. "What have we here?"

"Biscuits and minis." Meredith touched the tray. "Want some?"

"Why do you think I'm here?" Bronwyn grabbed two minis and took a bite. "Oh, sweet deliciousness. How I have missed you."

Meredith took a bite of a biscuit, then turned her attention back to Bronwyn. "How did you know?"

"That would be for me to know and you to never find out."

"Beep!"

Bronwyn grinned. "I saw him come in with them. Figured I'd give you a few minutes and then invite myself for breakfast. Looked like he had plenty."

"What do you mean, you saw him?"

"I mean, I saw him get out of his car with a tray. I said, 'Good morning, Gray, whatcha got there?' and he said, 'Morning. I got Meredith some CFA.' And I said, 'I'm totally going to eat some of it.' And he said, 'There's plenty.' Then he walked into your office. Twenty seconds later he walked out, smiled, got back in his car, and drove to the station."

"He went to CFA and got this for me? This morning?"

Bronwyn nodded and spoke around a bite. "Would seem so.

And, can I just say that if he keeps this up, you're going to have to marry him." Then she held up a hand. "Kidding. Kidding. Kinda."

"I heard there was Chick-fil-A in here." Mo's voice rang through the hall.

Bronwyn's eyes widened, and she took a step back from the desk. Mo barged into Meredith's office, eyes only on the tray. "Baby sister, don't ever forgive him." He popped a mini into his mouth whole, and it was only then that the realization that they weren't the only ones in the room hit him. For a moment, his eyes widened, and his body stiffened.

But he didn't turn and leave. Neither did Bronwyn.

Never underestimate the power of a chicken biscuit. Or, in this case, chicken mini.

"I'm kidding, of course. Forgiveness is divine and all that. But if you could not forgive him for a few more weeks? He might end up buying you a car."

"I don't need a car!"

"Who's getting a car?" Lucy walked in and went straight for the biscuits.

"Maybe Meredith." Bronwyn and Mo said the words at the same time, same inflection, same humor. They studiously avoided looking at each other, but Meredith couldn't stop the whisper of hope for a future that might include her best friend and her brother speaking to each other again.

"Not Meredith," she said. "Meredith likes her current modes of transportation just fine, thank you very much."

"He's brought flowers, coffees, and CFA." Lucy wiped a crumb from her lip. "What do you suppose he will do tomorrow?"

"Nothing." Meredith eyed the quickly vanishing tray of delights. "I'm going to put a stop to this."

Meredith stood in the door of Gray's office. "We need to talk."

"Words no man ever wants to hear, but okay. Close the door behind you if you will."

She did and took a seat in the chair across from his desk. She cleared her throat. "Thank you for the Chick-fil-A. It was delicious. I managed to save myself one biscuit from the rabid scavengers who helped themselves to the food. It was all wonderful."

"You're welcome."

"Why are you doing this, Gray?"

"Doing what?"

"Don't play coy."

Every sign he'd ever seen that told him he needed to get out of a situation blared in his brain. He ignored them all. She was here. She wanted answers. And he was done with any kind of dishonesty. Miscommunication and missed signals were for teenagers still trying to figure out who they were.

They were adults and adults could have hard conversations. He hoped. "Are you sure you want the answer?"

"Yes."

"Okay. But remember, you asked for it."

She eyed him warily as he walked to the chair beside her and sat on the edge.

"I'm sorry, Meredith. I'm sorry for leading you on. I'm sorry for being confusing. I'm sorry for being a jerk."

Her cheeks flamed. "You forgot about being sorry for kissing me."

"I most definitely didn't forget about kissing you. And I can't apologize for that because saying I'm sorry would be a lie. I *should* be sorry, but I can't seem to manage it."

Meredith tilted her head. "I think I might be more confused than I was when I walked in here."

"These aren't apology gifts, Meredith. Well, I mean, they can be. They partly are. But that's not the real reason for them."

"Okay." She drew the word out.

"This is my way of trying to break the ice between us. To open a path of communication. Maybe to give me a chance to worm my way into your affections? I'm trying to show you that I pay attention to you. That I've been watching you—in a completely non-creepy way, of course—since the first time you walked in. I know you love coffee and Chick-fil-A, and I wanted you to know that I know."

Meredith's brow crinkled adorably when she was confused. "I . . . don't . . . um . . . you're going to have to be more specific. Because I hear what you're saying, but I don't understand why you're saying it."

If he told her he was in love with her, that might be a step too far. Especially at this stage in the process. But he wouldn't, couldn't, lie to her. Not if he wanted them to have a chance.

"I made a huge mistake."

She watched him warily.

"I was so sure that there was no room in my life for relationships that whenever I was with you, or around you, I tried to convince myself that what I was feeling for you was friendship. And even though I've never felt this way about anyone else, I tried to tell myself that the intensity of what I feel for you was just the protective nature any man would have toward his best friend's sister, or cousin, or whatever."

Meredith pinched her lips together like she was trying not to say something.

"I know it was stupid, but it was a defense mechanism." He leaned closer to her. "I'm not afraid of love. But I am afraid of losing someone I love. I've survived so many losses that I'm not sure I could survive another one."

He leaned back. "I don't expect you to trust me. Or forgive me. But I hope you will. Because I want to see what a relationship with you looks like. I want to talk to you in the morning and hear your laughter over the phone in the afternoon. I want to love every moment of our lives here in Gossamer Falls, but I also want to visit Iceland and New Zealand with you."

Her eyes—her gorgeous, expressive eyes—told him he'd shocked her, and maybe not in a good way.

Too far. Too far. Time to pull this ship back to shore. "I'm not foolish enough to think that we're at that point. But I want you to give me a chance. I want us to have a chance."

Meredith's jaw moved up and down, but no words came out. When they did, they weren't what he was expecting. "I don't understand you at all."

The words nearly broke him, but he tried to keep his voice encouraging and light. "If you'd care to be more specific, I'd be happy to try to explain."

"I"—she waved a hand toward herself—"said horrible things to you. How did we get from there to here?"

"I—"

"No. Wait. Don't answer that yet. I need to apologize."

"You just did."

"No. I didn't. I stated a fact. I didn't ask for forgiveness. I didn't tell you how sorry I am. I—" She blew out a breath, her shoulders dropped, and she closed her eyes. "Wow. This is hard."

He waited. Giving her time, hoping that was the right call because he had no clue what she was about to say or what was hard. And he wasn't sure he wanted to know.

"I want to tell you that I'm not like that. That I'm kind and gentle. But obviously, you heard me say the words. And in the moment, I meant them."

He believed that. He'd seen it in her face, heard it in her voice.

"But the moment? It didn't last. By the time I walked in my door, I was horrified at myself. I could hardly believe I'd said those things to you. But I did. And I did it out of a mean, spiteful place that I rarely turn loose."

She looked at him with an obvious plea for understanding, so he nodded in encouragement while hoping she would keep explaining, because if he had confused her earlier, she had completely befuddled him now.

"And in response, you bring me all these gifts." She threw her hands up. "And tell me you . . . you . . ."

"I'm not sure that I spelled it out as clearly as I could have, but I would very much like to date you."

"That!" She shook her head. "Why? I mean, why now?"

"Why not now?"

"I was mean to you!"

"Have you forgotten that I was mean to you first?"

"That's no excuse!"

He rubbed his hands over his face. "Okay. Let's back up a little bit. No confusion. No mixed signals. No crossed wires. Full disclosure. Total transparency."

"That seems like a lot."

"You don't have to reciprocate, but please hear me out."

She nodded.

"The first day I saw you, I thought you were the most beautiful woman I'd ever seen. You laughed with Cal, and if I hadn't known you were cousins, I would have been consumed with jealousy on the spot. When I realized that I'd reacted to you so strongly, I made a conscious effort to minimize my contact with you. But you kept showing up. You redecorated and reorganized and painted and nearly killed me with kindness. Things were getting shaky on my end. But then your mom was diagnosed with cancer, and for a while you pretty much disappeared."

567d

"It was—"

"No apologies, Meredith. None whatsoever. Honestly, it was a bit of a relief for me. I thought I could use the time to get you out of my system. To clear my head of you. Build my walls higher to keep you from getting in. And I thought it had worked. But it turns out that when it comes to you, I might build walls, but they're flimsy. One little push from you and they didn't just fall. They disintegrated."

He leaned toward her again. "It took me a while to realize that I was wide open to you. That the reason I needed to protect you, to be around you, to know what was going on in your life, was because you had already set up shop in my heart. I just didn't realize it." He reached for her hand, and she slid her fingers across his.

"I want to rebuild the walls, but I want to build them with you. I want to build them around us, together. I want the walls to protect what we're building together. I want there to be things that go on behind the walls that are ours and no one else's."

He brushed a strand of hair behind her ear. "I would never try to separate you from your family or your friends, but there are things I don't want to share with Cal or Mo."

She shuddered. "I should hope not."

This time, he leaned until his forehead rested against hers. "I'm sorry, Meredith. I was a fool. Please consider giving me a chance."

She was quiet for so long, he feared her answer.

"If you hurt me again, I'm not sure I would have enough mercy in me for us to stay friends. I'm not sure Gossamer Falls would be big enough for both of us. You could lose everything, Gray. Everything. I'm not trying to be entitled or overdramatic, but have you thought it through? My family will choose me. And if you hurt me again, my father will do his best to have you run out of town." Her smile this time was sad. "I know this because he's already volunteered to do it. Also, you should know, Mo wanted to kill you or give your computer viruses."

Gray pressed a hand to her cheek. "What did you tell them?"

"I said to hold off." She leaned into his hand. "But seriously, Gray. You need to be sure. Because if you aren't, you could lose everything."

"You don't trust me." He could see it in her eyes. A wariness that spoke of pain and hurt. All of which was his fault.

"I . . . I want to. But I'm afraid to take the risk. And really, you should be too."

"As crazy as this is going to sound, I'm not afraid at all. And you won't let anyone kill me."

She wrinkled her nose. "I wouldn't. But I would probably let them run you out of town."

"Sweetheart, if I ever hurt you again, I'll run myself out of town."

TWENTY-TWO

Meredith tried to form coherent thoughts.

Failed.

Tried again.

And again.

Finally, she managed to say, "Gray?"

"Yes?"

"What happens now?"

He grazed her forehead with the lightest of kisses. "Right now? I'm afraid you have to go back to work."

The intercom buzzed on his desk. He stood and answered it. "Yes, Glenda?"

"I'm so sorry to bother you, sir, but Lucy is here. She's, um, well, a little concerned. She said Dr. Quinn has a patient in three minutes, and she tried to call but—"

Was it already time to be back in the office? Had her phone buzzed and she'd missed it?

Gray had his professional voice going when he said, "Tell her she can return to the office. Dr. Quinn will be a few minutes late, but she'll be there shortly. Thank you."

"Yes, sir."

Meredith was pretty sure she should say something at this point, but she was still having trouble getting her brain in gear.

Gray stood in front of her chair, took both of her hands in his, and pulled her to standing. He didn't move, and the motion brought her body flush against his. "Hi."

"Hi."

"Could I make dinner for you tonight? My place. Seven p.m.?"

She nodded.

"Okay. I'll pick you up at six forty-five."

"That's silly. If we're eating at your place, I can drive."

He shook his head. "I wouldn't say yes to that even if there was no danger at all. But given that you are in danger, that's not just a no. That's a no way, under no circumstances, absolutely not."

Well, that was . . . firm. "Okay. What can I bring?"

"Yourself."

"I can do that."

"Great."

"So, I should go."

"Yeah."

But she didn't move. They stood there. Bodies almost touching. Hands held between them. Eyes locked on each other.

The intercom buzzed again.

"I swear I'm going to throw that thing out a window." Meredith laughed as he answered, "Yes, Glenda?"

"Sorry to bother you, sir, but I thought you should know that Lucy called and is holding." Glenda's exasperation was evident. "She said she can see Dr. Quinn's patient waiting outside the office. I believe she's running down the sidewalk."

"Please tell Lucy that Dr. Quinn is on her way."

"Thank you, sir."

As he'd spoken to Glenda, Meredith had backed up until she was at his door. "Tonight."

"Tonight." Meredith had no idea how she managed to get out of Gray's office. Or out of the building. She walked down the street in a fog. It was a miracle she didn't get run over. When she entered her office, she was extra thankful that she had a back entrance and didn't have to walk in through the lobby. She landed in her office chair and dropped her head on the desk.

What had just happened?

She slid her phone from her pocket and texted Bronwyn.

I have a date with Gray tonight.

Bronwyn wasn't known for her lightning-fast responses to text messages, but the three dots began dancing almost as soon as Meredith hit send. Then they stopped, and her phone rang.

"Hello."

"Details. Now. Spill. Fast." Bronwyn's rapid-fire commands held concern and also a heavy dose of hope.

Meredith filled her in. "I don't understand him at all. I was so mean. And he's all, 'I want to go to Iceland with you.'"

"Oh, sweetie, you don't get it at all. But I think I do."

"Explain it to me. Please. Fast."

"Meredith, you're so gentle and loving that you don't lose your temper often. And the only time you're truly angry is when you've been hurt badly. He figured out that the reason you reacted the way you did isn't because you don't love him. It's because you do."

"That's messed up. I don't want to be mean to people I love."

"That's not what I meant. You don't bother getting angry about things that don't matter. You're angry with him because he does matter. And he's realized that. So now he has hope that he can fix things. And he's not wrong. I mean, really, of all of us, the only person who is worse at holding grudges than you are is Cassie. She can't stay mad to save her life. Literally."

"I love Cassie."

"So do I. Stay on track, sweetie. You were hurt. You lashed out. That doesn't mean you don't care about Gray. He understands that you took a risk with him by showing how you felt. You put yourself out there and got your nose smacked for it."

"More like a black eye."

"Fine. You got punched in the face. Or, more accurately, the gut, the heart, the feels. He kissed you and then claimed it was a mistake. And you reacted in anger while in pain. But if he hadn't been important, you wouldn't have cared."

"If he wasn't important, I never would have kissed him."

"Exactly. And now he's come to his senses. Took him long enough. If he's smart, he wants to restore things to the point where you'll be crazy for him again."

"I'm pretty sure that part never went away." Meredith fiddled with the calendar on her desk. "I tried to make it go away, but . . ."

Bronwyn sighed. "Yeah. I know. So, what time is your date?"

"Seven. He's picking me up at six forty-five. He says there's no way I'm driving to his house for a date, which is super polite but ridiculously inefficient."

"You sound like Mo when you say things like that. Love isn't about efficiency. Love is supposed to be inefficient, inconvenient, and even a little weird."

"What's with all the love talk? It's a date. A *first* date."

"But can it be a first date when you've already had your first kiss?"

"Not funny."

Bronwyn ignored her. "I'll be at your place at five thirty. We'll find the perfect outfit, freshen up your makeup, and have you ready to leave for the ball at six forty-five."

"I don't need help getting dressed for a date. I'm not fifteen. I'm thirty-two."

"I'm not coming to help you get dressed, although you should let me help you pick out your outfit. Maybe I'll bring a few things."

"Then—?"

"I'm coming to run interference."

"What?"

"As soon as Gray pulls into the driveway, Mo and Cal will lose their minds. If I'm there, I'll be able to smooth the way."

———

Meredith made it through the day in a blur. She focused on her patients and thanked the Lord, sincerely and fervently, that her entire afternoon was nothing but routine cleanings. If she'd had to do a root canal, she might have needed to reschedule.

At five thirty, she was waiting on her porch when Bronwyn brought her BMW SUV to a stop behind Meredith's 4Runner.

Meredith doubted that Bronwyn could see him, but she knew Mo stood in his doorway, watching as Bronwyn came toward her holding three garment bags and a makeup case.

"I don't need your clothes." Meredith opened the door for her to step inside and then followed.

"You might. You never know." Bronwyn divested herself of her burdens, turned, and threw her arms around Meredith. "How are you feeling? It's been a few hours. Are you sure you want to go out with him? Because I can head him off if you don't."

Meredith's phone buzzed, but she ignored it. "I'm excited. And terrified. I'm worried about whether my deodorant will hold up. What if I start sweating?"

"Sweat is a normal bodily function. And in your case, all Gray will see is that you have a translucent glow about you." Bronwyn slipped into a snooty upper-crust accent at the end, then dissolved into laughter. "Since when do you worry about sweat?"

"Since I started breaking out in one every time I'm around him," Meredith confessed.

Bronwyn gave her a shrewd look. "How long has this been going on?"

"Since the day I met him."

Bronwyn grinned. "Then I guess we should plan for you to wear layers. If you start glistening, you'll need to be able to bare some skin."

"No one bares skin in February."

"I'm not talking about wearing a bikini." Bronwyn shot her a look. "What is wrong with you? He really does have your brain scrambled. I'm talking about scarves, jackets, sweaters, etc. You can bundle up for the drive over there and in case he decides to take you on a walk."

"To Gossamer Falls?" Meredith snorted a laugh. "Pretty sure that won't be happening."

"Not to Gossamer Falls. He's too old for that. But there is that gorgeous spot in the park . . ."

"Yeah. And he's the chief of police. I doubt he's going to be big on public displays of affection."

"I wouldn't be so sure. The man has been spoiling you all week. Quite publicly."

"Fair point."

An hour later, Meredith was dressed comfortably, with layers, and her hair was extra shiny thanks to some miracle spray Bronwyn had pulled from her Mary Poppins makeup bag. She was sipping a chamomile tea that Bronwyn had assured her would help settle her nerves and her stomach.

Both of which had lost their minds in the last fifteen minutes.

Mo had come over earlier and checked everything for listening devices, so she was 99 percent sure she could talk to Bronwyn without anyone hearing. She'd have to risk it.

"What is wrong with me?" She blew on the tea. "I'm a grown-up. I'm not a teenager with a crush."

"You have more to lose. And you're smart enough to know that." Bronwyn's answer wasn't unkind or unfeeling. It was the truth Meredith needed to hear.

"Yeah. He's Cal's best friend."

"You've turned into a romance trope. You're dating your brother's best friend. Except he's your cousin. But 'cousin's best friend' doesn't have the same ring to it." Bronwyn sipped her own tea. A decaf Earl Gray. "Everyone knows the biggest problem with dating your brother's best friend is that if things go south, it's not just your relationship that suffers."

"Aren't you Suzy Sunshine this evening? You're supposed to be helping me."

"I am."

"I'm not feeling comforted at the moment."

"Gray wants to be with you enough to risk it. What was it you told me once? That you wanted someone to choose you?"

"Yeah." She did want that.

"Well, you have your wish. He's chosen you, the hope and the promise of what a relationship with you could be, over his friendship with Cal. That should settle your nerves. Those two are tight. Gray wouldn't take the risk if he wasn't serious about you, and serious about making your relationship work."

Meredith studied Bronwyn over her teacup, then caught a glimpse of a man approaching and hissed out a warning. "Incoming."

Bronwyn didn't miss a beat. She grabbed a magazine from the coffee table, settled herself more deeply into Meredith's sofa, and was in mid-sip when the front door to Meredith's tiny house opened.

Mo stood in the doorway. "Is there a reason you aren't answering your messages?"

Meredith gasped and pulled her phone from her pocket. "Sorry. Been busy."

Mo took in the room, including Bronwyn as she studiously read the magazine and didn't look up to acknowledge Mo's presence. "You don't look busy. Why did Bronwyn bring all that stuff? Is she in trouble?"

Meredith didn't miss the way Bronwyn's mug trembled at Mo's words. "No. Nothing like that. She came to help me get ready."

There was a slight lessening of the tension in Mo's jaw, and then he asked, "Get ready for what?"

Before Meredith could answer, another vehicle pulled in and parked beside the carport. Gray was here.

Mo rolled his head around in a slow circle. Meredith heard his neck crack twice. But all he said was, "Seriously?" Then he walked to the kitchen, poured himself a glass of water, took two cookies from her cookie jar, and planted himself in the chair opposite where Bronwyn sat on the sofa.

Now it was Meredith's turn to say, "Seriously? What is this? Go home. Both of you."

"I think it's good for him to see what he's up against if he hurts you." Mo took a bite of his cookie and spoke around it. "Oh, wait. He already did that."

Bronwyn pinched her lips together but didn't come to Meredith's aid.

"We've discussed it. That matter is between us."

"No, it isn't. He hurt you. You're my sister. That makes it my business."

"Told you." Bronwyn's murmur was just loud enough for Meredith and Mo to hear. Which was good, because Gray was almost to the door, a bouquet of flowers in his hand.

"Would you shut up?" Meredith spoke to both of them, then went to open the door. "Hi!"

Gray extended the flowers to her.

"These are gorgeous." She took them. "Let me set them in a vase and then we can go. Come on in, if you dare. My bodyguards are here."

TWENTY-THREE

Gray entered Meredith's home and acknowledged Bronwyn first. He'd seen her BMW, so her presence was no surprise. "Bronwyn."

"Chief Ward." She didn't get up. And she didn't use his name, even though he'd used hers. Did this mean she didn't approve? He had no idea, so he focused on Mo next.

"Mo."

"Ward."

Ooh. Last name only. Mo definitely didn't approve.

"Behave. Both of you." Meredith rolled her eyes and pulled a vase from the top of her fridge, filled it with water, and settled the flowers inside. "I'll take care of them when I get home." She grabbed her purse from the counter. "Ready?"

Gray looked from Meredith to Bronwyn to Mo, then back to Meredith. She didn't look at her brother or her friend. "They know their way out."

"Then yes, let's go." Gray opened the door, but Meredith went to Bronwyn first. She placed a gentle kiss on her hair and gave her a side squeeze. Then she went to Mo and repeated the process. But when she stepped back, Mo grabbed her hand and held on. Something unspoken passed between them. Then he released her

243

and, once her back was turned, glared at Gray until his view was blocked by Meredith's back.

Gray didn't speak until they were out of hearing range of her house. "Are you going to leave them alone?" he asked as he took her hand and rested it in the crook of his arm.

Her Machiavellian laughter had him seeing a whole new side of this woman who'd fascinated him from the start. "They deserve it for being nosy. Bronwyn claimed she was coming to help me and to run interference if needed. She's not opposed to us dating. What she really wanted was to have a front-row seat to Mo's reaction."

"Because Mo *is* opposed?"

"No . . ." She drew out the word like she was tasting it for truth. "I don't think he's opposed to you. I think Mo is less willing for me to take risks. And in his mind, you're a big one."

"And in yours?" Gray opened the door of his Explorer and stood back as she settled herself into the seat.

"Despite what people think about me, I happen to think taking risks is what makes life beautiful." She gave him a cheeky grin.

He closed her door and jogged to the driver's side. It was close the door or kiss her, and it was too soon for kissing. And way too soon for kissing with an audience, which they definitely had. He could feel two sets of eyes tracking his every move all the way down the driveway.

The ride back to his place was smooth and uneventful. She told him about a patient who'd brought her his first lost tooth and asked if she was friends with the tooth fairy. He told her about the Statons' cows getting loose again, and how it had taken two hours of his afternoon to get everyone back where they belonged. "If I smell like cow patties, you'll know why. I did shower. But some smells . . ."

"They linger." She grinned at him. "Remind me to tell you

about the time we got in a fight in the pasture and rolled through a few recent cow piles."

"You can't say something like that and leave me hanging. What happened?"

Meredith tried to tell him twice, but her laughter was too much and it took her several miles to calm down enough to speak. When she did, her words were punctuated with fits of giggles. "It was epic. Cal tells it best, so you should get him to give you his version. It was such a big deal that Cassie remembers, and she was only four at the time."

She blinked eyes that were brimming with laughter-induced tears. "We walked up to the front door of Papa and Granny's house covered in poop, smelling like, well, poop. We refused to answer questions about how we came to be that way."

Meredith ran a finger under her eye. "Granny made us strip and use the outdoor shower before she let us inside to use the indoor showers. The outdoor shower is freezing. She didn't care. She told me there'd better not be any poop left in my hair when I walked back in her house."

"How old were you?"

Meredith thought about it. "Fifth grade? Maybe sixth?" She laughed then. "I had to wash my hair in the cold water while keeping my body out of it as much as possible. There was a lot of squealing on my part. When I turned off the water and declared myself poop-free, Granny handed me a towel and told me to go to my room and shower again. Then she put Mo in, and Cal went last."

Gray held up a hand. "You had a room at your grandparents'?"

"We have our parents' rooms. More or less. Mo and I had our dad's old room. When we got older, he shared with Cal in Aunt Carol's old room."

Something tickled her again, and she laughed harder. "When

we were all clean, Granny informed us that she had thrown our clothes on the burn pile. I don't think I've ever seen her so mad. Granny put up with a lot, but we pushed her too far that day. We were supposed to be going into town to have dinner. We'd run out to play, and that would have been fine if we'd come back ready to go. As far as Granny was concerned, we were far too old to be going on with such nonsense. She lectured us all the way to dinner."

Meredith sighed. "We apologized profusely, of course, but that was the day we realized it was possible to tick Granny off."

"I'm surprised it took you that long. Your granny isn't a woman I would ever cross." Gray turned onto the road that led into town.

"Yeah, but she's my granny, and Granny spoils her grandchildren. I'm still spoiled. I know I am. I'm not sorry. My granny would turn the world upside down for me. So would my papa. My entire family. Not everyone has that."

"No, they don't." His comment wiped the humor from Meredith's gaze, but she didn't question him.

"Of course, Papa found out about it at dinner. He was most displeased. But not that we'd gotten in a cow-patty fight. He was disappointed that we'd disrespected Granny."

"Ouch."

"Oh yeah. The disappointment factor was the worst."

"How long were they upset?"

"Granny ordered us all desserts at the end of dinner."

Gray paused at one of Gossamer Falls' few lights. "That fast?"

Meredith's smile was soft and held a flirtatiousness he'd never seen from her. "Lucky for you, some Quinns take after Granny. She has a long fuse. When you make her mad, you will know it when she explodes. But then she's over it. She forgives quickly." The flirtatiousness faded away. "Papa pointed out that night that we had apologized, and that we had repented, and that God forgives and doesn't hold a grudge, so neither would they. I've never forgotten it."

She looked out the window. "Mom and Dad weren't quite so forgiving. Neither were Aunt Carol and Uncle Craig. They told us that while Papa and Granny had forgiven us and our relationships were restored, that didn't give us a pass on the consequences. We had to clean cow patties out of the pasture for the next four Saturdays. It was disgusting. Never forgot that lesson either. Forgiveness doesn't mean there aren't any consequences."

"Pretty sure I'm living that out right now." Gray pulled into his driveway. "Your family won't be quite as quick to forgive me as you've been."

"They'll come around. Someday it will be a funny story with a lesson. Something we'll be talking about for decades. Last Christmas, Cal found cow-patty ornaments. He gave one to Mo and to me each. But he also gave one to Granny Quinn. She thought it was hilarious."

Gray chose not to acknowledge the way Meredith had indicated that she had, in fact, forgiven him or the part where she expected him to be around decades from now. Both statements filled him with hope. He parked and rushed to where Meredith sat waiting for him to open her door. She tucked her hand into his arm without any prompting and, once inside, allowed him to take her coat and scarf. She left her purse, with her phone poking out the top, by the front door.

"Shoes on or off?" she asked him.

"Your preference. I tend to keep mine on. I know there are germs in the world, but I frequently have to run out the door. If my shoes are on, it makes it faster."

She slid her boots off, revealing feet clad in colorful wool socks. "I tend to take mine off, but only because I like to sit with my feet curled up in the chair. It makes me feel more comfortable."

"Fair enough." Whatever made her more comfortable, he was in favor of. He led her through his small front room and into the kitchen.

Gray poured Meredith a glass of water and set the tray of munchies he'd made earlier on the table. "I'm planning seared sea bass, risotto, and a wedge salad. Hope that's okay."

Meredith's expressive features lit with obvious delight.

He gave himself an internal high five. He'd gotten it right.

"That sounds amazing. I've never tried to cook sea bass or risotto."

"In the interest of transparency, the risotto comes from a mix, but it's very good. Wedge salads only require the knowledge of how to slice iceberg lettuce into, well, wedges. And Cassie made the dressing for me. She said you were a ranch girl and wouldn't touch blue cheese, so it's wedge salad with ranch, bacon, and tomatoes."

Meredith's laughter stopped him in his tracks. He'd heard her laugh like that twice since he picked her up. He wanted her to laugh that way, many times a day, forever, and he wanted to be the one who made her do it.

"Did Cassie make the sea bass as well?"

"Nope. That's all me. It's best right out of the skillet. I have everything prepped. It only takes a few minutes. I was hoping you'd keep me company while I cooked."

"Gladly."

She leaned against the counter as he pulled the salads from the fridge where he'd stashed them earlier, then started the risotto. "How did you have time for this? I don't typically have sea bass in my fridge. Wait." She narrowed her eyes and made an adorably disgruntled face. "Were you planning this meal for someone else?"

"Jealous, Dr. Quinn?"

"Yes." Her answer held no hesitation.

Oh, he liked the idea of a jealous Meredith. But he wouldn't tease her about it. Ever. "As a matter of fact, I threw myself on Cassie's mercy. I asked her if she had any sea bass, and she did."

Meredith pretended to clutch her pearls and spoke in a horrible Southern accent. "Why, Chief Ward, what is the meaning of this? Leading my baby cousin into a life of crime? Having her steal from her employer?"

He pointed a spatula at her. "I'll have you know that your baby cousin didn't steal from her employer. She orders seafood on Thursday and had time to add to the order for me."

"I didn't know that." The adorable disgruntled face was back. And the fact that he thought it was adorable was proof of how far gone he was.

"She stopped in a few weeks ago to see Donovan. I have no idea how it came up in conversation, but Donovan must have told her that I love fresh seafood. She offered to let me place an order with hers if I wanted something specific. It was a long shot today, but she caught the guy making the delivery before he left Asheville. They'd gotten fresh sea bass in this morning." He tapped the fillets he'd pulled from the fridge. "These babies were swimming yesterday."

"How does she get fish that fresh? It has to be outrageously expensive."

Gray gave her a look.

"Oh. Right. She isn't paying for it." She frowned. "But you are."

He stepped closer to her, lifted a curl from her shoulder, and rubbed it between his fingers. "I don't have a lot of experience with dating. It probably would have made more sense to take you to a nice restaurant, but I didn't want to give you a chance to change your mind. Since we don't have any fine dining in Gossamer Falls, at least none that we mere mortals can access, I thought I'd bring the experience to you. Here. In my home. Is that okay?"

Meredith trembled against Gray. He'd thought of everything. And he'd been so intentional about his decisions. "More than okay."

"Good." He didn't move toward her, but his eyes spoke of so many things she'd barely given herself permission to dream of.

"Now"—he reached for her waist, and with far less effort than it should have taken, he lifted her to the counter—"tell me more about your childhood while I cook."

So she did. She told him about growing up in Gossamer Falls, running around all over Quinn land, going off to college and being so homesick she thought she would die from the agony of it.

She watched Gray move around the kitchen with a grace that spoke of his confidence in his skills. And she discovered that she liked watching him cook.

And that wasn't something she'd ever thought about any man. Ever.

He plated the bass, risotto, salads, and crusty rolls and turned to her. "I'll be right back." He left the kitchen a few times, taking the dishes with him, and finally taking her water.

When he returned the last time, he stepped in front of her and placed his hands on her waist. "Dinner is served." He pulled her off the counter and set her feet on the floor but didn't move his hands.

She looked up at the way his Adam's apple bobbed in his throat and decided that she wasn't the only one drowning in sensation.

"We should eat." His voice was gruff, his hands still firm at her waist, his body unmoving.

"The food could get cold."

"Yes."

"Gray?"

"Yes?"

"Would it mess up your plan for the perfect date if you kissed me first?"

His eyes held hers as his hands traveled up to cup her face. "Meredith." The word was a whisper just before his lips brushed across hers. "You're supposed to make me wait." Another brush of lips. "You're supposed to insist on lots of dates, each one more extravagant than the last."

The next kiss held her lips a few seconds longer.

"Otherwise, I might think you've forgiven me." His lips traveled to her ear. "I don't deserve that."

She leaned into his caress. "Maybe I don't care what you think you deserve." She turned her head to capture his lips with her own. "You obviously need someone in your life who will appreciate you and take care of you."

"Are you volunteering?" His lips brushed her chin, then her nose.

"Is the position still available?"

He pressed his forehead to hers. "The position was only ever yours."

"It's filled now."

His smile soothed all the hurts and raw edges from the last few weeks. "You're still going to get the dates and surprises."

"I like surprises."

He closed his eyes and pulled in a long breath, then released it at the same time he released all of her except one hand. "Come on. Let's eat."

She followed him into the dining room on shaking legs and then had the most romantic meal of her life. The bass was perfection. The risotto creamy. The wedge crunchy and crisp. And when she couldn't possibly eat another bite, he cleared the dishes and returned to her, holding her coat. "Come on. Let's walk off dinner."

"Please tell me we aren't going to Gossamer Falls."

He laughed. "Too crowded. I have a better spot in mind."

Meredith slid into her boots, and for the next couple of hours, she let him convince her that she was the only one he wanted, the only one he would ever want, and the only one who could ever have pulled him out of the abyss he'd placed himself in.

As he drove her home, far too late for grown-ups with real jobs to be out at night but far sooner than she wanted to, she said, "Gray?"

"Hmm?" His thumb ran across her hand where he held it.

"Will you be my plus-one for the wedding?"

His hand clenched on hers. "I might have to work while we're there."

"I know. But I'm still asking you to please be my plus-one, as a date."

"Then yes, I'd love to be your plus-one."

"So it's a date."

"It's a date."

TWENTY-FOUR

Gray walked around to Meredith's side of the car and opened the door for her.

He offered her his hand and she took it, but she wasn't looking at him. She narrowed her eyes and tilted her head toward the firepit. Gray followed her gaze. Mo sat nursing what looked like a root beer, and Cal was beside him in Meredith's regular seat. The location gave Cal an excellent view of the driveway, and Gray had no doubt both men had been waiting on them to return.

Meredith touched his arm and whispered, "Do you want to join them? Or say good night here?"

"We aren't saying good night here. I'm not leaving you by the car just to avoid speaking to them."

Meredith looked from him to the two men by the fire. "Cal's your best friend. I don't want you to avoid speaking to him ever."

"I appreciate that, but tonight is about you. What do *you* want to do?"

She wrapped her hand around his. "Let's go chat."

They were ten feet away when Meredith pointed to Cal. "You're in my seat."

He stood and waved to the chair with a flourish. "My apologies, ma'am." Cal went to sit in the chair beside her and then it was Gray's turn to protest.

"Now you're in my seat."

Cal hovered over it, his hands braced on the arms of the chair. "Is it now?"

"Yes. It is."

Cal stood and moved to his normal seat across the fire.

"What, no apology for me?" Gray scooted his chair closer to Meredith's so he could continue to hold her hand.

"Nope." Cal quirked an eyebrow at him but didn't say more.

Meredith reached out her free hand to Mo. "You can't refuse to speak to him forever. No one can do that."

Mo didn't look at anyone. He stared into the fire and said, "Wanna bet?"

Meredith gasped. "Tell me you're joking. I left you in a room with her. How did you manage to leave without speaking?"

It took Gray a second to keep up. They weren't talking about Mo not speaking to him anymore.

"Wasn't too difficult." Mo's tone was calm. The tension in his body screamed frustration.

Meredith leaned toward her brother. "Please tell me you didn't get up and walk away."

"I did no such thing."

Meredith relaxed in her seat.

"But she did."

So Bronwyn had left without speaking? Gray had no idea what was going on between them, but that seemed harsh.

Meredith dropped her head on the back of the chair. "Seriously?"

"We sat there in awkward silence for a few minutes before she left."

"You couldn't have said something? Anything?"

"There's nothing to say. If she wants to open the lines of communication, that's up to her. I swore I wouldn't speak to her again until she spoke to me first. Unlike some people, *I* don't break my promises."

"You did what?" Meredith squeaked a little on the last word.

Meredith and Cal were on the edges of their seats. This must have been new information for all of them.

"You mean Bronwyn knows why you don't speak to her?" Cal looked at Meredith. "Did you know this?"

"No! What—"

"We aren't here for that." Mo cut her off and turned the tables. "We're here to discuss the fact that you're sitting here holding hands with a man who made you cry. A lot. For weeks. The same guy who made you so upset you didn't eat enough, who had you so twisted in knots that it impacted your sleep. I volunteered to kill him. I volunteered to give him computer viruses. I took your refusal of my offers to be yet another indication that you are a better person than I am. I did not think you were protecting him so you could date him." Mo said *date* like it was the vilest option available to anyone.

But Gray was hung up on one new piece of information. He brought Meredith's hand to his lips. "Please tell me you didn't stop eating."

"He's being dramatic. I didn't want dessert at dinner."

"For weeks." Mo glared at his sister.

"It's not like I was on a hunger strike. Let it go. I have plenty of extra to lose. It didn't hurt me."

Again, Gray pressed her hand to his lips. "Meredith, please don't ever let me hear you talk about yourself that way. Your body is perfection, and it houses your beautiful soul. You have to take care of it."

"Okay." Her response was breathy and a little bit of something that Gray didn't like. Meredith Quinn was confident, gorgeous, and kind. But his instincts screamed at him that at some point in her past, someone had made her question all of that.

"Amen, brother." Mo's comment confirmed what Gray suspected.

She turned to Mo. "You butt out of this."

"You can't make me."

"Wanna bet?"

And just like that, Gray could see the siblings they were. There was so little animosity between them under normal circumstances that he sometimes forgot that they must have squabbled as children.

Cal groaned. "If you two keep going, I'll tell Aunt Jacque on you."

Not Cal too!

The threat silenced them and had them turning identical glares in Cal's direction. He threw up his hands. "She doesn't like it when you fight. It upsets her. And none of us want that."

"Traitor," Mo muttered under his breath.

"Tattletale," Meredith muttered under hers.

Cal gave them all a devilish grin. "Years of practice. Now, Gray, brother, we need to talk."

Cal's comment brought Mo's attention fully onto Gray. But it also brought Meredith's to him. "Callum Shaw, you have no business talking to Gray that way," she said.

"Do so."

Here we go again.

"You do not." Meredith and Cal were both smiling now, and Gray realized they were teasing, not fighting.

"He's my best friend." Cal pointed to himself.

"Well, he's my . . . my . . ." Meredith looked at Gray, then back at Cal. "He's mine."

And Gray understood what it meant to melt for a woman. Because as long as Meredith Quinn claimed him that way, she could get him to do just about anything. And when she leaned over the arms of her chair and his to plant a soft kiss on his cheek, Gray didn't even try to hide his triumphant smile.

"Ugh." Mo groaned. "Great. Now I have to watch you both be all mushy and gushy." He pointed a finger at Meredith. "I'm telling you the same thing I told Cal. No PDA. I don't need to see you kissing and hugging and all that." He waved a hand toward her and Gray.

Meredith leaned toward Mo and kissed his cheek. "Okay. I'll be like Cal."

Cal kissed Landry at any time and in any place. If Landry was near him, he was holding her hand, running his hand through her hair, tapping her foot with his, wrapping his arms around her.

Mo must have come to the same realization, because he pointed at Gray this time. "I have plenty of my own nightmares and I'll thank you to avoid adding any more."

Taking his cue from Meredith, Gray said, "I'll do my best." Which he could already tell wouldn't be much at all.

Mo grumbled something unintelligible and took a long drink.

"Mo?" Meredith patted Mo's arm.

"What?"

"I'm sorry about Bronwyn."

He gave her a quick glance, then looked back at the fire. "Nothing for you to be sorry about." Before Meredith could argue, he leaned forward in his chair and looked around her to focus his attention on Gray. "You hurt her again, and I won't ask her permission to make your life miserable."

"If you think that's going to scare me or make me mad, you're wrong on both counts." Gray squeezed Meredith's hand. "I had a sister, and I couldn't protect her. I will never fault you for doing what I wish I could have done."

Mo looked to Meredith, then Cal, then back to Gray. Gray could tell he was torn between wanting to ask for more details and desperately trying to avoid getting into a sensitive conversation. "Fair enough." Mo stood, walked over to Meredith, and kissed her on the head. "Not trying to be bossy or anything, but you have to work tomorrow and it's getting late."

There was laughter in her voice when she said, "Good night, Mo."

He threw up a hand and walked to his house.

Cal settled back and they talked for another ten minutes before his phone buzzed. He hopped out of his chair, a sappy grin on his face. "My girls are on their way home. Gotta go."

"What were they doing out this late on a school night?" Gray asked.

"There's no school tomorrow or Monday, but one of Chad and Naomi's boys had a basketball game tonight in Waynesville. They went to watch and then went out to eat with everyone after."

"Why didn't you go?" Meredith asked.

"I had to work late tonight so I can be off while Eliza's off." Cal pointed his finger at Gray, then Meredith. "Behave." With that, he jogged down the path that led him home.

Gray followed Meredith's gaze as she watched Cal's retreating form.

An indulgent smile crossed her face. "That right there is the definition of domestic bliss."

"True enough. I'm so happy for him, I can't even tease him about it." Gray had walked with Cal through some of the hardest days of his life.

"God moves in mysterious ways, that's for sure." Meredith stood and walked around the firepit, straightening chairs. "Well, you survived Mo and Cal. Now you have to survive my parents, grandparents, and every Quinn you'll come into contact with over the next few weeks. Are you sure you're up for it?"

There was a teasing light in her eyes, but a definite hint of insecurity bled through the question.

"I'm sure." Running the Quinn gauntlet had never been a concern. Her loving family was one of the best things she had going for her.

"Meredith!" Mo's voice rang out across the open space between their homes.

"What?" She sounded a bit disgruntled. Gray couldn't blame her.

"I checked your house, car, and shop a little while ago. You're bug-free."

"Thanks."

Mo's response was a nod and another wave, then his door closed and left them alone by the firepit.

Gray appreciated Mo's efforts on Meredith's behalf, but now the danger Meredith was in was at the forefront of his mind.

Her family was never going to scare him off. It was the people who bugged her scarf, cut her fuel line, and tried to run her over who terrified him. He took her hand and pulled her close, then walked her to the door of her home. "Meredith?"

"Hmm?"

"I will do everything in my power to keep you safe and to never harm you again. I want you to live life to the fullest, but right now, with everything so up in the air, please help me hold it together by doing everything you can to stay safe."

Meredith pressed a kiss to his jaw. "I promise." Her thumb traced the spot her lips had been. "I'm not always going to check in with you about every move I make. But I also won't hold your fears against you. Right now, I'll keep you in the loop. And I'll pay attention to where I am and who's around me."

"Thank you." He held her close and breathed in the scent of her. Her shampoo had a citrus edge to it, but it was now almost completely obscured by wood smoke. "I'll do everything I can to get you back to your old life."

Meredith wrapped her arms around his neck. "If it's all the same to you, I don't want my old life back."

Her fingers were doing something glorious to the nape of his neck, and his eyes closed without his permission. He had to force his brain to concentrate when all he wanted to do was sink into her touch. "You don't want your old life back?"

"Nope."

Her body shifted against his and her lips brushed his. "I want a new one. With you."

He pulled her closer and took over the kiss. There was no more talking about lives, new or old. But for the first time in a long time, when he walked into his house an hour later and fell into his bed, he knew his days of being alone were over.

Meredith woke up wondering if she'd dreamed the events of the day before. She still wasn't convinced it had happened until she pulled into the parking lot of her office. Gray leaned against the sign that reserved her spot, and he held two coffees and a paper bag.

She pinched her arm. Not dreaming.

She grabbed her things, hopped out, and walked to him. She knew her smile was goofy, and she didn't care. "Good morning."

"Morning."

She hadn't needed to know how delicious he sounded early in the morning. But now she did. Mercy.

"Is one of those for me?" She nodded toward the coffee.

"Yes." He leaned toward her. "You should know that it's going to be all over town by midmorning. There were two middle-aged ladies in Mountain Brew eavesdropping on my conversation with Judy. One of them pulled out her phone and took a picture of me."

Meredith took the coffee. "Nosy Nellies."

"Intrusive and unacceptable is what it was. What do you think they're going to do with the picture?"

"Probably send it to Granny with a note explaining what was going on when they took it."

"What is wrong with people?"

Grumpy Gray was also rather appealing. Interesting that she didn't mind him like this as long as his grumpiness wasn't directed toward her.

She took a sip of her drink. "What is this?" She tasted it again. "It's delicious."

"I tried to order you a caramel macchiato. Judy said this was a new drink and that you wanted to try it. It's a maple praline latte, I think."

"Mmm." Meredith approved. "What are you drinking?"

"Americano with a splash of cream."

"I thought you would say black coffee."

"I had enough black coffee while I was overseas. I promised myself I'd never willingly drink it black again."

"Good to know." She entered the key code to her office, and Gray opened the door for her. "Thank you."

"My pleasure."

He followed her into her personal office and placed the paper bag and his coffee on her desk. She set her bag on the floor, and as soon as she put her coffee down, his hands came around her waist and he pulled her close.

She couldn't get as close as she'd been last night. He wore a vest under his uniform, and his belt held all the things cops usually had with them. It made the hugging a bit of a dicey proposition.

But she wasn't going to let that stop her. She let her hands land at his waist and made no protest when his lips found hers. He pulled away a fraction and whispered, "I woke up this morning and knew I wouldn't be able to focus today until I made sure this is really happening."

When he was done confirming that she was his, she blinked up at him and said, "Will you be able to concentrate now?"

He shook his head. "Not a chance. Might need to come over here a few times to be sure we're still good."

"Well, I would never shirk my civic duty. I want to be sure you can work at full capacity, so whatever you need . . ."

"I'll hold you to that." He kissed her nose and stepped away. "Although, too much of that might addle my brain permanently." He took the bag to the small table in her office and opened it.

"I'm pretty sure you'll get used to it."

His grin was positively devilish. "Oh, I don't think I'll be getting used to it anytime soon." He pulled out a muffin and a scone. "Which do you want?"

"Can we split them?"

"Of course." He broke each one in half, and she joined him at the table.

He took her hand. "Can I ask the blessing?"

Meredith wanted to say, "Yes, you can ask the blessing, and I love that this is how you want to start our first morning as a couple, and you don't realize it yet, but I'm so gone for you that I'm never, ever coming back." What she did was nod.

"Dear heavenly Father, thank you for this food and thank you for miracles. Amen."

She picked up her half of the scone. "Miracles?"

"You kissed me." He took half of the muffin. "If that isn't a miracle, I don't know what is."

She took a bite and waited until his mouth was full before she said, "The real miracle is that *you* kissed *me*."

262

They laughed and talked about their day, the wedding in Neeson, Cassie and Donovan's upcoming wedding, and Cassie's anticipated reaction to the monstrosity of a floral arrangement.

Breakfast was over far too soon, and when Gray reached for her hand and started playing with her fingers, she knew he was going to say something she didn't like.

"One of my officers called this morning. Stomach bug."

Meredith tried not to react but failed. She took in a deep breath through her nose and then pinched her lips together.

Gray laughed. "How is it possible that you put your hands in people's mouths, and the thought of a little regurgitation makes you squirm?"

"Don't use that word. Don't even say it."

"So the v-word is out?"

She shuddered. "All the way out." His smile eased her discomfort, and she tried to explain. "I don't know what it is. I can handle blood. I can pull teeth and drill out cavities. But not that. Sorry. I'll make a horrible mother. My poor kids will be in the bathroom all alone. And heaven help me if they don't make it to the bathroom."

She shuddered again, and that's when the expression on Gray's face registered. "What's wrong?"

"Nothing." His voice was a little gruff. "But you shouldn't joke about that. You'll make a phenomenal mother. Having a phobia about something doesn't make you a bad mother. You'd deal with it if you had to. You wouldn't leave them alone to suffer without help. Your children will be blessed beyond belief."

Oh, there was so much to unpack there. "First, thank you. That's very kind of you."

"Second?"

"You really don't like it when I say anything negative about myself, do you?"

"No, I do not."

"Care to elaborate on that?"

Gray ran a thumb across her hand. "Words have power. I've seen words used as weapons. I've been on the receiving end of the wounds. But most of them were self-inflicted. If you say something negative to yourself long enough, you'll start to believe it."

Meredith shifted in her chair. "Sometimes the negative stuff is true. It isn't healthy to think you've attained perfection."

"True. But it isn't healthy to think negative stuff all the time. You're beautiful exactly as you are. Loved exactly as you are. If you want to make changes to yourself because they're part of your personal growth, that's great. But only if it's because it's what you really want, not because you think it will make people love you more or accept you more. If they don't love you for who you are, present tense, then they're missing out."

She should have said something more eloquent, but all she managed was a low-voiced, "Wow."

"Does it bother you? For me to tell you I don't like it when you talk about yourself that way?"

She took his question seriously. "I'm not sure yet. I mean, no. Not at the moment. Ten years from now, it might be getting old."

He bit back a smile. "Ten years from now, huh?"

Her skin heated as the implications of her words sunk in, but she didn't backtrack. "Full disclosure. I'm in it to win it. If you aren't, you should run for the hills, or maybe the coast. The hills are sketchy."

"Indeed, they are."

TWENTY-FIVE

Gray stayed with Meredith until her first patient arrived. And when he walked into the police station, he was greeted by two of his officers, Donovan and Brick.

"Told ya," Brick said to Donovan.

Donovan grinned. "Is it too soon to say welcome to the family, boss?"

"Your wedding is still a few months away," Gray said. "Still plenty of time for Cassie to come to her senses."

"Are you kidding? I'm in, man. Got the approval of Granny Quinn. There's no stopping me."

Brick gave Donovan a fist bump.

"Don't you two have work to do?" Gray walked to his office. Donovan and Brick fell in behind him.

"Nope. We've scared all the criminals out of town." Brick buffed his nails on his uniform.

"Yeah," Donovan scoffed. "Sent 'em straight to Neeson."

Brick groaned. "Sad but true."

Gray turned to his men. "Do you really have a quiet morning?"

"We could set up a speed trap?" Brick rubbed the back of his

265

neck. "Or walk around town and be a comforting presence to our citizens?"

"Or"—Gray pointed to the whiteboard in his office—"you could help me brainstorm a few things."

Both men nodded enthusiastically.

"Get some coffee and your laptops. Give me fifteen minutes to check my inbox."

They left and Gray blew through his email in record time. Something had been niggling at the back of his brain for a few days now. Maybe if he talked it out, he could pull it to the surface.

Donovan was, like him, a transplant to Gossamer Falls. Brick Nolan was another animal altogether. He was a born-and-bred native, proud of his Appalachian heritage, proud of his state, and proud of the fact that he had no chill whatsoever when it came to March Madness.

Brick had proven to be an invaluable resource. He, much like Cal, knew everyone in town and in most of the towns around Gossamer Falls. He also had a mother who was known as the worst gossip in four counties.

Granny Quinn told Gray early on not to say anything to Brick's mama that he didn't want the whole town to know in less than forty-eight hours. Gray had been convinced it was an exaggeration, but Brick had confirmed it.

Donovan and Brick had completely different styles but had meshed well together. Gray hoped their unique perspectives would help him see what he was missing.

When they returned, he had the whiteboard pulled front and center. He'd written *Meredith* in the middle of the board.

"Um, boss, not trying to tell you how to do your job or anything, but if you have to write her name on a whiteboard, you might need to seek professional help." Brick slid into the chair closest to the door.

"Nah, man, you got that all wrong," Donovan added, "he was practicing his spelling."

He ducked and the marker Gray had thrown at him went sailing past. It hit the wall and left a small green streak.

"You'd better not let Meredith see that you've defaced her pretty walls. She'll be back in here with a paintbrush." Donovan set his coffee down, retrieved the marker, and eyed the mark. "Yo, Glenda?"

"Yeah?" Glenda called back from her desk.

"You got one of those eraser things? Chief's marked up the wall."

Her laughter filtered down the hall. "Hang on."

A minute later, Glenda had produced the requested item. Gray restored the wall to its previous pristine state, and they were finally able to return to work.

"I want to brainstorm who is after Meredith and why. Mostly why." Gray tapped the pen on the board.

An hour later, the board looked like a toddler had attacked it. There were lines, circles, squares, a few triangles, and a lot of random question marks.

There were, however, no definitive answers.

"Meredith Quinn is a saint. She makes children like going to the dentist. I'm sorry, but no one likes to go to the dentist." Brick stared into a coffee cup, his second of the hour, and took a sip. "I don't like going either, but I go twice a year because Meredith makes it okay. Also because I've known her forever and she will hunt me down if I don't show up."

"Brick's right, Chief. As Papa Quinn would say, 'You picked a good 'un.'"

Gray wasn't going to tell him that Meredith had picked him and that he had no idea how he'd gotten so lucky, but he wasn't going to complain.

"But," Donovan continued, "it's obvious someone wants her. Based on what you told us about her sneaky activities in pursuit of sainthood, I'd say it's either that someone wants that girl Meredith helped out of the arranged marriage or they want to scare her so bad she'll stop going to Neeson."

"You don't think they want to kill her?" Brick asked the question before Gray could. "Because that whole thing where they nearly ran her and Bronwyn down sure seemed like they wanted her dead."

"Too random. Too sloppy. Too likely not to work. They got lucky that they managed to catch them alone and in a place where they could do that. Plus, I'm not convinced Meredith was the target. I think Bronwyn has more to worry about when it comes to people who want her dead."

"I want to come back to the Bronwyn situation," Brick said, "but finish telling us why you're leaning toward them wanting to grab her more than kill her." Gray agreed, but he wanted to see if their reasoning was the same.

"The fuel line, the bug, the tracking, that's the thing you do if you either want to catch someone talking about something, or you want to snatch them. And, I hate to be blunt like this, Chief, but if they really wanted her dead, they could have done it before now. You didn't lock her down until the last few weeks. She's been rambling all over the mountains for years."

Donovan nodded. "I agree."

"Is the girl from the arranged marriage safe? Has anyone checked lately?"

Gray had intentionally left her name off the board, but he'd shared it with the men. Even so, he appreciated that they weren't using the name out loud now. "Mo knows how to find her. I don't think he knows where she is." Not because he couldn't find her if he wanted to, but because he'd chosen not to. "But he knows the people who helped her. He confirmed her safety a few days ago and sent a warning to her to be on guard."

"If we knew more about this girl, it might help." Brick ran his hands over his face. "I hate to say this. I really do. But it might be time for me to bring in the gossip group."

Gray groaned.

"I can be sly about it. But you know my mother knows all the dirt in a hundred-mile radius."

"Fine. I can't believe I'm saying this, but go have lunch with your mother."

Donovan raised his hand. "Can I go? Please? His mama is a phenomenal cook."

Gray tossed another marker at Donovan's head. "You're marrying a world-class chef!"

"I am aware." Donovan caught the marker and tossed it back. "And even she says Brick's mama makes the best chicken fried steak she's ever put in her mouth. Also the best chow chow."

"The best what?"

"Chow chow." Brick nodded sagely. "It's like a relish. Kind of. You can put it on anything. Mama cans it and gives it away. You haven't tried it?"

And that was how Gray found himself at Brick's childhood home two hours later, pulled up to the table as Lorraine Nolan showed him a small glass jar. "This is chow chow. You take this one on home with you later. We'll have some with our meal."

"Yes, ma'am."

When Brick called, she'd told him she had a pot of beans on, and they could come over for beans, country ham, and cornbread.

Mrs. Nolan sliced a tomato and some onion but mourned how awful the tomato would be because "you just can't get a fit tomato in February" and then set the food out for them to dig in.

Gray watched as Brick, Donovan, and Mr. Nolan, who had

made it a point to come home at lunch when he heard she was "fixing a spread," filled their plates, and he copied them precisely.

His first bite was tentative, but the chow chow turned out to be unbelievably good on the beans. And by the third bite, he understood why Brick and Donovan had been so excited.

"This is delicious, Mrs. Nolan." He took a sip of tea so sweet he could almost stand a spoon in it.

"Thank you, young man. I'm so glad you like it."

"Bet you didn't eat like this growing up, did ya, son?" Mr. Nolan asked.

"No, sir. Not like this."

The conversation was easy, and Mr. and Mrs. Nolan were gentle and sarcastic to each other in turns.

Gray intended to let Brick lead this dance, and he wasn't surprised when he didn't start with the main question. "Mama, you got anything we need to know about?"

His dad snorted. "I told you they wanted something."

Mrs. Nolan gave Brick a look that could strip paint. "What on earth do you think I know, young man?"

"Now, Mama, we all know you know everything. You can't deny it."

She pinched her lips together. "I know you'll not be getting any blackberry cobbler." She pointed her fork at all three officers. "Not a one of you. You'll watch him"—she pointed at Mr. Nolan—"eat it and you'll weep for being scoundrels."

"We're the good guys, Mrs. Nolan." Donovan clasped his hands together. "Please don't banish me from your kitchen."

"Mama, you're gonna get me in trouble with the chief," Brick implored, and Gray kicked him under the table.

But Mrs. Nolan wasn't having it. "Your chief should know better."

"Mama, we were talking about how good your cooking is. We

mentioned your chow chow, and one thing led to another. That's why we're here."

"Mm-hmm." She was miffed.

"Can you blame us for trying to see what's going on? While we're here, we might as well catch up."

That seemed to appease her. Slightly. "I know word has gone out that if you get caught with your honey at Gossamer Falls, the chief won't rat you out. But he will run you off."

Gray hid his smile in another sip of tea.

"And I know you"—she pointed a piece of cornbread at Gray—"are sparking Meredith Quinn. And it's about time too. What took you so long?"

Gray had never heard the term "sparking," but he figured it out in context. Given the way she was looking at him, he decided the question hadn't been rhetorical. "I'm an idiot, ma'am, but I've come to my senses."

"Glad to hear it. She's an angel." She narrowed her eyes at him. "Although, I heard tell that she's caused some stir in Neeson. You might want to tell her to take it easy up there."

Gray tried to keep his expression neutral. "I'll do that, ma'am. Is there anything specific?"

"Oh, I'll say there is. My cousin's second ex-wife is from Neeson. We talk. Dena said there's a rumor that old Johnstone's got himself a couple of kids that nobody knew about." She nodded grimly. "He's been married to the same woman for going on forty years, but rumor is there's at least two kids in town who look an awful lot like him, even though they're no relation. Or they aren't supposed to be."

"How old are these kids?" Brick asked.

"One's not more than five, but Dena says her mama says he looks just like Marvin Johnstone did as a kid. Same eyes. Same hair. There's a teenager, and then there's that girl that run off. She didn't look like him a bit. Spitting image of her mama. Not even sure if Johnstone knew about it for a long time."

Gray forced himself to take a bite. The food was delicious, but his gut was churning.

Mrs. Nolan buttered a piece of cornbread and kept talking. "The rumor is that the girl didn't know but found out somehow and that's when she disappeared. You'd think her mama'd be worried about her, but she isn't. Of course, the other rumor is that she ran off with some guy twenty years older than her. That one might have more truth to it."

"Why do you say that?"

"Now, Chief, you know Johnstone wouldn't have let her go. He won't let his other kids go either. Not if he knows they're his. I hear the ones he knows about, he helps take care of them. Not in person, of course, but he gives the mamas money."

"Why would he take care of them?" Donovan asked. "I mean, if they don't know?"

"Just 'cause they don't know doesn't mean everybody else don't know." Mr. Nolan shook his head. "It's not right. He doesn't acknowledge them, but at least he doesn't leave 'em to starve either. 'Bout the only good thing I can say about the man, and that's precious little."

"He can't very well claim them without ruining his reputation." Mrs. Nolan's mouth was pinched into a line so thin you couldn't see her lips anymore.

"That's rich." Brick took a big bite of his beans. "Everybody knows he's a criminal."

"Yeah, but they pretend they don't. Dena says he goes to church. Gives big to the building fund and missions. Has coffee with Kirby once a week."

"And runs drugs the rest of the time." Donovan set his fork down. "Do you think he would have hurt this girl? The one who ran off? If she found out he was her dad and was disgusted by him?"

"I don't rightly know. She was a pretty little thing. And such a pretty name. What was it?"

Gray tensed.

Mrs. Nolan snapped her fingers. "Amara. That's it. Isn't that pretty? And so unusual."

Gray shared a look with Donovan and Brick, and he saw the same realization in their eyes that he knew was in his.

Meredith had helped Marvin Johnstone's illegitimate daughter escape him.

And somehow, Johnstone knew.

TWENTY-SIX

Two days later, Meredith climbed from Mo's Jeep at Papa and Granny Quinn's house for their monthly Sunday dinner. Mo fell into step beside her.

They'd only gone five steps when Meredith stopped walking. "Really?" She put her hands on her hips and glared at her barely older brother.

"What?" Mo was all innocence.

"We're at Papa and Granny's." She hissed the words. "You don't have to stay within reach every minute of the day. No one is going to kill me here."

Mo stepped closer and his voice was a bare whisper. "Rein in the drama, baby sister." He cut his eyes to the porch where Granny and Aunt Rhonda sat, despite the fact that it was barely over forty degrees outside. "I know you're scared and you're tired of everyone hovering." He made a sour face. "And you haven't seen Gray all weekend." She started to speak, but he put a hand up. "Don't deny it. Don't even try."

She relaxed her body but kept her glare on full beam. A car parked behind them, but she kept her eyes on Mo. "Ever since Gray called on Friday, you and Cal have been insufferable. I didn't need anyone sleeping in my guest loft, but that's where you've been. I didn't need a ride to church, but you gave me one. You think I'm scared? You're right. But your incessant hovering isn't helping."

Mo was unrepentant. "We can discuss my perfectly rational levels of caution later. But not here. Papa and Granny don't know, Mer. If you don't calm down . . ."

"Maybe I could help with that." Gray stepped out from behind Mo and inserted himself into the very small space between Meredith and her brother. Mo immediately stepped back. Meredith didn't move.

Gray brushed his thumb across her cheek, an action that was becoming familiar and welcome. "I thought I told you not to worry."

The sound of fake retching came from behind them.

"Mo, I've got her," Gray said, not taking his eyes off Meredith. "Why don't you go inside and give us a minute."

Mo grumbled something unintelligible and then reached in between them and pulled her away from Gray.

"Hey!" she protested.

But Mo squeezed her close and whispered in her ear, "I won't apologize."

Then he released her and took off toward the house.

Gray put an arm around her waist. "I've never known you two to fight the way you've been lately."

She looked at Mo's retreating back. "We don't usually. I guess mortal danger is bringing out the worst in us." She dropped her head to Gray's chest, careful to choose a spot that wouldn't involve poking herself in the face with his badge.

"I missed you." Gray's lips brushed her outer ear. "I wanted to be with you this weekend."

"Same." She pulled away and linked her arm with his. They started toward the porch. "Not that I'm upset about it, but why are you here? Aren't you on duty?"

"I've been on duty for the past seventy-two hours. I might have to dash out of here, but I'm hopeful that Gossamer Falls can hold it together for a few hours." He waved at Granny Quinn. "And I have a standing invitation for Sunday lunch."

As if talking about lunch triggered it, his stomach rumbled loud enough for her to hear.

"Have you eaten today?"

"Does coffee count?"

"No," she said. "Did you eat yesterday?"

"I think I ate a pack of crackers last night."

"Chief Ward, there's to be none of that mess." Granny Quinn's voice was a combination of sharp and concerned. They must have gotten close enough to the porch for her to overhear. "Why didn't you eat breakfast?"

"Sorry, ma'am. Duty called."

Granny humphed. "I heard you got called by a bunch of hooligans who got drunk last night and then woke up in the wrong house."

"What?" Meredith looked from Granny to Gray. "And how would you know, Granny?"

"It was all over the church this morning. If you'd been early, you'd have heard all about it." There was a hint of censure in the comment.

"You can take that up with Mo, Granny. I was ready to go. He made me late."

"Mo!" Granny's voice pierced through the gathering Quinns. Mo came at a jog. "Yes, ma'am."

"You best be getting to church a little bit earlier, young man."

Mo's jaw twitched, but he gave Granny a sharp salute. "Ma'am, yes ma'am." And then he made a quick retreat.

Granny looked after him, then turned back to Meredith. "Something you're not telling me?"

"Meredith!" Aunt Minnie careened down the porch steps and straight into Meredith's welcoming arms. Saved by Aunt Minnie.

"Minnie Moo! How are you?"

Aunt Minnie looked at Gray. "You brought your policeman."

Meredith decided not to try to explain that Gray had just appeared. "I did."

Aunt Minnie looked at Granny. "See, Mama. She got it sorted."

Granny gave her daughter the same smile she'd been giving her for over sixty years. "Yes, she did. You were right."

Aunt Minnie's face was lit with the joy that she almost always seemed to carry with her. "Come on, Merry. Mama made my favorite."

"Can Gray come too?"

Aunt Minnie gave her a look. "He's yours, Merry. Of course he can come."

Granny and Aunt Rhonda made no attempt to hide their glee. "Well, I do believe Minnie's got the right of it." Aunt Rhonda nudged Granny. "How many grandmother-of-the-bride dresses do you have to buy this year?"

Meredith grabbed Gray's hand and indicated that Aunt Minnie should lead the way to the kitchen before her grandmother and aunt had them going to the chapel before they had their second date.

They made it into the house and hit a wall of heat and people. "Now I understand why they're sitting on the porch." Meredith saw her dad and he saw them.

"Minnie. Bring my baby girl over here, won't you, sweetheart?"

Aunt Minnie tugged on Meredith's hand, and Meredith clung to Gray with her other hand. This was so not how she'd envisioned introducing Gray to the family. Not that everyone hadn't already met him, of course.

But in the Quinn family, if you showed up with a date, that

person had to be prepared. Everyone was always welcome at the Quinn table, but if your relationship status had moved beyond friendship, an entirely different level of scrutiny was brought to bear.

Aunt Minnie reached her brother first, and he grabbed his older sister and pressed a kiss to her temple. "There's my first girl. How are you today? You didn't even speak to me at church."

Aunt Minnie preened under his attention. "I helped in children's church."

"Well, then that's okay." He looked at Meredith and very obviously allowed his gaze to linger on her hand, firmly clasped in Gray's. He returned his attention to Minnie. "Could I borrow Meredith and Gray for a minute?"

Aunt Minnie grinned. "I'm taking Merry into the kitchen for some ham."

"Minnie, you haven't been sneaking ham, have you?"

She giggled and ran off.

Meredith faced her father. Gray stood straight at her back, and she got the sense that if he could stand beside her, or even in front of her, he would. But they were in a corner, and there wasn't anywhere to go.

She wasn't sure what to say. She had nothing to be ashamed of. She'd done nothing wrong. And for that matter, neither had Gray. Well, okay, so he'd broken her heart. But he was sorry.

Yeah. That was not the argument to use with her dad. But how could she explain it? Gray had hurt her. But he apologized. And he explained. And she believed him. And she cared about him—okay, fine, she'd been in love with him for a while. So she was willing to see where things went.

If her family couldn't get on board with that, then they were going to have a problem. And by "they," she meant her family. She and Gray would be fine. "Hi, Dad."

"Hey, baby girl." Her father pointedly looked over her shoulder. "Gray."

"Sir." Gray didn't sound nervous.

"You hurt her again, you'd better not show up for lunch. You hear me?"

"Dad—"

"Won't happen, sir."

"Better not."

"Dad—"

"Glad we got that straight. One of the kids messed with the thermostat and it's hot as blazes in here. Dad opened a few windows. Should cool off soon enough. Granny and Rhonda went to the front porch, but it's too cold for your mom. She went to the sunroom. Go see her before lunch. She's got it in her head that you and Mo are fighting."

He kissed her cheek, slapped Gray on the shoulder, and maneuvered through the crowd. He called out, "All the little hooligans, let's go outside and burn off some energy." And like some kind of mountain-man pied piper, he led most of her cousins under the age of fifteen into the yard.

Meredith turned to face Gray. "I'm so sorry."

"For what?" He seemed genuinely confused.

"My dad. He's usually nicer than that."

"He's looking out for his daughter. I respect that. If some man treated my daughter the way I treated you? I don't know that I would be so forgiving."

"That wasn't forgiving. That was putting you on notice."

"Oh, I know." Gray smiled. "But I'm not worried."

"He didn't have to be so blunt."

"What's the matter?" Gray studied her. "Are you worried about me? Do you think I'm upset?"

"Clearly you aren't. But I am. He should treat you better than that. I hope he doesn't plan to act this way for long. I won't stand for it."

———

Gray would have given up dessert for a decade to be alone with Meredith in this moment. As it was, he leaned toward her and whispered, "Sweetheart, I love the way you're trying to protect me from your family. I really do. But I promise you, I'm fine. Your dad and I are fine."

He stepped back, but her expression still hadn't cleared. Was this what it was like to have a woman care about you? Was this protectiveness, this worry, going to be part of his life? Was this what he'd been missing? Because if so, he'd been a fool.

The warmth in his chest trickled through his entire body, and it was a heat that had nothing to do with the stifling temperature of the room.

"Let's go find your mom and then we can go for a walk."

Meredith was quiet as she led him toward the back of the house. They entered a room that had probably been an open back deck at some point but now was enclosed with large windows. This space was noticeably cooler than the rest of the house, but significantly warmer than it was outside. Gray concluded there was no heat or A/C in this room.

Jacqueline sat in a rocking chair, and when they entered her face lit. "Oh, there you are." She stood and gave Meredith a hug, and then hugged Gray. He patted her in what had to be the world's most awkward hug. For one thing, he was in full uniform, which made all hugs a bit weird.

But the real issue was that she was hugging him. Why?

"Oh, don't look so surprised." She winked at him and patted his arm. "Mothers take a different approach. Dads get grumpy.

Brothers get dramatic. But a mother? She sees the way her daughter's spark has grown brighter, and the way she's all fierce and determined to defend you. I bet Doug gave you a hard time, didn't he? And it got her all riled up."

Jacqueline returned to the rocking chair. "She's protective of those she loves. You'll get used to it. Or maybe you won't. That might be better. A lifetime of delight is hardly a bad way to live. I should know. My husband's the same way."

She turned her attention on Meredith, then patted the arm of the chair beside her. "Now, come here and tell me why you're fighting with Mo."

Meredith, her expression a bit befuddled, took the seat her mother had indicated. Gray took up a post leaning against a window, where he could see both women.

"What makes you think we're fighting, Mama?"

"I'm not as strong as I used to be, but my brain works just fine, Meredith Catherine Quinn."

Uh-oh. She'd full-named her.

"You were almost late for church. You sat by Mo, but you both looked like little thunderclouds. You didn't speak to him. You didn't turn your head in his direction even once. While he—what's the term?—oh yes, he had his head on a swivel."

Gray coughed a little. Jacqueline knew her children well.

"Spill." There was command in that word, and Meredith dropped her head.

"He won't leave me alone. He follows me everywhere. He's convinced someone is going to jump out of the trees and grab me. He's making me paranoid."

"It isn't paranoia if the threat is real," Gray muttered.

Jacqueline pointed at him. "Exactly." She shifted in her seat. "He's trying to protect you, Merry-girl. He's lost so much. He can't lose you. You know that."

Gray wasn't sure what loss they were discussing, but now wasn't the time to ask.

"He's suffocating me."

"He's a Quinn." Jacqueline winked. "It's a family characteristic." She leaned back in her chair and rocked a few times. "As I recall, I had to have a conversation with you about the very real possibility of *you* loving *me* to death."

Meredith looked at the ceiling. "That was different."

"How so?"

"I wasn't . . ."

When Meredith didn't say anything more, her mother prompted, "What's that, dear? Oh, wait. Let me guess. You've just realized that he's making you mad because he does the same thing you do. And you don't like that at all." She stood and patted Meredith's hand. "I'm going to see if they've got things sorted so we can eat. I'm starving. You be sure to make up with your brother before you run off with Gray."

"Mama!" Meredith flushed.

"Please. I'm not an idiot. You'll be dragging him out for a walk by the river before we're halfway done eating."

"He's on call, Mama."

"Well, that changes things. Better get that walk in first." She grinned a sly grin, patted Gray's arm, and disappeared into the house.

Gray took the seat she'd vacated and waited for Meredith to speak.

"I wish I could tell you this is abnormal behavior, but I can't. My family's always like this."

"If by 'this,' you mean exuberantly loving, wildly protective, and fiercely loyal, then, yeah, they are. And you are the luckiest woman in the world to have that."

"True, but today they're driving me bonkers." Meredith popped to her feet. "Come on. Let's go eat. You're starving, and I need to find Mo."

Gray hadn't seen her in two days. They were in an empty room at the back of the house. And he had no plans to wait for a walk that might not happen.

He stood, spun her around, and placed his hands on her shoulders. "Meredith." Her eyes were wide, her mouth parted, and she made a soft sound that indicated that she'd heard him. "I'm not that hungry."

She slid her hands up his arms and laced them around his neck. "In that case . . ." She pressed her lips to his, and he knew no one else would ever touch him the way she did.

And when she ended the kiss far sooner than he wanted her to and insisted that he get some food before someone in Gossamer Falls did something stupid that required his assistance, he knew that no one else would ever be protective of him the way she was.

She bullied family members to clear a path and made sure he had a full plate of food and a separate plate for dessert. Holding her own plate, which held nothing more than a green salad, in front of her, she led the way to one of the tables set up in the garage. They sat beside each other, and while he inhaled the first real meal he'd had in two days, she picked at her salad.

Until Mo sat down across from her and slid a full plate of food to her. "Eat."

Gray made note of the items on the plate. Deviled eggs. Mac and cheese. A yeast roll. Mashed potatoes. Ham. Green beans.

Meredith slid her salad to Mo and said, "Then you eat this."

Mo grinned and took a huge bite of the salad. Meredith took a big bite of mashed potatoes.

Jacqueline walked by, saw the three of them, and smiled. "It makes me so happy to see you getting along."

Mo blew her a kiss, and she caught it and then walked away.

"What am I missing?" Gray asked.

Mo spoke around a bite. "Meredith doesn't like salad, and I only like salads when someone else makes them."

"You don't like salad?" She'd seemed to enjoy the wedge salad he'd made for her Thursday night.

"I like salads, but not at Granny's. Why would I eat a salad when I can eat this?" She waved a forkful of mac and cheese in his direction.

She had a point. And he had a lot to learn. He thought he'd been paying attention. Thought he had catalogued many of the things that made Meredith tick, but there was still so much he didn't know.

Cal and Landry joined them at their table a few moments later.

Landry had a roll, mashed potatoes, and a piece of ham on her plate. Nothing more. Weird. Landry usually had a little bit of everything.

For a few moments, everyone ate, and the conversation was light and innocuous. Cal scooped up a spoonful of corn and asked, "When will you have time for some target practice?"

Gray wasn't sure if the question was meant for him or Meredith.

Meredith's grumbled "Never" answered the question for him.

"Come on. It wouldn't hurt you to get some practice in."

Landry placed a hand on Cal's forearm. He looked at her, and even from where Gray was, he could tell she was saying "Shut up" without uttering a single word.

Mo, oblivious to the tiny drama happening on the other side of him, nodded enthusiastically. "Maybe some hand-to-hand? Or grappling?"

Meredith was coiled so tight beside him, Gray imagined that if Cal or Mo said one more word, she was going to start pinging around the room like she was in a pinball machine.

"Will y'all excuse us? I'm going to have to go back to work soon, and I need to talk to Meredith."

"Talk?" Cal and Mo said the word, with the same incredulous inflection, at the same time.

Meredith stood, slid her chair in, grabbed her plate, and high-tailed it away from the table without a backward glance.

Gray leaned across and spoke to Mo and Cal. "Back off."

Both men's expressions hardened, but Gray didn't stay to chat. He followed Meredith outside. Once they were away from the house, he took her hand. She rested her head on his arm, and he happily followed her lead.

When the well-worn path they were on led them to the river, then to a bench that overlooked it, he took a seat beside her. She didn't seem to be in a hurry to talk, so he put his arm around her shoulders and held her until she rested against him.

"I don't want to die, Gray." Her broken words sent a shaft of terror into his heart.

"I can't promise you complete safety, but between me, Mo, Cal, your dad, and pretty much your entire family, we're going to do all we can to be sure that won't happen. I just got you, Meredith. There's no way I'm going to lose you now."

He got another ten minutes to cuddle her, to whisper things like "I've got you" and "We'll be okay" in between pressing kisses to her hair, twisting his fingers with hers, and doing everything he could to comfort her.

Then his phone rang. He answered.

"Sorry, boss," Brick said. "I'm okay to man the fort, but I can't go out on any calls. The stomach bug that's been going around got me."

"I'll be there in twenty."

He put his phone back in his pocket.

"I'm sorry I dumped this on you. You have so much on your

plate. But if I tell my parents or Mo that I'm scared, they'll freak out." She dropped her head against his chest and took a few deep breaths.

"It's probably too soon for this, but I'm going to put this out there."

She looked up at him.

"I want to be the one you run to. The one you call when you're overwhelmed. The first person you want to see when you're scared. I don't want to replace your family or your friends. I don't want to take their place in your life. But I want to have my own place. And I want it to be the safest place you've ever known."

He'd told Brick it would be twenty. It was more like forty.

TWENTY-SEVEN

Meredith led their caravan to the church at seven Saturday morning. There were so many plants in her 4Runner, it was like driving a mobile greenhouse up the mountain.

Gray followed her in his Explorer. He had all the bridal party flowers. Lydia's bouquet was much like the young woman herself. Classic and mostly traditional, but with unique touches that set them apart. Her flowers were white, nestled in lush greenery, with one rose so red it leaned toward black. The bridesmaids' bouquets were similar to the bride's but on a smaller scale. The boutonnieres were all the deepest red, and they were going to pop against the gray tuxes.

Everything was tucked into boxes designed to protect it from being squished in transit, but today, the need for the boxes was even more crucial.

Meredith's windshield wipers whipped back and forth. The rain hadn't stopped for four days. Papa said if it didn't quit soon, the Appalachians might float off somewhere new.

Lydia had made the tough call to cancel her river reception. The wedding guests would be invited to the church's fellowship hall for a smaller gathering, and then the bride and groom would hit the road.

Meredith had worked nonstop to make a few arrangements that would spruce up the fellowship hall. Thankfully, she'd been inside it enough that she didn't need to make a trip to Neeson.

A landslide had blocked a road in Gossamer County last night. Gray should have been handling the scene, but when she hesitantly suggested that Mo come with her instead of him, he refused to consider it. "I have faith in my men, Meredith. They can handle the town for a few hours."

"But you're exhausted and cold."

"It's nothing coffee and a shower can't fix."

He'd been outside most of the night, wearing one of those head-to-toe rain slickers, boots, and a huge hat. It had helped him stay dry but hadn't helped him stay warm. The temperature had insisted on hanging out in the upper thirties all week, making for miserable outdoor conditions.

But there'd been no point in arguing. The only redeeming factor about this wedding was that it was scheduled for 11:00 a.m. The ceremony would be over by 11:30, and when it was over and the pictures had been taken, she and Gray would pack up all the live greenery from the church and hightail it back to Gossamer Falls.

The new reception plan would be a simple affair with cake and punch only. The bride and groom planned to spend their wedding night in Asheville, then fly to Jamaica for their honeymoon. With everyone crammed into the small space, Meredith had no qualms whatsoever about leaving early.

Meredith's tires hit standing water and lost traction for a moment. She gripped the steering wheel tighter and focused on the road. Ten more minutes to the church and then she could trade her "driving in the rain" anxiety for the fancier "hope I don't get kidnapped at the wedding" anxiety.

Mo had been in her living room when she woke up, sipping his expensive coffee and pecking away at his computer. He'd made her breakfast and hugged her hard before she left.

Her dad had called and prayed for her over the phone, then he told her he loved her and he'd see her and Gray for supper that night.

Her mom had joined in on the conversation and there'd been no hint of fear in her voice when she said, "I'm so proud of you, Merry-girl."

Meredith had to go fix her makeup after that.

Landry let it slip that Cal and Mo intended to drive toward the county line so they could react faster should there be a need.

And Cassie let it slip that the patrol route for today had been modified and included a heavy Gossamer Falls police presence in the area bordering Neeson County.

Of course, that had been before the mudslide.

But still. Gray was with her.

The church was one of the first buildings you came to as you drove into Neeson from Gossamer Falls, and Meredith unclenched her jaw when she saw it. She parked as close as she could to the side door, and before she could gather her phone and keys, Gray was at her door, huge umbrella overhead, ready to assist.

They didn't talk as they raced to the door and found it, as promised, unlocked. "You stay right here where I can see you," Gray shouted above the rain. "I'll unload the cars."

"That's ridiculous," she shouted back. "I can—"

"Meredith!"

"What?"

He kissed her. Hard. Fast. Then said, "Please let me do this."

She stood to the side while he went out into the storm.

"This could be a problem," she said out loud. She'd been

prepared to stand her ground, and that kiss had short-circuited her arguments.

When he brought in the first load of flowers, she stepped closer to him. "Just so you know, you can't get your way by kissing me."

He put one hand on her chin and pressed his lips to hers again. This kiss was slow and a little bit teasing. "You sure about that?" He winked and went back outside.

"Is it hot in here? It can't be hot in here." She spoke aloud again. Great. Not only did she have a spine that was about as stiff as cake batter, but now she was asking herself questions and answering them . . . out loud.

This time, when he came back in, she stayed several steps back and waited for him to set his burdens down.

"Why are you standing way back there?" Gray's expression was entirely too smug for his health. "Scared?"

"No."

He laughed so hard she could hear him over the rain.

He would be insufferable now. And if he clued in to how his kisses made her dizzy? She'd never hear the end of it.

She waited until he put everything down and then she made her move. She grabbed the sides of his rain slicker and leaned into him. She claimed a kiss of her own and was gratified when he made no move to take over. In fact, when she finally turned him loose, he seemed to be a bit unsteady as he returned for another trip to the car.

And it hit her. It was okay if his kisses left her confused and discombobulated because hers did the same to him. They were on even ground.

And it was fun.

And helped settle her nerves.

She had a goofy grin on her face as she organized the flowers Gray brought inside. After he made his final trip, he parked both of their vehicles and stripped off his rain slicker at the door before coming all the way in.

He'd brought his own change of clothes, as well as hers. They'd talked about it last night and each packed a dry set of clothes that they could change into so they wouldn't have to work while soaking wet. Then they'd change into their finery for the wedding itself.

He insisted on checking the bathroom to be sure it was empty before she went inside to change, then waited in the small sitting area around the corner. They switched places so he could change, and then they went to work.

Gray quickly caught her vision for the space and turned out to have an excellent eye for where the arrangements would work best. "You're a much better helper than Mo or Cal," she told him.

He brushed imaginary lint from his shoulders. "I'm a man of many talents."

With his help, everything was arranged in record time. "I may have to hire you for future events."

He took a photo of the space and said, "As long as I can hang out with you, I'll do anything you want."

"What I want for today is to go back to your place, put on our comfiest clothes, get a fire roaring in your fireplace, curl up in that ginormous chair you have, and take a nap."

"You really are the perfect woman."

Their conversation was interrupted by the arrival of the bridal party. And from that moment on, chaos reigned.

An hour before the ceremony, Gray stood with Meredith at the back of the sanctuary and watched as a frantic bridesmaid ran down the center aisle and disappeared through the doors to the right of the platform, only to emerge thirty seconds later through the doors at the left of the platform holding a hair dryer like she'd been in a shootout. She ran back down the center aisle, and when she reached the doors to the foyer, she called out, "I got it."

Beside him Meredith sniggered, then leaned close to whisper, "There are no words for me to express to you how relieved I am that I only agreed to coordinate the flowers."

"Why is everything so disorganized?" Gray hadn't been to many weddings, but Cal and Landry's wedding hadn't been like this.

Meredith lifted her hands up. "Who knows? They're young and they're winging it. I'm not sure if anyone is in charge."

"This scenario makes a strong case for elopement." Gray hadn't given much thought to having a wedding of his own until quite recently. But was this level of drama worth it?

Meredith cleared her throat. "Connor and Carla did that over twenty years ago, and Aunt Carol still gets a pained look on her face anytime it comes up. I might be jumping the gun here, but if you have any thoughts of marrying into the Quinn family, you should know that elopements are frowned upon."

Gray turned so he was facing Meredith. "Just so we're clear, I don't have thoughts about marrying into the Quinn family. I have detailed plans. Step one was getting you to go out with me. Step two was getting you to kiss me."

"You're two for two." There was a husky quality to her voice that Gray couldn't dwell on. "What's step three?"

"Winning over the family."

"Three for three."

"I don't know about that."

"I do. Papa stopped by on Monday to pick up Aunt Minnie to take her to one of the boys' basketball games. He said, 'You've got a good one, Meredith. I like him.' Coming from Papa? That's high praise."

"What about your dad?"

"He's always going to be protective. Doesn't mean he doesn't approve."

"Mo?"

Before Meredith could answer, Gray's phone buzzed. "Excuse me." He accepted the call. "Ward."

"Chief, we got the road cleared, but Glenda got three calls within five minutes of each other. All three are up near the Neeson County line. All three called to report a loud noise. One said it sounded like an explosion. One said it sounded like a sonic boom from a military aircraft. And one said he thought it was another landslide. Given what we just saw, my vote is door number three."

"I agree."

"Want me to check it out?"

"Not alone."

"Brick can come with. Glenda is staying at the office to field any calls."

"She doesn't typically work on Saturday. Why is she staying?"

Donovan's voice dropped in volume. "I got the feeling she didn't want to discuss it, but she broke up with that guy she's been seeing in Boone."

Gray bumped his head on the wall. "She only dated him for a few months."

"I guess she thought it was serious."

"And he didn't."

"Not serious enough. Cassie says he cheated on her."

All Gray's protective instincts kicked in. His men would be feeling the same way. "Make sure it's clear that no one is to take matters into their own hands."

"Yes, sir."

"Okay, you and Brick check it out. Let me know. The ceremony starts in forty-five minutes. Don't call me unless it's an emergency."

"Got it."

Gray slid the phone into his pocket. "You heard all that?"

Meredith nodded. "I feel bad for Glenda, but she needs to make better choices. I wish she and Brick would get together."

Gray shook his head. "No. Nope. Bad idea. Office romances are complicated at best, and nuclear-level explosive at worst. Maybe we can find her someone local."

"Yeah, like Brick."

"I like Brick." Gray tried to picture the officer with the young woman who kept them all organized and was surprised when the image worked. "Huh."

"Told you." Meredith was smug. "I have matchmaking skills. I know things."

"If they didn't work together, I'd be all for it. As it is? Please, no."

Meredith laughed as she walked away from him to change. Lydia had invited her to join her and her bridesmaids in the room they'd converted into their dressing chamber. He didn't like having Meredith out of sight, but she should be safe with the bride.

He changed his own clothes in record time and returned to his self-appointed station outside the bridal area. Ten minutes later, Meredith put him out of his misery.

She breezed out of the room in a navy dress. The long-sleeved top was some kind of squishy material. Velvet maybe? And it fit tight to her body from the neck to her waist. The skirt material was something shimmery and hit her at mid-calf. On her feet were two barely-there high heels that matched the color of her skin. She was glorious. "I know you can't help it, but it's bad form to upstage the bride." He brushed a lock of hair from her shoulder.

Meredith's smile was warm and inviting. "Trust me. No one can upstage her. Not today. She's radiant."

"You like her."

"I do. I want her to make it. She and the groom have a tough

294

road ahead. They know they need to break some generational curses, and I believe they can do it."

Thirty minutes later, as Gray sat beside Meredith and watched the couple marry, he hoped she was right.

He also hoped that whatever was happening that had someone blowing up his phone wouldn't mar the beauty of this day.

TWENTY-EIGHT

The moment the couple—eyes glowing, faces shining—made their retreat down the aisle, Gray slid his phone from his pocket. He had multiple texts, but the strand from Faith stood out.

Please call me.

We need to talk now.

I tried to call you. Why aren't you answering?
The wedding. You're at the wedding. Call me as
soon as it's over. Johnstone is back in Neeson.

Meredith, reading over his shoulder, gasped. "He's here?"

"We need to leave. Now." Gray didn't want to upset her or mess up the couple's day, but right now he would gladly do both if it meant Meredith made it out of Neeson safely. "Please—"

"Let's go." She crammed her phone in her small bag and grabbed his arm.

He'd been willing to beg. And if that didn't work fast enough, he wasn't ashamed to admit that he was prepared to throw her over his shoulder and carry her away. Her willingness to follow his lead humbled him. It wasn't what she wanted to do, but she wasn't giving him a hard time, and when they were safely back in Gossamer Falls, he would thank her.

He glanced at the back of the church. It was packed with wedding guests who were reluctant to head out into the stormy weather. He didn't blame them, but getting jammed up in that crowd was a recipe for disaster.

He picked up the bags that held their clothes in one hand, took Meredith's hand in his other, and instead of joining the throng headed to the back of the church, he moved them toward the front. He had no idea what his face looked like, but something must have been telling people to move out of his way because they cleared a path.

When they broke free, twenty feet from the platform, he leaned down and whispered in Meredith's ear, "Are your keys in the big bag or your small one?"

She patted the small bag.

"Good. Our cars are still at the side door. You lead the way. I'll follow you."

"Okay."

They moved quietly to the side door and opened it. The rain was heavier than it had been this morning, and the wind had picked up. He looked to his left.

Looked again.

Meredith's 4Runner wasn't there.

She leaned around him. "Where's my car?"

Gray closed his eyes for a moment. *Lord, we're going to need some serious help here.*

He ran through his options. They could stay in the church. Call Chief Kirby to report the missing vehicle and deal with the fallout. But if they did that, Kirby might hand them over to Johnstone. The risk was too high.

They could take his car and head to Gossamer Falls. But that might be playing right into their hands. They stole Meredith's car. Were they trying to force them to use his SUV? If so, they'd probably done something to his vehicle. Best-case scenario it was a tracker. Worst case? A bomb. Unbidden, a vision of the desert appeared in his mind. Flames billowed from a vehicle. Cal was there. Their friends. Not all of them got out. No way he could take that risk.

They could leave on foot and head into the woods, then hunker down until someone from Gossamer Falls could come to get them. They'd get soaked, and the potential for hypothermia was high given the cold temperature. Meredith could wear his rain slicker. It wouldn't keep her warm, though. But at this point, hypothermia was less dangerous than Johnstone.

They could always call in his people and sit tight. But if someone came after them in the church, they might have to shoot their way out. Meredith had her personal firearm. But she'd never shot anyone and wasn't trained to do it. She would probably fire in self-defense, but her hesitation could be fatal.

He looked at Meredith. She was afraid, but she wasn't panicking. He shoved her bag toward her. "Change. Fast. Start with the pants and boots."

If they had to run, her heels—which would quickly turn into bare feet—would be the biggest problem.

She didn't argue. She took the bag and looked around. "Where?"

"Right here." He pointed to the corner. "I'll stand in front of you. Be fast."

He turned his back to her and faced the hallway. Behind him, she rummaged through her bag. Her breathing was slightly elevated, but otherwise she was handling this better than he could have ever imagined.

He looked at the remaining messages on his phone.

From Donovan:

When that wedding is over, we need you out here. Sorry.

Cal, Mo, Mo, Mo, Cal, and then Mo: All variations on the theme of "we need to talk to you" and "call us."

From Faith:

You may need this number.

Attached to it was a contact number that could only be one thing. The phone number for the undercover agent.

Behind him, Meredith grunted, then hissed, "Gray. Help me."

He turned around. Where Meredith had looked like royalty a minute earlier, now she looked a bit like a Picasso. All the pieces were there, but they were in the wrong place. She had boots and pants on. The dress was partly over her head. Her arms stuck out the top. Her head was in there somewhere. If things hadn't been so serious, he would have laughed.

"Um . . ." He had no idea where to start.

She turned her back to him. "Unzip me. I tried to pull it over my head without unzipping it. But now I'm stuck."

Lord, this is not helping. He had to shift fabric around to find the top of the zipper. When he finally got it between his fingers, he tugged it down, only to have it catch before he'd gone two inches. "Hang on."

"Just rip it," Meredith said from somewhere inside the dress.

"I appreciate your confidence in my strength, but tearing fabric is harder than you might think."

"Pull at the zipper. The seam will come loose."

What did he have to lose at this point? He grabbed the fabric above the zipper and yanked out and down. On one side, the seam gave way and the zipper broke away from the dress, leaving it open another four inches.

He reached down to the mass of shiny skirt and yanked it up and over Meredith's head. She squeaked.

He shut his eyes. "I'm not looking." He turned to the hallway, arms full of her dress, and scanned the area around them.

He dropped the dress and called Cal.

"Where—"

"No time."

Cal stopped talking.

"You need to drive into Neeson. Meredith's car is missing. Mine may be compromised. I'll call back." He didn't say more. He disconnected that call and pulled open the contact info from Faith.

He hit call and waited.

"What?"

The voice was familiar, but Gray didn't want to say anything compromising. "Might need an assist."

"I'm sure you do."

"Any ideas?"

No answer. Gray looked at the screen. "He hung up on me."

"Give me that." Meredith took his phone. "Change."

Meredith wasn't wearing enough clothes to last long outside, but she'd last a lot longer than she would have in her dress. While he'd had her start with her pants and boots, he did the opposite. He pulled off the jacket and dress shirt, left the undershirt he never went anywhere without, and pulled a performance long-sleeved shirt on over top of it. He followed it with the hoodie he'd had on. He didn't bother changing his pants, but he kicked off his dress shoes and shoved his feet into his boots.

"We have to go!" Meredith grabbed his arms. "Now!"

He didn't argue with her. He paused only long enough to throw his rain slicker around Meredith. He grabbed his heavy coat, and they dashed outside. Meredith was still talking. "The text said, 'Run!' Then it said, 'Get into the woods. I'll find you.'"

She made a horrified sound. "Gray! What if it was the wrong people? What if I just—"

"What was the number?"

"It was local. Five-five-five-seven-seven-three-eight."

"That was the agent. We're good."

"Oh, thank you, Jesus. He's helping us."

The Lord knew they needed his help on this one indeed.

He maneuvered them through the cars in the parking lot, then through the small graveyard, dodging stones and plaques and narrowly avoiding a broken kneecap when a small bench appeared out of nowhere.

The goal for the moment was simple. Get out of sight. He'd figure the rest of it out after they made their escape.

Ten feet into the wooded area around the church, their pace slowed to a fast walk. Another ten feet and they were moving slower. There was no path, no trail, and the farther into the forest they went, the thicker the trees, vines, prickly thorns, and undergrowth.

He looked for a place they could pause. He needed to check his phone. He needed to check Meredith. He needed to get them out of this situation. Once again, his nightmares had come to life while he was wide awake. If he lost Meredith . . .

They kept moving for five of the longest minutes of his existence when he expected to hear gunfire ringing out every second, and then he found a spot that was far from perfect but would do for a few moments. Several trees had fallen and there was enough room for them to squat down behind them and have some protection on at least three sides.

Meredith hadn't spoken since they hit the tree line, and as he maneuvered her into the safest spot he could manage, the only sound she made was labored breathing.

He glanced at his phone.

They know you're gone.

He showed the screen to Meredith.

Her eyes were wide, and her breathing was more like panting. She hiked often and was in good shape. She wasn't winded. She was scared.

So was he. Not only of the men chasing them, but of what he might become if he lost her. This was why he didn't do relationships. This was why he'd done his best to stay away from Meredith. If he failed to protect her tonight, he wouldn't survive.

He couldn't risk a phone call, but he put Cal, Mo, Donovan, and Brick on a group text.

> Had to make a run for it. No time to explain. We're in the woods behind the church. Pretty sure they're looking for us.

Gray had to hope his signal was strong enough.

Meredith's phone buzzed at the same time his did. She looked at it.

Gray looked at his.

The message was from Mo and had been sent to both of them.

> Look around. Anything familiar?

What kind of random remark was that? Gray went to fire back a message, but Meredith was doing exactly as Mo had requested. The next message was a bit more logical.

> Do you have a compass? If you do, head SSW until you know where you are.

South-southwest would put them deeper into the woods and not toward any road that Gray knew of.

But Meredith nodded and her thumbs flew on her phone.

"I'll explain later." She took her phone and tapped the screen a few times. "Ready?"

"Lead on, Sacajawea."

Her smile was wan. She showed him her compass app, and they took off. He dug in his pocket for the compass that he kept on a key ring along with his Swiss Army knife. Apps were great, but they didn't always work.

He oriented himself as they walked.

It was slow going.

And it was cold.

The only thing saving them right now was that the rain made it hard to see them and muffled the sound of their passage.

TWENTY-NINE

Meredith had never been as cold as she was in this moment. Never. She'd also never spent so long convinced she was going to die.

And she had thoughts.

Zero stars. Would not recommend. Would give a negative rating if possible.

But they pressed on. SSW. She knew what Mo had been reminding her of, but it had been fifteen years since they'd pulled that stunt. The forest wasn't like a subdivision. It changed. Trees grew. Trees fell. And the season mattered too. They'd come up here in the fall before the leaves fell.

It was winter now. While there were plenty of evergreens, the forest looked like someone had filled the land with drawings of stick figures. Gray. Slim. Barren.

Lord, help me see.

She kept that prayer on loop as they pushed through the woods.

What felt like hours, but according to her watch was only forty-five minutes later, she heard it.

But she shouldn't have been able to. She stopped moving.

Gray froze beside her. "Is that a river?" She mostly had to read his lips, because neither of them wanted to yell but speaking in a normal voice barely carried.

Realization hit her. Oh, God was really, really good. So good. She pressed her lips to his ear. "Not normally. But I think today, yes. Come on." She followed the sound until they came to the edge of the angry, roiling water. She'd never seen anything more beautiful. "Hello, old friend."

This was her river. At least, it would become her river as it flowed toward her property. In this area, it wasn't much more than a creek except for days like today, when it was swollen from the rain. She studied the area. Nothing looked familiar, but it didn't matter. Now that she'd found the river, she could find her way home.

Unfortunately, home was miles away and she was losing feeling in her fingers.

The good news was that Mo and Cal would know where to look. Wandering around in a forest was never a good idea. Even experienced hikers could get lost. But someone would find them now.

She prayed it would be the good guys who found them first. She had no doubt that Gray would die before he'd let anyone take her, and that was unacceptable.

She pointed downstream and again spoke into Gray's ear. "Home is that way."

He twisted his head so he could speak to her. "Please tell me you aren't planning to hike all the way home."

She leaned in again, and despite the circumstances, couldn't quite ignore the little thrill that zinged through her at the contact. Mercy, but she had it bad for this man. "There's a cabin. Old. Won't do more than give us a chance to catch our breath. But Mo and Cal will head toward it and then come upstream."

Gray gave her a look that sent another, darker zing through her.

"What?"

"You are incredible." Before she could respond to that random remark, he took her hand again. "But we have to keep moving."

They kept the river on their right and headed downstream. Sometimes they had to move a good bit away from it, but she wasn't worried. As long as it was nearby, she could make it home.

Meredith never would have dreamed that long-ago, ill-advised adventure would have ever paid off.

They were fifteen and sixteen years old. Bronwyn had taken off. Meredith and Cal were in shock. Mo vacillated between fiery anger and terrifying despondency. He never lashed out at her or Cal, but he beat the stuffing out of several punching bags and chopped so much firewood that he kept the whole family in split logs that entire winter.

Meredith and Cal hadn't known how to help. As an adult, she understood that they were grieving in their own way, Mo was grieving in his. And none of them had the emotional capacity to help anyone.

Their compromised state probably helped explain why they decided to hike the river. Meredith had grown up traipsing all over the forests with Mo, Cal, and Bronwyn. But they'd always stayed on Quinn land. There was plenty of it, and she'd never been tempted to venture beyond it.

But they were feeling some weird mix of reckless and brave, and they started out early on a Saturday morning and hiked up the river. They knew when they'd left Quinn land. There were markers all over the place if you knew what to look for. Some of them marked one person's personal property from another. Some marked the boundary between Quinn land and non-Quinn land. The ones to be most wary of were the ones that marked the line between the Quinns and Pierces, but there were others.

That day, they'd ventured on past the boundary that marked

their home territory. And on. And on. Mo hiked like a man on a mission. Cal and Meredith followed him. She still didn't know why they'd done it, but she did know that she'd been terrified to leave him. In hindsight? She suspected that God had been protecting all of them, but Mo especially, from doing something rash.

Not that hiking into Neeson County hadn't been rash.

Although to be fair to their teenage selves, they hadn't done it on purpose.

It wasn't like the county lines were marked through the forest the way they were on the road. They hadn't realized they were out of the county until they came to a ramshackle hut. Cabin was too fancy a word to describe it. And because they were young, stupid, and emotionally compromised, they went inside.

Ten seconds later, they were back outside and moving back toward home as fast as they could manage it. They didn't stop or talk until they were back on Quinn land.

"Should we tell someone?" Meredith asked as they stood by the river.

"What are we going to tell them?" Mo's voice was low, his anger simmering just below his fear. "So, Mom and Dad, we decided to hike up the river and we saw a hut and when we went inside there was a sign that said 'Get out,' and we're pretty sure it was written in blood. We got out."

"Yeah. That's exactly what we tell them."

"We were way off our own land. Probably trespassing." Cal ran a hand over his hair. "Private property and all that."

"So?"

"There's nothing illegal about putting up a sign that tells people to get off your property, Meredith."

Mo nodded. "While there *is* something illegal about trespassing."

"You aren't going to tell?" Meredith looked at them.

"Not a chance." Cal shook his head.

Mo agreed. "My lips are sealed."

Later, they'd asked random, innocent questions and learned there were small hunting huts all over the mountains. Spots where people could hole up if they needed to for reasons that had nothing to do with criminal activity.

But they also learned that sometimes those huts were hideouts for people with nefarious ideas. Uncle John had said, "If you see one, stay away from it unless it's on our land."

She shared the story with Gray as they walked. "I haven't thought about that hut for years. We have three that I know of on Quinn property. I can confirm that as of three years ago, none of them had signs written in blood."

"Are you sure it was blood?"

"Until recently I would have told you it was some old geezer's idea of a good way to keep kids out of his hunting hut. That it was red paint and that it was an effective, albeit horrific, method of protecting his space."

"And now?"

"Now? Now I wonder if we should have said something."

He bumped her elbow with his. "Well, see, now you have. You've reported it to law enforcement. And it looks like we're going to have the opportunity to check it out for ourselves."

"Yeah." She couldn't drum up any real enthusiasm. She was so cold. When they reached the hut, she was going inside. She didn't care if there were signs all over that thing.

"You okay?" Gray asked.

She nodded.

"We're going to get home tonight, baby. It will be warm. We'll sit by the fire."

"I'm not sitting outside tonight." She rubbed her hands together. "I may never sit outside again."

"Sure you will but not tonight. Tonight, you're coming to my place. We'll have the fire roaring. We'll snuggle under a blanket. We'll put a movie on, and you'll fall asleep in the big chair. And I'll have to explain myself to your dad and your brother and your cousin tomorrow."

"Why?"

"Because I'm not letting you out of my sight."

THIRTY

An hour later, Meredith paused. "I think we're close."

Gray looked around them. The trees, the river, the forest—it all looked exactly the same as it had for the last hour. The only thing keeping them going was that they were still moving. But he was soaked. Meredith shivered and stumbled. The last time they spoke, she repeated the story of their long-ago hike. He hadn't stopped her, and he hadn't told her she was repeating herself. It wouldn't help to panic her further.

Her eyes were wide, and her breathing was ragged. If they didn't get dry and warm soon . . .

What if they'd gotten in his car? It might have been okay.

Was he dragging the woman he loved through horrific conditions out of fear? Was it all for nothing? She'd fallen four times. He'd fallen twice. One time, she'd slid almost ten feet down a small incline before she got enough traction to stop. It was a miracle she'd stayed on her feet. What if she was injured? What if she suffered something permanent because of him?

What kind of protector was he, anyway? If it hadn't been for her, they'd be wandering around in circles. He was a city boy. He'd learned navigation in the Marines, but he wasn't an outdoorsman. He didn't know these mountains the way she did.

He'd been all but useless up to this point, but when—he refused to think *if*—they reached this so-called hut, he could put a few skills to use. He might not know how to navigate through a forest the way she did, but he did know how to clear empty buildings in hostile territory. Starting with one simple rule: Never assume the building is empty.

"Why do you think we're close?"

She pointed across the river. "See those trees?"

He almost said something about how they were surrounded by trees and that she might need to be more specific. But one glance explained it all. Someone had painted the trunks of the trees in multiple neon shades.

Meredith stopped moving and leaned into him. "That is exactly the way I remember it. The pattern is the same: yellow, green, orange, green, orange, yellow, orange, yellow, green."

The fact that she remembered the pattern made his brain hurt.

"We always figured that it was some kind of signal. The hut is nearby."

"Okay."

"Not okay!" He hadn't realized it was possible to whisper and yell at the same time, but she'd managed it. "It shouldn't look the same. It should be faded and most of the paint should have peeled off by now. It's been at least fifteen years. This paint looks like someone did it last week."

"Agreed."

"Or it could mean that someone painted the same pattern in a different place and I'm completely wrong." She put her hands on her temples and squeezed her eyes closed. "I'm sorry, Gray. I'm trying to think, but everything is getting muddled in my brain."

"It's okay. You're doing great. Is there anything besides the trees that makes you think we're close?"

She pointed to the river. "The main thing I remember about the hut was that it was in a place where the river made a sharp turn. Not quite a right angle, but close."

He squinted through the rain and the trees and saw what she meant. Instead of the river stretching out before him, it appeared to stop at a point in the distance. If the riverbed made a sharp turn, that would make sense.

Meredith shivered against him.

"I know you're freezing, but this is close enough. Let's see if we can find a place to stop for a few minutes."

Her teeth chattered. "I don't think I can stop. If I stop, I might not go again. Ever."

He pulled his phone from his pocket. Still no signal. "I think we should back away from the river and see if we can make a big enough circle that we don't run into anything near the hut."

"Okay." Her eyes were huge in her pale face.

"You're amazing. You got us to the river. And you got us to the right spot. Will you let me take over from here?"

She nodded. "Please. I'm so afraid I'm going to get us killed."

He pressed a kiss to her wet forehead. "You've done great. Now it's my turn to keep us alive."

She dropped her head to his chest. "Okay."

Her trust in him nearly broke him. He had no idea if he could keep her alive or not. All he knew for sure was that he would die trying.

They'd been walking roughly downhill for a while now, and the ground was oversaturated. It took several minutes to make the wide loop he wanted to make. He caught one glimpse of the hut. Eight months of the year, it would have been completely hidden. You could walk within fifty yards and miss it.

How had the Quinn cousins ever found it?

And why was it so weirdly marked but hidden?

Questions he might never get answers to.

A rush of sound filtered through the rain and the river. A motor. No. Several motors. Not car engines. Motorcycles? ATVs? How could anyone drive either of those through this mess?

There must be a trail, narrow and intentionally allowed to be somewhat overgrown. He'd seen things like that, and unless you knew exactly where they were, like this hut, they were difficult to spot.

He pulled Meredith against him. The rain made the acoustics tricky, but he thought their company was coming from their left. If he knew more about where he was and who was after them, they could run. As it was? The safest option was to hide.

He looked around them and made for a small copse of evergreens. The white pine had branches that came almost to the ground. But the pine needles were mostly on the ends of the branches. If they climbed under the branches and got up against the trunk, they could probably sit on the lower branches and be completely hidden.

It took a few minutes to find the best spot. He motioned to Meredith to go first. She wrinkled her nose but dropped to her hands and knees. He held the branches back and she crawled through them. When she was far enough in, he followed her, then allowed the branches to close around them.

Meredith's body shook from the cold. Her lips were blue.

Panic gnawed on the edges of Gray's mind. He had to get her warm.

Doubts flooded him again. The hut they'd been looking for was a few yards away. From what Meredith said, it was unlikely that it would have heat, but it would give them a chance to get out of the elements. Maybe even get dry. But instead, they were hiding in a tree.

Had he made the right call? He couldn't explain why he'd been so sure it was best to take off on foot. Or why he'd been determined to avoid the hut.

But as the revving engines grew even closer, he prayed. *Protect us. Show me how to protect her. I'll die for her if I need to, but I'd much rather live with her for the rest of my life. Please don't let us have made it this far just to lose each other.*

A new sound filtered through the forest. People running. Yelling. And then the unmistakable sound of machine-gun fire.

Meredith grabbed him and held on.

He pressed into her and drew his own weapon.

Private citizens weren't permitted to own machine guns in North Carolina. Gray wasn't naive enough to believe that meant there weren't any in his jurisdiction, but he also didn't think any of the people he suspected of owning one were out here today, in the rain, shooting up the forest.

The gunfire continued sporadically for the next three minutes. From the sound of it, Gray feared that at least one shooter was nearing their position.

Then three men emerged from the left. They were dressed in camo, and each held a weapon. One had an M16. One a handgun. He could only see part of the third man's weapon. Best guess was another handgun.

They paused near enough to the tree that Gray could hear them talking.

"It shouldn't be that hard to track them," the tallest man said. "They've been sliding all over the woods. How could we have lost them?"

Meredith's hands tightened on him, and the way her body shook behind him . . . they were running out of time. Whether

her tremors were from cold, panic, or both, he had to get her out of here. Fast.

"I don't care about the girl." This came from a man who looked like he could bench-press a small car. "I care about those idiots on the dirt bikes. Who are they? And what are they doing here?"

"You're gonna care when Johnstone finds out we lost her," the third man—shorter, thinner, and with an accent that screamed "not from around here"—said. "I don't care what's happening as long as they don't kill her in the crossfire."

"She's been out here a long time," Bench Press said. "If we don't find her soon, there may not be much left of her to take back."

"The cop will protect her." Tall Man waved a hand at the trees around them. "We'll have to take him out."

"Fine by me." Skinny Dude spat out a string of curses. "We'll bury him with the others. We'll play it off that they took off after the wedding and never made it home."

"No one will believe that." Tall Man ducked as another stream of gunfire erupted to their right.

"No one will be able to prove different." Bench Press pointed toward the river. "But we have to get out of here first."

Gray strained to hear more, but the men moved off and disappeared from view.

Meredith's body continued to tremble, but this time, he suspected it was more from fear than anything else.

An explosion ripped through the forest. If Meredith cried out, Gray couldn't hear it. The tree they'd taken shelter in shook so hard Gray wondered if it would fall. He turned so he was pressing Meredith into the tree, his arms around her. She had her hands over her ears and her head tucked against his chest. The tree stopped shaking, but the ringing in his ears kept Gray from processing what was happening.

When he could hear again, the air filled with the sounds of men screaming in agony. Then shots. Two at a time. Then everything went quiet for twenty seconds before engines revved, and the dirt bikes sped away.

The silence left behind was more terrifying than the gun battle.

THIRTY-ONE

Meredith wasn't as cold as she'd been before, and she was pretty sure that was a problem. Before the explosion, she'd zoned out several times. Then Gray would shift, or pinch her leg, or press an elbow into her side, and she'd refocus. After the second time he pinched her, she realized he was doing everything he could to keep her awake.

She'd been sitting on a branch a few feet off the ground. It was uncomfortable, but better than sitting on the wet ground. At some point, Gray had shifted so his feet were on the ground and he'd been holding on to her. Or maybe holding her in place so she didn't fall? She wasn't sure.

Her head spun. Gray pulled away slightly and looked at her. "We have to try to get home, Meredith. We can't stay here any longer. Do you think you can walk?"

"Yes." She had no idea if she could or not, but that didn't mean she wasn't going to try.

"Okay, here's the plan. We keep following the river. We keep our eyes open. The gunfire will have brought Cal and Mo this way. Donovan and Brick too. We keep moving until we find some friendlies."

"Gray? What are the chances—"

He stopped her question with a quick kiss. "We don't think that way in battle. We can't. Our friends are fine. Our family is fine. And we'll see them soon. Okay?"

Having never been in a battle before, she decided to borrow his survival mechanism. Because if she thought too much about Cal or Mo lying somewhere nearby? Bodies torn apart? With two bullet holes for good measure?

She blinked back hot tears. "Okay."

She climbed down from her perch, crawled out from under the branches Gray held for her, and followed him as he slowly made his way toward the river while still keeping them a good distance from it.

They'd walked for three minutes when they found the first body. Gray held up his hand. "Don't look." But it was too late. She'd already seen. The man on the ground was missing an arm, and the blood had turned the rainwater around him into a pink puddle.

Gray pulled his phone from his pocket and snapped a photo.

They kept walking. A minute later, another body was leaning against a tree, eyes wide. Gray took another photo.

The path he took must have been on the edge of the carnage because there weren't any more bodies until they'd walked past the bend in the river.

What she saw sent Meredith to her knees, stomach heaving. Five bodies. Or, more precisely, what was left of them. Gray helped her up, and they kept moving.

They hadn't seen a body for five full minutes when a man stepped in front of them.

She wasn't sure who was more shocked, him or her. Gray shoved her out of the way. She slid, lost her balance, and rolled several feet as the man's weapon came up and he fired.

Gray went down. Meredith screamed. The man turned toward her.

She tried to stand, but her legs gave out, so she crawled toward Gray. She couldn't leave him.

The shooter raised his weapon again, and she knew it was over. She reached Gray and fell across his chest. She felt movement under her, and a shot rang out. Or were there two?

But she felt no pain. Was she dead? She really hadn't expected heaven to be this wet. Or cold.

She looked up to see the man fall, but before he went down, she saw the hole in his forehead, and blood blooming on his chest.

Meredith didn't know if she was next. She didn't know who'd killed the man who'd shot Gray. She couldn't think about it.

She turned to Gray. His chest continued to rise and fall. He had a heartbeat, but his eyes were closed.

A man knelt beside her. His weapon was drawn, but it wasn't pointed at her. "That was some shot, man. Where are you hit?"

What was this guy talking about? He was the one who'd done the shooting. She tried to focus. Her brain was so fuzzy.

Gray stirred under her hands. "Meredith?"

"Gray!"

"You're okay." He reached up and pulled her against him. "You're okay."

"Yes, she's okay, but we need to get her out of here." The man pulled off his raincoat, then pulled a heavy sweater over his head. And without so much as a "Hello, my name is . . ." he pulled Meredith to her feet, ripped her raincoat off of her, and slipped the sweater over her head. Then he manhandled her back into her raincoat.

She moaned in relief. The warmth was so intense it was almost painful.

Gray sat up and looked at a spot behind her. "Thank you."

"You had it under control." The man—she needed to get his name because she couldn't keep calling him "the man" in her head—extended a hand and pulled Gray to his feet. Then helped steady him. "Can you breathe?"

Was he talking to Gray? Her? Who was he? What was happening?

Gray bent over at the waist, hands on his knees. "Give me a second." He pointed to Meredith. "Meredith, meet Carlos. Carlos, Meredith."

"Ma'am." Carlos shook her hand.

Gray straightened. His face was contorted, and he rubbed his chest. "That's gonna leave a mark."

"Beats a hole."

A mark beats a hole? Meredith didn't understand what they were talking about. But when she tried to ask, her voice didn't work right.

"No doubt." Gray retrieved his weapon from the ground, then wrapped an arm around Meredith's waist. "We've been cut off from all communication since we left the wedding. What are we walking into?"

Meredith leaned into Gray and tried to concentrate on what the man was saying. What was his name? Carl? No. That wasn't right. Whoever he was, he was pointing into the trees. "I have a bike parked a few hundred yards back."

A bike? Like they could ride a bike out of the forest. What good would a bike do?

"There's a trail. It's not much, but it will take you to the road and dump you out solidly in Gossamer County. You ride out, get your girl warm. I'll hike out."

Gray didn't argue with him and followed the man where he led them. "I'll send someone after you."

"No need."

Gray studied the man's back, then nodded. "How about I put someone on the road who can give you a ride?"

"That would be appreciated."

They reached a dirt bike. Ah. That made more sense. It would be a tight squeeze for the two of them. Would they fit?

Gray straddled the bike. "I think it's time for you to call it quits on this gig, man."

What gig?

The man gave him a grim smile. "If I don't get out of here"—he pointed to Meredith—"inside pocket. Has all she needs."

What would she need that was in the pocket? Meredith patted the sweater. There was something in one pocket, but it was tiny, and she couldn't think of how it would be helpful. Nothing was making any sense.

"I'll let her know, but you're going to get out. We'll come back for you." Gray kickstarted the dirt bike and patted the back.

The man helped Meredith climb on behind Gray, pointed out the trail, and disappeared into the forest.

Meredith dropped her head against Gray's back and tried to hold on.

Gray rode as fast as he could through the forest. The trail was barely more than a deer path, but it was enough. When he popped out onto the highway, he could have cried in relief.

But when a big truck flew around a curve in the other direction, then screeched to a halt, he had to bite back a sob. Mo and Cal jumped from the truck and ran toward them. "Hypothermia. Get her warm." He pressed a kiss to Meredith's forehead, then handed her to Mo.

He needed to stay with her. But he couldn't. "I have to go back."

"I'm with you." Cal tossed the keys to Mo.

"No."

"Not up for debate. Mo will call it in and get us more backup."

Mo nodded at them both and settled Meredith into the front of the truck while Cal grabbed a backpack. Gray could hear Mo talking before Cal closed the door.

"Let's go."

Gray filled Cal in as they walked back to the bike. Dirt bikes weren't made for two men their size, but it would be faster than walking. Before they climbed on, Cal handed Gray a heavy sweater, gloves, and a dry jacket. Gray stripped out of everything except the ballistic undershirt that had saved his life, put the dry, warm clothes on, and then climbed on behind Cal.

Cal was better at bikes, and Gray was a better shot. It only made sense.

They made it back to the spot where he'd left Carlos in twenty minutes and found the man sitting by the river.

They approached slowly. "Carlos?" Gray called out. He didn't want to get shot. Again.

Carlos raised a hand but didn't turn. Cal stayed back, gun in hand, scanning the area. Gray joined Carlos by the raging river.

"You were supposed to send a car. Not come back in here. What's wrong with you?"

"I'm a Marine. We never leave a man behind."

"Oorah." Carlos handed a small phone to Gray. "I recorded everything. But you should probably go look for yourself." He pointed to the spot where the hut had probably stood.

Nothing was there now. Gray stood and walked in that direction. Cal joined him.

"I don't know what we're about to find, but it won't be pretty," Gray said to Cal. "You can stay back."

Cal ignored him. Typical.

Thirty feet from what he assumed had been the footprint of the hut, there was evidence of a small mudslide.

Stuck in the mud were bones.

Lots and lots of bones.

"I think we found Johnstone's burial ground."

———

It was another eight hours before Gray finally walked into his house. Carlos was safely en route to Raleigh. It wasn't safe for him to be anywhere near Neeson.

Faith Powell had arrived an hour after they walked out of the woods, and she'd brought friends. A forensics team from the State Bureau of Investigation, based out of the Asheville area, descended on the woods. They established a large perimeter and set up huge tarps over the most obvious burial sites. They worked until after dark getting the bodies out. In all, there were nine fresh corpses, including the man who'd shot Gray. There were three female bodies whose decomp indicated that their deaths had been in the last month. Gray suspected that they were the three women Carlos had told him about.

Everything else would have to wait for daylight. The rain had stopped around dark, but the temperature was going to drop into the teens tonight. The SBI team set up high-tech surveillance and planned to spend the night in a warm van, watching monitors, rather than in the forest with the skeletons.

Gray supported that decision.

Faith Powell had taken the opportunity to storm the castle. Literally. She'd brought a team with her, and they arrived at Marvin Johnstone's home to find the place in chaos. She took him into custody, placidly ignoring his insistence that he would have her badge, that her career was over, and that she would regret the day she took this action.

Dennis Kirby didn't say a word when she arrested him and took four Neeson officers into custody.

Tonight, Faith and her team were headed back to Asheville, along with the prisoners. She would be back in the morning, and she'd probably wind up staying for several days. He would be glad for the help.

Gray stumbled into his kitchen. He was tired in a way he'd never been before. Everything hurt. Dr. Shaw had said to expect muscle pain from the hours of intense cold, and that he had a bruised rib from the bullet he'd taken to the chest. But otherwise, there was nothing wrong with him that sleep wouldn't fix.

Except that he needed to see Meredith. He'd talked to her twice. The last time had been two hours earlier, and he'd told her he would see her tomorrow. She was fine. She'd warmed up nicely and her head had cleared. Dr. Shaw told her there would be no permanent damage, but she'd also prescribed a sedative because she was concerned about how keyed up Meredith was.

He glanced at his watch. 10:00 p.m. He could call her. If she'd taken the sedative, she'd be zonked. But if she answered—

He stepped into his living room and dropped the phone.

A fire roared in the fireplace. On his coffee table sat two steaming mugs. And in his oversized chair sat Meredith, wrapped up in blankets. "Hi."

She threw the blankets off, but he reached her before she could stand. He pressed a knee into the seat beside her and kissed her.

There was no passion or intensity in this kiss. This was a kiss filled with relief and gratitude and the need to reassure his heart that she was alive. When they broke apart, she patted the seat beside her. "I won't stay long. We both need to sleep. But I couldn't let the man who took a bullet for me be greeted by a cold, empty house."

He settled in beside her, and when she curled into him, her head on his chest, he draped the blanket over them both and knew he was finally home.

THIRTY-TWO

MARCH

"Please, make yourselves comfortable." Meredith indicated the chairs that ringed the firepit. They'd brought in extras for their guests so everyone had a seat available to them.

Tables were set up nearby with a chili bar, soft drinks, bottled waters, and brownies. It was simple but welcoming.

Dr. Sabrina Fleming-Campbell was easy to pick out of the crowd. She and Mo were in an intense discussion about computers that made no sense to anyone else. Sabrina's husband, Adam, stood nearby talking to Donovan and Cassie about the scuba diving they were planning for their honeymoon.

FBI Special Agent Faith Powell was talking to Gray and Cal, while her husband, Secret Service Special Agent Luke Powell, and Bronwyn talked about the possibility of a presidential visit to The Haven.

Meredith leaned against the porch rail of her tiny house and thanked God, again, that she'd made it out of the forest alive.

Carlos joined her on the porch. A month after returning to his real life, he carried a somewhat haunted expression.

"Are you okay?"

He pulled in a long breath. "No."

"Is there anything we can do to help?"

He pointed to the groups of people talking. "This helps. Normalcy. Good people who do the right thing. It helps me remember that I'm one of the good guys."

"You're definitely one of the good guys."

Gray looked away from Faith and caught her eye. His smile sent warmth flooding through her.

Carlos pointed his water bottle in Gray's direction. "He's one of the good guys too."

"I know." She didn't know Carlos, but she'd been wanting to talk to him, and now was as good a time as any. "Thank you."

"For what?"

"For the warning to run."

"Ah."

"How did you know they were coming for me?"

"Once upon a time, I would have said it was luck. Now? I think it must have been from God. I was in the right place at the right time and realized they'd decided to grab you."

He rested his elbows on the porch rail. "I had a bad feeling from the time Johnstone told us he wouldn't be at the wedding. Johnstone left town plenty of times before. The man likes the finer things in life, and he likes to see the world. But he'd never announced his absence before. Most of the time, no one knew he'd been gone until he was back. It screamed setup to me. But I didn't know how it would play out."

He took a sip of water and when he spoke again, the intensity of his tone sent a chill racing over Meredith's skin. "What I did know was that if they got their hands on you, Johnstone would have tortured you until you told him where Amara was, and then he would have killed you."

Carlos sucked in a breath and blew it out hard. "I owe you an apology, though. I didn't realize how many pieces were moving on the chessboard. I thought if you hid in the woods for a bit, it would all blow over. I didn't expect Johnstone to use the opportunity to clean house."

It had taken several days to sort it all out, but eventually the pieces had clicked. The men who'd been coming after her were Johnstone's men. They'd stolen her car and sabotaged Gray's. If she and Gray had tried to leave in his car, they would only have made it a mile or so before they would have been on the side of the road and easily accessible. That had been the original plan, but Gray's refusal to take his car had scuttled that.

The men hiding out in the hut had been the Atlanta drug dealers. Johnstone had been none too happy about the way they'd killed the women who were brought to them. So Johnstone planned to get payback by using them as cover. Johnstone's people planned to plant evidence that showed the Atlanta drug dealers had captured and killed Meredith and Gray, and then blown themselves up cooking meth.

It would have been a pitiful story anywhere else, but Johnstone had Kirby in his pocket. And the arrogance to believe he could get away with it.

Johnstone's crew timed the explosions to go off during the reception, not knowing that Meredith and Gray would be in the woods. They'd had no way to predict that anyone would be there to see and hear the fight, and later to find the bodies.

And neither Johnstone nor Ledbetter had anticipated that blowing up the hut would have the unintended consequence of dislodging so many corpses. It probably wouldn't have happened in dry conditions, but the explosion had triggered a small slide, and once the bones were visible, it was like opening Pandora's box. Chaos had ensued.

"Do you think it's over?" Meredith voiced the question that had haunted her for weeks. "Really over?"

Carlos held his hands out. "I think it's over for Johnstone and Kirby. And for Ledbetter. As for the drugs and trafficking? That's never really over. The Atlanta gangs will find someone else to help them move their product. But I don't think it will be in Neeson. At least, not on the scale it has been."

"So for you, does it feel like a success?"

"It feels like we won a battle, but the war rages on." Carlos patted her hand where it rested on the porch rail. "But for the people of Neeson, I think it was a success. They'll have new oversight, new law enforcement, new structures. Some of them will go to jail for their involvement. Most, hopefully, will take the opportunity to start fresh." He shoved away from the railing. "As for me, my fresh start begins with a bowl of that chili, some of those brownies, and an evening with people who don't want to shoot me."

Meredith grinned. "By all means, don't let me stop you."

Two minutes later, Faith joined her on the porch. "I'm going to be nosy. Is Carlos okay?"

Meredith waved her hand back and forth. "According to him, he is not. But I think he will be." This must be her day for thank-yous. "I haven't had a chance to say thank you yet, but I hope you know how much I appreciate what you did for Neeson."

"I did my job." Faith sipped a Cherry Coke and looked around them. "Did you hear the latest theory about Kirby and Johnstone?"

"No."

"There's a rumor going around that the thing that tied them together was a criminal act from fifty years ago. Something about a friend of theirs who took a beating and never recovered."

"I know that story."

"The rumor is that at some point, Kirby found out who did

it, killed the men, and hid the bodies. Then, like an idiot, he told Johnstone, thinking Johnstone would be thrilled."

Meredith frowned. "He wasn't?"

"Oh, he was, but not in the way Kirby expected. He used the knowledge to blackmail Kirby, and that started the chain of events that led us to today."

"Do you think the evidence is strong enough to win cases against them?"

Faith nudged Meredith's arm. "Don't you worry. You can sleep at night. Those two won't be coming back anytime soon. And when I was in Neeson this week, the people there were so relieved to be free of the corruption, you could feel it in the air. It's like a completely different town. We've cleared two of their officers of any wrongdoing. The one you were worried about, Nichols, never caved. He'll keep his job. And I think he'll be an asset to the new administration there."

"That's wonderful to hear."

Faith sighed. "The good news is a little thin on the ground. But it's there. It will take years to heal the wounds, but I think there's hope for the town now. I heard that the church wants you to come back with your dental van and that they want to open up the building so people have a place to wait. There was even talk of allowing the kids to play on the playground equipment."

"Wow. That is progress."

Faith's husband, Luke, came to stand beneath where they stood. "We have to come back here. This place is gorgeous."

Cal joined them and pointed to his tiny house. "That one will be available as soon as my cousin gets married. And my guess is that this one"—he tapped Meredith's porch—"will be empty soon too. We'd love to have you. Come on up anytime."

JUNE

Gray loved the mountains in all their seasons, but summer nights might be his favorite. Tonight, he sat by the firepit outside Meredith's home. It had been warm today, but the June evening had cooled off enough that the fire made everything cozy. They had the place to themselves for once. Cassie and Donovan were on their honeymoon. Cal and Landry were at the beach with his brothers, their wives, all the kids, and his parents.

Bronwyn was overseeing everything at Hideaway because, with Cassie out of the country, she didn't fully trust the temporary chef to keep things under control. Especially on a Friday night.

Mo was in New York City on a job for some clients and had messaged Meredith eight times today telling her that if he ever hinted at wanting to move to a city, she should shoot him because he'd been abducted by aliens.

Meredith came to sit beside Gray. She'd replaced their Adirondack-style chairs with a larger one big enough to sit in together. She snuggled in beside him and rested her head on his chest in a position that had become so familiar to him that he wondered how he'd ever lived without this connection.

"Long day?" she asked.

The forensics team had found another body at the Neeson site today. That brought the body count to thirty-nine. Any other night, he would have told Meredith all about it, but he didn't want to bring that into their time together.

"Busy. You?"

"Same. This working on Fridays is for the birds." She yawned. "I'm looking forward to tomorrow, though. Me, you, and a hike that doesn't involve people trying to kill us."

"My favorite kind."

They watched the fire for a few minutes of what should have been comfortable silence, but he couldn't take it anymore.

"Meredith?"

"Hmm?"

"I love you."

She cuddled closer. "I love you too."

He kissed the top of her head and slid the ring from his pocket. "Can I ask you something?"

"Anything."

"Will you marry me?"

"Of course I will. All you have to do is ask."

"Pretty sure I just did."

Her body went stiff beside him, and she slowly pulled away from him. "You did?"

"I did."

Her smile was slow and huge. "Gray! Are you serious? Because if you aren't serious—"

He grabbed her left hand and slid the ring on her fourth finger.

"You *are* serious." There was a hint of wonder in her voice, and when she looked away from her hand and into his eyes, he saw the forever he'd never allowed himself to dream of.

"Till death do us part."

"Yes!"

LOVE LYNN H. BLACKBURN'S WRITING?

Turn the page for a sneak peek at the
next book in the GOSSAMER FALLS series.

AVAILABLE MARCH 2026

Whoever said blood was thicker than water hadn't known about the Pierce family. Bronwyn Pierce could think of several people she could trust more than her own family, and one of them despised her.

But he was the one she needed now.

He would come. She knew it in a place so deep in her core despite the pain they'd inflicted on each other for the past seventeen years.

After close to two decades of hostility, she still knew that while he wouldn't speak to her, he *would* keep her secrets and do everything he could to keep her safe.

"This is so messed up." She muttered the words into the silence of her office, then clamped her mouth shut.

For all she knew, someone was listening.

She propped her elbows on her desk and rested her face in her hands. Her head ached. Her heart was . . . numb. It had been bruised and beaten so often in her thirty-three years that even the magnitude of this current betrayal barely registered.

The light tap on her office door jolted her from her musing, and she barely stopped the scream that bubbled up in her chest. Who was wandering around The Haven at three in the morning?

She slid open the middle drawer of her desk and rested her left hand on the small gun that she kept there. And yeah, wasn't that just a kick in the pants. She was the CEO of an exclusive resort. She prided herself in how her staff protected the celebrities, politicians, and uber-wealthy visitors who rested in blissful slumber in the elegant cabins that dotted the property. They knew no paparazzi would approach them and no one would harm them while they were here.

But she couldn't expect the same level of security for herself. She gripped the gun.

"Ms. Pierce? Are you in there?" The deep voice of Randall, one of the night watchmen, filtered through the thick door.

"Yes. Come in."

He eased the door open and took one step inside. "Ms. Pierce? Are you okay?"

She understood the confusion she saw on his face. She put in well over sixty hours a week, sometimes closer to eighty hours, but even she didn't make a habit of being in her office in the middle of the night.

"I'm fine. Thank you." She didn't owe him an explanation, but she gave it anyway. Or part of one. "I thought of something that needed to be done on this computer."

It was no secret that The Haven computer network carried some of the most advanced security available. And that some information couldn't be accessed from remote locations. Not even by her.

"Gotcha." Randall's tense smile sent a chill skittering across her skin. "I guess it's in the air tonight. Mr. Pierce is in his office as well."

The chill turned into an arctic blast through her soul. "Which Mr. Pierce?"

"Nathan."

"I see."

Randall regarded her with an expression she couldn't decipher. Was it concern? Distrust?

"If it's all the same to you, ma'am, I'm going to stay in this area for a bit. I'd appreciate it if you'd allow me to escort you back to your home when you're done here."

And that didn't sound ominous. Not at all.

Did he want to see her safely back to her home? Or did he want to take the opportunity to . . . what? What would he do? Surely the situation hadn't devolved to the point where physical violence was on the table.

She gave herself a mental shake. No. Randall was good people. He was looking out for her. Nothing more. She hoped.

"Sure. I'll probably be another ten minutes. I need to send a few emails."

Randall lowered his head. "In that case, I'll wait outside."

With that, he stepped back and closed the door.

Now what?

Her cousin Nathan was in his office on the other side of the property doing who knew what at three a.m.—probably plotting world domination. Or her painful death. Or both.

Lord, how did we get here? And how do I get out of this mess?

She didn't know the answer to the first question, but she knew the answer to the second. Or at least, she knew the first step on the path.

She twisted to her computer and typed out an email.

With shaking fingers, she hit send, gathered her things, including her weapon, and walked out to meet Randall.

There was no turning back now. She'd placed the charges and lit the fuse. Her walls were coming down. She had to trust that he'd stand with her when the last one fell.

ACKNOWLEDGMENTS

No one ever writes a book on their own. My eternal gratitude to:

Christy Hart, owner and designer of Bloomphoria, for sharing the beauty and colorful chaos of your workshop with me. I know my readers will love your wooden floral designs as much as I do!

My family—Brian, Emma, James, Drew, Jennifer, Mom, Dad, and Sandra—because none of these books would ever happen without you!

Lynette Eason, for being my #SamePerson.

Deborah Clack and Debb Hackett, for memes, socks, laughter, and being a soft place to land.

Kelsey Bowen, for pushing me and the story to be better.

Robin Turici, for getting my little side jokes and finding every single mistake I never wanted to make.

The remarkable team at Revell, for being the absolute best in the business and the best to work with!

Tamela Hancock Murray, my ever-supportive agent.

Most of all, to my Savior, the ultimate Storyteller, for allowing me to write stories for you.

> Let the words of my mouth and the meditation of my heart
> be acceptable in your sight,
> O Lord, my rock and my redeemer.
>
> Psalm 19:14 ESV

LYNN H. BLACKBURN is the award-winning author of *Never Fall Again*, as well as the Dive Team Investigations and Defend and Protect series. She loves writing swoon-worthy Southern suspense because her childhood fantasy was to become a spy, but her grown-up reality is that she's a huge chicken and would have been caught on her first mission. She prefers to live vicariously through her characters by putting them into terrifying situations while she sits at home in her pajamas. She lives in Simpsonville, South Carolina, with her true love, Brian, and their three children. Learn more at LynnHBlackburn.com.

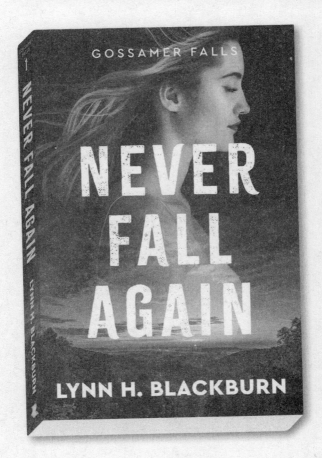

MEET LYNN

LYNNHBLACKBURN.COM

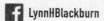 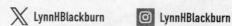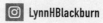